Anonymous

Spring 1898

Anonymous

Spring 1898

ISBN/EAN: 9783742864895

Manufactured in Europe, USA, Canada, Australia, Japa

Cover: Foto ©Andreas Hilbeck / pixelio.de

Manufactured and distributed by brebook publishing software
(www.brebook.com)

Anonymous

Spring 1898

JOHN A. SALZER SEED CO.
LA CROSSE, WIS.
SEED CO.

Spring 1899

SALZER'S ODDLY ODD GOURDS.

INDEX.

PLANTS.

FLOWER SEEDS—Pages 22 to 30.

TREES AND SMALL FRUITS—Pages 18 to 21.

VEGETABLE SEEDS.

FARM SEEDS.

IMPLEMENTS AND SUNDRIES.

(Complete list, page 134.)

TO OUR FRIENDS AND PATRONS.

We wish here to publicly express our sincere thanks to you, kind patron and friend, for the lively interest you have taken in speaking a good word to your neighbors for our seeds and plants, as also for your liberal patronage, and for your efforts to increase the sale of our plants and seeds in your neighborhood. To you it is due largely that our business, from a small beginning, has grown to be the LARGEST MAIL BUSINESS OF ITS KIND IN AMERICA, and we shall take every pains that our business, if duly kind to be lasting, and we assure you that all orders intrusted to our care by you will receive prompt attention and many extras.

Our trade, more especially for the past season, was next to enormous, so much so that we have been obliged to (we like this) to double the capacity of this already mammoth (largest in the world) seed house establishment. With this new address and enlarged office rooms, we are in a position to fill each and every order for 1899 at once after receipt. We hope to be favored with many of your kind orders during the future.

FREE!

With each order of 60c or more for anything out of this catalogue we give free one package of our

Salzer's Oddly Odd Gourds.

A sensational mixture of rare, strange, droll, curious, singular, comical, fantastical, queer, comely, funny, big, little, long, thin, fat, round, oblong and oddly odd shaped gourds. Just the seed you will want to plant for the children and for your own fun and pleasure.

Given free with each order.

Pkg., 20c; 3 pkgs., 40c; 1 oz., 25c.

Wild Rice Seed.

This was omitted from the body of our catalogue. Sown along creeks, lakes, marshes, etc., to attract wild ducks, geese, etc. 1 lb., 25c, postpaid; by express, 5 lbs., 90 lbs., $1.20.

On pages 9 and 10 you will find a beautiful illustration of handsome blooming and ornamental plants. This Rainbow Collection we sell so cheap, and plants are so beautiful, that we can't see how possibly without these plants...

11 for 60c, or 21 for $1.00.

CHOICE PLANTS FOR THE GARDEN $1.00

Seven Giant Monthly Carnations, only 75c.

There is no flower so sweet as the carnation and no flower is more highly esteemed by gentlemen for buttonhole bouquets than the carnation. Their fragrance is quite so sweet and lasting as that of the carnation. Our varieties are free bloomers and very choice.

1. Helen Keller, silent bloom, white, slightly splashed with red; each, 15c; seed, pkg., 25c.
2. Flora Hill, the giant bloom, one among the whites; each, 20c; seed, pkg., 15c.
3. Jubilee, a magnificent bright red, free blooming variety; each, 20c; seed, pkg., 15c.
4. Meteor, the darkest red imaginable; each, 20c; seed, pkg., 15c.
5. William Scott, the prince of all pink varieties, very showy; each, 15c; seed, pkg., 15c.
6. Daybreak, peculiar color, pale salmon pink, elegant; each, 15c; seed, pkg., 15c.
7. American Flag, beautifully variegated with red and white; each, 15c; seed, pkg., 15c.

One each of above 7 for 75c; your selection of sorts for 40c.

AMERICAN FLAG. EACH, 15c.

SEND ALL ORDERS TO   **JOHN A. SALZER SEED CO.,**   LA CROSSE, Wis.

EVERY SEEDSMAN IS READY TO ADMIT

1. That we own more floor room for storage and packing than any three Western seedsmen put together (with the Detroit Commission Seed House excepted), and larger than any New York, Philadelphia, Chicago or Illinois or Iowa, Minnesota or Wisconsin house.

2. That our improved methods of packing, mailing, and shipping give us the advantage of filling an order faster than any other house in America, without exception.

3. The cellar is the largest of its kind for seed potatoes in the world. *See sectional view under Potatoes.*

4. *The Freight Shipping Department* is under the supervision of an expert. The farm seed orders are filled on the 2d, 3d, 4th and 5th floors, properly labeled and addressed. They are then let down to the 1st floor by means of two mammoth elevators. On this floor the several railroads, steamboat lines and express companies have apartments. The packed order is then placed in the apartment of the railroad which runs to the city in which our customer resides. From these apartments, during the busy season, many teams, each making nine trips daily, haul the freight to the different depots, boat landings, express offices, etc.

5. *The Mail Order Department* is complete in all its details. Every invention possible to quickly and accurately facilitate the prompt dispatch of an order has been made. In this department scores of women pick out the orders, check them, pack them, weigh and stamp the packages and then deposit the same in U. S. Mail bags furnished in large numbers by the Government. This department can fill and dispatch 6,000 orders daily, and during the busy season is open day and night.

View of the John A. Salzer Seed Co.'s establishment at LaCrosse, Wis., said to be the largest of the kind in America, if not in the world.

OUR PRICES.

It is our constant aim to make HIGHEST QUALITY A FIRST CONSIDERATION, and then make our PRICES AS LOW AS GOOD, HONEST SEEDS CAN BE SOLD FOR. OUR PRICES, THEREFORE, will in all cases be as LOW as those of any other RELIABLE HOUSE for seeds of the highest standard of excellence. OUR DETERMINATION to grow and distribute nothing but the VERY BEST SEEDS THAT IT IS POSSIBLE TO PRODUCE has increased our business to its present LARGE PROPORTIONS, and gained for us the largest trade enjoyed by any house in America, direct with critical market gardeners and experienced planters who cultivate for profit, and whose trade always seeks the source where the highest quality can be obtained. "OUR SUCCESS ACHIEVED CAN ONLY BE MAINTAINED BY THE METHODS THAT OBTAINED IT."

Any dealer, market gardener, market farmer, farmer's club or any individual wishing seeds in large quantities is requested to mail us a list of what he wants, and we will promptly return it to him with the very lowest prices marked. A letter of inquiry may save you dollars, if you want to buy in quantity, as We are the largest growers of choice vegetable and farm seeds. Please send in your large list for estimate.

NOW, THEN, FOR 1899!

WHAT WE DO.

FREE DELIVERY BY MAIL.

All seeds ordered at the packet, ounce, quart or pound mail prices, also bulbs, roses, vines and such goods as are offered postpaid and at catalogue prices, will be sent by mail, postage prepaid by us to any address in America. We sometimes send by express (prepaid) instead of mail, but only when there is a saving of cost to ourselves, and at no extra cost to purchaser to receive these that way. The exceptions to this rule are goods by peck or bushel, and all goods and seeds listed from page 6 to 67 [illegible] of catalogue) on these, unless specially stated postpaid, the customer pays freight charges—that is from page 6 on. From page 6 to 67 we pay postage as per above.

PLANTS OR SEEDS BY EXPRESS OR FREIGHT.

On plants ordered by express purchasers pay the express charges. When the distance is not too far, they can well afford to pay the express charges, for we always send larger and finer plants by express than can be sent by mail, and always add extra plants to help pay express charges. By mail the earth is washed off the roots; by express, the earth is retained, so there is no standstill whatever.

Our plants are uniformly large for the price, are thrifty, strong and healthy, grown on this cold process—not forced. Nine-tenths of our competitors force their plants; such plants look well while in the greenhouse, but soon after arrival drop their leaves and die. Ours are hardy, will stand a ten days' trip across the country, fresh and green, and will smile at you with their pretty leaves upon reaching the box.

EXPRESS RATES.

These have been greatly reduced for us. The express companies, recognizing our claims as their largest shippers, have given us, for our customers, very low rates. Thus a

TWENTY-FIVE POUND PACKAGE.

Would cost, to points in Illinois, Nebraska, Missouri, Indiana, New York, Pennsylvania, Kentucky, the Dakotas, Kansas, Michigan and Ohio, from 40c to 90c.
To points in Alabama, Maine, Rhode Island, Arkansas, Massachusetts, Tennessee, Connecticut, Mississippi, New Brunswick, Delaware, New Jersey and Virginia, from 85c to $1.35.
To points in the Far West and South—Arizona, $3.00; New Mexico, $2.50; Idaho, $2.00; Oregon, $2.50; Montana, $2.00; Utah, $2.00; Nevada, $2.50; Washington, $2.50.
Above gives you a fair idea of express charges. All seeds quoted by express or freight mean that you pay the transportation charges; by mail, postpaid, that we prepay.

DISCOUNTS.

AMONG YOUR FRIENDS there are many who want good seeds and fine plants. Well, if you will go and see them and urge them to order with you, we allow you in sending us

| If $2.00 is selected, plants or seeds in packages, amounting to $2.25 | a profit of $0.25, page 1. |
| 3.00 " " " " 3.30 " " 0.30 " |
| 5.00 " " " " 5.75 " " 0.75 " |
| 10.00 " " " " 11.75 " " 1.75 " |
| 20.00 " " " " 24.00 " " 4.00 " |
| 50.00 " " " " 64.50 " " 14.50 " |

Above terms apply only to plants at single rate or in group prices, and not in 10, 12 or 100 prices; and to seeds in packages only—not by pint, ¼ lb. or lb. *See page 37 regarding premiums on pints, pounds, etc.* We advise the formation of large clubs, and the above discount will certainly pay any one for some trouble in that direction.

WHAT YOU SHOULD DO.

MONEY—We prefer all money sent by Express Orders, as these are absolutely safe and sure. If you cannot get these then use Bank Drafts, Money Orders or Registered Letters. Do not send loose money in a letter without registering it; it is not safe, and if it is lost we are not responsible for it. Silver coin should be sewed or pasted upon strong cloth or paper to prevent breaking through Registered Letter.

Private Checks.

Do not send your check—because it costs 15c to collect same, which is deducted from the amount, and, besides, orders are held till our bankers report private check is paid. This causes needless trouble and delay in filling orders.

Postage Stamps.

We accept postage stamps when other modes of remittance are inconvenient, but only in 1 and 2 cent denominations. Be very particular to use discretion so that they do not get damp and stuck to the order.

Those Who Send

A neat, plainly written order will be sure to be filled correctly and with dispatch, and will also receive some valuable "extras." Always copy out the price of each article, and, after adding the amounts together and deducting the discount, remit the exact sum.

Important.

It occasionally happens (very seldom) that an order is lost in coming to us, or the goods in going to the customer. Therefore, if any who order do not hear from us within a reasonable length of time, they should send a duplicate order, naming the date on which the former was sent, and the amount of money enclosed, and in what form. DO NOT simply say, "I sent you an order 14 days ago, and have not heard from same," but be explicit. This will enable us to investigate the matter and fill the duplicate order with dispatch.

Prepaid Railroad Stations.

Many of our farmer customers live on Prepaid Railroad Stations, where there are no agents. In such cases we can ship the goods to the nearest station to the Prepaid Station, as we never pay freight charges on to any roads. This insures quick delivery and no danger of loss.

JOHN A. SALZER SEED CO., LA CROSSE, WIS.

RAREST OF RARE PLANTS.

These pages contain the rarest of rare plants. This collection is so complete that we doubt whether any many rare things are found in any one catalogue in America. They are all choice, low-priced, and we hope to make many a heart glad in purchasing these beauties.

Abutilon.

Plants of continuous bloom for house culture.
1. **Golden Sunset**—Imagine a plant with fully 120 massive, clear, golden, yellow bells pendant to every branch; that's a one-year-old Golden Sunset. 20c.
2. **"Pearl of the Sea"**—Grows rapidly and compact, and its large white flowers in profusion. In fact, it is almost an "everbloomer." Each, 25c.
3. **A. Selsum**—Cut up want of 5,000 massive dark crimson blossoms from a one-year-old plant. Each, 20c.
☞Above 3 Rare Abutilons, 40c.☜
Thompsonii Plena—Double yellow. Each, 25c.
Souvenir de Bonn—Bright green leaves, distinctly margined with white. Long yellow flowers. A magnificent foliage plant. Each, 20c.

Alyssum White Lily.

The trusses are enormous, measuring at times 1 inch in diameter and 5 inches long. Flowers perfectly double, of delightful fragrance; splendid for baskets. 10c; 6 for 50c.

Alternathera.

Dwarf class of plants, with exquisitely colored foliage; fine for edging. Each, 8c; 12 for 15c.

Bryophyllum.

The air plant. It's a very odd plant, grows oddly and likes odd places to flourish its oddity. A leaf will send out a dozen little plants. Each, 15c.

Giant Achillea.

Please turn to page 9 for full description of this most wonderful plant—hardy 3,000 blossoms at once. No plant will give so more pleasure and one will bloom more easily. Price only, each, 20c; 3 for 30c; 5 for 60c; 12 for $1.00.

Banana.

A tropical plant, producing a grand effect when planted on a lawn. A bed of 53 banana plants on a lawn was admired more by our thousands of visitors than anything else in our garden. Each, 40c; 3 for 25c.

THE GREAT BANANA.

Bridal Rose.

The Bridal Rose is charming, resembling white roses. Blooms in the early spring in great profusion. One of the best house plants known. Absolutely sure of bloom in the winter months. Each, 25c.

Balsami Sultani

Or single balsam. Each, 25c.

Aspidistra.

Silver Shield.

Beautifully variegated. The rarest silver leaf variegation of same. Very scarce. Each, 25c.

"Sea Green."

A glorious deep sea green colored Aspidistra. Does well in water or earth. Very fine. Each, 25c.

ASPIDISTRA.

Asparagus (Climbing.)

The finest of all plants for floral decoration. The foliage is so fine, so fairy-like, so graceful, so much like a soft, vapory fern, that as a decorative vine it cannot be compared with anything we know of. Each, 20c.

Anthurium.

A magnificent pot plant. Beautifully variegated white and green. Sure to please. Each, 15c.

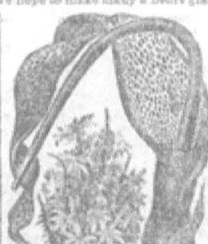
CLIMBING ASPARAGUS.

ANTHURIUM.
Aqua Reineckea—Grows to perfection in water or aquaria. Bright green foliage, surmounted by a crown of pale, yellow blossoms. Each, 15c.

ACALYPHIA, 30c.

Acalyphia.

Has large leaves which are colored like the finest autumn foliage. The colors are dark brownish red, light olive green and tongue scarlet. Mixed in an irregular manner, exactly like the finest specimens of autumn leaves. Each, 30c.

Agapanthus.

A blue African Lily, an exquisite flower going to well everywhere that we heartily recommend same. Scarce from 10 to 50 spikes of bright blue lily-like flowers each year. Each, 25c.

Amorphophallus Simiense.

This plant has been immensely popular on account of its very remarkable flower. The most long-like bodies of which is of peculiar golden color, spotted purple, while the back is of mottled brown. Very palm-like tropical foliage; large bulbs. Each, 40c; 3 for $1.00.

Amorphophallus Rivieri.

Another species, having a flower the shape of a Calla Lily, but of enormous proportions. Stems and stalks green, spotted rose; leaves deep green, and often 4 feet across. Flowers usually a yard in length. Each, 50c.

Ageratums.

Bloom almost continuously. Mrs. Garfield, the white, the Amore, best, largest blue, 10c.

Achania.

One of the handsomest house plants grown, bearing innumerable scarlet blossoms. Frequently termed "Bright Fuchsia." Each, 20c.

Alocasia.

Another one of the so rare plants, seldom found, and we doubt whether there is one in your town. It is a plant of such magnificent tropical foliage, bearing great blotches of a peculiar tint, with powerful pineapple fragrance, that it is worth a place in the rarest collection. We do not too strongly recommend same. It makes a magnificent pot plant, as also a rare plant; ornament. There is not another plant in the world to rival this, so rare, so fine, of so many a culture and still so rare. Price, for each, large plants from $1.50 to $5.00.

ALOCASIA—THE GRAND, 50c.

Ananassa.

Pineapple.

We have a fine stock of this gorgeous decorative plant, which, when in fruit, is quite unsurpassed by any, very easy of culture. Each, 40c.

Philodendron.

The rarest of rare plants. A tropical grandeur! Found in no other plant. Great massive, triangular, deep green leaves transcendent beautiful. Rarest culture. Rarest of all. Each, $1.00; large plants, $5.00 to $10.00.

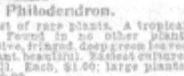

☞ Azalea Indica.

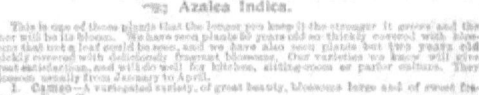

This is one of those plants that the longer you keep it the stronger it grows and the finer will be its bloom. We have seen plants 50 years old so thickly covered with blossoms that not a leaf could be seen, and we have also seen plants but two years old thickly covered with deliciously fragrant blossoms. Our varieties we know will give great satisfaction, and will do well for kitchen, sitting room or parlor culture. They blossom usually from January to April.

1. Cameo—A variegated variety, of great beauty, blossoms large and of sweet fragrance. Each, 25c.
2. Pearl—This is the finest of all single white Azaleas. The blossoms are large, of pearly whiteness, and of a delicious fragrance. Each, 25c.
3. Ruby—A beautiful Azalea of a rich deep pink, almost red color, very fragrant; a strong grower and sure to please. Each, 25c.
One each of above 3 beautiful Azaleas, for 60c.
Five different Azaleas, our selection, including above 3, for $1.00.

Salzer's Charming Rex Begonias, Always Beautiful.

Our Jewel Collection.

Composed of our selection of rare Rex sorts, we offer, post-paid:

3 Charming Sorts, postpaid, 40c.
6 Charming Sorts, postpaid, $1.00.

Among the rarest, choicest plants that grow are found the Rex and Blooming Begonias. Indeed, to-day no collection is complete without these exquisite beauties. The leaves of the Rex varieties are massive and grand, while the foliage and blossoms of the Blooming sorts are unrivaled.

Countess Louise Erdody. See Cut No. 1.—The striking peculiarity which distinguishes it from all other Begonias consists in the fact that the two lobes at the base of the leaf do not grow side by side, but one of them winds in a spiral-like way until in a full-grown leaf there are four of these twists lying on the top of the leaf. Each, 25c.

Drops of Blood—This is a superb new variety recently imported. The leaf is dark, well-center blotched with red of a blood hue. Is without question the finest Begonia grown. Each, 30c.

Queen of Hanover—Leaves silvery white, sometimes greenish white border veined; very fine. Each, 30c.

Scepter—One of the finest dark-leaved variation. Each, 30c.

Silverplate—A bright, silvery leaf; rapid growth. Each, 30c.

American Beauty—The grandest of all new Begonias Rex. It is simply perfect, both in growth and appearance. Each, 30c; 3 for $1.00.

Common Rex Begonia sorts, 20c each; 3 for 50c.
3 charming plants, 40c, or 6 elegant varieties for $1.00.

Rare Blooming Begonias.

10 for $1.00.

This collection is immensely popular, and thousands of our customers have taken this opportunity of getting 10 GRAND BEGONIAS FOR ONLY $1.00. This collection of blooming Begonias is strictly our selection, all different in style, growth and colors. They are free bloomers and splendid throughout, and are sure to please the eye. At the low price we cannot allow selection of sorts, hence all are strictly our selection. Please! We should say they would. The annals of pleased ladies write us of the genuine pleasure derived from growing this collection. They are so pretty and so sure to give satisfaction that we send them out with great confidence.

10 SPLENDID SORTS, POSTPAID, $1.00.
5 SPLENDID SORTS, POSTPAID, 50c.

A Few Rare Named Blooming Begonias.

Bertha—Resembles 12; flowers bright red. Each, 20c.
Incarnata—1. Dark leaves and silver dots; pink flowers. Each, 20c.
Ingramii—Resembles 8; great winter bloomer; flowers carmine. Each, 20c.
Dregii—Resembles 5; never out of bloom. Each, 20c.
Weltoniensis—A great bloomer; pink flower; resembles 10. Each, 20c.
Sanguinea—13. Top of leaf deep green and bottom soft crimson. Each, 20c.
Metallica—8. A great novelty; fine foliage; rose blossoms. Each, 20c.
Schmidtii—9. Flowers white, tinged with pink; extremely floriferous. Each, 15c.
Palm Leaf—9. Named from its tropical shaped leaves; always rare. Each, 15c.
Alba Picta—2. A splendid Begonia; leaves spotted, flowers white. Each, 20c.
O. Scandens—The running Begonia; a great rarity; fine for vases. Each, 20c.
Rubra—4. Grandest of all Begonias; most growers; flowers pink. Each, 20c.

Our Brilliant Begonia collection of 10 Plants postpaid,

FOR ONLY $1.00.

Tuberous Begonias.

The tubers rest in the winter, like the Gloxinia, but start early in the spring. They thrive best treated as a pot plant, when the massive, brilliantly colored blossoms will both please and astonish you. For garden culture, plant June 1st.

Victoria — Mammoth, double; white; very rare. Each, 20c.
Prince Albert—Very large, double; yellow. Each, 20c.
Gladstone—(immense blossoms of) brightest red. Each, 20c.

The 3 double sorts, postpaid.

SINGLE SORTS.

Alba—Very large blossom. Each, 20c.
Rosea—Pink; immense blossoms. Each, 25c.
Red—Finest quality; brilliant. Each, 20c.
Yellow—Very fine indeed. Each, 25c.
Mixed Bulbs—For 3, 50c; each, 20c.

Fancy Caladium.

No plant excites more admiration than the Fancy Caladium. A few of these plants in a conspicuous place, with their wonderful and gorgeous leaf-markings, will attract constant attention. They are marvelous, grandly, gloriously beautiful—nothing like them in the floral world!

Bicolor — Gorgeous, red center. Very choice, 30c.
Beethoven—Green, spotted white. Each, 30c.
Prince — Green, crimson mid-ribbed. Each, 30c.
Mozart—Green, spotted and dotted red; fine; 25c.

Our selection 5 rare Fancy Caladiums for only 60c, postpaid; 6 for 90c.

FANCY CALADIUM. EACH, 30c.

Caladium Esculentum.

The foliage of this tropical plant is of immense size, frequently measuring from 5 to 10 feet in circumference. It is particularly striking when grown either single or in a group on the lawn, with Cannas as the center. Each, 20c; 3 for 50c.

Camellia.

Ports rare over the purity and simple grandeur of the Camellia. Whose pure and spotless blooms boasts no fragrance and conceals no charm.

Queen Esther—Pure double white. Each, 50c.
Mt. Vesuvius—Elegant scarlet. Each, 50c.
Intricata—Variegated. Each, 50c.
The 3 for $1.00; any 2 for 75c.

The Bismark Apple is the Novelty of the Century. See Page 99.

Brugmansia Arborea.

This is one of those plants of which words fail to convey a true idea of its magnificence, and people who see it for the first time are bewildered. It blooms freely at all times of the year, both winter and summer, in a window or conservatory, or it can be cultivated in the garden during the summer, and wintered in a cellar or pit. The flowers are over a foot long, and 8 or 9 inches wide, of a creamy-white color, and very sweet. The striking beauty of these gigantic, enormous, glorious blossoms cannot be described. They make magnificent lawn plants when plunged in the ground during the summer. 25c.

BRUGMANSIA—ANGEL'S TRUMPET. EACH, 25c.

Each, only 25c. Large Plants, $1.00.

PRICE OF BRUGMANSIA, ONLY 25 CENTS.

Cuphea Hyssopifolia.

Entirely distinct. Bushy habit; myrtle-like foliage; lilac blossoms. Each, 20c.

Cigar Plant—Tube of flowers; scarlet; tip white and black; very free-blooming. Each, 20c.

Red, White and Blue—A new Cigar Plant; very large blossoms. Each, 20c.

CIGAR.

Do You Farm? Then Try the "Big 4" Oats.

Dracaena.

One of the hardiest, most satisfactory decorative plants known; of easy culture; always looking well.

Indivisa—Splendid for vases or center plants. Each, 30c.

Terminalis — Foliage green; very showy indeed for center plant. Each, 25c.

INDIVISA.

Cooperii—Leaves richly covered with scarlet, often edged with white. Each, 50c.

Brasiliensis—Massive green leaves, gracefully recurved. Each, 40c.

A PAGE OF ODDITIES.

No class of plants gives more satisfaction than the Cacti.

Rainbow Cactus—The plant is covered with a network of spines which range in color from creamy white to deep crimson, hence its name "Rainbow." When in bloom its grandeur is unsurpassed, bearing flowers inches across, bright crimson with a white center. Each, 75c.

Phyllocactus—The most brilliantly beautiful blossom among Cacti is found on this plant, often bearing 20 blossoms annually. Each, 20c; large, $1.00.

C. Frutescens—Blooms profusely and carries itself with a great number of small red fruit. Must be kept moist. Each, 20c.

Pilocereus Senilis, or Old Man—Is superbly beautiful; the long, white hair, so thickly grown, resembles the hoary head of an aged man. Each, 50c; second size, $1.00.

Rhipsalis Mes (1 cent "bloom"). Cacti—Each, 15c.

Aloe Variegata—Too well represented to call to mind further description. Leaves equally arranged, here concave, striped. The curve, channel, dense, colored of all mottled plants, of very easy growth. A noble plant. Each, 20c; large, $1.00.

Night Blooming Cereus—This gorgeous Cactus usually opens at 7 o'clock evenings, attaining its greatest beauty at 11; blossoms sometimes 12 inches in diameter. The leaves of a very free-blooming, and of easy culture, requiring little care. It is in our collection. Each, 25c.

Cereus Flagelliformis—Also called "Rat Tail," of dwarf, drooping habit; admirably suited for hanging baskets; beautiful reddish pink blossoms, very free bloomer indeed. Each, 20c.

Agaves, or Century Plant—Green, 25c variegated, 50c.

ALOE VARIEGATA, 75c.

Gasteria—One of the rarest of rare plants. Grows rapidly and bears odd blossoms on long stems. Each, 40c; large, $1.00.

FLAGELLI FORMIS.

GASTERIA. EACH, 40c.

Lobster—A wonderfully free bloomer; frequently blooming three to four times a season. Of drooping, weeping habit; remarkable! Blooming time. Each, 50c.

Candle Cactus (Opuntia)—This is the Candle Cactus of New Mexico. Wonderfully beautiful blossoms; yellow and purple. Each, 20c.

Texas Fence Cacti—Massive large leaved, rapid growing. Very beautiful. In great demand. Each, 20c.

STAPELIA, A RARE BEAUTY. EACH, 20c.

Stapelia—Very odd indeed, bearing beautiful deep yellow colored blossoms, with deep maroon markings, and of wonderful construction. Each, 20c.

Old Man Cactus and His Family, for $1.35.

PHYLLOCACTUS. IT'S GRAND. EACH, 20c.

OLD MAN CACTUS AND ——.
12 SORTS, INCLUDING OLD MAN, POSTPAID, $1.35.

CACTI COLLECTION.

12 Plants for $1.00.

Now, then, do you want a lot of pleasure for but little money? Then you will want our "Old Man Cactus and His Family" collection. They are fine for summer, fine for winter; indeed they seem to come just to best use in winter, when their curious growth and magnificent blossoms come into full play, always showing new forms and blossoms.

12 Beauties for only $1.00.

These will all be different, curious shapes and beautiful blossoms, and will be strictly our selection of 12 fine varieties.
　Our selection of 12 sorts, $1.00; including Old Man, $1.35.
　Our selection of 6 sorts, 50c; including Old Man, 95c.
　Our selection of 3 sorts, 25c; including Old Man, 75c.

Cactus Seed.

There is much pleasure derived from growing Cacti from seed. Our mixture of seed is very fine. You will be surprised at the odd looks of Cacti just sprouting from the earth. Sow in flat boxes filled with coarse sand. Keep moderately moist. Choice mixed, pkg., 10c; Wonder Mixture of Cacti seed, pkg., 25c.

4 Sacred Scenes (Bible) Plants, 75c, Postpaid.

1. Crown of Thorns, or Euphorbia.

On the wild, rocky hills of Judea, and in the Immediate neighborhood of Jerusalem, this curious shaped plant is found, like a peculiar plant, thorny, with a few bright leaves and a sharp issue of light rose blossoms, of the easiest possible culture, and can be trained to assume any shape; as a crown, anchor, harp, wreath, cross, etc. "The Crown of Thorns worn by our Saviour," was made out of this plant, and the thorny branches were frequently used for the banishment of offenders. Indeed, some sacred histories assert that the dried gives us our Saviour before his death was made from the bush of this plant. Get one for your child and see with what love and pleasure it will be watched and trained. Each, 25c; large size, 50c.

2. The Fig.

Nothing will please the children more than the Fig Tree or Crown of Thorns. The fig is of the easiest culture; can be placed in soil during winter, and set out early in spring. We ship the fig during summer (in catalogue); to California August 25th, we have a fine with it well developed figs. Each, 50c; second size, $1.00.

3. The Resurrection Plant.

Among the pines and cedars of Palestine, in the thickets of the India, this circular plant is found. Imagine a bunch of withered-looking shoots, brown, stiff and apparently dead; place it in water, and within an hour it is transformed from a withered-looking bunch into a lovely patch of green anew. Each, 25c; 3 for 50c.

4. Star of Bethlehem.

In the valleys of Jezreel and Hebron, at the foot of Mount Tabor and the Lebanon Mountains, so, also, throughout the plains and valleys watered by the Jordan, this pale blue, almost white, star-like, bulbous plant grows wild, and it is a favorite among the Palestinian inhabitants, and also among the travelers who annually visit these sacred scenes. Each, 15c; 3 for 30c. 1 plant each above 4 (from Sacred Scenes), postpaid 75c.

JAVA COFFEE PLANT—This is imported from Java, and is a great rarity. It will grow in the house to perfection and will bear coffee when quite young. Each, 20c.

MOCHA COFFEE—These two plants resemble each other very much, only that one is from Java and the other from Mocha. Each, 20c.

TEA PLANT—From the plant the celebrated tea of China is gathered. 50c.

THE VANILLA PLANT—This is a thick, pineappel great with fine blossoms from which the vanilla of commerce is obtained. Each, 20c.

WAX PLANT—A rare climber, bearing large clusters of wax-covered, delicately scented flowers. Each, 20c.

Orchids.

Elegant sorts, choicest blossoms. 50c to $2.00 each.

Agave or Century Plant.

Variegated—Each, 25c; large plants, $1.50, $2.00, up to $25.00 each.

Green—Each, 25c to $5.00.

CENTURY PLANT.

UMBRELLA PLANT—A great beauty. Splendid for vases and pots, where a magnificent effect is desired. Even will in water. The plain green variety. Each, 15c; 2 for 25c.

Yucca.

Grows more beautiful and blooms more freely each succeeding year. It grows and also forever, bearing great quantities of white blossoms, very desirable for a lawn ornament. Each, 20c. Yucca seed, pkg., 10c.

THE JAVA COFFEE PLANT, 20c.

Solanum.—Always pretty. Its bright red berries lend to this pot plant a great charm. Each, 20c.

YUCCA, 20c.

CALLAS.

Salzer's Ever Blooming Calla.

Gloxinia.

The Water Hyacinth.

CALLA, EVER BLOOMING.   EACH, 20c.

Black Calla.

Spotted Calla.

Climbing Violet.

Cyclamen.

Cardamom Plant.

Royal Coleus.

Croton.

ROYAL COLEUS.

Billbergia.

CROTON, EACH, 20c.

Camphor.

Peperomia.

Farfugium Grande.

Strobilanthes.

Thyrsacanthus (Carmine Fountain).

Sanseveria.

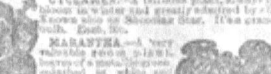

Swainsonia.

Mexican Tradescantia.

Haemanthus.

Crimson Violet.

Genista, or Shower of Gold.

Ficus Elastica.

Physalis Francheti.

Feverfew.

BRIDAL VEIL.

CHRYSANTHEMUMS.

MRS. MCKINLEY—PREMIUM CHRYSANTHEMUM.

Seven Giant Chrysanthemums.

These Seven giant colossal bloomers contain absolutely the cream of "Mums." None finer, none grander, none more glorious, none larger, none stronger, none surer to please—seven sorts—the golden number—'tis enough!

1. Mrs. McKinley—Pure white; honors the spotless name it bears. Great, pure white blossoms. Each. 20c.
2. Gold Standard—Giant trusses, enormous blossoms; golden color. Bewilderingly beautiful. Each, 20c.
3. The World—Wonderful size; noble bearing. Color, pink ; a giant blossom. Each, 20c.
4. Mrs. John A. Logan—A superb beauty; great blossoms of intense orange red. Enormous size. Each, 20c.
5. Free Silver—Colossal blossoms, pure snowy white, a veritable snow white silver giant. Each, 20c.
6. Pink Giant—A grand flower; colossal size; beautiful pink trusses, wonderfully grand. Each, 20c.
7. Setting Sun—Noble, largest, broader, bolder, grander among the giant yellow. Each, 20c.
Above 7 postpaid $1.00. Any 3 for 40c.

15 for $1.00.—Combines varieties of Chrysanthemums, we sell all colors at 10c. each, 3 for 50c; 15 for $1.00.

HELIOTROPE.

This delicate and delicious perfume stands unrivaled; nothing can take its place in bouquets. You cannot miss it, even if you plant a dozen, for no perfume is considered quite so lovely.

White Coral.

This is the finest light Heliotrope that we have ever seen. Its great clusters of light, deliciously-scented blossoms, often 32 inches in circumference, are borne in great abundance. Each, 20c ; 3 for 50c.

THE QUEEN. EACH. 15c.

The Queen Heliotrope.

Enormous trusses of deep purple giant blossoms ; very sweet ; one of the very finest. Each, 15c.
Snow Wreath—Nearly white. Each, 15c.
Negro—Dark. Each, 15c.
Our selection, 3 Heliotropes for 25c.

Clerodendron Balfouri—
Flowers are borne in elegant profusion, and are rarely beautiful and distinct. The outside petals are pearly white, and in high contrast, the inserted stamens are reddish purple, with somewhat chocolate-colored stamens. Each, 25c.

MelonPear or Pepino
A rare plant from Mexico, bearing delicious fruit all fall and winter. Great novelty. Each, 20c.

Lobelia.
Pretty plants for baskets, vases, etc. Nothing just like this ; flowers blue. Each, 5c ; 3 for 15c ; 12 for 50c.

CANNAS.

1. Wisconsin—A very dwarf Canna, which will show bloom every day in the year, its flowers being borne in great compact panicles, often as large as a man's hat, and of the most intense deep scarlet color. Each, 15c.
2. Mad. Crozy—The flowers are produced in large branching stems, closely set with bloom ; individual flowers very large ; dazzling crimson scarlet, distinctly bordered with yellow. Finest of all blooming Cannas. Each, 15c.
3. The Tiger Canna—Deep foliage ; dwarf habit ; begins blooming when very small. Flowers extra large, yellow color, thickly spotted with crimson. The most striking novelty of recent years. Each, 15c.
4. Flamingo—An intense light blood red. Each, 20c.
5. Burbank—Orchid flowers, enormous trusses ; clear yellow, crimson center. It's immense. Each, 20c.
6. Chicago—Grand sort ; great blossoms ; finest red. Each, 20c.
7. Italia—Colossal blossoms ; center brilliant red, surrounded by wide band of clear yellow. Each, 25c.
Above 7 grand Cannas, one each, $1.00.

THE WISCONSIN CANNA. 15c.

DAHLIA.

The choicest of these great favorites are becoming more and more known, and the inquiry for same assumes enormous proportions. Our stock is fine ; yes, magnificent. We find our strong rooted cuttings give great satisfaction. General favorite, growing from 2 to 5 feet high, and producing a profusion of flowers in the most perfect form. Very double.

DAHLIA PLANT.

Eva—30c   or—Delicate white and colored.
Finkert   A beautiful, large blooming pink.
Herbert—Jager is shaded ; beautiful.
Louis Philip—Rich velvety crimson ; large.
Perfection—Clear yellow—fine.
Triumphant—Dark velvety brown.
Vivid—Bright red ; very double.
White Bedder—Host white ; very double.
H. W. Ward—Old gold, tinged at times with scarlet or white ; very double.

Rooted Cuttings (these bloom this summer)
Price, 10c ; 3 for 25c ; 13 for 75c.
Dahlia Bulbs, 20c. each ; $1.50 per 12.

Single Dahlias.

These are seedlings raised from the rarest European Dahlia collectors' seed. They are fine, rare and beautiful. Each, 35c ; 3 for 30c.
Rooted Cuttings Single Dahlias, 15c. each ; 3 for 30c ; 12 for $1.20.

FERNS.

We associate Ferns with wild and romantic scenery ; where mountains and valleys, rocks and shaded rills combine their fascinating influences upon the imagination. They thrive best in a warm room, if kept moist and shady. Shower frequently.

Sword Fern. Each, 20c.

In it we have the most satisfactory of all ferns—hear what we say, the most satisfactory of all ferns. It's the very best to grow for house use. It does exceedingly well everywhere. It's charming, graceful, magnificent, healthy fronds are limitable. Just the thing for baskets and jardineers.

No picture, no illustration, no description can do justice to this most magnificent of all graceful, hardy, easily kept ferns. Mrs. Salzer would not part with her Sword Fern jardineers for $25. Its great fronds are often six feet long, and the very essence of beauty and grace.

Price of Sword Fern, 20c. each ; 3 for 50c. Large, 40c. to $1.00.

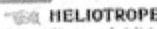
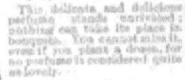

SWORD FERN. EACH, 20c.

India Fern—From the East Indies. "The rarest, most graceful, loveliest darling you ever saw," is the way a pleased lady calls it. Each, 20c.
Silver Fern—An exquisitely beautiful silvery foliage. See bottom leaf. Each, 25c.
Gold Fern—Stems covered with gold dust. Each, 20c.
Lycopodium—Runs 20 feet ; fine. Each, 25c.
Maiden Hair Fern—Very fine. Each, 20c.
Tremanla—Trembles easily. Each, 25c.
Petris Fern—A handsome foliage. Each, 25c.
Oak Fern—A great beauty ; thick, yes, very odd thick leaves. Each, 25c.

COLLECTION OF FERNS.
Our selection of 2 sorts, 25c.   Our selection of 3 sorts, 35c.
5 sorts including India Fern for 75c.

MOSES.
Especially adapted for creeping over soil, ferneries and the like. Unexcelled for this purpose. Each, 10c ; 3 fine sorts for 25c.

Jasmine Grandiflora.

Foliage fine ; flowers white, star-shaped. It is easy of culture, and should be in every collection. Blooms continually ; will climb, if desired, 20 feet high. It is a great beauty. A profuse bloomer ; very fragrant and sweet. It's the ideal of the poet and painter. Assume the sweet ; it must be grown to fully appreciate its fragrance and beauty. You cannot help falling in love with it, if you once grow same. Each 20c ; 3 for 50c.

Revolutum—A yellow-flowering Jasmine of exquisite fragrance ; grows rapidly to the height of 10 feet. Each, 10c.

Night-Blooming—This beautiful Jasmine is of no little merit ; in a vigorous grower and free bloomer ; the blossoms are small, creamy white, but borne in dense clusters. Each, 20c.

Vines, Creepers and Climbers.
We are constantly asked for running vines for rockeries, window boxes, vases, etc., and we have grouped together a large assortment of different vines and plants suitable for this purpose, which we offer at a remarkably low price. Price, our selection of sorts, each, 15c ; 5 for 50c ; 6 for 45c ; 10, all different, 65c ; 20 for $1.20.

LORBEER BAUM

Lorbeerbaum—Mirica.

A grand German favorite ; its leaves have a pleasant fragrance, and are used largely by Germans to flavor meats, soups, etc. A plant furnishes leaves for a family, and its rich green leaves are a source of constant pleasure to the grower. Each 20c ; 2 for 35c.

THE GRAND FUCHSIA TRIO, 50c.

[illegible] Cloud— This is [illegible] doubt the grandest double white Fuchsia grown. We have a bed of several hundred large plants, that is, at the time of writing, one solid mass of great, glorious snow-white balls, and is a sight worth coming miles to see, and hundreds of city visitors have been here daily, admiring its grandeur. It is the largest, finest double white Fuchsia, and its great snow-white balls, borne in such prodigal profusion, almost completely hide the foliage of the plant. Each, 20c; 5 for $1.00.

2. Midnight — This is an acquisition. Grows somewhat taller than its companion, Storm Cloud, but for genuine beauty its deep midnight blossoms are hard to beat, and is certainly the largest, finest, most [illegible] dark purple Fuchsia grown, having good habits, very healthy, bushy, and covering itself with great blossoms. Each, 20c; 5 for $1.00.

3. Red Dragon— Pre-eminently beautiful. While Storm Cloud and Midnight are great balls of Fuchsia blooms, Red Dragon produces an elongated shape, the blossoms often measuring 4 to 5 inches in length, and of an original new crimson red hue. It is [illegible] [illegible] the original seedling when 3 months old bore at one time [illegible] large, long, lovely buds and blossoms of a peculiar, indescribable vermilion velvety crimson color that must be seen to be appreciated, as no gem can in quality describe this "bloom[illegible]" novelty. Each, [illegible]

Above 3 Incomparable Fuchsias, 50c.

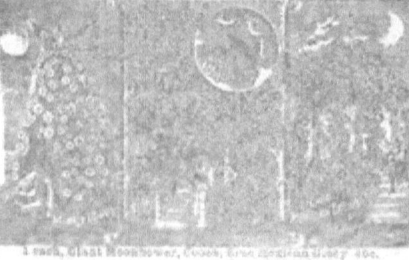

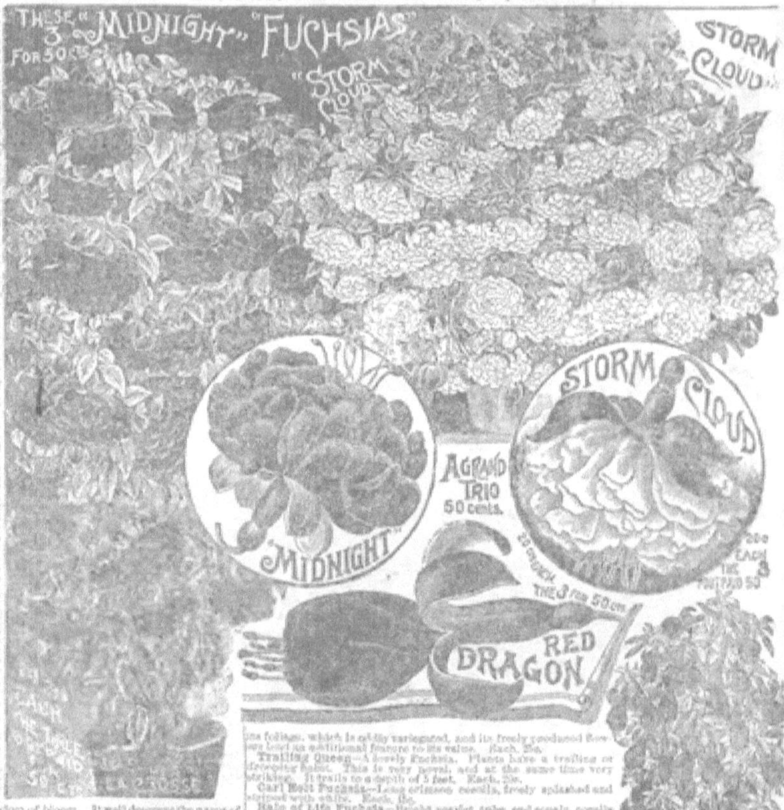

Speciosa Fuchsia— [illegible] blush-rose tube and sepals, reddish corolla; extra free bloomer. This is the best ever-blooming Fuchsia we know of. Nothing like it for freedom of bloom. It well deserves the name of [illegible] bloomer, as it is rarely seen without scores of blossoms. Each, 15c.

Purple Glory Fuchsia— Enormous trusses of double deep purple blossoms. Each, 20c.

Earl of Beaconsfield— Is very vigorous, fine in appearance, and [illegible] great, long, [illegible] trusses of orange rosy sepals and [illegible] carmine corollas. Each, 20c.

Storm King Fuchsia (also known as Weeping Fuchsia)—Pure [illegible], very double. Each, 20c.

[illegible]array— The most valuable decorative Fuchsia, on account of its foliage, which is oddly variegated, and its freely produced flowers lend an additional feature to its value. Each, 25c.

Trailing Queen— A lovely Fuchsia. Plants have a trailing or drooping habit. This is very novel, and at the same time very striking. It trails to a depth of 5 feet. Each, 20c.

Carl Holt Fuchsia— Long crimson corolla, freely splashed and striped with white. Each, 15c.

Halo of Life Fuchsia— Bright scarlet tube and sepals, corolla deep scarlet. Each, 20c.

THREE GREAT CLIMBERS.

1. New Giant Moon Flower.

It grows anywhere where there are old trees, walls or strings to cling to, growing 30 feet in one season; blooms continuously from June to November, the moon-like flowers being of the purest white, of giant size; blooming only at night or on dull days; gives out a delicious odor similar to the Jasmine.

Extra Strong plants—Each, 20c; 3 for 50c; 12 for $1.75, by mail. Seed, 15c per pkg.

2. Cobea Scandens, or Mexican Glory.

Three or four plants placed on the side of a house, will cover it fully twenty feet wide, and rival each other as to which will reach the top of the roof first, and will all the while display a purple blossom glory unknown to any other flower or vine, continually lavishing its mass of great purple, bell-shaped, perfect pendant blossoms, borne on long stems, during the whole season. Its leaves are fresh green, of unusual beauty of cut, while the gorgeous glory of its great purple blossoms stands unrivaled in the wide domain of Flora.

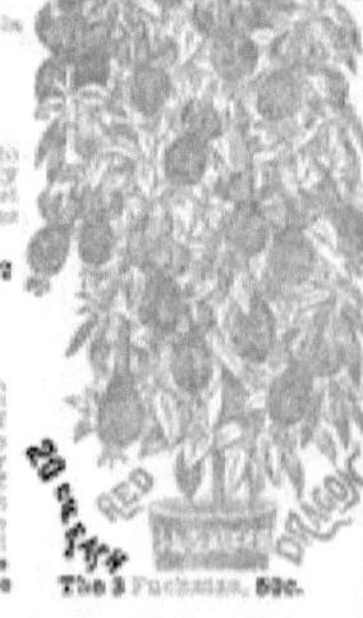

The 3 Fuchsias, 50c.

Each, 20c; 3 for 50c; 12 for $1.25; seed, 15c per pkg.; free by mail.

3. Blue Brazilian Glory.

This magnificent blue blooming Glory blossoms in great profusion. It is similar to the Moon Flower in growth, with blossoms from 8 to 9 inches in diameter. Each [illegible]

1 each, Giant Moonflower, Cobea, Blue Brazilian Glory, 40c.

[illegible] ONE EACH ABOVE THREE GREAT LIGHTNING CLIMBERS, 40c. [illegible]

RAINBOW COLLECTION OF 21 PLANTS FOR $1.00.

This great plant collection, beautifully illustrated on next page, composed of the best the greenhouses of America or Europe can furnish. A rainbow of colors, we offer at a price so completely within the reach of everybody, whether rich or poor, that we predict it will take

2,000,000 PLANTS.

to fill our orders for 1899. Well, no matter, we have them. We are the largest growers in America of rare-blooming and ornamental plants. To meet the demand of our large plant trade, we are obliged to grow enormous stocks of all kinds of roses, plants and bulbs—often more than necessary—to make sure that we have enough so after the heavy spring business is about over in May, we take this stock of various rare and good things and make it into a Rainbow Collection, and offer them to our customers at 11 plants for $1.00, or 11 plants for 60c., giving them 3 to 5 times the value of their money. They will be sent free by mail. All Rainbow collections are booked and will be shipped as early in the season as our stock permits.

This collection is immensely popular among our customers, and we append hereto a letter from Mrs. Jane Russell Ayers, of Ohio, who obtained from us last season our collection:

"JOHN A. SALZER SEED CO—Gentlemen: I have purchased plants for twenty years. It's safe to say that I have spent over $200 during this time, but never before have I really felt that I got more than my money's worth until I bought of you. All the plants I obtained from you were A No. 1 first and your Collection beats anything I ever saw. Yes, I got five times more than my money's worth. These twenty-two plants (you threw in one extra) contain Carnations, Cannas, Achillea and Begonias, Palms, Roses, Azaleas and Geraniums, Carnations and Chrysanthemums, Gloxinias and Salvias, Oranges and Coffee; yes, all of these choice, well grown, rare plants. It's the grandest surprise I ever had in plants. You are positively too generous. My neighbors, Mrs. Wilson, also Mrs. Mallory and Harry, each when they saw my plants ordered a collection, and they are more than pleased therewith. You will have large orders from here."

What is the Rainbow Surprise Collection?

It is composed of everything we have a surplus of, our selection consisting of rich, rare beautiful plants and bulbs. We send such fine plants that you are sure to be pleased. These we sell

11 plants, postpaid, for 60c.　　　　21 plants, postpaid, for $1.00.

With every collection of 21 plants we throw in our great Chrysanthemum Seedling, Mrs. McKinley, 20 cents, or the Climbing Violet, 25 cents, free.

SALZER'S NEW GIANT ACHILLEA.

SALZER'S GIANT ACHILLEA ALBA

Each year adds thousands of friends to this queen of all hardy free-flowering, constantly blooming pure white flowers. We cannot too strongly urge you to plant a few of our Achillea, as there is no flower than this. It is hardy as oak. A profuse bloomer, and will do well in any garden in the land than this. It is a hardy perennial, the top dying down to the ground every winter. Its many branches grow to the length of 1 or 2 feet, rooting on the ground and holding their great mass of pure white flowers about a foot above the soil. A plant well produce hundreds and over, thousands of flowers the first summer, but when established the second year we have had them with more than 5,000 perfect flowers on a plant at the same time. For cemetery planting it is the most valuable of all flowers, as it is sure to thrive and bear its great profusion of snow white flowers the whole treasure for years and years.

If there was to be but one white flower in our garden the Achillea Alba would be the one. Its 5,000 pure, snow white, perfect blossoms would accord it the place. It is hardy as oak. and blooms from May until snow flies.

Price of Salzer's Giant Achillea, each, 20c; 2 for 50c; 5 for 60c; 12 for $1.00; 25 for $1.50.　Common Achillea, each, 10c; 3 for 25c.

5,000 Blossoms in 6 Months From One Plant.

New Myrtle Bridesmaid.

This is the greatest Myrtle sensation of the age, and to show the value of the plant—the whole stock consisting of only a few plants, brought $600! It's a rare plant, a plant that will captivate everybody. The variegation of this plant is marvelous. A bright, light white surrounds the green of each leaf. It is extremely lovely and attractive. While the Bride's Myrtle is a deep rich glory we see the Bridesmaid is a flashy variegated leaf, found nowhere else. Fine, small plants. 50c; large, 75c.

New Variegated Myrtle. Each, 50c.

Bride's Myrtle.

An evergreen greenhouse shrub, with pure white flowers, blooming in early spring; used in Jewish religions rites. Our stock is fine. Each, 25c to $1.00.

BRIDE'S MYRTLE. EACH, 25c.

Hibiscus Glory of the Indies.

No doubt the greatest of all hibiscus, it is so free of bloom, so sure to please, so healthy and strong in growth, that it should decorate every home. Each, 25c.

Mr. Horsh (New) A large very double scarlet free blooming variety. Each, 25c.

Hibiscus. Single Red, 15c. Double Red 25c. Double Yellow, 50c.

Hibiscus Cooperii.

The rich glossy foliage has the greatest variety of variegation—showing light and dark green, pink, carmine, creamy yellow and white, and not two leaves show the same markings, some being all green, some nearly all pink and carmine, and others with nearly all the colors blended. It's a beauty. Each, 20c.

CLIMBING VIOLET

21 PLANTS FOR $1.00 POSTPAID

Send all orders to JOHN A. SALZER SEED Co., La Crosse, Wis.

GERANIUMS.

.his list contains the cream of old and new sorts; no poor variety fin ds a place in this list.

Helen Salzer.

It is pre-eminently beautiful, a seedling of an entirely new type, which we are sure will please every one. The upper petals are crystal white, margined with rosy carmine, which shades to a peach-blossom pink. The lower petals are a deep coral color, with a blotch of pure white in the center. This gradually merges into the coral, producing again the peach blossom pink, or on the upper petals, the whole forming a charming combination, so unique as to compel admiration at first sight. Price, 20c; 3 for 50c.

Irvin Salzer Geranium.

It is safe to say, right here, that it is by all odds the finest double Geranium in culture. The color of this remarkable Geranium is hard to describe, and we will not make an attempt at it, only state that it is a peculiar light violet color. The flowers are enormous, while the clusters are very large. Price, 20c; 3 for 50c.

3 Giant Trusses.

Wonderful—(Single). Intense scarlet, bright, dazzling, brilliant! Blossoms often, 9 inches in circumference. Wonderful in every respect. Retail customers seeing the plant in bloom gladly pay 50c each for small plants. Price 25c each.

Early Richmond—(Double)—Intense deep red, a great bloomer, color of the ripe Richmond cherry, splendid for variety. Each, 25c.

Queen Lil—A giant among blooms! Blossoms often 8 inches in circumference, of a soft, light salmon and deeply variegated with rose. Elegant. Each, 30c.

☞ Above 3 Giants, 75 cents.

Double Sorts.

Belle of LaCrosse—Magnificent, blue pink; very double; free bloomer. Each, 20c.

Las Gray—Double, bright salmon dwarf. Each, 15c.

Morning Star—White centre, rich pink, shading to white; very large, double. Each, 20c.

Brunatti Semi-double, light scarlet; 150 blossoms were counted on a 6-months-old plant. 1 c.

White Swan—Immense florets, pure white, double. 15c.

Mrs. Hoffman—Bears great trusses, of a clear, coppery red. Each, 20c.

Single Sorts.

Lady White—The finest single white. Each, 15c.

Dazzler—Rich scarlet white eye. Each, 15c.

Master Christine—Enormous trusses, beautiful pink; very free bloomer. Each, 15c.

General Grant—Bright scarlet; great bedder. Each, 20c.

☞ Our selection, 12 Fine Geraniums, postpaid, $1.50.

New Rose Geranium.

Angelus.

Sweet Scented.

It has the feature of the Rose, but, with the exception that it is a more vigorous grower, a freer bloomer, while the blossoms are larger and of a brighter red, resembling a small Pelargonium, in so respects; its most striking characteristic is... Nothing exceeds this in beauty and fragrance. Each, 20c.

NEW SWEET SCENTED ROSE GERANIUM, ANGELUS. 20c.

Salzer's French Hybrid Gladiola.

Go where you will the world over and you will find nothing more brilliantly beautiful than our French Hybrid Gladiola. They are simply incomparable. This mixture is taken from upward of 300 charming varieties, and is indescribably good.

Salzer's French Hybrid—Each, 5c; 12 for $1.00; postpaid, 50c; 100 for $5.00; 500 for $4.50.

Lemoine Hybrids.

Each, 6c; 12 for 60c.

	Each	Per 12	Per 100
Red shades	4c	35c	$2.25
Scarlet shades	4c	35c	2.00
Yellow shades	5c	50c	3.00
Variegated shades	4c	35c	2.00
Light shades	4c	35c	2.00

The Lily of the Valley

is the sweetest, most delicate flower. Reproduces readily, being perfectly hardy, and each succeeding year rewards the grower with a greater abundance of deliciously fragrant snow white blossoms. Each, 5c; 12 for $1.00; 100 for $5.00.

Imported, each, 10c; 12 for 60c; 100 for $3.75.

Hyacinth Candicans—Produces pure white bell shaped flowers on long stalks. Bloom in fall. Each, 10c; 3 for 25c.

Tri-Colors.

Mrs. Pollock—The ground color of leaf is deep green; next comes a zone of dark crimson, the margin of which is tinted (if scarlet), then a belt of green, the margin of being a clear yellow. As an ornament for the period of ornamentary, nothing but excels Mrs. Pollock. The flowers are dark scarlet. Each, 20c.

Mountain of Snow—The foliage is green, handsomely bordered with white. Each, 20c.

Dwarf Mme. Salleroi.

This is the greatest acquisition in silver variegated Geraniums for bedding and pot purposes that has ever been introduced. Each, 10c; 6 for 50c.

SALLEROI. 10c.

Distinction—The leaves are nearly circular, of a dark green, and have a narrow band of jet black near the margin. Each, 15c.

Happy Thought—Universally admired; new style of leaf. Large yellow blotch in the center of leaf, with an outer band of green. Each, 15c.

Fanny—House Zonale, tri-color. This is a fine strain. Each, 15c.

Sweet Scented Geraniums.

Apple fragrance, each, 20c; Rose fragrance, 10c; Oak Leaf, fine foliage, 15c; Hazleton Leaf, rose, very pretty, 10c; Nutmeg, the Mrs. Taylor (large rose), 15c.

Pelargoniums.

Of this most beautiful class of plants we have a fine collection, but give no description of the varieties, as it would be impossible to convey any idea of their varied markings. Each, 25c.

Ivy Geraniums.

This magnificent class of Geraniums is one of the most glorious gems in the floral world. Their bright, glossy, ivy-like leaves, graceful and trailing habit, and numerous trusses of large, double gay-colored flowers combine to form an object of the utmost striking contrast and beauty.

Mrs. Palmer—Flowers enormous size, full double white, borne in great profusion. Each, 20c.

World's Fair—As the World's Fair was the greatest event of its kind in history, so is this ivy Geranium the greatest of its kind ever introduced. Blossoms of enormous size, pink red color, borne in profusion. Each, 20c.

Blue Blood—Something new in ivy Geraniums—blooms early, grows rank and bears innumerable giant blossoms of a blue blood color; great. Each, 20c.

Above 3 to one address, 50c, postpaid.

LILIES.

1. **Auratum**—An exquisite beauty. The finest of all lilies, bearing 15 to 40 great white flowers, marked with a band of gold, spotted with maroon. Extra each, 30c; 3 for $1; 12 for $3.

2. **Tenuifolium**—This dazzling vermilion flower is simply exquisite. Each, 25c.

3. **Candidum**—White, very sweet, hardy as oak; grows against fast and blooms astoundingly. Each, 15c.

Above 3—Lovely for outdoors, 60c.

Harrisii—A bulb planted in spring, bears from 8 to 30 grand, white, trumpet-shaped blossoms. Extra size, each, 30c; smaller, 20c.

White Day Lily—Large blossoms, hardy. Each, 25c.

Blue Day Lily—Each, 15c.

Variegated Day Lily—Each, 25c.

Amaryllis Johnsonii—A grand scarlet lily. Each, 60c.

Lantana. Continuous blooming plants, affording a great variety of color and bloom.

Victor Hugo—Grand beyond description; immense yellow changing almost to blood red. Each, 20c.

Alba Perfecta—Pure white; fine. Each, 15c.

Luella—Beautiful light purple. Each, 15c.

Schleggili—Yellow, orange and purple. Each, 15c.

Thos. Meehan—New and valuable from the most exquisite coloring of the superb blossom just now beginning to be fully appreciated; the color is of deep orange, changing to deep vermilion, flowers often measuring 3 inches in diameter. Each, 20c.

Laurestinus.

An elegant plant adapted to house culture, producing a great abundance of white flowers during the holidays. We advise all to buy one for winter bloom. Each, 15c.

Ledebergia.

A house shrub of free growth; upper surface of the leaves bronze green; lower, deep, crimson. Each, 20c.

Lemon Verbena.

This plant is indispensable for the delightful fragrance of its leaves. Grows to the height of 4 feet, scenting the air, especially after a shower, for many yards with its deliciously sweet aroma. Each, 15c.

Lemons.

Florida Lemons—Growth of plant similar to Orange. Each, $1.00.

Linum Trigynum.

This plant must be seen to be fully appreciated. Its large, bright, golden yellow blossoms, borne so freely, astonish all who plant it. Each, 20c.

Mahernia Odorata.

One of the prettiest, rapidly growing hanging vines of today. It is one of those lovely plants you will never want to get along without when you once possess it. Each, 15c / 4 for 50c.

Maurandia.

Very graceful climber, with fine foliage and handsome large tubular flowers of a blue color; growth from 4 to 6 feet. Each, 10c.

Mackaya Bella.

A superior plant, with metallic green leaves. Grows very bushy, to the height of 2 feet, and covers itself in winter with bell-shaped, lilac colored blossoms. Very pretty indoed. Each, 20c.

Mimosa.

SENSITIVE PLANT.

A very interesting and curious plant, its leaves closing if touched or shaken, creating much amusement for children. Each, 10c.

Music Plant.

Strong musk fragrance; of good growth. Each, 10c.

Nierembergia Grandiflora.

Large bluish flower; requires plenty of sunlight to open its flowers. Each, 15c.

The Alamo Oleander.
LARGE SEMI-DOUBLE PINK. 25c.

THE ALAMO. NA., 25c.

In one of our travels through Texas we found growing near the Alamo, the birthplace of Texas liberty, a magnificent group of Oleanders. The grandest of them all, and we obtained the finest of them all, and have named same "The Alamo." It is a large, semi-double pink blossom, very free and of unusual vigor. No matter how badly the Oleander is treated, whether it be put in the cellar during the winter or in a cold room, it rewards the grower in the summer and fall with a great abundance of blossoms, so that one almost feels guilty in storing the plant away in the cellar during the winter. Price, The Alamo Oleander, each, 25c; Double Semi-White, 25c; Common Pink, 20c.

Madeira Vine.

Also known as Mignonette vine on account of its sweet fragrance. Rapid climber. Each, 10c / 3 for 25c.

Passiflora.

A glorious vine of flowers, said to represent the Crown of Thorns. Each, 15c. See page 9 and 10 and you will be glad if you order them.

Panicum Variegatum.

A variegated plant of creeping habit, valuable for vases, baskets or fern. Each, 20c.

PANSY

Pansies.
Our strain has no equal anywhere. It is known all over America and Europe. All large, fine blooming and exquisite coloring. Each, 5c / 12, 60c; 25, by mail, $1.25; 50, by express, $2.40; 100, by express, $4.50.

PASSIFLORA COERULEA.

Plumbago.
Plumbago Capensis—Produces large heads of light blue flowers, frequently 5 to 6 inches in diameter. It is a very fashionable flower. Each, 20c.

Solanum Jasminoides Grandiflora.

Its flowers are star-shaped, pure white, like a Clematis, and borne in enormous panicles or clusters, often a foot across. 20c / 3 for 50c.

The Manettia Vine.

Flowers intense scarlet, tipped with yellow, the most brilliant and striking combination, and borne by the thousand, each flower keeping perfect over a month before fading. It can be trained on a trellis, strings, or used for drooping from hanging baskets. Each, 20c. One each above two, 35c.

ORANGES.

Florida Oranges—We have distributed a great number and everywhere they have given satisfaction. Keep in a cool, sunny place, watering frequently, sprinkling leaves with Soulway's Soluble. They will do well in the house. Bear easily. Each, 60c; large, $1.00 to $10.00.

Dwarf Hardy Orange, Trifoliate.
Its great abundance of beautiful white fragrant flowers and then a golden mass of oranges, make it desirable for all purposes. It is hardy as far north as Ohio, Indiana and New York, and will do well as a pot plant removed to cellar for the winter. Each, 35c.

Otaheite Orange.
A grand pot plant and one of great beauty and novelty. It is magnificent in all its bearings. It's a dwarf orange, which grows, blooms and fruits freely in pots, even when only a foot or two high. The fruit is about one-half the size of ordinary oranges, and very sweet and delicious. The blossoms are produced in great abundance, delicate and beautiful in color and rich in delicious perfume. As a pot plant this lovely dwarf Orange is one of the most novel and beautiful that can be grown. It blooms most freely during winter, though it is likely to bloom at any and all times of the year. With one or two pots of it, anyone can raise an abundance of far-famed delicate and fragrant orange blossoms. The plants we supply are strong and ready to bloom and fruit at once. Price of Otaheite Orange: Each, 20c / 3 for 50c.

LEMONS.

Florida sorts. Very fine. Each, $1.00.

Oxalis, Gen. Howard.

POT WITH GEN. HOWARD OXALIS.
This is the finest pink Oxalis. Blooms frequently 3 inches in diameter, continuously in bloom. Today we have a 5-inch pot plant with 1,500 buds and blossoms on. It is a floral wonder. Each, 25c.

Oxalis Original.
Grows several feet tall and literally covers itself each beautiful. Orange colored, suddenly its bloom. Each, 25c; mixed sorts, each, 5c; 15 for 50c.

Primrose.
The single varieties bloom more profusely than the double. Are especially adapted for winter gardening, often yielding 1,500 blossoms per plant.

English Primrose.
Primula Obconica—The ever-blooming Primrose. Each, 20c.
Single Red or White Primrose—Each, 20c.
Double White—This is the most profitable of all plants we cultivate for winter flowers, well-grown specimens yielding often over 100 flowers from November 1st to April 1st. Each, 25c.

Great Mexican Primrose.
The plant grows 10 inches high; is neither too tall drooping nor too erect, so that their unsurpassed beauty is seen to best advantage. As a window plant it combines great hardiness and easy culture with immense showy blossoms. Each, 25c / 3 for 60c.

Salvia—Scarlet Sage
No plant grows such brilliant display of flowers as the calyx.
Salvia Gordoni—Dwarf scarlet. Each, 20c.
Splendens—This scarlet variety. Each, 20c.
Dauntless—Flowers of the richest blue. Each, 15c.
Variegata—A fine variegated variety. Each, 20c.
Maroon Queen—deep maroon. Each, 15c.
Snow Prince—an exquisitely beautiful white. Each, 20c.

Apple Salvia.
"Oh, what a delightful fragrance!" is the expression we continually hear when persons who visit our green houses pass the bed of Apple Salvia that we are growing. It is a strong grower, and will make a magnificent pot plant by fall, when it will do splendid service all winter in the house. The price is ridiculously cheap for such a splendid acquisition. Price, each, 15c / 3 for 30c.

Hardy Climbers.
Ampelopsis Veitchii.

It clings firmly to any wall or tree; needs no support. The leaves at first are of an olive green color, then brown, changing to bright scarlet in the autumn. Indescribably grand. Would not part with a 3-year old plant (20 feet tall) covering the north side of our house, for $25.00. Each, 20c; 3 for 50c; 7 for $1.00.

Ampelopsis Virginia.

A vine well known; climbing in one season to the height of 20 feet. It is as hardy as oak; does well anywhere. Each, 20c.

Climbing Wisteria.

See page 14. A glorious hardy vine, climbing 100 feet and blooming in great profusion. Can be trained shrub-shaped. 25c.

Honeysuckles.

For real home vines, to be near your, climbing over your windows and doorways, there is nothing prettier than the sweet-scented Honeysuckles.

1. **Royal Scarlet**—The prince of all Honeysuckles; climbs rapidly, attaining the height of 20 feet, and bears innumerable bright scarlet, fragrant blossoms. Each, No. 1; 3 for 50c.

2. **Happy Childhood**—Our new, pure white seedling. Grows very rapidly and bears great quantities of pure white, very fragrant flowers. Hardy. Each, 20c; 3 for 50c.

3. **Golden Beauty**—Bears very large, golden yellow blossoms in great profusion. Each, 20c; 3 for 50c.

4. **New Honeysuckle**—"Monthly." So named because it blooms every month, scarlet; no other. Each, 25c.

One each Nos. 1, 2 and 3, 40c; the 4 for 55c.

3 Hardy Rapid Climbing Vines 35c.

1. **Mountain Rose**—Native of China. Blooms two inches in diameter, light pink, extremely double. Plants hardy. Climb 25 feet in one season, reappear the next spring with renewed vigor. Each, 20c; 3 for 50c.

2. **The Great Cinnamon Vine**—It is safe to say that there are a million ones of this vine distributed than any other. It's "THE GRAND OLD VINE," beautiful, shiny, heart shaped leaves. The vine cannot be described, so beautiful is its rapid growth, a single plant having

vine and laterals in one season fully 3,000 feet long. The blossoms are fine of a rich cinnamon fragrance. They die down in fall but spring up in early spring with greater energy than before and are sure to please. Each 20c; 3 for 50c; 12 for 70c.

3. **Apios Tuberosus**—A matchless beauty, hardy as oak, having clusters of rich deep purple flowers, of delicious violet fragrance. Grows stronger each year. Each, 15c; 3 for 30c.

One each above 5, 35c; 3 each, 9 plants, for 90c.

Clematis.

By all odds the most popular of all hardy garden climbers of easy growth; needs but slight protection, and rewards the grower with innumerable blossoms.

1. **Clematis Jackmanni**.

It begins blooming usually the same season, and thereafter it is lavish with its floral glory. On a 3-year-old plant it is not unusual to see from 100 to 200 blossoms at one time. The Jackmanni begins to bloom early and continually. The blossoms are very large, thick in texture, and of rich, deep purple. The $1.00 sizes are strong, and will, with ordinary care, bloom freely this summer.

Price, large size, $1.00 each; second size 50c.

2. **Claret**—Wine color. Each, 50c.

3. **Snowflake**—Very fine white variety, blooming freely, bearing hundreds of blossoms. Each, 50c.

1 each above 3, $1.25.

Coccinia Clematis—Immensely popular, growing fully 15 feet high, covering the walls with bright coral scarlet flowers. Each, 25c.

Crispa Clematis—Free, robust growth, blooming from June until frost. Blossoms are large. Each, 25c.

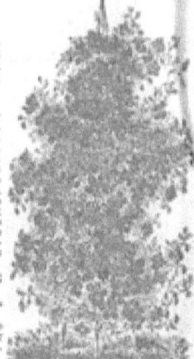

JACKMANNI CLEMATIS.

COMMON VINE.

One each of these 3 rapid climbing vines, 35c.

1. Hydrangea Grandiflora.

Its equal has yet to be found. Indeed it is the finest hardy shrub in cultivation; flowers are formed in large white trusses, 5 to 10 inches in length, remaining in bloom until killed by frost. They change from creamy pink to rosy pink in the fall. It is hardy as oak and a profuse bloomer, grows 5 feet high. Too much cannot be said in favor of this plant. Had a bush on our grounds 3 years old, in bloom last fall, and there were on it over 300 great trusses of flowers. It is to all means the best hardy shrub we know of, and we cheerfully recommend it. Splendid for Cemetery, as shown in the engraving, the plant is of compact and sturdy habit, and when laden with its great masses of bloom is exceedingly striking and attractive. This noble shrub is none grading alike with its superb presence the cottage, farmyard, large lawns, extensive grounds, parks, and it specially desirable when grown as tree specimen plants, as shown in our illustration. A universal favorite. Stands 50 degrees below zero. Price according to size.

Each, 25c;	5 for $1.00.
2d size, 50c;	3 " 1.00.
3d size, 75c;	1.50.
4th size, $1.00;	3 for $2.00.

2. **Common Snowball.** Well known. Each, 25c.

3. **Deutzia.** Flowers white; on long stalks. Each, 25c; 3 for 60c.

One each above, Hydrangea, Snowball and Deutzia, 50c.

Noble hardy Hydrangea Grandiflora. Each, 25c; 5 for $1.00.

New Japan Double Snowball.

Grandest of all double white shrubs—Noble in this climate. Don't confound it with the Common Snowball; it's immeasurably superior! Enormous balls of great snow-white blossoms, born in matchless prodigious profusion. Hardy as oak. This and the Hydrangea Grandiflora are noble companions. Each 35c; 2 for 60c; Large, 75c each. One each Japan Snowball and Hydrangea Grandifl., 50c.

RED BRANCHED, PRICE, 25c.

Hydrangea for House Culture.
Red Branched—The queen of all House Hydrangeas, big, giant pink blossoms. Each, 25c.
Thos. Hogg—Pure white, fine. Each, 25c.

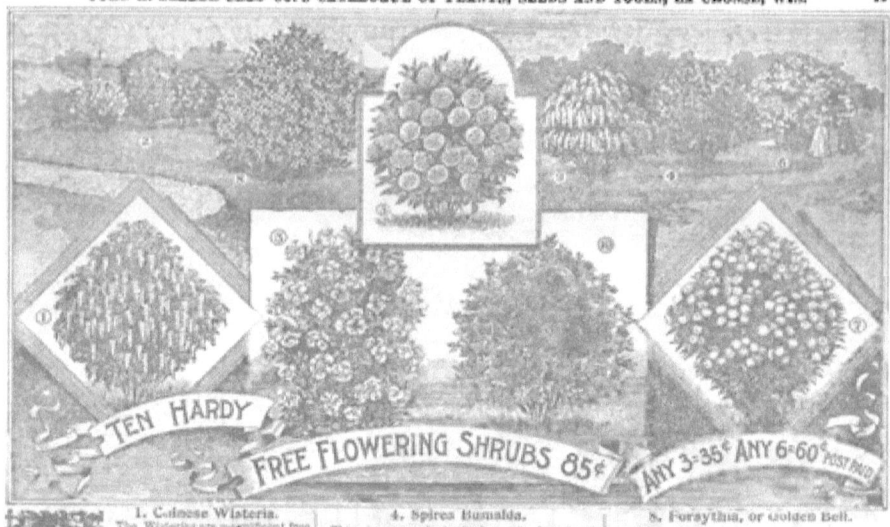

TEN HARDY FREE FLOWERING SHRUBS 85¢ ANY 3=35¢ ANY 6=60¢ POST PAID

1. Chinese Wisteria.

The Wisterias are magnificent free flowering climbers, blooming freely early in the season. Can we not urge upon our customers the superiors and immense beauty of deliciously sweet and lovely flowers from porches, balconies and verandas; grows 100 feet high. Nothing can be finer. It is considered perfectly hardy everywhere. Can be grown as a shrub as in illustration—or as a climber. White, or, 30c; 3 for 85c; 6 for 60c.

2. California Privet.

A noble shrub with beautiful blossoms and rare foliage. It is a shrub that is sure to please. Each, 20c.

3. Persian Lilac.

Hardy as oak. Bears its enormous trusses of pure white flowers in great profusion. Great improvement on the common variety of lilacs. Our best ever has made a poor cut of this; the blossoms are long, pointed, often ten inches long, of magnificent beauty. Each, 20c; 3 for 50c.

II. WISTERIA, No. 4y and fragrance. Each, 20c; 3 for 50c.

4. Spirea Bumalda.

This is a grand shrub, from the fact that it blossoms late in the season, blooming from June till affected and killed by frost. The blossoms are large and of a bright rose color. Is a shrub from Japan; perfectly hardy and will give satisfaction. Each, 20c.

5. Weigelia.

Roses—A grand shrub, which is a mass of fine bell-shaped pink blossoms during June. It is one of the most popular and beautiful of all shrubs. 25c.

6. Philadelphus.

One of the handsomest and at the same time hardiest shrubs in cultivation. The blossoms are large, pure white, waxy, of delicious orange fragrance and borne in prodigal profusion. 20c; 3, 50c.

7. Purple Fringe.

Greatly admired on account of its long feathery flower stalks giving the shrub the appearance of a cloud of smoke. Each, 20c; 3 for 50c.

Price the 10, mail size, 20c; any 3 for 50c; any 6 for $1.00, postpaid. 10, large plants, $1.75; any 3 for 50c; any 6 for $1.00, by express.

8. Forsythia, or Golden Bell.

Robes itself, during April and May, the length of its branches, in mammoth bells of a bright yellow color. It is such a mass of brilliant yellow that it can be seen for a long distance, and lights up a lawn as nothing else can at that early season. 20c.

9. Spirea Van Houttei.

The most showy of all the Spireas. The plant is an upright grower, with long, slender branches that droop gracefully with their weight of foliage and flowers. Flowers pure white, in great clusters and whorls, forming plumes 2 feet long. It blooms freely. Each, 20c.

10. Calycanthus.

This is the well-known "sweet-scented" shrub. It bears, in May, a great profusion of double purple blossoms, which have a strong, delicious pineapple fragrance. Very popular. Each, 20c; 3, 50c.

PÆONIES.

Now, there is no hardy plant more justly popular, more beautiful and serviceable than the Pæony. They increase in beauty and size with each succeeding year. Three or four plants will give from 200 to 600 great, gorgeous blossoms.

1. La Crosse—A glorious, fragrant, very double pink of giant, colossal, magnificent size. Each, 20c; 3 for 50c.

2. Goethe—Magnificent dark red variety, of great freedom of bloom, blossoms intense in color and large in size. Each, 20c; 3 for 50c.

3. Snowdrift—A Pure white, very large and finely formed blossom. Each, 20c; 3 for 50c.

4. Gicalot—A rich deep pink, of great beauty. Each, 20c; 3 for 50c.

One each above four for 70c, postpaid. Any 3 of above for 45c.

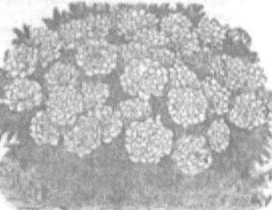

SNOWDRIFT, EACH, 20c; 3 FOR 70c.

Perennial Phlox.

It is impossible to describe the following quartet; they are as hardy as oak, and of great freedom of bloom. Plant anywhere in the garden; they will flourish, increase rapidly and bloom forever.

1. Phlox Diana—Bright, deep pink, with crimson center; giant blossoms; indescribably grand. This is the finest Phlox we have ever seen bloom. Each, 15c.

2. Heroine—Giant blossoms; magenta red; large florets; great trusses; very fragrant. Each, 15c.

3. Silver Lake—Peerlessly beautiful; blossoms large, pure snow-white; profuse bloomer. Each, 15c.

4. Elmira—Lilac, suffused with pale white, with splendid pink eye. 15c.

The above 4 Phlox, postpaid, 50c.

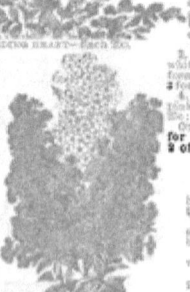

PERENNIAL PHLOX.

An old-fashioned, hardy flower, but one that deserves a place everywhere. Of it, it can be truly said, "A thing of beauty is a joy forever."

Rudbeckia—Golden Glow.

The most distinct large flowering hardy plant. A wonderful grower, very branching and each branch bears from six to twenty great shining golden yellow blossoms. A plant is literally covered with bloom. Hardy as oak. Increases rapidly. Each, 20c; 4 for 60c.

... more liberal and free in bloom than this. It will stand the coldest winters and flourish, and a single plant will bear from 200 to 300 long spikes of blood-red, heart-shaped, drooping flowers, hence the name Bleeding Heart. Price, postpaid: Each, 20c; 3 for 50c; 10 for $1.00.

BLEEDING HEART—Each 20c.

THE ROSE.

Our Premium Rose. 40c.

"NAMELESS BEAUTY"
Many years ago a German gardener brought from Germany a seedling Rose of great bloom, vigorous health and sweet fragrance. This was guarded carefully, no stock sold, and no name revealed. At last we have secured a generous supply of plants and we send it out as our great Premium Rose. It's a Rose of transcendent beauty, large and proud, of rich fragrance and exquisite pink color. It's a Tea Rose and blooms as freely as does the Bella Siebrecht, Bridesmaid, The Bride, etc. Price, each, 40c; 3 for 75c.

American Beauty.

Proudest and noblest of all Roses, that's what The American Beauty can truly claim. It has the true hybrid fragrance, and with a large size (blossoms often 5 inches in diameter); rich deep crimson colored free-blooming properties, makes it the finest Rose in America to-day. Each, 20c.

Hundreds of new Roses are being offered to the people of America at present by florists, and of the long list but few are really of lasting merit, or such that will reward the ordinary grower with dazzling like "paying buds." One or two buds a year from a new Rose with a high, commanding title is certainly not as good as 100 or more buds from a trusted, tried, standard Rose; hence our list this year contains only the cream of free bloomers.

Culture

Give the Rose good loamy soil, enriched with rotten cow manure or bonedust. Apply plenty of water, sunshine, and it is we sure to bloom and flourish as a Geranium or Fuchsia. A dozen of the following Roses planted in open ground in full exposure, with sufficient moisture, will reward the grower with bushels of blooms during the summer. For fertilizer, use Salzer's Pulverized Sheep Manure.

1. Bella — The sweetest freest bloom. Each, 20c.
2. Louis Philip — The grandest crimson blossom. 20c.
3. Isabella Sprunt — No freed so fine yellow Rose on free of bloom. 20c.
4. Sofrano — Grand. Saffron or buff colored; exquisite buds; free bloomer.

☞ THE ABOVE 4, 60c.
With each order for above 4, we add 1 Nameless Beauty Rose, 30c.

Marshal Niel.

Incomparably the finest Rose in any section or of any color. In the South, where it luxuriates in a genial soil and climate, or in a home where these conditions are supplied, it develops charms possessed by no other Rose. The flower is extremely large; rich golden yellow. Each, 30c.

5 Ever-Blooming Roses, 70c.

1. The Bride. — Flowers large and double, on long stems of finest texture and substance, lasting a long time in beauty. Magnificent buds. Each, 20c.
2. Wootton. This is a remarkably striking and brilliant ever-blooming Rose; bright magenta red, passing at the base to rich violet crimson, richly shaded; flowers are large, full; exquisite, with thick petals and delicious tea scent; very beautiful buds. Each, 20c.
3. Clothilde Soupert. — Flowers of large size, very full, produced of the most perfect form; very double and beautiful. The color is pearl-white, deepening to carmine at the center, and it certainly surpasses all other varieties as a pot Rose, and so far as its blooming qualities are concerned, it cannot be equaled for either in or outdoor culture. Each, 20c.
4. Perle des Jardins. — A magnificent Rose. The flowers, full, of globular form, very double and highly perfumed; clear, golden yellow. Its finest buds are very large. Each, 20c.
5. Catharine Mermet. — One of the grandest Roses; a bright flesh color; large, full, of beautiful form, of cultivation; buds very large. Each, 20c.

With each order for 5 Rare Ever-Blooming Roses for 70c, we add free 1 Nameless Beauty Rose, 30c.

The Three Belle Roses, 50c, postpaid.

Here we have 3 hardy, ironclad, climbing Roses of different form and color, that cannot be beat where abundance of blossoms, delightful fragrance and hardy vigor are desired. The price is so low — only 50c postpaid — that every farmhouse, every city home, every cottage and every palace should be graced by them.

1. Prairie Belle, or Prairie Queen — Grows to 30 feet long. Clear, bright, pink; sometimes with a white stripe; large, compact and globular; very double and full; blooms in clusters; one of the finest. Each, 30c.

2. Baltimore Belle — A large magnificent Rose of good growth, bearing its beautiful, almost white, blossoms in such profusion as to cover the blossoms even in blast. It is a splendid climber. Each, 30c.

3. Tennessee Belle — Deep rosy pink; shoots slender and flowers in clusters prodigally. Each, 30c.

1 each of above 3 Belle Roses, 50c, postpaid.
☞ With each order for above 3 we add free our "Snowcap" Rose, 30c.

THE THREE BELLES
THE THREE BELLE ROSES. ONE EACH, POSTPAID, ONLY 50c, AND "SNOWCAP" FREE!

The 4 Ramblers.

1. Crimson Rambler — The greatest Rose of the century. It is said to be hardy as oak, to withstand every caprice of climate, to grow rapidly, to remain outdoors even in Wisconsin's cold climate, and to bloom, and bloom all season long. A one-year-old plant, from which our stock was propagated had a single branch upon which there were 300 crimson blossoms, and over 3,000 blossoms during the first year. This Rose is offered at a lower price by many, but we trust to be careful to get the genuine. A plant under favorable conditions grows 10 feet the first season. Everybody growing some perennials it the rose wonder of the century. We cordially recommend same. It is hardy even with slight protection. Each, 20c; 3 for 50c; for $1.50.

2. Yellow Rambler — What is said of the Crimson Rambler applies equally to the yellow, only that the color is rich yellow. Each, 20c; 3 for 50c.

3. White Rambler — A transcendent beauty, a great climber, otherwise like the Crimson, except in color. Each, 20c; 3 for 50c.

4. Pink Rambler — A Rose of great merit, a rapid free blooming Pink Rambler — rambles everywhere. Each, 20c; 3 for 50c.

1 each above 4 Ramblers, only 75c.
3 each above 4 Ramblers, only $1.25.

☞ With each order for the 4 Ramblers we add our "Snowcap" Rose, free.

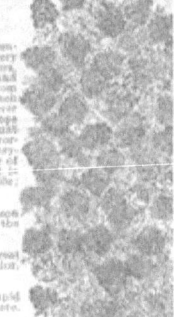

Crimson Rambler, the Prize Rambling Rose. Each.

Three Hardy Moss Roses

The Moss Roses are known in England and song. The graceful bud and stem are sought everywhere, varieties are hardy and very floriferous.

The Pink — Beautiful shade of pink .... Each
The White — Pure white, large buds .... Each
The Red — Deep color; fine form .... Each

One each of these 3 grand Moss Roses, 65c.

THREE HARDY MOSS ROSES 65c

PRINCELY HARDY GARDEN ROSES.

The Hybrid Perpetual Roses

Are justly popular, as they combine perfect hardiness with the most perfect forms and the most brilliant colors; surpassing the Tea Rose in rich perfume; blooming two and three times a season.

1. General Jacqueminot.

Rich, velvety, scarlet crimson; magnificent bud, often 4 inches in diameter; the most popular hardy Red Rose grown; blooms several times during the summer. Each, 20c.

2. Magna Charta.

A splendid rose; extra large, full flowers, very double and sweet; color clear, rosy red, beautifully flushed with violet crimson; a sure bloomer; one of the hardiest. Each, 20c.

3. Mad. Plantier.

It is perfectly hardy, and withstands the cold winters of Wisconsin without protection. It is a pure white, perfect flower, fine buds, very fragrant; especially suitable for cemetery planting. If grown very fast, and a two-year-old plant will bear from 300 to 500 beautiful blossoms. Each, 20c.

Above 3, only 45c.

4. Hardy Yellow Rose.

The old-fashioned Hardy Yellow Rose is one of the finest pure, deep yellow hardy Roses ever grown. It is perfectly hardy, blooms profusely, requires no protection; rich golden yellow flowers; very handsome and desirable. Each 30c.

Above 4 for 55c.

☞ With each order for above, we add free our Snowcap Rose, 30c.

Full culture directions for Hardy Hybrid Perpetual Roses, also Climbing Outdoor Roses, with each collection order!

ABOVE SEVEN MAGNIFICENT HARDY ROSES 85¢ ANY 3 FOR 40¢ POSTPAID
LARGE STRONG PLANTS EACH 30¢ FOUR FOR 90¢ THE SEVEN FOR $1.50 BY EXPRESS

1. Paul Neyron.

We ask special attention to this grand Rose; the flowers are immense; probably the largest and finest Rose; bright shining pink, clear and beautiful; very double and full; finely scented; blooms the first season and all summer; no collection is complete without this magnificent variety. 30 cts. each; 3 for 60 cts.

2. Fisher Holmes.

A glorious Rose; the only fit companion of the peerless, matchless General Jacqueminot. It blooms freely; buds large and intense crimson. Each, 30c.

3. Snowcap.

A colossal Rose in every respect. It's a colossal grower and bears its great pure white double blossoms in prodigal profusion. It's a grand freedom of bloom reminds one of the eternally snowcapped Mountains of the Alps. It is our Hardy Premium Rose. Price, 30c.

4. Captain Christi.

A giant Rose, large pointed buds, deliciously sweet. Peach colored, a grand sort. Each, 25c; 3 for 60c.

5. Mad. Alfred de Rougemont.

White flowers, finely tinged and clouded with pale rosy blush; large, full and double; borne in large clusters, fragrant and good. 30c each; 3 for 60c.

6. Boule de Neige.

A lovely Rose; clear white color; very free of bloom; hardy and with all a grand Rose. You will like it! Each, 30c; 3 for 60c.

7. Dinsmore.

A magnificent Rose unparalleled in its variety of scarlet color. Blooms prolifically. This is an everbloomer, almost always showing its intense scarlet blossom. Each, 30c.

☞ One each above 7 Glorious Roses, postpaid, 85c.

THE

1. Martha Washington.

Over a hundred years ago George Washington planted this Rose in honor of his bride, at Mount Vernon. Color, pure white; perfect; is double to the center, and of unsurpassed fragrance; buds beautiful and long pointed. It is a rapid grower, especially the second season, when it attains a height of from 8 to 12 feet, and is so literally covered with pure white fragrant flowers as to completely hide the foliage. It is a magnificent Rose for outdoors, splendid for cemeteries, hardy as oak, and will do everywhere. Each, 30c; 3 for 50c.

2. Memorial Rose.

The great points in favor of this Rose for cemetery purposes are that it creeps on the ground like ivy, has dark green leaves, with numberless satiny white flowers, is as hardy as grass, and will grow in sun or shade. One could wish for no greater recommendation than the above description. We know of no three better Roses for cemetery purposes than the Memorial, Martha Washington and Mad. Plantier, and we trust every one to give same a thorough trial. Each, 25c; 3 for 50c.

Pink Memorial.

In every respect the same as the white Memorial except the color which is pink. Each, Hybrid Perpetual. Each, 30c.

FOR 55 CENTS we will send one each of the three great white-blooming hardy Roses for cemetery or lawn effects, namely, Memorial, Martha Washington and Mad. Plantier.

3. Mad. Plantier.

This pure white hardy Rose is fully described above under this tier.

Sweet Briar Roses. These Roses from the land of Burns give a powerful fragrance to both leaves and flowers. They are hardy and fine. Each, 30c.

The Martha Washington.

THE GRANDEST WHITE ROSE EACH, 30c; 3 FOR 50c.

PALMS.

Many persons have an idea that Palms are hard to grow. This is entirely wrong. There is no decorative plant that will stand such varied and rough usage as the Palm. Ordinary moisture, partial shade and warmth are the requisites in the tropics, and as nearly as we can give the plant these three requisites in our homes, the better they will flourish. The sorts that we list in this collection are hardy, rugged, vigorous, thrifty, beautiful varieties, such as will flourish in any home in America. They grow more beautiful with each succeeding year.

1. Phœnix Canariensis.

A magnificent Palm. The leaves are pinnate, spreading and recurved, and form one of the handsomest species of Palms. It is eminently graceful and peculiarly adapted for decorating the home. Each, 25c; 3 for 50c.

2. Lantania Borbonica.

Chinese Fan Palm—A glorious Palm; indeed, one of the best house varieties known. The leaves are large, fan-shaped, deeply divided and of a beautiful green. It is extremely hardy. Each, 25c; 3 for 50c.

3. Kentia Balmoriana.

One of the very best Palms for every purpose. Splendid as a decorator, beautiful as a grower, hardy in the extreme. You will like this variety. Each, 25c; 3 for 50c. Seed pkg., 10c; the 5 sorts, 25c.

4. Corypha Australis.

One of the grandest Palms cultivated. Its leaves are stately and massive, especially when the plant attains the age of 5 or 6 years, growing more beautiful with each succeeding year. Hardy and of easy growth. Each, 25c; 3 for 50c. Seed pkg., 10c; the 5 pkgs., 25c.

5. Filifera, the Weeping Palm.

The leaves are dark green, fan-shaped, from which hang thread-like fronts, as seen in cut. It will grow where the threatens flourish. All Palms when young have long, narrow leaves, developing the round, fan-shaped ones as they grow older; therefore, when you get your plants and see long leaves instead of round ones, do not think that the Wrong sort has been sent you. They will assume their shape as they grow. Each, 25c; 3 for 50c. Seed, 10c per pkg.; the 5 pkgs., 25c.

1 EACH ABOVE 5 PALMS, ONLY 60c.

PALM SEEDS—The 5 varieties of Palms are of easy growth from seed. Full directions "How to Grow" with each package. Each variety, per package, 10c. The 5 packages, 25c.

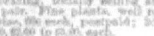

Cycas Revoluta, the True Sago Palm—Any one having seen this most magnificent Cycas, will admit that no other plant can equal it in grandeur. Leaves much used by florists for decorating, usually selling at $2.50 per pair. Fine plants, well rooted (of size, 60c each, postpaid; 30 size, $1.00, $2.00 to $3.00 each.

Zamia Integrifolia.

Similar to above; finer foliage and smaller stems; a very beautiful plant. Price reduced to 40c.

Pandanus Utilis.

Called Screw Pine from arrangement of leaves on stem. A stately plant similar to the Vetchii, well adapted for centers of vases or baskets. Easy to keep, rapid in growth; a constant source of pleasure. 1st size, $1.00 each; 2d size, 50c each.

Pandanus Vetchii.

The handsomest of all variegated plants. In every respect like Utilis, only handsomer. It's a stately plant. See cut. Each, $1.50; large plants, $2.00 to $3.00.

Poinsetta Pulcherrima.

Largely grown for cut flowers; blossoms scarlet, often a foot in diameter. Each, 30c.

Large Palms.

There is an increasing demand for these. There is no plant more beautiful, more serviceable, more hardy for house culture. We can furnish Palms of above sorts in 3 inch pots by express, for 50c each; 4 inch pots for 75c each; and 5 inch pots for $1.00 each. These will be noble plants, and are such as are sure to give to each grower great satisfaction and constant pleasure.

Aracaria Excelsa.

The grandest of all evergreen house plants; a regular beauty, very graceful, fine and rare. Easily taken care of. Small plants, 50c each; large, $1.00.

P. VETCHII. $1.00.

The Guava.

This magnificent pot plant, bearing blossoms and fruit continuously is a native of West Indies. In our home an eighteen months old plant bore five hundred fruits. A prosperous plant for house, parlor or kitchen. Does well everywhere. Fruit splendid for jellies, pies, etc., etc. The Guava has thick, climbing evergreen. Flossoms, the foliage, with pure white flowers of an agreeable odor. The fruit is large, about the size of an English walnut, and of a beautiful claret color, while the flavor is most delicious—sweet and aromatic, resembling that of the strawberry. It is used for dessert fruit, also for preserving, and is considered a rare delicacy. Each, only 30c.

The Dwarf Papaya.

No plant has so completely captivated us as this. It is a wonder in every respect. It grows rapidly, attaining to but a few weeks so large a size as a palm does in three years. It produces big, tropical leaves, the green trunk is spotted red. It is one of the most remarkable products of the vegetable kingdom. The fruit is borne in great profusion. Price, each, 30c.

DWARF PAPAYA—THE WONDERFUL. EACH, 30c.

GUAVA THE RARE BEAUTY. EACH, 30c.

Saizer's Peerless Petunias.

1. Defender—A pure white sort, having taken many first prices as the handsomest double white Petunia. Each, 20c.

2. Red Rover—A magnificent variety; blossoms giant in size and of a bright red color. Each, 20c.

3. Thankful—This is a pure white seedling of enormous blossoms, most beautifully shaped and fringed flowers. It is very fragrant and a continuous bloomer. It's thankful. Each, 25c.

4. Favorite—Intense double, very large; beautiful color; very fragrant, and a free bloomer. You will like it. Each, 20c.

5. Brightness—Beautifully variegated; blossoms large; flowers sweetly fragrant. Each, 20c.

Any 2 for 35c; 3 for 50c; the 5 for 65c.

Rosemary.

This pretty German house. It is not without merit; leaves very fragrant, becomes small, blue color; stock fine. Can be grown to assume any shape. Very fine for buttonhole bouquets. Each, 20c; 2 plants, 35c.

Smilax.

Though grown principally for its elegant green foliage, so indispensible for floral work and house decoration, it nevertheless bears flowers by the thousand, which, for graceful beauty and delicate fragrance, cannot be excelled. It grows very quickly from seed. Price, 1 plant, 10c; 3 for 25c. Smilax, Extra Fine Seed. Pkg., 10c.

2

SALZER'S TUBEROSES.

BELLE OF SOUTH CAROLINA, TUBEROSE. EACH, 10c.

There is nothing that will give you more satisfaction and more pleasure, for less money, for less care and attention, than a dozen of our Tuberoses. For there is no Tuberose that has the reputation of blooming more freely than ours; indeed they will average 99 bloomers out of every 100 bulbs. They should be planted early, in 5-inch pots, in rich, sandy loam, watered moderately, beginning to bloom as early as July or August, and continuing for some months. A good way to have succession of bloom would be to plant bulbs every second week.

Pearl—Dwarf habit, free blooming. Extra. Each, 8c; 3 for 15c; 10 for 40c; 25 for $1.00.

Double—Each, 5c; 3 for 15c; 10 for 35c.

Belle of South Carolina—This new Tuberose is magnificent in every respect. Blossoms very large, perfect and of purest white. Indeed it is the most wonderful Tuberose in cultivation. It is not unusual to count from 50 to 90 beautiful, snowy white, waxy, fragrant, blossoms from a single bulb. We hope that everybody will give these splendid flowers a trial. Bulbs solid, sound and bring forth quantities of bloom. Each, 10c; 2 for 15c; 10 for 60c.

Stevia.

White, **winter-blooming** plants of great value.

Stevia Variegata—Finely **variegated.** Each, 15c.

Spirea Japonica.

One of the finest garden plants, **with** feather-like spikes of purest white flowers. Each, 15c.

Vinca.

Pre-eminently beautiful. Its bright pink and white flowers are borne continually on low bushy plants. Always in bloom, summer and winter. Each, 15c.

Running Vinca—A running vine with small lilac blossoms. Each, 10c.

Vinca Variegated—Like above. Each, 15c.

Wax Plant.

A fine, succulent, trailing plant; star-shaped blossoms. Each, 15c.

Verbena.

VERBENA.

The prettiest and most popular of all flowering plants suitable for beds. It commences to flower and spread from the first day the plants are set until late in the autumn, every day becoming more handsome. Our colors are white, pink, blue, purple, rosy crimson, red, maroon, striped, scarlet, dark red, etc. Each, by mail, 10c; 12 for 75c. By express, each, 5c; 12 for 60c.

☞SEED—Star Verbena Seed, all colors. See page 30. Pkg., 15c.☜

VIOLETS.

"Sweeter than all the roses." Easy culture.

New Climbing Violet—See page 4.

New Violet, "Modesty"—The grandest double white violet ever offered. A modest beauty. Each, 20c.

VIOLET, "MODESTY," 20c.

Swanly White Violet—Flowers frequently 1 inch in diameter and pure white color. Each, 15c; 3 for 40c.

Giant Russian Violet—This is single. Blossoms often 2 inches across. Very fragrant and hardy. Each, 15c; 8 for $1.00.

Marie Louise—One of the finest Violets grown; very double and large; color, dark lavender blue. Each, 15c; 3 for 30c.

Blue Alsatian—New. The finest, sweetest, purest, blooming dark blue double Violet grown. Imagine a pot with large, sweetly fragrant blossoms, and you have the Blue Alsatian. Each, 15c; 3 for 40c.

Belle de Chattenay—Light blue, often white. Each, 15c; 3 for 35c.

BLUE ALSATIAN. PRICE, EACH, 15c.

IRONCLAD FRUIT TREES AND TREE SEEDS.

What is more delicious in early June than a dish of sweet Strawberries and rich cream, and lots of Raspberries, Dewberries, Blackberries, Currants, Gooseberries and Grapes in their season! A small bed of Strawberries, a patch of Raspberries, a row of Currants, a few hills of Blackberries, a half-dozen Grapes, will keep a family in fruit almost all summer. These are as easily cared for as the Cabbage, as sure of yield as the Potato, and as hardy as the oak.

Tree Seeds for the Dakotas, Iowa, Nebraska, Etc.

Repeatedly the inquiry comes to us, which tree seeds shall we plant in order to get quick returns from same for our prairie soil? This inquiry comes to us from the Dakotas, Iowa, Nebraska, Kansas, Missouri and other states, and invariably we answer: If you want the quickest growing tree take the Locust, next the Box Elder and then the White Ash; indeed, these three varieties rival with each other as to which can grow the fastest. They are just the trees to plant in the West, and are trees whose wood in less than 25 years will be greatly sought. Planted now will, in 20 years, be worth $1,000 or more.

Seeds Required per Acre—Of Box Elder and White Ash we usually plant 4 pounds of each per acre; of Black Locust, 5 pounds per acre.

White Ash.

A splendid tree, growing rapidly and withstanding the dry atmosphere of the Western prairies to a remarkable degree. Price of the seed: Pkg., 5c; ¼ lb., 10c; lb., 25c, postpaid; by express, lb., 15c; 5 lbs., 75c., 10 lbs. or more at 12½c per lb.

Black Locust.

This tree is grown in great quantities in Nebraska, Colorado, Kansas and other Western states, and in a few years is large enough for fence posts. Price: Pkg., 5c; ¼ lb., 10c; lb., 30c, postpaid; by express, lb., 20c; 5 lbs., 90c; 10 lbs. at 15c per lb.

Box Elder.

A tree that does usually well, growing rapidly, and makes wood that is at present in great demand in the East for boxes, etc. Price: Pkg., 5c; ¼ lb., 10c; lb., 25c, postpaid; by express, lb., 15c; 5 lbs., 75c; 10 lbs. or more at 12½c per lb.

The American Linden.

This tree does well in all parts of the country. It grows rapidly, has a large size, extremely handsome; a special favorite for large lawns. Price: Pkg., 5c; oz., 10c; lb., 50c, postpaid; by express, 5 lbs., $1.75; 10 lbs., or more 30c per lb.

Tulip Tree.

This is a most magnificent tree, of rapid and beautiful growth, and bearing in May and June thousands of yellowish white flowers the size and shape of Tulips, from which it derives its name. Plant one or two by all means. Each, 25c; 3 for 60c; 10 for $1.25, postpaid.

TREE SEEDS.	PKG.	OZ.	LB.	BY EXPRESS. LB.	BY EXPRESS. 10 LBS.
American Beech	$0.05	$0.10	$0.75	$0.65	$ 5.00
Scotch Pine	.05	.30	1.50	1.35	12.50
Linden	.05	.10	.75	.65	5.00
Elm	.05	.10	.75	.65	5.00
Yellow Locust	.05	.10	.60	.45	3.50
Mulberry, Czar of Russia	.15	.50	6.00	......	......
Mulberry, Russian	.10	.25	3.00	2.65	25.00
Catalpa, Speciosa	.10	.15	1.00	.85	6.50
Ailanthus, or Tree of Heaven	.15	.50	......	......	......
June Berry	.15	.40	4.00	......	......
Buffalo Berry	.10	.30	2.50	......	......

Arbor Vitæ European Larch Balsam Fir Norway Spruce Scotch Fir Austrian Pine White Pine Silver Fir Swiss Stone Pine Mediterranean Pine Upright Cypress	Prices of Seeds: Pkg., 10c. Oz., 25c. ¼ lb., 60c. Lb., $2.00.	Hemlock Spruce White Spruce Red Cedar European Beech Common Alder White Birch European Elm Catalpa, Tea's Jap. Hybrid	Pkg., 10c. Oz., 40c. ¼ lb., $1.25. Lb., $4.00. Pkg., 10c. Oz., 20c. ¼ lb., 40c. Lb., $1.25.

Osage Orange.

The great Hedge Tree of America, grows to the height of 15 to 20 feet, forming a very dense hedge. Pkg., 5c; 1 oz., 10c; ¼ lb., 20c; 1 lb., 65c, postpaid; by express, 1 oz., 10c; 1 lb., 50c; 5 lbs., $2.00; 25 lbs., $4.25.

Small Fruit Seeds.

Many families would like to experiment with growing small fruits, apple and hardy pear trees. The seeds of these are the choicest obtainable and are indeed fine. We offer these at a low price:

Apple Seed—Pkg., 10c; oz., **15c**; ¼ lb., 50c; lb., $1.00; 3 lbs. for $2.00.

Pear Seed—Pkg., 10c; oz., 20; ¼ lb., 60c; lb., $1.80.

Crab Apples—Mixed varieties. Pkg., 10c; oz., 35c; lb., $1.25; 3 lbs. for $3.00.

Apricots—Mixed varieties. Pkg., 10c; oz., 25c; lb., $1.25.

Quinces—Mixed. Pkg., 10c; oz., 25c; lb., $1.25.

Cherries—Many mixed varieties. Pkg., 10c; ¼ lb., 30c; lb., 60c.

Plums—Mixed. Large pkg., 10c; lb., 60c.

Peaches—Mixed. Pkg., 10c; lb., 60c, postpaid.

Blackberries—Mixed. Pkg., 10c; oz., 50c; ¼ lb., $1.00; lb., $3.00.

Currants—Red. Pkg., 10c; oz., 40c; ¼ lb., $1.00.

Currants—White. Pkg., 10c; oz., 40c; ¼ lb., $1.00.

Currants—Mixed. Pkg., 10c; oz., 40c; ¼ lb., $1.00.

Cranberries—Swamp. Pkg., 10c; oz., 50c.

Dewberries—Pkg., 10c; oz., 40c; ¼ lb., $1.50.

Gooseberries—Mixed. Pkg., 10c; oz., 75c.

Grapes—Mixed. Pkg., 10c., oz., 25c; ¼ lb., 75c.

Raspberries—Mixed. Pkg., 10c; oz., 40c; ¼ lb., $1.00.

Strawberries—Pkg., 10c; oz., 75c.

Salzer's Everbearing Strawberry—Pkg., 25c.

Salzer's Ponderosa—Pkg., 25c.

Salzer's Earliest—Pkg., 25c.

Cotton Seed—Pkg., 5c; oz., 10c; ¼ lb., 25c; lb., 75c.

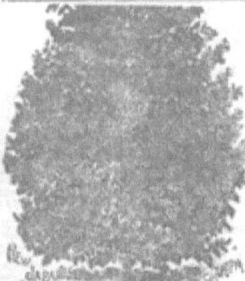

New Japanese Catalpa.

The most wonderfully luxuriant foliage imaginable adorns the Catalpa, but not only is the foliage grand, large and majestic, but the whole growth and appearance of the tree is massive. It is a wonderful grower; a budding plant grows to 7 feet the first summer and a 5 year-old tree attains the height of 25 feet; grows symmetrical and is loaded with 300 to 500 immense panicles of massive white dotted with purple blossoms. It is truly a regal tree, and its appearance reminds one of the luxuriance of the tropics. It is hardy in Wisconsin—yes, everywhere. It is a grand tree.

By mail, postpaid: Each, 10c; 3 for 25c; 10 for $1.00; 25 for $2.00, by express: Large trees, 7 to 10 feet tall, each, $1.00; 3 for $2.50; 10 for $5.00.

Allanthus.

Called in China the Tree of Heaven, grows from seed, on good soil, 20 feet high the first season, it is laying a wealth of immensely large, magnificent leaves. It is "majesty" itself. Seed pkg., 10c; oz., 20c; small plants, each, 10c; 3 for $1.00; 5 for $2.00, by express.

New Mulberry, Czar of Russia.

A magnificent introduction from Western Russia. It grows as freely anywhere and can be planted anywhere. They bear when but two or three years old, according to size, from 1 to 10 bushels of fruit, which, when ripe, falls to the ground and is eagerly eaten by fowls and pigs, which thrive on same remarkably. A few trees will establish a large flock of fowls and a drove of pigs for 2 or 3 months, as they bear and ripen their fruit for a long period. The Mulberry, especially this sort, makes delicious pies and preserves, and is also used in Russia for wines. The fruit has a subacid, sweet taste, and is most for dessert, as we use Blackberries or Raspberries. Price, each, 25c; 3 for 50c; 10 for $2.00, postpaid.

Siberian Giant Mulberry.

The fruit is very large, solid and of delicious flavor, and it remains on the bushes a long while; indeed the plant looks as though it were an everbearer, as the fruit hangs on from the time it begins to fruit until it is ripe—fully 4 months. Price, each, 25c; 3 for 50c.

Russian Mulberry.

The trees of seed planted 7 years ago are now 12 feet high, and this year past laden with fruit. The fruit is very valuable, about the size of Blackberries, and is used for dessert or preserves, similar to the Raspberry or Blackberry. Each, by mail, 25c; 3 for $1.00, postpaid.

THE 8 ORCHARD BEAUTIES, BY MAIL, $1.00.

1. Apricot—Mammoth Russian.

It is extremely hardy, having flourished as far north as Siberia, during a temperature of 40 degrees below zero. Adapts itself to all soils, and is reliable. Each, 20c; 3 for 75c.

2. Cherry—Russian Colossal.

It is early, large size and remarkably hardy. The fruit is shiny, deep red, globular, tender and very rich. Each, 20c; 3 for 75c.

3. Champion Peach.

Originated at Nokomis, Ill. The flavor is delicious, sweet, rich and juicy, surpassing all other early varieties; skin creamy white with red cheeks; strikingly handsome. It ripens at Nokomis about Aug. 5th. Each, 25c; 3 for 50c.

4. De Soto Plum.

This great variety was discovered a few miles south of La Crosse, at DeSoto. It is claimed that French explorers in the 17th century dropped the seed, and that this Plum is the result. It is certainly one of the very finest, hardiest, prolific, best Plums in cultivation. Each, 25c; 3 for 50c.

5. New Crab Apple—Ashland.

Originated in Wisconsin. It is perfectly hardy, of a fine color, glossy green, marbled with carmine; very firm, juicy, pleasant and a great bearer. Each, 25c; 3 for 50c.

6. New Apple—Early Northern.

It is of beautiful appearance, color is a deep crimson, form regular, almost round and of fine size. It is especially valuable for family use. Each, 25c; 3 for 50c.

7. Wisconsin Pear.

This is a seedling of the celebrated Lawson Pear, and has demonstrated its adaptability to Wisconsin soils. The fruit is very large, of fine shape, and of beautiful brownish carmine color, and most excellent quality, very fine grained and tender. Each, 40c; 3 for $1.00.

8. Quince—Meech's Prolific.

A vigorous grower and immensely productive, frequently bearing fruit when but two years of age, increasing in quality yearly. The fruit is large, lively orange yellow, of great beauty and of identical fragrance. Each, 30c; 3 for 75c.

Above 8 Orchard Beauties, Catalogue value, $2.30, we mail for only $1.00.
Above 8, Large Trees, 3 to 7 feet, by freight, each, 50c; the 8, $2.50.

The Banana Apple.

A wonderful apple. Large size, selling quickly at from $5.00 to $10.00 a barrel, on account of extreme beauty. Fully described in our wholesale list of choice fruits. Send 4c for same. Price of Banana Apple: Each, 50c, postpaid.

THREE HARDY FRUITS.

1. Buffalo Berry.

A most remarkable shrub, found in the mountains of the Rockies. In the early spring its fragrant blossoms appear, liberally holding the foliage in their blooming glory; then comes the fruit, in the shape of great clusters of berries, similar to the Currant in appearance, but borne so profusely that a single plant often yields 2 bushels. The fruit makes excellent pies, jellies and preserves, but the most remarkable part is that, as soon as the frost appears, it changes the flavor of the berry to the richness and quality of the best Cranberry. By mail, each, 25c; 3 for $1.00. Seed, pkg., 10c; oz., 20c.

2. New Dwarf Juneberry.

They bloom and bear fruit when very small, not over a foot in height. The berries are of fair size, about like ordinary Cherries, dark purple in color and exceedingly sweet and delicate in taste. It is one of the finest fruits to eat raw that ever grew. It blooms very early in the spring, before the leaves start, and so numerous are the flowers that the whole bush is clothed in a robe of snowy whiteness. Each, 25c; 2, 50c; 10, $1.50. Juneberry Seed—Pkg., 10c; oz., 40c.

3. Tree Cranberry.

A pleasing ornament on the lawn or shrubbery. Its juicy acid fruit is of a beautiful bright red, and in used as an excellent substitute for the swamp Cranberries. When growing in a wild state, it forms a dense bush, but responds readily to judicious pruning, and may be made to assume either the tree form or that of an open bush. Survives anywhere. Each, 25c; 3, $1.00, postpaid. Seed Pkg. 10c.

One each above 3 Hardy Fruit Novelties, 50c.
Large Plants of above 3, Buffalo Berry, Juneberry and Tree Cranberry (should bear in 1899).

HOPS.

Muenchen Giant.

We were fortunate in obtaining a very fine large-clustered Hop in Germany. When we saw same growing there, we immediately purchased a large lot of plants of Muenchen Giant for our American trade. Does splendidly well here. Each, 25c; 2 for 40c; 10 for $1.50.

Salzer's Prolific.

This is a rapid and beautiful climbing vine, bearing great clusters of golden Hops, which are not only beautiful and fragrant, but useful for medicinal purposes for yeasts, tea, etc. Each, 10c; 3 for 20c; 10 for $1.25.

Large Plants (by Express)—3½ to 5 feet in height, of each, 50c; the three for $1.25; 3 sets, or 9 plants, for $3.00.

THE WONDERFUL BISMARCK APPLE.

If on our recent trip to Europe after rare things and novelties for our trade, we had obtained nothing else than this wonderful Apple, we would feel repaid many times, for we believe that nothing has yet been offered to the American public in the Apple line that will equal this magnificent new Apple. It originated in New Zealand, and is, therefore, as hardy as oak, and capable of withstanding the rigors of the Northern climate and the changes of Eastern, Southern and Western climes.

The most remarkable fact about the apple is that you do not have to wait until you are gray before it bears. The illustration above no Apple bearing the second year after grafting. The Apples are very large in size, of excellent quality, and will keep well until January. The great point of merit is that it will bear at once. Plants set out this year will give you fruit next, while the second year following you will have lots of it. We consider it the greatest novelty ever offered in America.

PLEASE READ THIS LETTER.

SHEBOYGAN, WIS., June 13.

JOHN A. SALZER SEED CO.:
Gentlemen,—I purchased from you, in the spring of '95, a Bismarck Apple, planted same in May, received a few Apples the same season, and this year it is fairly loaded with choice fruit. My garden is in the center of the city, and thousands of people pass same, and everybody is struck with the beautiful appearance of the Bismarck Apple. What can you let me have 50 trees for this fall?

JACOB HENNE.

PRICE OF THE SALZER BISMARCK APPLE.

First size	50c each,	3 for	$1.00.
Second size	15c	3	1.00.
Third size (bear in 1900)	$1.00	3	2.50.

There is nothing in the Apple world that begins to come up to this great novelty. You can plant it in your home in a pot on your front lawn or anywhere in your garden, and be just as sure of a rich harvest of delicious Apples, as you are of the coming of Summer! It's an Apple that bears! It bears quickly, freely and prolifically. It's hardy here in Wisconsin and everywhere. We got it while in Europe and are the only seedsmen whom we know have the genuine Bismarck Apple in America. Get the right Apple when you plant.

THE BISMARCK APPLE IS POSITIVELY THE MOST WONDERFUL HARDY APPLE NOVELTY IN THE WORLD.

SMALL FRUITS—Ironclad.

A small bed of Strawberries, a patch of Raspberries, a row of Currants, a few hills of Blackberries, a half-dozen Grapes, will keep a family in fruit almost all Summer. These are as easily cared for as the cabbage, as sure of yield as the potato, and as hardy as the oak. Strawberry plants, early planted, will frequently give a good crop of berries same season.

Our prices may seem high, but they are cheap for hardy, ironclad stock that laughs at 40 degrees below zero, appeared last spring early, fresh and green, and bore heavy enormous crops the past season.

BLACKBERRIES.

The Snyder.—This is a standard, ironclad sort; very productive. Each, 15c; 10 for 50c; 50 for $4.00, by express.

Early Wilson.—A splendid early blackberry. Each, 15c; 10 for 50c.

Large Wisconsin.—A very hardy, large yielding sort. Each, 15c; 10 for 50c.

The Governor.—A new blackberry, wondrously prolific and hardy. Each, 25c; 3 for 60c.

Colossal Blackberry.—The most marvelously productive of all blackberries. Very large, luscious, of excellent flavor and splendid for shipping. Each, 20c; 3 for 50c; 10 for $1.50; postpaid.

The Minnesota King Blackberry.—A magnificent sort, very hardy and enormously prolific. Each, 20c; 10 for $1.50; postpaid.

Eldorado Blackberry.—One of the finest late blackberries. Each, 20c; 10 for $1.50.

Salzer's Early.—The earliest blackberry known. A tremendous seller. Each, 20c; 3 for 50c; 5 for 90c.
One each of the last 5 named, $1.00, postpaid.

Ancient Briton.—One of the best hardy varieties for Wisconsin and other Northern states. Large berries. Each, 15c; 5 for 50c; 10 for 90c, postpaid.

Japan Tree Blackberry.—A great novelty. Hardy, bearing innumerable berries, resembling in flavor and quality our great Colossal Blackberry. Each, $1.50; 6 for 50c.

DEWBERRIES.

Lucretia.—One of the best. Each, 15c; 10 for 75c.

Salzer's Mammoth.—Grows rapidly, bears quickly, fruit enormous size, delicious flavor. Each, 15c; 5 for 50c; 10 for $1.00.

CATALOGUE OF NURSERYSTOCK, APPLES, GRAPES, ETC. Lowest Wholesale prices to large buyers. Send 4c Postage.

1. The Great Japanese Tree Blackberry.

A transcendent novelty; grows to the height of 50 feet; very bushy; bears innumerable berries resembling in flavor and quality our great Colossal Blackberry. It is not unusual to take 50 bushels from a single tree in Japan. It is hardy, and will surely surprise, delight and please. Each, 50c; 3 for $1.00.

2. Golden Japanese Mayberry.

A great fruit novelty, ripening in May. Very large berry. Of the Raspberry family. Each, 25c; 3 for $1.00.

3. The Strawberry Raspberry.

Foliage like a rose bush. Very early in the season the plants are covered with the most white, single rose-like flowers in its large number as to present a very ornamental appearance. The fruit is very, very early. They are of a very bright red color, in the shape of a strawberry, standing upright and without the foliage, thereby being easily gathered. Each, 25c; 4 for 75c.

One each above 3 Novelties, 75c.

STRAWBERRY RASPBERRY.
Each, 25c; 4 for 75.

CURRANTS.

Salzer's Red.—Very large fruit. Each, 5c; 10 for 15c; 100, by express, $5.00.

Salzer's White.—Fine fruit. Each, 5c; 10 for 15c; 100, by express, $5.00.

Black Cherry.—Fine black. Each, 15c; 10 for 15c; 100, by express, $6.00.

Crandall Tree.—Black. Fruit size of grapes. Very fine in flavor. Each, 25c; 4 for 75c.

Fay's Prolific.—Remarkably prolific. Berries often as large as cherries. Each, 2c; 10 for $1.55.

Salzer's Red Wine.

The grandest of all new currants. The berries are large, bright red and of excellent quality, selling at no advanced price over common sorts everywhere. Fall price for 1898. Each, 25c; 6 for $1.00; per 100, $15.00.

SALZER'S RED CHERRY CURRANT

GOOSEBERRIES.

Houghton.—Well known old sort, large berries. Each, 15c; 10 for $1.00.

Downing.—Excellent berry; large yielder. Each, 15c; 10 for $1.00.

Industry.—Very large. Each, 20c; 5 for $1.25; 10 for $2.50.

The Erfurt Giant Gooseberry.

The most wonderful of all gooseberries; grown berries of enormous size, delicious flavor, and singularly free from insects, mildew, etc. Each, 30c; 2 for 50c; 5 for $1.00.

Triumph.—An American seedling. Very productive. Each, 30c; 3 for $1.00.

Keepsake.—Very popular in England. Extremely delicious. Each, 40c; 2 for 75c; 5 for $1.50.

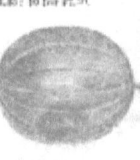

WHOLESALE CATALOGUE OF SMALL FRUITS, APPLES, CHERRIES, ETC., ETC., FOR 4c POSTAGE WRITE FOR IT.

GRAPES.

These sorts stood 40 degrees below zero and are bearing heavily in our garden this season. There is no fruit more delicious than this, and none that yielded a more prompt and generous return. Everybody who has a few feet of vacant ground, a bare wall, fence or outbuilding, can plant a few grape vines and have annual returns of the most delicious under the sun.

231 FINE BUNCHES FROM 3 YEAR OLD VINE.

Salzer's Concord.—This is our favorite. It is very prolific, hardy as oak and has never failed to ripen at La Crosse. With each succeeding year it gains new friends; indeed, there is no dark-colored grape except Salzer's Earliest that is its peer. It is early, luscious, large and hardy. Each, 20c; 3 for 50c; 7 for 75c; 10 for $1.10; 100 for $8.00, by express.

Moore's Early.—The finest early grape known; fruit very large, of delicious flavor. Each, 25c; 3 for 60c; 10 for $2.00.

Pocklington.—No golden white grape exceeds this in yield, lusciousness and earliness. This wonderful grape has fairly leaped into popularity, and is one that we sell with a great deal of pleasure. Of course, the berry is not as large, nor is it as luscious, nor as prolific, as our Sunbeam; nevertheless, where two white varieties are desired, we can heartily recommend the Pocklington as the second. You will certainly like this grape. Each, 20c; 3 for 50c; 10 for $1.50.

Elvira.—The hardiest, finest, sweetest and most prolific white. Each, 20c; 10 for $2.50.

Salzer's Earliest Grape.—This new grape was sent out last spring. It is the earliest grape we know of; the finest fruit we know of; the finest flavored variety we have ever tasted, and much more prolific than the Concord. Each, 25c; 3 for $1.00; 10, $2.25.

Salzer's Sunbeam Grape. This magnificent new white grape we referred to the first time last spring, and everywhere it was received with joy, for hundreds upon hundreds of customers availed themselves of the opportunity of buying this finest of all white grapes. It is perfectly hardy. The bunches are of enormous size, fruit very large and of luscious quality. Extremely prolific, and will do well everywhere. Each, 30c; 3 for $1.00; 10 for $3.00.

One each Salzer's Earliest and Sunbeam, only 50c; 10 each, $4.00.

5 HARDY IRONCLAD GRAPES, ONLY 90c.

1. **Wyoming Red.**—A new red, large, grand variety. Each, 20c.
2. **Brownsville (white).**—A very large white grape; very delicious; hardy. Each, 20c.
3. **Ambrosia (black).**—Perfectly hardy; fruit delicious, almost melting in one's mouth. Each, 20c.
4. **American Beauty (red).**—A magnificent new red grape; very hardy; large berry. Each, 20c.
5. **Janesville, Early White.**—An early grape; white color, large berry. Each, 20c.

Above 5 hardy grapes, 90c. Any 10 for $1.75.

RASPBERRIES.

The Gregg.—A superior late black berry, very productive and hardy. Each, 10c; per 10, 50c; 100, $3.00.

Souhegan.—The earliest and finest black. Each, 15c; per 10, 90c.

Colossal.—The finest, hardiest red raspberry grown. Each, 15c; per 10, 60c.

Turner.—The standard red sort. Each, 10c; per 10, 60c; 100, $2.50.

Red Raspberry.

King of the Reds (novelty).—This is a new, oily, great berry; very hardy; splendid for the North. Each, 20c; 10 for $1.50.

New Raspberry.

Orange Jelly.—A great berry, golden, yellow color; delicious quality; very hardy. Each, 20c; 10 for $1.50, postpaid.

Royal Church.—A large, red raspberry; very hardy; highly recommended. Each, 20c; 3 for $1.50.

Child's Japanese Raspberry.—A magnificent berry, imported from Japan. Hardy as oak. 50 to 100 berries from one cluster. Glossy scarlet color. Each, 20c; 3 for 40c; 10 for $1.00.

SALZER'S FOUR GREAT HARDY RASPBERRIES FOUR 50c

ONE EACH ABOVE FOUR GREAT RASPBERRIES, POSTPAID, ONLY 50c.

1. **The Arctic.**—New; one of the finest black. Each, 20c; 3 for 50c; 10 for $1.50.
2. **Wineberry.**—Large, delicious, red fruit; very hardy. Each, 20c; 3 for 40c.
3. **Golden Alaska.**—Hardy, yellow, very large, perfect fruit. Each, 20c; 3 for 40c; 10 for $1.40; 100 for $12.50.
4. **Salzer's Everbearing Raspberry.**—The fruit is of a large size, a beautiful, rich red color, of excellent quality and begins to ripen the latter part of June, fruiting into Fall. So long does this excellent fruit remain that it has received the name "Everbearer." Hardy as oak; very prolific. Each, 20c; 3 for 50c; 10 for $1.40.

One Each Above Four Great Raspberries, Postpaid, Only 50c.

STRAWBERRIES.

Salzer's New Everbearer Strawberry.

This is a most wonderful and valuable novelty, producing delicious fruit the entire season, and is, therefore, very desirable for family use, and sells at a high figure in the market. Bears every day from June 20th until frost sets in—berries all the time, and good ones, too. 3 for 25c; 10 for 90c; 100 for $5.00.

NEW EVERBEARER STRAWBERRY.

SPECIAL OFFER ON STRAWBERRIES.

10 Salzer's Earliest	$0.50
10 Sharpless	.40
10 Perfection	.40
10 Late Mastodon	.40
10 Belle of La Crosse	.40
	$2.10

All for $1.50

The 50, postpaid, as an introduction, for only...$1.50
Or for $1.85, we will add to the above:
10 New Pondorosa.................................$0.50
10 New Everbearer................................ .50
In all, 30 plants of 7 of the grandest berries known in the world, all for $1.85, postpaid.

Catalogue of rare nursery stock, apples, plums, pears, grapes, etc., at lowest wholesale prices. Send 4c postage for same.

Salzer's Earliest Strawberry.—The earliest strawberry in cultivation. Offered for the first time in 1893. Bears enormously. Very hardy. Luscious fruit. A splendid variety for family use and early market. 3, 20c; 10, 50c; 50, $1.75; 100, $3.00; 1,000, $25.00.

Pondorosa.—Of this giant novelty 12,000 quarts have been gathered per acre, of rarest quality, excellent for all purposes. 3 plants, 25c; 10 for 50c; 100 for $1.00, postpaid.

Three each of Salzer's Earliest and Pondorosa, in all 6 plants, for 25c; 25 of each for $1.25.

Perfection Strawberry.

It is the perfection in strawberries. It cannot be improved upon as a family berry. It is very hardy and prolific. This wonderful novelty can be had only of us. 3 or 5, 20c; per 10, 50c; per 25, $1.50; per 100, $4.50.

Wisconsin Giant Strawberry.

A very popular berry, for 20c; 10 for 60c; 100 plants $4.50.

Salzer's Late Mastodon Strawberry.

The latest strawberry known. Fruit of enormous size; delicious; quality fine. Grows rank and is perfectly hardy. 3, 20c; 10, 50c; per 25, $1.25; 50, $2.50; 100, $4.50; 1,000, $22.50.

SALZER'S EARLIEST STRAWBERRY

Salzer's Earliest Strawberry is the earliest in the world.

Belle of La Crosse.—This is a dwelling. Upon a single two-year-old plant 142 berries were counted at one time. 10 for 50c; 100 for $4.00.

Wilson.—A standard. 10 for 30c; 50 for 75c; 100 for $1.25.

Longfellow.—Large, deliciously sweet. 10 for 50c; 100 for $2.00.

Princess.—Well known. 10 for 50c; 100 for $1.50.

Sharpless.—Enormously productive, of immense size. 10 for 40c; 100 for $2.00.

CHOICE FLOWER SEEDS.

From early childhood we have been passionately fond of flowers. The summer days were always spent in our parents' garden. Great beds of Phlox, Pansies, Verbenas, Portulacas, Sweet William, Four O'clocks, Candytuft, Balsam, etc., were our daily delight. Our boyhood was spent in the garden (our father being a nurseryman and gardener), our young manhood found us there; indeed, there is no place we feel so completed at home as when surrounded with plants and flowers. We have for long years tested every flower obtainable; and our list is full of choice sorts—and we pride ourselves that no flower seeds offered in America, have a higher reputation among gardeners and all lovers of beautiful blossoms than Salzer's Choice Northern grown, and we trust that every reader of these lines will let us help make their garden beautiful by sowing our splendid flower seeds. And in order that you may gather large orders among your friends, we offer:

SPECIAL RATES ON SEEDS IN PACKETS.

This Offer is by mail, Postage Paid by us to any Postoffice in America.

For a remittance of $1.00 you may select Seeds in Packets only, or Plants, valued at $1.35	PRICE OF ALL
For a remittance of $2.00 you may select Seeds in Packets only, or Plants, valued at $2.50	FLOWER and VEGE-
For a remittance of $3.00 you may select Seeds in Packets only, or Plants, valued at $3.00	TABLE SEED COL-
For a remittance of $4.00 you may select Seeds in Packets only, or Plants, valued at $5.10	LECTIONS are NET.
For a remittance of $5.00 you may select Seeds in Packets only, or Plants, valued at $6.75	

SOWING FLOWER SEED.

Nine-tenths of the failures in the flower and vegetable garden occur from improper sowing and treatment. We want everybody buying our seeds to have success with them, and we urge upon them to carefully read the culture directions on each package, and the following rules:

Soil.—Prepare this carefully; have it smooth, fine, mellow and well enriched. It is well to choose a south, sunny location of the house; make your seed bed even by means of a smooth board. Do not sow on wet, cold soil—have it warm and mellow. Put a little stick at each end of each row, so as to mark it, then pull up all weeds that appear between the rows the first day they can be seen. When plants are large enough, remove some where you want them to remain, and they will reward you with flowers all summer, and vegetables, fine and large, to gladden your heart.

Collection of Flower Seeds.

We desire to introduce our flower seeds into every home and garden in America, and hence make three collections, one for 25c, one for 50c, the other for $1.00. These, in quantity, variety and quality cannot be excelled in America. We grow these varieties in great quantities, hence our ability to sell them so cheap—as an introduction.—for when once you try our flower seeds you will want no other.

1. A BEAUTIFUL GARDEN FOR 25 CENTS.

These 10 exquisite varieties, brilliant and varied in colors, we offer, postpaid, for only 25c. They are all full bloomers.

1. Acroclinum,	4. Mignonette,	7. Petunia,
2. Ageratum,	5. Marigold,	8. Pansy,
3. Convolvulus.	6. Sweet Peas,	9. Calliopsis,
	10. Poppy.	

2. BRILLIANT DISPLAY OF FLOWERS FOR 50 CENTS.

The following 19 varieties of elegant, brilliant, dazzling flower seeds, composed of choicest varieties and strains known to florists, we offer for only 50c. You will be surprised at the great beauty, fragrance and freedom of these flowers. And what is more cheering than a garden full of flowers?

19 Pkg's CHOICEST FLOWER SEEDS ONLY 50¢

50 CTS. These 19 packages, brilliant varieties, postpaid, 50c.

1. Asters,	8. Celosia,	15. Lobelia,
2. Balsam,	9. Clarkia,	16. Mignonette,
3. Bartonia,	10. Collinsia,	17. Poppy,
4. Brachycome,	11. Eschscholtzia,	18. Phlox,
5. Candila,	12. Four O'Clock,	19. Zinnia.
6. Calliopsis,	13. Gypsophila,	
7. Candytuft,	14. Linum,	All for 50c.

3. A MAGNIFICENT GARDEN FOR $1.00.

The following 40 packages of beautiful flower seeds, choice sorts, we offer postpaid (net) for only $1.00. This collection contains the cream of all flower seeds and cannot be beaten. It's what you will need if you want a great garden of choice flowers.

1 Abronia,	21 Gaillardia,
2 Acroclinum,	22 Gilia,
3 Adonis,	23 Godetia,
4 Ageratum,	24 Helichrysum,
5 Alyssum,	25 Kaulfussia,
6 Amaranthus,	26 Larkspur,
7 Antirrhinum,	27 Lobelia,
8 Asters,	28 Lupinus,
9 Balsam,	29 Marigold,
10 Calendula,	30 Mignonette,
11 Calliopsis,	31 Nasturtium,
12 Celosia,	32 Nemophila,
13 Candytuft,	33 Pansy,
14 Canterbury Bell,	34 Phlox,
15 Chrysanthemum,	35 Poppy,
16 Clarkia,	36 Stock,
17 Convolvulus,	37 Sweet Peas,
18 Crosea,	38 Scabiosa,
19 Eschscholtzia,	39 Verbena,
20 Forget-Me-Not,	40 Zinnia.

The 40 Packages only $1.00 with Package Flowers of Paradise thrown in free.

This Grand Collection only $1.00. (The catalogue price is $2.50.)

4. FINE FLOWER SEEDS 55 CENTS.

We have grown very largely of the following annual flower varieties, and have concluded to offer them at a remarkably low price in order to introduce our flower seeds into every home in America. We believe to-day that we have the largest mail trade in seeds in the world, and yet we would like to extend same, in order to make more people happy; for we believe where flowers grow and plants abound discontent vanishes and happiness and sunshine and brightness in life take place. Try any of these 4 collections, either 25c, 50c, $1.00 or this 55c collection and be happy.

Amaranthus, good mixed, per pkg..5c	Centaurea, good mixed, per pkg..5c
Alyssum, good mixed, per pkg...5c	Four O'clock, good mixed, per pkg..5c
Asters, good mixed, per pkg 5c	Gilia, good mixed, per pkg......5c
Antirrhinum, good mixed, per pkg..5c	Eschscholtzia, good mixed, per pkg..5c
Asperula, good mixed, per pkg ...5c	Lobelia, good mixed, per pkg...5c
Bartonia, good mixed, per pkg.....5c	Mignonette, good mixed, per pkg..5c
Acroclinum, good mixed, per pkg..5c	Ageratum, good mixed, per pkg..5c
Ageratum, good mixed, per pkg..5c	Nemophila, good mixed, per pkg...5c
Calliopsis, good mixed, per pkg..5c	Petunia, good mixed, per pkg...5c
Balsam, good mixed, per pkg...4c	Pansy, good mixed, per pkg..10c
Candytuft, good mixed, per pkg...5c	Poppy, good mixed, per pkg...5c
Convolvulus, good mixed, per pkg..5c	Sweet Peas, good mixed, per pkg..5c

Abutilon—P.

A plant of great beauty, bearing quantities of dazzlingly brilliant colored flowers the entire season. It's ordinary cultivation flowers bell-shaped. Elegant mixture. Pkg., 10c.; finest mixed, 20c.

Abronia—A.

A charming trailer with Verbena-like clusters of sweet-scented flowers; elegant finest mixed. Pkg. 20; mixed colors, 5c.

Acrolinum—F.

Very pretty, half-hardy annual, with rose and white daisy-like flowers. They grow about 1 foot high, and should be planted in the open. Pkg., 5c.; good mixed, pkg., 5c.

Adonis (Pheasant's Eye)—A.

The flowers are very brilliant; mixed. Pkg., 5c.

Adlumia—Mountain Fringe.

An attractive climber with pale green foliage; rose-colored blossoms; mixed. Pkg., 5c.

Ageratum—A.

Flowers bush like; indispensable for the garden. Aster—The great Ageratum, dwarf blue. Pkg., good mixed, 5c.
Conspicuous — White, pkg., 5c.; finest mixed, 5c.

Agrostemma.

Perfectly hardy plants, producing pretty pinkish blossoms on long slender stems. Pkg., 5c.; good mixed. Pkg., 5c.

Agrostis (Ornamental Grass)—It's a hardy ornamental grass, much used in connection with everlastings, for winter bouquets. Pkg., 5c.

Ampelopsis.

A climbing vine of great beauty. Perfectly hardy. Pkg., 10c.

Amaranthus—A.

Of remarkably attractive foliage, producing striking effects in connection with grasses and other ornamental foliage or beds, etc.

Caudacus (Love Lies Bleeding)—Drooping red. Pkg., 5c.

Tricolor (Joseph's Coat)—Pkg., 5c.

Abbysicinus — Is splendid as solitary specimens. Pkg., 5c.

Bicolor—Foliage green and dark red, striped with yellow. Pkg., 5c.

Melancholis Rubra—Finest mixed. Pkg., 5c.; all colors mixed, 5c; good mixed, 5c.

Ammobium—F.

One of the grandest of everlastings, and desirable for the garden, but more valuable for winter bouquets in connection with grasses and other everlastings. The flowers are rather small; pure white. Pkg., 5c.

Anemone (Windflower)—R.

Brilliant beauties; indescribably grand. Pkg., 5c.

Anagallis—A.

Grandly beautiful as a border plant; a profusion of richly colored blossoms. Pkg., 5c.

Asperula.

Low-growing and produces blossoms. Flowers sweet-scented, lavender; well adapted for bouquet making. Pkg., 5c.; good mixed, Pkg., 5c.

Alyssum, Sweet—A.

The sweet, sweetest of all pure white blooming annuals; no garden complete without it. Fine mixed sorts. pkg., 5c. Good Mixed, 5c.

Salzer's Ocean Spray.

The grandest of all Alyssums. Very large blossoms of delicious fragrance, and lavish on its pure white flowers a prodigal profusion. INDEED, few or three hundred blossoms FROM A SINGLE PLANT IS NOT UNCOMMON. Pkg., 15c.; 2 pkgs., 25 cts.

Alyssum (Saxatile)—P.

Flowers brilliant golden yellow, completely hiding the foliage; grows 1 foot high. Pkg., 5c.

Antirrhinum

(Snap Dragon)—A.
Unsurpassed for summer and fall flowering.
White—Pkg., 5c.
Brilliant—Scarlet, grasses and white. 5c.
Striprum — Finest striped sorts; mixed colors. Pkg., 5c.
"Carnation Rival" — A new strain grandly beautiful, of the most wonderful colors imaginable. Pkg., 10c; fine mixed, pkg., 5c. Good mixed, 5c.

Anchusa—A.

One of the few plants that will do well in the shade. Splendid for bouquets. Pkg., 5c.

Aquilegia (Columbine)—A.

Very popular and distinct flower; blooms in early summer; exceedingly showy. Pkg., 5c.
Erfurt Prize—This mixture contains nothing but the finest free-blooming varieties, and is peerless. Pkg., 10c.

Argemone—A.

Flowers large, poppy-shaped; very free. Pkg., 5c.

Salzer's Splendid Asters.

Salzer's Asters have a high reputation for freedom of bloom, richness of color, beauty of form and rapidity of growth.
White Bouquet—The finest dwarf pure white Aster known: A plant resembles a large bunch of white Asters. Pkg., 10c.
New White Rose—A pure white, large flowered, beautifully formed Aster. The color petals are recurved like a rose. Pkg., 10c.
Pansy-Flowered Perfection—A superb class; large and double-petaled; beautiful (plume-like). White, 10c; all colors, mixed, 10c.
Needle or Hedgehog—Large, perfect beauties; twelve finest colors, 10c.
Salzer's Goliath—Asters of enormous size, measuring from 5 to 7 inches in diameter; unexcelled for every guard. Pkg., 10c.
Vesuvius—New. Intense dark scarlet blossoms. Pkg., 10c.
Crown-Fine; very double, with white centers, bordered with many bright, rich colors. 10 inch. Pkg., 10c.
Salzer's Prize Bouquet—This charming class, containing over 20 colors, grows to the height of 6 inches, and literally hides the plant with its scores of beautiful blossoms. Pkg., 10c.

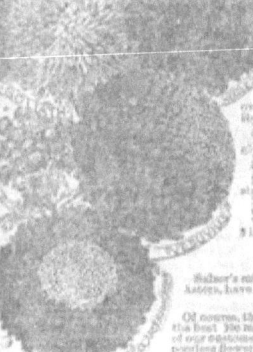

Dwarf Pyramidal—the plants form a complete bouquet of flowers; 1 foot, 10c.
Victoria—One of the finest; very large; of perfect double form; imbricated, and of rich colored flowers; of pyramidal habit and richest colors; 20 inch. Pkg., 10c.
Dwarf Chrysanthemum—A splendid variety of dwarf compact habit. Pkg., 10c.
Tall Chrysanthemum—Very tall; blossoms largest and finely formed. Pkg., 10c.
Large Flowering Rose—Very large blossoms of every imaginable hue; in form similar to Salzer's New White Rose, but of endless variety of colors. Pkg., 10c.
Imbricated Pompon Sorts—Very fine; excellent for bouquets; mixed. Pkg., 10c.
Queen—A splendid white dwarf, enjoying an extended sale. Pkg., 15c; 2 for 25c.
Washington—Sprang from the Victoria class; flowers of enormous size, often 5 inches in diameter. Pkg., 10c.

☞ Any 6 Packages of above for 50c. ☜

MIXTURE OF ASTERS.

Salzer's mixtures, for the price, quality and quantity of choice, beautifully formed, free-blooming Asters, have no superior anywhere. Gorgeous Prize is an Aster Mixture Wonder.

ASTERS, ALL COLORS, MIXED. PKG., 10c.

Of course, this mixture is not equal to our Gorgeous Prize Mixture, but we say this for it, that it is the best 10c mixture offered in the world. We have taken special pains with same, in order that those of our customers who do not wish to pay 25c for the grandest mixture known to florists can have these peerless flowers at a price within the reach of all. We do not know of a 10c package of seed that will give you more genuine pleasure, from August on until killed by frost, than Salzer's All Colors, mixed. Colors are brilliant, varied and charming. Pkg., 10c; 3 pkgs., 20c.

GORGEOUS PRIZE ASTER MIXTURE.

This mixture we have greatly improved the past season; it contains over 70 varieties of elegant sorts and colors; nothing like it in the floral world; wonderfully beautiful. Pkg., 25c; 2 pkgs., 40c.

No. 3 Mixed—Very fine for the price; indeed, equal to nine-tenths of other seedsmen's choicest. Pkg., 20c.

Dwarf German Mixture—Contains over 30 choice sorts; very elegant and particularly choice. Pkg., 15c.

Perennial Asters — This is one of the great beauty, medley of bloom and hardiness; live for many years. Pkg., 10c.
Good Mixed Asters, 4c per package. F—

BRANCHING ASTERS.

A new race of Asters with long branches bearing flowers of glorious form, exquisite shape and color. Package, 30; seeds, 15c.

Auricula.

Our seed of this grand perennial plant is from one of the best English collections. Finest mixed, Pkg, 15c. Salzer's Auricula—Gathered only from choice flowers; grandly beautiful. Pkg, 25c.

Aristolochia A. (Dutchman's Pipe.)—A quick-growing, hardy climber, attaining a height of 30 feet, with large, heart-shaped foliage; flowers singularly formed, curved like a siphon; mixed. Pkg, 25c.

Begonia.

Pkg.

Extra fine tuberous double mixed 15c
Rex castoties extra fine 25c
Extra fine blooming sorts, mixed 15c

Balloon Vine—A.

Remarkable for its inflated membranous capsules, and sometimes called (erron) a Puff. 5 feet high. Pkg, 5c.

Brachycome.

(Swan River Daisy)—A; free flowering plants covered all summer with a profusion of flowers like blossoms; fine; finest mixed. Pkg, 5c.

Pride of Australia—Wonderfully beautiful; very attractive color, tint and tone in this mixture. Pkg, 15c.

Browallia—A.

One of the finest annuals grown. The blue variety is especially handsome; blooms profusely; white, blue or fine mixed. Each, 5c.

Bachelor's Buttons—A. Pkg, 10c.
Bromus Brizaeformis—A, very fine grass with elegant, hanging ears; well adapted for winter bouquets. Pkg, 5c.

Briza Maxima—An elegant shaking grass; one of the best ornamental grasses for winter use. 5c.

Gracilis; A.—Smaller, very finely and is always desirable. 5c.

Bellis—(Daisy)—P.

Charming plants for borders and beds. The flowers are quilled; white, pink, red and variegated. Pkg, 5c.

Longfellow—A new, large flowered double daisy of enormous size; flowered dark rose color. Pkg, 25c.
White Wing—The most double white. Pkg, 20c.

Salzer's Extra Daisy Mixture.

Composed of every obtainable kind known, indeed, peerless as a mixture. Pkg, 15c; 4 pkgs, 30c.
Daisy—Double mixed; very fine indeed. Pkg, 10c.

SALZER'S BALSAMS

Are justly popular. They combine in one golden whole beauty and perfection, solidity and fullness of form, strength and rigor of growth, prodigal freedom in bloom and exquisite richness of colorings.

1. Apple Blossom—Beautiful apple blossom shading. Pkg, 10c
2. Salzer Snowball—The flowers are large, full, of immense size, and are the most thoroughly double and perfectly solid flowers of all the purest white. Pkg, 10c; ½ oz. 25c.
3. Crimson Mottled—Perfection in the mottled line. Pkg, 10c
4. Salzer's Crimson King—The finest of all deep blood red Balsams; magnificently adapted for groups; it is without a peer for this purpose. Pkg, 15c.
5. Solferino—White, striped with scarlet and purple. Pkg, 10
6. Scarlet Spotted—Spotted. Pkg, 10.
White Perfection—Flowers snow white, round as a ball; double. Pkg, 10c.

Balsam Mixture.

These mixtures, for beauty and freedom of bloom and varieties of colors cannot be beat. No. 1 is grand.

	Pkg.
Good Mixed	5c
No. 1 Mixture, very fine	5c
No. 2 Mixture, over 15 sorts	10c
No. 3 Mixture, imp. 30 colors	15c

Salzer's Superior Mixture.

Brilliantly beautiful, combining upward of 60 sorts of coolish varieties, colors and forms; nothing like it in America. At the Interstate Fair, in presence of 15,000 people, Salzer's Superior Balsams were awarded first prize for beauty and great variety of color. Pkg, 25c; 3 pkgs, 50c.

CANDYTUFT—Summer Glory.

Hundreds of people this past summer and autumn admired our independent, ever-blooming candytuft, Summer Glory, and many saw the exquisite beauty of the flower; charming, brilliant, delightful; met their eyes. We bespeak for it more glad planting. This ever-blooming variety can be had only of us. Pkg, 10c; ¼ oz. 20c; oz. 30c.

White Wave.

The finest hiennia white Candytuft. Splendid for cemeteries. Pkg, 10c.
Rocket—Mixed, 5c.
Fragrant—White, 5c.
New Crimson—Fine, 5c.
New Carmine—Fine, 5c. A plant producing a profusion of vivid and rich blooms. Pkg, 10c.
Finest Mixed Candytuft—Many brilliant sorts and colors. Pkg, 5c; oz. 20c; ¼ lb. 60c; lb. mixed, pkg. 5c.

Brionopsis—A.

A beautiful plant of the gourd species, with ivy-like, pale green foliage, and showy scarlet fruit, striped with white; 10 feet. Pkg, 5c.

Calendula.

Very beautiful annuals, resembling Double Asters, of rich colors and rapid growth; fine mixed. Pkg, 5c.

Calceolaria.

Hybrida—A, superb ornamental, greenhouse plant, producing a mass of beautiful pocket-like flowers early in spring. Pkg, 25c.

Floribunda—Yellow. Pkg, 10c.

Salzer's Show Calceolaria—Saved only from the largest blossoms of grandly beautiful and superbly colored, spotted and maculated spots. Pkg, 50c.

Beautiful free-blooming plants, with tassel-shaped flowers; sometimes called Devil's Paint Brush, fine mixed. Pkg, 5c; cheapest mixture, 10c.

CALLIRHOE.

Splendid for bedding out. The plants begin to bloom early, and continue to produce their wonderfully colored flowers all season. Pkg, 10c.

CACTI SEED.

See page 27 for description of Cacti seed. Pkg, 10c.

Calandrina.

Creeping plants, well suited for planting in rockwork or similar situations. Blooms freely. Pkg, 5c.

Calampelis.

A quick-growing climber, attaining a height of 10 feet in a season and bearing profusely clusters of orange-colored, tube-like flowers. Pkg, 10c.

Centaurea—Dusty Miller—A.

Plants with silvery foliage. New in house. An unusually fine for bordering. Pkg, 10c.
Cyanus—Very pretty. Pkg, 10c. Mixed pkg, 5.
Salzer's Korn Blume—Pkg, 5c.

Campanula—Bell Flower.

Beautiful bell-shaped flowers of various colors. If sown in the early spring they will bloom the first season.

Media—Pkg, 5c.
Speculum—(Venus Looking Glass) Colors finely mixed. Pkg, 5c.
Canterbury Bell—P. Very handsome white, blue and rose, bell-shaped flowers. Pkg, 5c.

Canna—P.

One of the grand and most effective foliage plants grown, with large leaves similar to the banana, growing from 4 to 20 feet high; fine mixed. Pkg, 5c; dark varieties, choice 15c.
Salzer's Prize—Contains 27 varieties of the newer imported sorts, and for beauty and tropical effect stands without an equal. ½ oz. 15c; oz. 50c.
Crozy—Grand mixture. Pkg, 30c.

Carnations.

Flowers are large, of delicious fragrance, **and of brilliant** and beautiful colors. Use heavy soil.

Marguerite Mixture—Pkg, 5c; 2 **pkg., 25c.**

Remontant—saved only from the choicest double named varieties. Pkg, 25c.

Grenadin—Blossoms three weeks earlier than other sorts. Color, deep salmon-red. Pkg., 20c.

German mixed seeds from prize pot plants. Pkg., 25c.

Italian seed, choice, 30c.

Fine mixed 10c.

Chrysanthemum.

For late autumn blooming in the home there is no flower to take the place of this. It blooms just at a time when there are but few other flowers, and furnishes several hundred flowers on each plant.

Salzer's Japanese Chrysanthemum.

This mixture of Japanese and Chinese sorts is without an equal, and comprises an endless variety of color and form. Pkg., 25c; choicest mixed, 10c; finest mixed, 5c.

CHRYSANTHEMUM.

Cypress Vine.

Everybody is acquainted with the Cypress Vine, its finely cut foliage and brilliant flowers. Pkg., 5c.

Cyclamen.

Salzer's Show Mixture of Cyclamen—Pkg., 25c. Finest Mixed, 10c.

Cineraria—A.

A free-flowering house plant, of wondrous beauty with flowers of great richness and diversity of color, blooming during the winter.

Salzer's Show—They are perfect in growth and form, and produce a great abundance of large blossoms exquisitely rich in and wonderfully colored. The finest of all Cineraria mixtures. Pkg., 20c.

Cineraria—Fine mixed. Pkg., 10c.

Datura (Angel's Trumpet).

Hardy annual with purple and white flowers, attaining a height of 5 feet. Mixed pkg., 5c. Choicest Mixed—Pkg., 10c; 3 pkgs., 25c.

Cacti Seed.

See page 27. Pkg., 10c.

Dahlias—A.

So well known that they need no description. Blooms same season from.

Single—This contains seeds of the finest single sorts known. Pkg., 15c.

Double—Fine sorts. Pkg., 20c.

Salzer's Superb—A mixture of 50 sorts and colors. Double and single. Pkg., 20c.

Finest Mixed, 10c.

SINGLE DAHLIA. PKG., 15c.

Delphinium—A.

Larkspur—Slender growth, with finely laciniated foliage and bright flowers in splendid spikes, perfectly hardy; blooming continuously. Sow early.

White Dwarf, double. Pkg., 10c.

Blue Dwarf, double. Pkg., 10c.

Dwarf Rocket, mixed. Pkg., 10c.

Show Mixture—Composed of all obtainable sorts and brilliant colors. Pkg., 10c.

Finest mixed. Pkg., 5c.

Eutoca—A.

Foliage full green, covered with hair; blossoms blue; about three quarters of an inch across. Excellent for cutting, becomes a branch, placed in water will bloom many days, and the blue is intense in color. Pkg., 5c.

DELPHINIUM.

REMEMBER !

Remember, a 40-cent order or more entitles you to a package of Salzer's Oddly Odd Seeds. *See cover page.*

Catchfly—Silene—A.

A continuous bloomer. The plant is covered with a glutinous moisture from which flies cannot disengage themselves, hence the name Catchfly. Mixed; pkg., 5c; show mixture, 10c.

Clarkia.

Among the most desirable annuals for bedding purposes; growing freely and blooming profusely; double and single; many colors mixed. Pkg., 5c.

Clematis—P.

Jackman's Large Flowering Hybrids—very choice and fine. Pkg., 25c.

Flammula—White, fragrant; 15 feet. Pkg., 10c.

Integrifolia—Blue sorts. Pkg., 20c.

Mixed—Pkg., 15c.

LADIES'ING CLARKIA.

Convolvulus (Morning Glory).

A magnificent class of climbing annuals.

Major—(tall sorts; mixed. Pkg., 5c.

Minor—Dwarf sorts; mixed. Pkg., 5c.

European—Contains every obtainable sort; mixed. Pkg., 15c.

The Bride—Pure white; beauty. Pkg., 5c.

Mauritanicus—Grandly beautiful, 10c.

All Sorts Mixed—Pkg., 5c.

Good Mixed—Pkg., 3c.

JAPANESE MORNING GLORIES—No words, no painter's brush, no imagination can do full justice to this wonderful new race of morning glories. Pkg., 10c.

CONVOLVULUS.

SALZER'S DIANTHUS.

D. Laciniatus—Grandly brilliant; beautifully fringed; single sorts. Pkg., 5c.

D. Laciniatus (double)—Wonderfully tasseled and fringed; rich colorings. Pkg., 10c.

Salzer's Superb—Composed of all Laciniatus sorts; double and single. Pkg., 20c.

Dianthus Mixtures

Salzer's Show—Composed of upward of 50 sorts; gay, charming, bright, brilliant; single and double sorts; unequaled for richness of colors. Pkg., 15c; 4, 50c.

No. 1 mixed, composed of double sorts. Pkg., 5c.

No. 2 mixed Dianthus, very fine; single and double. Pkg., 3c.

Digitalis, or Foxglove—P.

Showy and useful perennials for the border. New plants may be obtained by dividing the roots; mixed. Pkg., 5c. Splendid sorts. Pkg., 10c.

Edelweiss.

The alpine favorite, which every tourist delights in carrying home as a souvenir from that indescribably beautiful country. Beautiful silvery white perennial. Pkg., 10c.

Fern Spores.

Our mixture of Ferns, comprising some of the rarest and most desirable varieties. Pkg., 20c.

Four O'Clock—A. (Marvel of Peru.)

The plants are large and make a pretty hedge. The flowers are funnel-shaped, white, red and striped; very fragrant; open about 4 o'clock in the afternoon and remain open all night.

Fine Mixed—Indeed, pretty colors. Pkg., 5c.

Show Mixture of Four O'Clock—Composed of every variety obtainable. Pkg., 10c.

Good Mixed—3c.

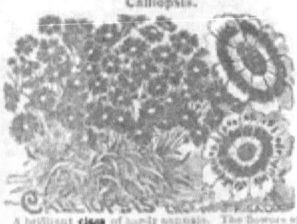

CELOSIA PRIZE WINNER

J. A. SALZER LA X. WIS.

Prize Winner Mixtures.

This is the most gorgeous of all Celosia mixtures. It is pre-eminently beautiful, bearing enormous rich, brilliant, magnificent heads. It is a "Prize Winner" at every fair; gorgeous in all respects. Pkg., 10c.

Celosia—Choicest mixed. Pkg., 5c.

Celosia (Cockscomb)—Fine mixed. Pkg., 5c.

1½-inch sorts as Glasgow Prize, Empress of India, Carlston and Feathered. Pkg., 5c.

Canary Bird Flower—A.

Grandly beautiful, climbing rapidly and producing a great abundance of yellow fringed flowers. If grown to run up an evergreen tree, the blossoms resemble canary birds hiding in the branches. Pkg., 5c.

Calliopsis.

CYPRESS VINE.

A brilliant class of hardy annuals. The flowers are of every shade of yellow, orange and rich reddish brown; very showy; finest mixed. Pkg., 5c.

Show Mixture—This is our novelty mixture, and contains seed of every procurable sort of this brilliant, beautiful annual. Pkg., 10c.

Crepis—A.

Crepis—A very fine double flower of striking colors. Mixed sorts. 5c.

Croix Lachrymæ.

Job's Tears—Grows about 4 feet; broad, corn-like leaves. Pkg., 5c.

Coleus.

Beautiful ornamental foliage plants for bedding and during the summer.

Finest Mixed—Pkg., 15c.

Salzer's Hybrid Wonder—Composed of rare, large leaved Coleus sorts. Pkg., 20c.

CROIX LACHRYMÆ. 5c.

Eschscholzia.

(California Poppy.)

A bed of Eschscholzias in the sunshine makes a blaze of brilliant colors. Sow plants where wanted to bloom, as they do not bear transplanting. Use foot high. Eschscholzia mixture, pkg., 10c. Fine mixed, pkg., 5c. Good mixed, pkg., 3c.

Fuchsia.

Our seed of this well-known and beautiful plant has been saved from a splendid collection of named varieties, double and single. Finest mixed pkg., 25c; also good mixed, 10c.

ESCHSCHOLZIA.

Gilliardia—A.

A striking-looking class, natives of this country, and presenting quite a diversity of color; mixed. Pkg., 5c.

Fenzlia.

A dwarf-growing plant, suited for rustic baskets and vases; flowers, rosy, lilac, with orange. Pkg., 10c.

Feverfew.

(Pyrethrum.)

Golden Feather—Beautiful, gold-leaved bedding plant; splendid for edging. Pkg., 10c.

Feverfew Bridal Veil—White, rare. Pkg., 15c.

Finest Double Boris—Mixed. Pkg., 10c.

GILLIARDIA.

Geranium.

Sow in dwelling in spring in shallow boxes; transplant when the seedlings are fit to handle.

Geranium — Extra choice, mixed. Pkg., 20c; finest mixed, 10c; gold and bronze, 20c; finest Zonale, 20c.

Pelargonium—Large flowered; pansy-shaped blossoms. Pkg. of 20 seeds, 25c.

Gloxinia.

A superb genus of house plants; profuse bloomer, of great beauty and diversity of colors. Finest Mixed—From a splendid collection of drooping and erect varieties. Pkg., 20c. Salzer's Show—Unsurpassed in grandness. Pkg., 30c.

Godetia—A.

Well worthy of extended cultivation; their delicate purple and pink have long made them favorites. Finest mixed. Pkg., 5c.

Duchess of Albany—A new, beautiful variety, with glossy, satiny white flowers of enormous size. Pkg., 15c.

Salzer's Show Mixture—Of every obtainable sort. Pkg., 10c.

Helipterum —

Charming plants, producing great clusters of richly colored, beautiful, everlasting flowers; mixed. Pkg., 10c.

Hunnemannia —A brilliant yellow annual from Mexico. Flowers large, tulip-shaped and grand. Pkg., 10c.

HELIPTERUM.

GOURDS.

This is a wonderfully interesting climber. Every garden where children romp and play should have them, and no vine will be more carefully watched and make the young hearts more glad than this.

Orange—Mock Orange shape. Pkg., 10c.

Dipper Gourd—Grows in shape of a dipper. Hollowed out, it can be used as such, lasting for years; ornamental. Pkg., 10c.

SALZER'S HERCULES CLUB.

Lufta, or Dish-Rag Gourd.

The peculiar lining is sponge-like, porous, tough, elastic and durable, making a natural dish-cloth. The fruit grows about 2 feet in length. Many ladies prefer this dish-cloth to anything that can be made. It also makes a lady's handsome summer bonnet; very unique and tasteful, suitably trimmed and ribboned. For the bath, and for all uses of the toilet in general, the "Dish-Rag Gourd" is taking the place of the sponge. Pkg., only 10c. Salzer's Oddly Odd Seed. See Cover Page. Pkg., 20c.

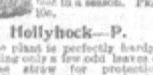

SHIRT MADE FROM DISH RAG

Big Hercules Club—Enormously large-growing, club-shaped gourd; the wonder and admiration of all. Pkg., 10c.

Gypsophila.

(Angel's Breath.)

When once planted not known, no garden will be without this graceful, elegant, and above all, beautiful pure white flower. Pkg., 5c; choicest mixed, 10c.

ANGEL'S BREATH

Hyacinth Bean—A splendid climber with abundantly clustered spikes of purple and white flowers; runs 20 feet in a season. Pkg., 10c.

Hollyhock—P.

The plant is perfectly hardy, needing only a few odd leaves or coarse straw for protection, standing, with this, our hardest winters.

Variegated—Beautifully variegated. Pkg., 15c.

Yellow—Very double. 15c.

Crimson—Fine double. 15c.

Rose—Splendid double. 15c.

Pink & White—Fine, 15c.

Double Mixed Hollyhock—Our mixture is wonderfully grand, containing all old and new sorts. In dozen brilliant Hollyhock plants, each 8c; $1 for 15c. Pkg., 10c.

HOLLYHOCK.

Heliotrope.

Well known, deliciously fragrant plants; excellent for bedding purposes or pot culture; finest, fine mixed. Pkg., 15c.

HELIOTROPE.

Salzer's Show.

A mixture of every obtainable color and sort of Helichrysum. 10c.

HELICHRYSUM.

Helichrysum—The finest among the everlasting flowers; of fine forms. Cut the flower before the color fully opens; fine mixed. 5c.

Ice Plant—A.

A singular trailing plant; the leaves and stems are covered with crystal-like globules, giving it the appearance of being covered with ice. Pkg., 5c.

Kaulfussia—A.

Desirable; dwarf habit and compact growth; richness and freedom of bloom. Pkg., 5c.

Lantana.

The flowers are borne in Verbena-like heads, embracing every shade of color; finest mixture. 10c.

Leptosiphon.

Low, pretty, hardy, free-blooming annuals. 5c.

Lobelia—A.

A continuously blooming plant, of easy culture; well adapted for bedding, edging pots or rockeries.

Cardinal Flower—Light red. Pkg., 5c.

Star of Ischl—Of erect growth, only 5 inches high, and forming dense balls of dark blue flowers. Pkg., 10c.

White Gem—Purest white blossoms. Pkg., 10c.

Emperor William—Light blue; compact. 5c.

Blue Bird.

A splendid Lobelia, blossoms large and intense blue. 10c.

Grinfilia—Very fine for baskets, trailing gracefully. All colors. Pkg., 5c.

Lobelia Mixed—All colors, very fine. Pkg., 5c; good mixed, 3c.

FINE MIXED GOURDS. 5c.

Marigold.

The newer sorts of Marigold are great beauties, and are beginning to be widely cultivated. Finest colors, mixed. 5c.

Salzer's Superb—Contains a mixture of many sorts and colors; especially adapted for garden culture. 10c.

MARIGOLD.

Myosotis.

Forget-Me-Not. Likes a moist location; extremely beautiful, low-growing plants; fine mixed. Pkg., 5c.

Azorica—Dark blue flowers; produced in greatest abundance. Pkg., 10c.

Eliza Fonrobert—Large blue. Pkg., 10c.

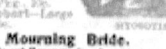

MYOSOTIS.

Mourning Bride.

One of the finest flowers for bouquets; great variety of colors, borne on long stems. Pkg., 5c.

Forget thou not that an order for 40c or more entitles you to a package of Oddly Odd Gourd Seeds. See Front Cover Page.

Nasturtium.

No annual gives more and finer blossoms and is so serviceable, cut and placed on the table in vases; while for wearing on corsage or neck bouquets they are extremely fashionable and valuable on account of their rich colors and their property of retaining their freshness so long.

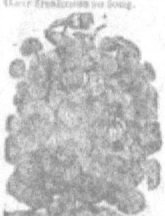

EMPRESS OF INDIA. 20c.

Empress of India—The plant has a very dwarf habit, while the flowers are of the most brilliant crimson color, so freely produced. Pkg., 5c.

Majus—Elegant profuse flowering plants, growing 10 feet in one season. Tall sorts mixed. Pkg., 5c.

Minus—Dwarf Nasturtiums in the yard are very brilliant and attractive. Mixed. Pkg., 5c.

Black Eye—Very dark; choice. Pkg., 5c.

Tall Yellow—Beautiful golden yellow. Pkg., 5c.

Tall White—Elegant pearly white. Pkg., 5c.
Tall Rose—Beautiful in the extreme. Pkg., 5c.
Tall Crimson—Extremely beautiful. Pkg., 5c.

Salzer's Perpetual Blooming.

Pkg., 10c.; oz., 20c.

Salzer's Perpetual Blooming Nasturtiums—We control all the seed of this wonderfully free-blooming Nasturtium. It blooms early and continually throughout the season. This mixture contains many brilliant and fashionable colors that are particularly adapted for dress bouquets. The flowers are large, proud, beautifully and exquisitely colored, borne on long stems. The endless variety contained in the Perpetual Blooming populates them as the most beautiful of all Nasturtiums, and thousands of ladies who have grown them extoll their great beauty and peerless colorings. Pkg., 10c.; oz., ½ lb., 50c.

Fine Mixed Colors.

This mixture of Nasturtiums is exceedingly beautiful and justly popular. Pkg., 5c.; oz., 15; ¼ lb., 20c; lb., 60c.

MISCELLANEOUS.

Alonsoa—Mask Flower. Pretty shrublike annual, bearing scarlet flowers in profusion. Pkg., 5c.

Abobra—Pretty, hardy perennial climber, glossy green foliage, bright scarlet fruit; 10 feet. Pkg., 10c.

Althea—Hardy, with odd little flowers. Pkg., 5c.

Bartonia—Showy summer-flowering annual. Pkg., 5c; good mixed pkg., 5c.

Baptisia—False Indigo. Flowers bright blue or yellow, borne on spiked inches long. Pkg., 5c.

Beta—Gorgeous, showy-leaved Beets. Pkg., 10c.

Cacti Seed.

Now, there is a great deal of genuine pleasure in growing these odd plants from seed. It is sure to chain your attention and interest you right along.

Choice Mixed Cacti, Pkg., 10c.

Cacti Wonder Mixture—The finest of sorts. Pkg., 25c.

Chiron Grandiflora—Brilliant yellow flowers. Pkg., 5c.

Coccinea—A handsome Gourd. Scarlet fruit. Pkg., 10c.

Coleostea—Free-flowering, hardy annuals. Pkg., 5c; good mixed pkg., 5c.

Cosmos—Plant 4 to 6 feet high, literally covered in the autumn with large, single flowers resembling Dahlias. A group in bloom is a gorgeous sight. Colors range through many shades. Pkg., 10c.

Cuphea—Cheer plant. Very attractive. Pkg., 10c.

Cucumis—Ornamental Cucumbers. Pkg., 5c.

Cosidaethera—Brilliant crimson. Pkg., 20c.

Cosidaethera—A climbing plant bearing oval-shaped fruit, exploding loudly when ripe. Pkg., 10c.

Dicentra—Bleeding Heart. Well known. Pkg., 10c.

Didiscus—A—Delicate skyblue blossoms. Pkg., 10c.

Erica—(Cape Heath)—Beautiful and interesting greenhouse shrubs, flowering most profusely. Pkg., 10c.

Erysimum—Showy, free-flowering annuals, very effective in beds. Pkg., 5c.

Eulalia—Unlike all other variegated plants, this has the striping or marking across the leaf. Pkg., 10c.

Eupatorium—Very hardy perennials, bearing large clusters of white bloom. Pkg., 5c.

Glaucium (Horn Poppy)—A showy plant with silvery leaves, orange blossoms. Pkg., 5c.

Golden Rod—The nation's favorite flower. Who does not admire this beauty? 10c.

Gnaphalium — Immortelles bearing clusters of bright golden blossoms. Pkg., 5c.

Gomphrena—Beautiful everlasting flowers, mixed colors. Pkg., 5c.

Gynerium—Pampas Grass. Pkg., 5c.

Humea—Great climbers, mixed colors. Pkg., 5c.

Gilia.

A beautiful annual; splendid for borders and show. Pkg., 5c.

Snow Mixture—The very finest. Pkg., good mixed, 5c.

Malope—A gem in blooming. Pkg., 5c.

Hibiscus, Garden—A branching plant of the easiest culture; blooms freely. Pkg., 5c.

Honesty (Moon Wort)—Interesting summer-blooming plants, suitable for shrubberies or woodland walks. Pkg., 5c.

Kolchia—A rapid-growing, graceful, cypress-like plant; flowers yellow. Pkg., 5c.

Jacobæa—Annuals of the easiest culture. Pkg., 10c; mixed, 5c.

Loasa—Pretty, hardy climbing annuals. Pkg., 5c.

Lavender (Lavandula)—Much prized for its fragrant violet flowers. Pkg., 5c.

Lophospermum—Exceedingly ornamental trailing plants with large flowers. Pkg., 10c.

Linum—Very graceful flowers, especially pretty when branched. Pkg., 5c.

Torenia, "Bird in the Swing."

Upon a small bed, 3 feet by 14, produced from a 10c package of Torenia, our head gardener estimates that from May 15th to frost there were upward of 30,000 blossoms, all of intense porcelain blue and rich violet, throat bright yellow, presenting a magnificent sight. Pkg., 15c; 2 for 25c.

Lychnis—Handsome and strikingly effective perennials; mixed. Pkg., 5c.

Lupinus—A—Bearing long and graceful spikes of various shades of scarlet, purple, yellow and white; fine mixed. Pkg., 5c.

Oxyura—This is a pretty little hardy annual, best in beds. Pkg., 5c.

Martynia—Handsome, large-flowering. Pkg., 5c.

Maurandia—P—Finest of all pot climbers, bearing quantities of bell-shaped blossoms. Pkg., 5c.

Malope—A package of Malope seed sown in the open ground in April will begin unfolding its rich pink blossoms early in June. Pkg., 10c.

Mimulus.

Strikingly handsome flowers of easiest cultivation.

Ave Maria—Grand; produces myriads of beautiful spotted blossoms. Pkg., 10c.

Musk Plant—Well-known fragrance. Pkg., 10c.

Show Mimulus—Contains grandly beautiful free-flowering sorts. Pkg., 20c; fine mixed, 5c.

Nemophila—Good mixed. Pkg., 5c.

Nigella—Love in a Mist. Pkg., 5c.

Nicotiana—Flowers pure white. Pkg., 20c.

Nycterygia—Star-shaped flowers. Pkg., 5c.

Odalis—Fine mixed. Pkg., 10c.

Oxalis Tropæoloides—Yellow flowers with brown foliage. Pkg., 10c.

Pink.

PINK.

Closely related to the Carnation and Picotee; but smaller flowers; plant dwarf and quite hardy; flowers beautiful and very fragrant.

Pink—Grand mixture. Contains many new and old varieties. Pkg., Fine mixed, 5c.

Picotee.

Very much like the Carnation; as fine and pure doubles in coloring. Choicest imported. Pkg., 15c; finest mixed, 10c.

Carnation Pinks—Superb in fragrance; finest sorts. They are sure to please, and will—

PICOTEE.

Peony—Grandly beautiful; mixed. Pkg., 20c.

Palava—A beautiful annual, flowering abundantly. Pkg., 5c.

Pentstemon—Continuous bloomers. Pkg., 10c.

Perilla—Beautifully fringed bloomers; 5c.

Phaseolus (Scarlet running bean). Pkg., 5c.

Rhodanthe.

Beautifully formed, very ornamental plants; bell-shaped and very everlasting flowers. Pkg., 5c.

Ricinus—A.

Tall growing giants, whose luxurious tropical foliage renders them exceedingly ornamental and desirable. Mixed, 5c; finest mixed, 10c.

RICINUS. Pkg., 5c.

Salvia.

Flowers in spikes of fiery rich crimson and blue, and continues to blossom until checked, when the plants can be removed to house for bloom.

Salvia Coccinea—Fiery scarlet; fine. Pkg., 10c.

Salvia Splendens—Pkg., 10c; fine mixed, 10c.

Salvia Bluebird—Finest blue. Pkg., 10c.

Fragrant Apple Salvia—Pkg., 10c.

Scyphantus—A free-flowering plant. Pkg., 5c.

Sievia—F—Plants producing white and pink flowers; largely used in bouquets. Pkg., 10c.

Solanum—Beautiful ornamental fruit-bearing plants of various forms; fine mixed. Pkg., 5c.

Sweet Sultan—Fragrant flowers of purple, white and yellow. Pkg., 5c.

Statice—Free-flowering. Pkg., 5c.

Viscaria (Rose of Heaven)—A fine, free-blooming annual of brilliant colors; fine mixed. Pkg., 5c.

Vinca (Madagascar Periwinkle)—Ornamental free-blooming plants. Pkg., 10c.

PANSIES.

Wisconsin soil and climate are specially adapted to the growing of splendid blossoms and hence our strain is recognized among florists as the finest by all odds in America. It is grown on the new process of growing enormous blossoms for seed, with experience, soil, climate, etc., all in our favor of producing the best Pansy seed in the world.

Pansies in Separate Colors.

These separate colors contain all known varieties and shades of each. Pkg., 10c each.

Blue Shades.   Mahogany Shades.
Brown Shades.   Margined Shades.
Bronze Shades.   White Shades.
Black Shades.   Yellow Shades.
    Black (King of the Black)

Pkg., 10c.; any two pkgs. of above, 15c.

Angel's Robe.

This pure white Pansy is a novelty of the first

water; is especially adapted for cemetery planting or edging in the garden. It's the sweetest of all white Pansies. Pkg., 10c; 3 pkgs. 25c.

Louis Odier—Beautifully blotched; extra large. Pkg., 10c.

Trimardeau — The largest race of Pansies; enormous blossoms. Pkg., 10c.

Lord Beaconsfield—Large flowers of deep purple velvet. Pkg., 10c.

The Fairy Pansies.

There are the spotted, the dark and light marble varieties, mahogany shades, the deep brown, the maroon crimson, the intense yellow. When the black, the blue and the bronze, the colored, striped and spotted, and of striking beauty, are found there. Indeed the fairy pansies contain so many colors, variegated, blotched, veined, mottled and margined, and in a combination of colors that would be thought impossible until the flowers are actually seen. Over 40,000 ladies have tested our wonderful Fairy Pansy, and everywhere they do well and bloom gorgeously, calling forth praise everywhere. Pkg., 15c. 2 pkgs. 25c.

Pansy Mixtures.

No. 1—Choice mixed Pansy; very choice. Pkg., 10c.; 3 pkgs. 25c.

No. 2—Mixed Pansy. This mixture is as fine as many modrsen's 10c and 20c mixtures; some giant blossoms found therein. Pkg., 5c; ½ oz., 50c.

Home, Sweet Home Mixture.

Pre-eminently distinct; indeed, they can well be named "Fragrant Everblossoms," because it is a distinct strain of exquisitely beautiful, very free blooming Pansies. They are specially adapted to house culture, and hence the name, for a package of these beauties and we are sure that no pot in your garden will be more carefully watched or more often visited by your house than and these gotten than your bed of "Home, Sweet Home Fancies. Pkg., 20c; 3 pkgs., $1.00.

Salzer's Superb Pansy.

This strain is gathered from mammoth flowers only, and is made up to accommodate fancy of our customers who want giant flowers, regardless of price. Pkg., 20c.; 3 pkgs., $1.00.

Giant Peacock Pansies.

Salzer's new race of colossal Pansies. Blossoms gigantic, thick, full texture, with single blossoms measuring the past season attaining the enormous size of 12 inches in circumference. The colors are marvelous. No pen can describe, no artist's brush depict their transcendent brilliancy and beauty. They blend in perfect forms of monstrous size all the colors known in art and nature. We wish at once to popularize this new race of fragrant, colossal beauties and have here placed the price very low.

Price, pkg., 30c; 2 pkgs., 50c; 6 pkgs., $1.00; ¼ oz. seed, $2.00; ½ oz. $3.75.

GIANT PEACOCK PANSY. PEO. 30c.

Petunias.

New Fancy Hybrida Sorts—Composed of thick-petaled, extremely beautiful, single, new varieties, giant blossoms. Pkg., 20c.

Belle Etoile—Striped and marbled. Pkg., 10c.

Ellesmere—Dark rose for massing. Pkg., 10c.

Pure White—Fine single for cemetery. Pkg., 10c.

Giltwood—A good per cent. of the seed full and very double, but it comprises the widest possible range of colorually perfect blossoms, many of them wonderfully beautiful. Pkg., 20c.

Single Petunias.

A brilliant plant for outdoor decoration, as ribbon bedding, for window boxes, in fact for anything where gorgeous and brilliant show and quick, early flowering is desired.
Fine mixed sorts of Single Petunias. Pkg., 5c.

Salzer's Imported Mixture of Petunias.

Seeds gathered only from show flowers and contains every imaginable sort—brilliant in colors, perfect in habit, and profusely free in bloom. It is incomparable as a mixture, and contains some semi-double sorts. Pkg., 15c; 2 for 25c.
Good mixture, pkg., 5c.

FROM SALZER'S IMPORTED MIXTURE OF PETUNIAS. PEG. ONLY 15c.

Mignonette—A.

The delightful fragrance of the Mignonette has been applauded for centuries.

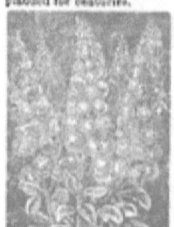

Snow Queen—The flower spikes of this magnificent novelty are long, often ten inches, pure white, and beautiful in form, the fragrance is delightful, rich and powerful. Pkg., 10c ; ¼ oz. 25c; oz. 50c.

Victoria—Dark red flowers, distinct and larger than the old varieties. Pkg., 10c; oz. 30c.

Macket—The plants are of pyramidal growth. Spikes of brightest red. Pkg., 10c; oz., 30c.

Double White—Nothing can equal a bed of this snow white sort. Pkg., 10c; oz., 30c.

Crimson Giant—New. The largest and sweetest of all Mignonettes. Pkg., 10c; oz., 30c.

Golden Queen—Literal mass of gold; continually in flower. Pkg., 10c.; oz., 35c.

Salzer's Giant White Spiral—Grows 2 or 3 feet high, perfectly erect, and we measured spikes of bloom on our grounds last season which were 15 inches long. It in color is pure snow white. Pkg., 10c.; oz., 30c.

Salzer's Snow—In this mixture we have placed every known variety, old and new. A package will furnish bloom and fragrance all season. Pkg., 10c; oz., 30c.

Mignonette—All sorts mixed. This mixture contains all known sorts and colors. Pkg., 5c; oz., 20c; ¼ lb., 50c.

Portulaca.

There are poured any flowers in cultivation that make such a dazzling display of bravery as a bed of our most brilliant colored Portulacas. Double mixed, for edge and double mixed to make a bed, Pkg., 5c.

Portulaca Mixture—Thirty sorts in the prettiest, choicest sorts. Pkg., 10c.

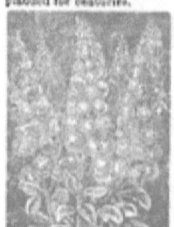
DOUBLE PORTULACA.

Salzer's Perpetual Pot—This strain covers every imaginable shade of scarlet, crimson, rose, white, yellow, etc., bearing innumerable large, full, double blossoms. It is indeed popular, whether grown as a pot plant or as a bed on the lawn or garden. The show is brilliant. Pkg., 10c.

SALZER'S PHLOX.

Of all annuals Phlox makes the finest beds, and every garden should have them. Flowers are vivid, rich and of wonderful hues, borne in clusters freely.

Phlox Drummondi.

Alba, pure white, fine for cutting. 10c
Purpurea, deep purple 10c
Rosea, bright rose; good 10c
Scarlet, very brilliant and showy. 10c
Phlox Drummondi, all sorts and colors; mixed; very fine. Price, ¼ oz., 35c; oz., 60c; pkg., 5c.

PHLOX DRUMMONDI.

Phlox Grandiflora.

The beauty of this grand Phlox is its gigantic blossoms, brilliant and showy.
Phlox Grandiflora, pure white.. 10c
Phlox Grandiflora, bright scarlet ..10c
Phlox Grandiflora, striped and blotched 10c
Phlox Grandiflora, deep purple. 10c

GIANT STAR PHLOX, 15c.

Phlox Grandiflora—Finest Mixed.

This mixture, for 10c, must not be compared with that offered by most seedsmen. Ours is composed of giant blossoms in endless colors. It is particularly fine, and we do not see how a garden can be called quite complete without a small bed of these brilliant beauties. Pkg., 10c; 2 pkgs., 15c; ¼ oz., 30c.

Phlox Snowbank—This is the grandest pure white Phlox in cultivation. Pkg., 10c.

Phlox D. Nana—Our mixture of this new dwarf, compact, free-blooming. Pkg., 10c.

STAR OF QUEDLINBURGH—Novelties in Phlox. The petals are charmingly fringed, often star-shaped, long-pointed, with borders margined, etc., and its oddity and beauty of colors will find for itself a place in many a garden. Don't try to get along without it, you will miss one of the rarest treats in annuals if you do. Pkg., 15c; 2 pkgs., 20c.

Giant Star Phlox.

A brilliant novelty on which we paid $250.00 in prizes three years ago. The blossoms are very large, beautifully shaded, of all manner of hues and colors, and are star-shaped. Indeed, this Phlox makes a brilliant display. Pkg., 15c.

Primrose, Evening.

The Œnothera, or Evening Primrose, produces large blossoms, 3 to 4 inches across, usually yellow or white; very showy; mixed. Pkg., 10c.

English Primrose—See Auricula. Pkg., 25c.

Primula.

Sown in spring or summer will make excellent pot plants for winter use.

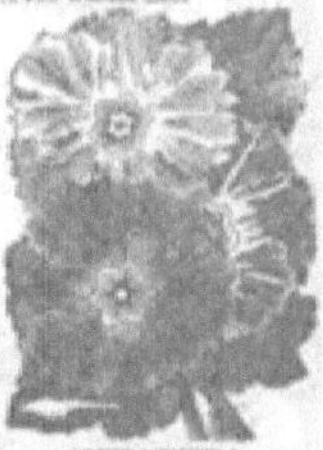

PRIZE PRIMULA.

Grand Sorts, Mixed—Pkg., 20c; 6 pkgs., $1.00.

Chinensis—Pkg., 20c.

Fringed Varieties—extra fine mixed. Pkg., 40c. Finest double sorts; mixed. Pkg., 50c.

Salzer's Prize—They are beautiful beyond description, are large, full and in endless colors. A splendid mixture for florists or for the house, as a package will give you many varieties. Pkg., 25c; 5 pkgs., $1.00.

SAMPLE FLOWERS OF "BLOSSOM EVERMORE."

POPPY SORTS.

Paeony, large, full double sorts.......... 5c
Oriental, dazzling scarlet, double.......10c
White Shades, best white sorts..........10c
Poppy, all sorts mixed..................... 5c
Poppy, double sorts mixed................. 5c
Poppy, single sorts mixed................. 5c
Poppy, hardy, perennial sorts mixed.... 10c
Opium Poppy, pkg., 5c; oz................25c
Good Mixed, pkg.............................. 3c

Poppy Blossom Evermore.

Noted for its brilliancy of color, charming and delicate tints, for beauty and variety of form, for oddity and richness, as well as uniqueness of its great single and double blossoms. Pkg., 15c; 2 pkgs., 25c.

Peacock Poppy Mixture.

Offered as a premium last year, and 126,000 packages were taken. It became at once unusually popular. Contains the most brilliant hues imaginable. Pkg., 15c; oz., $1.00.

Smilax.

A beautiful and graceful perennial climber, none surpassing its glossy deep green, wavy and most delicate foliage. Pkg., 10c.

Sensitive Plant.

An interesting plant, well known for the extreme irritability of its leaves and foot stalks, which close and droop at the slightest touch. Children's delight. Pkg., 10c.

Stipa Pinnata—E.

Feather Grass—A hardy perennial plant, with beautiful, delicate white, feathery-like stems of bloom; in great demand for ornamental work; flowering the second season from seed. Pkg., 10c.

Sweet William—A.

A very beautiful class of plants of extreme richness and diversity of color. The varieties have been greatly improved of late years. Hardy as oak. Cover with a few leaves in fall; in spring they will bloom with increased beauty. Fine mixed. Pkg., 10c.

Tritoma Uvaria.

Red Hot Poker, splendid perennials, bearing tall spikes of red bloom. Pkg., 10c.

SALZER'S SPLENDID SWEET PEAS.

For long stem; large, full, bright flowers; subtle, yet intense fragrance; hardy, free-flowering, ever-blooming varieties, we commend to you Salzer's Sweet Peas. Nothing quite like them anywhere.

Salzer's Ever-Blooming Sweet Peas.

Our Ever-Blooming is something especially rare, of unusually large blossoms, brilliantly shaded, deliciously fragrant, that bear continually until destroyed by severe frosts. It is impossible to describe the rare beauty of the brilliant tints. For personal wear during summer and autumn it is the most fashionable flower grown, as this strain retains its freshness for hours. We control the entire stock of Ever-Blooming Sweet Peas in America. Don't be misled by some seedsmen offering you a substitute for same, as "just as good." Pkg., 10c; oz., 20c; ¼ lb., 60c; lb., $1.50.

Cepopoco Sweet Peas.

This strain is remarkable for largeness and clearness of blossoms, rich, varied and marked colors, and great freedom of bloom and delicious fragrance. Pkg., 20c; oz., 30c; ¼ lb., 50c.

Cupid, the Dwarf Sweet Pea.

The famed dwarf Sweet Pea. Our stock is grown from the original. Pkg., 10c; 3 pkgs., 25c; oz., 50c.

We can furnish the following at 5c per pkg.; oz., of any variety, 20c; ¼ lb., 40c, postpaid; lb., 90c.

Apple Blossom—Pink and white.
Blanche Burpee—Pure white.
Blanche Ferry—Pink and white.
Blushing Beauty—Best pink.
Boreatton—Velvety maroon.
Bronze King—Bronze standard white.
Butterfly—Blue and white.
Captain of the Blues—Best blue.
Cardinal—Old red.
Countess of Radnor—Light lavender.
Duchess of York—Nearly pure white.
Duke of Clarence—Claret purple.
Duke of York—Pink and white.
Emily Eckford—White with blue edge.
Emily Henderson—White.
Firefly—Finest scarlet.
Gaiety—Red and white striped.
Her Majesty—Large; rose color.
Ignea—One of the best reds.
Lady of Penzance—Delicate salmon.
Lemon Queen—Blush pink and lemon.
Lottie Eckford—White, blue edge.
Meteor—Best salmon.
Mrs. Jos. Chamberlain—Red and white flaked.
Mrs. Eckford—Light lemon.
Mrs. Gladstone—Large pink.
Mrs. Sankey—White.
Novelty—Very dark rose.
Orange Prince—Beautiful shade of orange.
Ovid—Rosy pink.
Peach Blossom—Pink.
Primrose—Straw color.
Princess Beatrice—Light pink.
Royal Robe—Dark pink.
Stanley—Best maroon.
Venus—Salmon buff.
Waverly—Rosy, claret color.

Sweet Peas—Special Mixtures in Separate Shades.

White Sorts, mixed..........Pkg., 5c
Striped Sorts, mixed..........Pkg., 5c
Black Sorts, mixed..........Pkg., 5c
Pink Sorts, mixed..........Pkg., 5c
Blue Sorts, mixed..........Pkg., 5c
Blush Sorts, mixed..........Pkg., 5c
Carmine Sorts, mixed..........Pkg., 5c

☞ These special sorts by weight: Oz., 15c; ¼ lb., 25c; lb., 75c. ☜

Fine Mixed Sweet Peas.

This mixture, for the price, challenges an equal. It is composed of many sorts and colors, and will surely please. Pkg., 5c; oz., 10c; ¼ lb., 20c; ½ lb., 35c; lb., 65c, postpaid.

Good Mixed—As fine as Seedsmen's Choice. Pkg., 3c; oz., 6c; ¼ lb., 15c; 1 lb., 50c, postpaid.

Perennial Sweet Peas—Resembles Sweet Peas. Perfectly hardy; climber. Pkg., 5c.

Stock, Ten Weeks.

For fragrance and perfect blossoms, brilliancy and diversity of color and long duration of bloom, this annual is unsurpassed.

Stock, Giant Perfection.

This **plant** of the new Giant Perfection is pyramidal **in shape,** 1½ feet high; produces long spikes **of double** flowers, much finer and larger than ordinary sorts, and of delicious fragrance. **See cut.** Pkg. 15c.

Large Flowering—Grows tall, full of branches and blossoms; very sweet. Pkg. 10c.

Tree Stock—Grows tall; literally fills its many branches with **great, large blossoms.** Pkg., 10c.

Kaiserin Louise—Pure white novelty...... 20c
Snow blue, white or flesh color, each 10c
Rose or carmine, each 10c
Black Brown 10c
Imported Dwarf (large blossoms) 20c
Fine Mixed 5c

Salzer's Select Mixture—This mixture stands unrivaled. It contains every imaginable sort and color known to the trade. On our own grounds, where we grow stock in large quantities, nothing gives better satisfaction and more pleasure to our thousands of visitors than the Select Mixture Stock. Pkg., 25c; 2 pkgs., 35c.

Violet—P.

Sweet Violet—The culture of this humblest and most fragrant of plants is easy; it requires that of the Pansy. The temperature must not be too high, the soil moist and rich in loam.
White Perfecta, Pkg., 15c. | Alba.... Pkg., 15c.
Blue ....Pkg., 15c. | Choice Mix'd. 15c.
Salzer's Prize Violets — (contains some double seed and every single color and sort obtainable. It is without a superior. Pkg., 20c.

Whitlavia—A.

An elegant annual, with delicate foliage, drooping clusters of rich dark blue and white, bell-shaped blossoms. Pkg., 5c.

GIANT PERFECTION, 15c.

VIOLET, BLUE. PKG., 10c.

SPECIMENS FROM FRAU GRETE MIXTURE (¼ SIZE). PKG., 15c.

Star Verbenas—Package 15 Cents.

The best way to get a large variety of fine Verbenas, splendid colors, is to get strong, to to grow these from seed. Indeed, they grow easily and so sure, and do so well that everyone wonders that so few, comparatively, grow Verbenas from seed. A teaspoon of seed, sown early, give enough splendid plants to cover a large bed and furnish these lovely flowers all season. Our Star Mixture is the finest obtainable. It is a prize mixture throughout. In it you have included all of the finest giant strains known. Pkg., 15c; 2 for 25c; 5 pkgs., 50c.

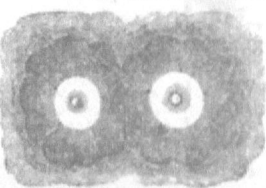

STAR VERBENA, PKG., 15c.

Mammoth Verbena—On perfect flowers, they reach the size of a silver quarter of a dollar. Pkg., 25c.
Candidissima—Purest white, Pkg., 15c. | Defiance—Deep scarlet. Pkg., 15c.
Bluebird—Blue black. Pkg., 10c. | Striata—Beautifully striped. Pkg., 10c.

Verbena Mixtures.

Fine Mixed—Pkg., 5c. | Star Mixture—The finest in the
No. 1 Mixed—Very fine indeed; many colors. Pkg., 10c. | world. Pkg., 15c; 2 pkgs., 25c.

Wahlenbergia.

Seeds sown in the house or early in the ground will, by June 1st, form a plant 12 inches high, very bushy and compact, deep green leaves, beautifully edged and lit nby covered with deep porcelain blue, four pointed, saucer shaped exquisitely and charmingly colored blossoms. Pkg., 15c.

Wall Flower—P.

A very fragrant and desirable class of winter bloomers. Sow seeds in hotbed, and while plants are small place in pots. In fall, remove to the house.
Dark Brown—Extra rose-formed, grand. Pkg., 25c.
Golden Yellow—Splendid. Pkg., 25c.
Choice Imported Mixture—Pkg., 25c.

Xeranthemum—E.

Annuals, dwarf, compact and free-flowering. The flowers are blue, white and purple. Pkg., 5c.

Zinnia—A.

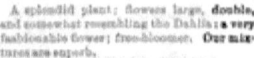

A splendid plant; flowers large, double, and somewhat resembling the Dahlia; a very fashionable flower; free-bloomer. Our mixtures are superb.

Double White—Pure, full. Pkg., 5c.
Double Striped—Pkg., 5c.
Double Crimson—Pkg., 5c.
Single sorts, mixed, very fine, pkg., 5c; tall sorts, mixed, 5c; dwarf sorts, mixed, 5c.
Salzer's Show—Contains every imaginable color, sort and kind obtainable in

Europe and America, and is for variety and gorgeousness, without an equal. Pkg., 10c.

Frau Grete—Peerlessly beautiful, of endless variety and color. This mixture is named in honor of ex-Gov. Hoffman's charming and estimable wife. The Zinnia is Mrs. Hoffman's favorite flower, and this mixture contains the finest in the world. Pkg., 10c.

Fine Mixed Zinnia—Extra. 5c.

SALZER'S VEGETABLE SEEDS.

The year 1898 was one of great plenty, especially in the vegetable line. Onions, Cabbages and Potatoes yielded abundantly, while prices ruled fair. The future must be judged by the past; years of plenty are followed by seasons of want. It therefore behooves YOU, if money-making is a pleasure to you, to sow plenty of Onions, Cabbage, Peas, Beets, Potatoes, etc., because many of your neighbors were disgusted with growing them last year, on account of the prices, and will not grow many in 1899. Look out for 1899. Plant a plenty,—prices may be high—yes, way up; that is the time to have plenty on hand to sell. It will fatten your bank account and give you money to do good with.

With us QUALITY IS FIRST, price secondary.

How good, not how cheap. Thus it comes that we have thousands of market gardeners and market farmers as customers who want our THE BEST, regardless of cost. Some of our prices may seem a trifle high; but it is not better to pay a fair price and get a GOOD ARTICLE than to pay but little and get a poor, worthless lot of seed. Is it not better to pay 10c for a packet of Salzer's Northern-Grown Giant Flat Dutch Cabbage and grow 500 solid, large, salable heads, than to pay 5c for some worthless, imported clover Cabbage seed offered by seedsmen who do not grow, but buy where they can get the cheapest? It costs 10 per cent. more than we could buy seed at, to grow seeds in the far North, but it pays our customers to have us do so—that is, in big vegetable yields and enormous farm crops. Remember, that cheap imported seeds, such as are frequently offered by seedsmen and dealers who are not growers, are dear at any cost. Seeds were never known to be grown in big cities—it takes the country to do so. It pays to buy direct from the grower. Try it this year by buying Salzer's Northern-Grown Seeds. They will prove best.

Club Terms—
Discounts and Premiums.

EVERYBODY NEEDS SEED. So if you go and see your neighbors, many of them never think of sending for seeds, and when the time comes, go to the nearest store and buy old, worthless Commission Box Seeds that have wandered over the land these 10 years or more—they will gladly give you their orders for Salzer's Fresh Seeds, if you show them our catalogue. In this way you can make Money besides getting all your own seed free.

Club Terms—We allow You in Sending Us

For $1.00 to select plants or seed packages amounting to $1.25, a profit of $0.25.

1.50	"	1.85
2.00	"	2.55
3.00	"	3.90
4.00	"	5.10
5.00	"	6.15
10.00	"	14.00
20.00	"	28.00

FREE! In addition to the great reduction of Seeds by purchasing at club terms we allow you, 1st, always to select Salzer's oddly odd goods from our front cover page, with each order of 40c or more. In addition we always throw in lots and lots and lots of extra goods, depending upon the size of your order—the larger the more EXTRA.

Discount on Seeds by Measure and Weight.

Above terms apply to Flower and Vegetable Seeds by the package (and plants at the single rate price) only. On each $1.00 worth of Vegetable seed ordered by the ounce, ¼ pound or 1 pound, or in pints, quarts, pecks (bushel prices are strictly net), we allow you to select 25c worth extra seed on each $1.00 cost. Thus, if you bought 1 peck Salzer's Earliest and Best Peas at $1.25 net per peck, we would be allowed to select the worth extra seeds. All farm seeds are net. As regards this you will find full instructions under Farm Seeds. Wholesale prices to market gardeners. Write to-day for same—make out your list of seed desired and send to us for special wholesale prices.

VEGETABLE SEEDS.

L. D. HAYFORD,
Rhinelander, Wis.

Mr. John Hauser, of La Crosse **Co. captured** *the First Prize at the West Salem fair, exhibiting 100* **different kinds** *of Vegetables, all grown from Salzer's Seeds.—"That's the* **reason,"** *he adds, "that* **I was** *able to take first prize. You see Salzer's Seeds furnished the germ, the vigor, the growth, the beautiful specimens—all I had to do was to furnish the ground for them to grow in and a little care in cultivating them! It was Salzer's Seeds that did it! And I can cheerfully recommend same to every market gardener who wishes the earliest, the best medium and best late vegetables—all true to name—to plant Salzer's Seeds. They never fail with me, they are always money makers for me."*

Joe H. De Roy, Cawker City, Kansas, says: "The Early Bird Radish is the earliest and best radish I ever saw.

"Your Lightning Cabbage is a world beater. It is the earliest."

"Your Giant Flat Dutch is magnificent."

Wm. Harberts, Little Rock, Iowa, says: "Your Giant Flat Dutch Cabbage cannot be excelled. Its large, solid, magnificent heads are just the size and quality we Germans like."

"Your 30-Day, the Earliest Tomato, is the earliest and best that we have ever used."

Wm. J. Murphy, Blessing, Iowa, says: "Your Wisconsin Hybrid Watermelon cannot be beat. Reserve seed for me for 5 acres."

Mr. August Freible says: "I have used your seeds for years. They produce the finest vegetables in the market. I bring in my crop ahead of the others and generally get double the price. I always take the first prize at fairs. Last year I exhibited 110 varieties of vegetables and of course carried off the first prize, all grown from Salzer's Seeds. Now, at the Interstate Fair, in the presence of thousands, I carried off first prize on 120 different kinds of vegetables from Salzer's Seeds. If you want fine show vegetables for fairs, Salzer's Seeds produce them."

MR. JOHN HAUSER,
The Great Vegetable Grower
of La Crosse Co.

L. *D. Hayford, Rhinelander, Wis., has this to say regards Salzer's Tools: "Your Matthews combined Drill, Wheel Hoe and Plow is positively the grandest tool of its kind on earth. I would not part with mine for* **an even $100.00,** *unless I could get another. It does its work splendidly. Your Seeds are A No. 1."*

C. A. Palmer, Lincoln, Neb., says: "I am a market gardener and have used your Seeds the last few years. Your 30-Day the Earliest Tomato and Salzer's Lightning Cabbage are the greatest money makers I ever struck. I had tomatoes thirty days ahead of the best gardeners of this place, and beat them all on cabbage."

Ginseng Roots.

GINSENG.

The inquiry for Ginseng Roots the past few years has been very large, so large that it has become a source of extremely profitable culture. There is probably no root that is in greater demand and paid for at fancier prices than the Ginseng Root, selling at $2.50 to $6.00 per pound. The average price of this root paid at La Crosse for the past five years has been over $3.00 per pound. It is of comparatively easy culture and is sure to pay the farmer, whether grown in large or small quantities, a handsome profit.

Roots, per 12, 40c, postpaid; per 25, 75c; per 100, $2.75; per 500, $10.00.

Salzer's pamphlet on Ginseng Culture, postpaid to any address for 15c. This little pamphlet gives full culture directions and should be obtained by all intending purchasers—or better get the "American Ginseng: History and Culture" by Hauser—for which he charges $1.00, but we have a large lot of copies and offer same for 60c each, postpaid.

HOW MUCH SEED TO SOW.

The following table gives a fair idea of quantity of seed to sow per row of 100 yards long; also, seeds required per acre. The amount given is a great plenty.

	Per Row.	Per Acre.		Per Row.	Per Acre.		Per Row.	Per Acre.		Per Row.	Per Acre.		Per Row.	Per Acre.
Asparagus	8 oz.	6 lbs.	Carrot	2 oz.	3 lbs.	Egg Plant	¼ oz.	10 oz.	Okra	12 oz.	5 lbs.	Radish	8 oz.	8 lbs.
Beans, Bush	3 qts.	1½ bu.	Cauliflower	¼ oz.	4 oz.	Endive	2 oz.	1 lb.	Onion, for large bulbs	2 oz.	5 lbs.	Rhubarb	4 oz.	4 lbs.
Beans, Lima	5 qts.	20 qts.	Celery	1 oz.	8 oz.	Leek	2 oz.	10 oz.	Onion, for sets	5 oz.	25 lbs.	Salsify	4 oz.	8 lbs.
Beans, Pole	1 pt.	15 qts.	Collards	½ oz.	10 oz.	Lettuce	2 oz.	25 oz.	Parsley	2 oz.	1 lb.	Spinach	4 oz.	10 lbs.
Beet	5 oz.	8 lbs.	Corn, Sweet	1 pt.	8 qts.	Melon, Water	2 oz.	3 lbs.	Peas	3 qts.	2 bu.	Squash	3 oz.	3 lbs.
Broccoli	¼ oz.	1 lb.	Cress	2 oz.	2 lbs.	Melon, Musk	2 oz.	2 lbs.	Pepper	½ oz.	½ lb.	Tomato	1 oz.	4 oz.
Brussels Sprouts	¼ oz.	1 lb.	Cucumber	2 oz.	3 lbs.	Mustard	4 oz.	3 lbs.	Pumpkin	2 oz.	5 lbs.	Turnips	2 oz.	2 lbs.
Cabbage	1 oz.	½ lb.												

☞ With each 50c order a package of Salzer's Oddly **Odd** Gourds! On larger orders, see page 30.☜

OUR SPLENDID 50c. LATE COLLECTION.

50 Cents. 18 packages of best late vegetables for only 50c. This package cannot be broken. They are choice. Look up their description in catalogue.

1. Beans, White Wonder.
2. Beet, Long Smooth Blood.
3. Cabbage, Premium Flat Dutch.
4. Carrot, Long Orange.
5. Cauliflower, Autumn Giant.
6. Celery, Boston Market.
7. Cucumber, Long Green.
8. Corn, Mammoth Sugar.
9. Kohl Rabi, Salzer's Mammoth.
10. Lettuce, Prize Head.
11. Melon, Ironclad.
12. Melon, Montreal Market.
13. Onion, Yellow Danvers.
14. Peas, Telephone.
15. Radish, White Strasburg.
16. Spinach, Long Standing.
17. Squash, Marblehead.
18. Tomato, Favorite.

Catalogue Price, $1.30. Special Price, Only 50c.

☞ **This collection has fairly leaped into popularity!** Everywhere it is receiving hearty indorsement. The sorts are splendid—the quality A No. 1. We **furnish the Late Collection and the Earliest** with great **pleasure,** for they **are sure to please** everybody, even the most critical.

The Great $1.00 Collection of Earliest Vegetables.

There are thieves even in the seed trade. There are men who are so unprincipled as to steal our cuts, our descriptions, in order to sell their inferior seeds. Thus they will try and palm off MEDIUM EARLY VEGETABLES, claiming them to be "just as good" as Salzer's Northern Grown Earliest. Well, they are not. This collection of 35 packages Earliest and Best Vegetables is without an equal. It is composed of our specialties—varieties we have cared for and improved for the past 20 years. There is nothing like it in the seed trade. That's the reason some seedsmen try to copy it. That this collection pleases; that the seeds therein are the earliest in the world, that it gives satisfaction everywhere, we introduce here only a few of THOUSANDS OF TESTIMONIALS:

Thus we could keep on with testimonials from Europe, Asia, Africa, South America, Australia, and from every county and state of our grand United States. Everybody praises this collection as the earliest in the wide, wide world. Try them for 1899. They are fine and cheap. Think of it! Postpaid, for only $1.00; not 5c per package, and every sort a gem.

THE GREAT ONE-DOLLAR COLLECTION.

This collection of 35 grand vegetable sorts is without question the very finest offered in the world. Many seedsmen, of course, will imitate this, but in quality it is impossible to reach it, because many of the seeds contained herein are our specialties, and cannot be had from anyone else.

The following 35 sorts of vegetable seeds,—sufficient for a family garden,—the very best and the very earliest of their kind,—for only $1.00 net. No slab rates. This gives everybody an opportunity to test our superior Northern Seeds and have the very earliest vegetables grown. If you want choice, early vegetables on your table, WAY AHEAD (yes, 10 to 15 days ahead) of your neighbors, get this collection. This lot is put up in 35 packages—the catalogue value, $2.50—and will not be broken. Look up their description. There 35 packages for $1.00 are a great bargain.

$1.00

1 Asparagus, Barliner. 2 Beet, Dewing's Red. 3 Beans, No Plus Ultra. 4 Borecole, Dwarf German. 5 Corn, Early La Crosse. 6 Cabbage, Salzer's Earliest. 7 Cabbage, Red Pickling. 8 Carrot, French Forcing. 9 Cauliflower, E. Paris. 10 Celery, White Plume. 11 Celery, Turnip Rooted. 12 Cucumber, Early Market. 13 Cucumber, Pacific Pickle. 14 Cress, Extra Curled. 15 Endive. 16 Kohl Rabi, Early Vienna. 17 Lettuce, Early Simpson. 18 Lettuce, German Butter. 19 Leek, Salzer's Earliest. 20 Melon, Water, Phinney's. 21 Musk, Jenny Lind. 22 Onion, New Queen. 23 Parsnip, Long Sugar. 24 Pepper, Ruby King. 25 Peas, Salzer's Earliest 8 Best. 26 Parsley, Early Moss Curled. 27 Radish, Scarlet Dark Red. 28 Radish, Long Scarlet. 29 Rutabaga, Early Yellow. 30 Sage. 31 Spinach, Early Summer. 32 Squash, Early White Bush. 33 Sweet Marjoram. 34 Turnip, Early La Crosse. 35 Tomato, Early Conqueror.

THESE 35 Packages for $1.00, POSTPAID. These 35 Packages will not be changed.

This collection gives you the choicest of the choice in Early Vegetables, and gives you lots of them for but little money. Thousands have tried them and thousands chant their praises. You will certainly do the same if you order them this spring. Nothing in the world quite so early and so fine. They are the rarest of all rare, rich, luscious vegetables, just the kind that you will delight in. We throw in a package of Salzer's Oddly Odd Gourds with each collection order. Try this Collection in 1899 for EARLIEST.

Earliest of All Collection.

POSTPAID ONLY... **50** CENTS.

This is the earliest of all vegetable novelty collections. Will produce vegetables 20 days ahead of others. All grand novelties and rare sorts. Try them.

Beans, Earliest Wax $0.15
Beet, Red Beauty .... .10
Cabbage, Lightning ...... .10
Corn, First of All ...... .10
Carrot, First of All .... .10
Melon, Salzer's Earliest . .10
Pea, Early May .... .10
Radish, Salzer's Earliest .10
Tomato, Earliest of All .. .20
                         $1.15

50 Cents.

The whole lot, worth $1.15, on trial, for 50c.

FOR 70 CENTS.

We are frequently asked for a collection of vegetables for a small garden, and we cordially recommend the following, which we send, postpaid, for only 70 cents. The varieties contained therein are all A No. 1, of choicest qualities, and will surely please and delight. Some of the best sorts in the world are found in this 70c collection. You will surely be delighted with same:

Beans, Salzer's Six Weeks, 5c.
Beans, Case Knife, a gold Bean, 10c.
Beet, Best of All, 5c.
Carrot, Guerande, 10c.
Cabbage, Salzer's Ideal, 12c.
Celery, Self-Blanching, 10c.
Corn, Eggplant Sweet, 10c.
Cucumber, Salzer's Perfection, 10c.
Cucumber, Boston Pickling, 5c.
Lettuce, All Cream, 5c.

Muskmelon, The Osage, 10c.
Watermelon, 5c.
Onion, Prize Dancers, 5c.
Parsnip, Salzer's Crown, 5c.
Peas, Telephone, 10c.
Radish, Scarlet Olive, 5c.
Parsley, Moss Curled, 5c.
Tomato, La Crosse Seedling, 15c.
Squash, Improved Hubbard, 10c.
Turnip, Early Six Weeks, 5c.

ALL FOR 70c.

In all, 20 packages, with a retail value of over $1.85, postpaid, for only 70c. If you want a complete garden, take our great $1.00 Collection, found on page 32, and this 70c collection. The two we will mail to one address for $1.50.

ASPARAGUS.

Asparagus—Berliner Freude.

(Our own introduction.) A superior Hybrid Asparagus, maturing fully the third year, with a bountiful crop already the second year, from seed culture. Extremely early. Pkg., 10c; oz., 20c; ¼ lb., 50c; lb., $1.50.

New Asparagus—Frankfurter Speck.

A new, large white variety of great beauty and yield. Immensely prolific; giant size stalks; rich, juicy, tender—just the Asparagus you want.
Price of Seed: Per pkg., 10c; oz., 20c; ¼ lb., 50c; lb., $2.00.

Baer's Mammoth.

A bunch of 25 edible shoots weighed 13 lbs. It is of a very fine flavor; the shoots are very tender almost to the stem. Pkg., 5c; oz., 15c; ¼ lb., 40c; lb., $1.25.

Giant Palmetto.

It is an enormous yielder, very even and regular in its growth, and of very large size. Pkg., 10c; oz., 20c; ¼ lb., 50c; lb., $1.50.

Conover's Colossal.

Large and rapid growth. The well known sort; used for many years. Pkg., 5c; oz., 10c; lb., postpaid, 60c.

Asparagus Roots.

ALL ONE YEAR OLD.	FREE BY MAIL. Per 25	Per 100	EXPRESS. Per 25	Per 100	Per 500
Berliner Freude	$0.50	$1.25	$0.50	$0.50	$2.00
Frankfurter	0.50	1.25	0.30	1.00	2.00
Conover's	0.30	1.25	0.30	1.00	1.00
Baer's Mammoth	0.50	1.25	0.30	1.00	1.00
Palmetto	0.50	1.25	0.30	1.00	2.00

For 500 ..... $3.50. Per 1000..... $5.00.

Plant one-year-old roots on rich, deep soil, 12 inches apart, and in 1000 you can cut fair crops.

☞ **Two-year** old Asparagus 75c per 100 more than one-year.

Salzer's Hamburg Brussels Sprouts.

We saw immense fields of this splendid vegetable while in France and Germany. It is used there in great quantities. It is the very **best** winter vegetable that **can be sown.** No matter how hard the frosts of November and December, it does not injure the Sprout. The plant remains in the garden until desired for cooking, and then are taken in, to greatly improve them. Strip off the outer covering of the Sprouts, cook them whole—ah! such Sprouts melt in the mouth, and are a delicacy not surpassed by the finest Cauliflower. For early use, plant in May and June, **for late, in July.** Full culture directions on package. Pkg., 10c; oz., 20c; ¼ lb., 75c; lb., $2.50.

Brussels Sprouts.

Improved Dwarf—Very fine. Pkg., 5c; ¼ lb., 50c.

Corn Salad or Fetticus.

An excellent vegetable; used as a salad; largely grown for market. Sow early in spring in rows 1 foot apart, and fit as fit for use in six weeks. Pkg., 5c; oz., 20c; lb., $1.00.

Chervil.

Well known. Used like Parsley. Pkg., 5c; oz., 15c; ¼ lb., 40c.

Cardoon.

Used blanched like Celery. Pkg., 10c; oz., 30c.

☞ **Chives, Horseradish and Eggplant**—See description.

COFFEE.—Good, too. (See page 51.)

☞ **Hop Roots**, page 19.
☞ **Chicory**, see page 51.

ARTICHOKE.

A delicious vegetable. The **blossom is cooked** and prepared, and **furnishes a great** utility in food.

Large Globe—Pkg., 10c; oz., 25c; lb., $2.50.

Salzer's Eaw.....cut—The earliest Artichoke known. It is a great improvement on Large Globe. Pkg., 10c; oz., 45c; ¼ lb., $1.00.

Borecole or Kale.

A hardy, useful winter vegetable. Sow in the middle of April, or in the fall. Improves in taste when touched by frost.

Salzer's Erfurt Dwarf Kale or Borecole. Pkg., 10c.

Salzer's Erfurt Dwarf Kale.

This magnificent novelty we introduced from Erfurt, where Kale is grown to great perfection. It is extremely prolific, of the richest color and most delicious flavor. If you haven't given Kale a trial, do so this year, you will relish it. Pkg., 10c; oz., 20c; ¼ lb., 60c; lb., $2.00.

Scotch Green Kale—Very fine. Pkg., 5c; oz., 10c; lb., $1.00.

Dwarf German Green Kale. Grown in large quantities by our German friends, who thoroughly understand the preparation of this splendid vegetable. Pkg., 5c; oz., 20c; ¼ lb., 50c.

BROCCOLI.

Nearly allied to Cauliflower, but more hardy, of excellent flavor, and greatly relished by all who grow them.

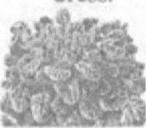

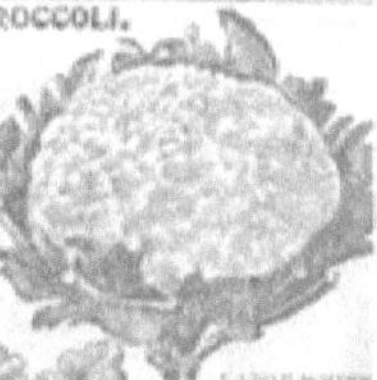

Large White. The finest, largest and best cropping sorts. Pkg., 10c; oz., 30c; lb., $2.00. **Purple Cape**—Standard sort, too. Pkg., 5c; oz., 30c; ¼ lb., $1.00.

Cress.

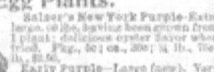

Extra Curled—Fine flavor, and can be cut two or three times. Pkg., 5c; oz., 10c; ¼ lb., 25c; lb., 50c.

True Water—A perennial aquatic plant of low growth. Pkg., 10c; oz., 50c; ¼ lb., $1.00.

Upland Cress—Shows its bright green leaves among us when winter begins to melt, and is eaten of all others. Pkg., 5c.

UPLAND. greens in the spring be fall; of taste, and is relished as a salad. Pkg., oz., 40c.

Egg Plants.

Salzer's New York Purple—Extra large, of the heaviest been given from 1 plant; delicious purple flavor when tried. Pkg., 5c; oz., 30c; ¼ lb., 75c.
Early Purple—Large (new). Very early and prolific; fine for family use. Pkg., 5c; oz., 40c; ¼ lb., $1.00.
Long Purple—Pkg., 5c; oz., 25c.
White Egg Plant—A novelty. Very ornamental, white and fine. Pkg., 15c.

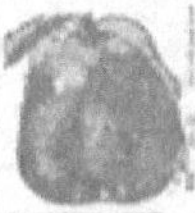

NEW YORK PURPLE.

Andiven, or Endive Lettuce.

Endive is one of the best salads for fall and winter use. Blanch by tying up the leaves in a conical form with bass or twine.

Salzer's Moss Curled—Very fine indeed. The very best for family use. Of excellent flavor and quality. Pkg., 10c; oz., 35c; ¼ lb., 90c; lb., $1.50.

Broad-Leaved Batavian—Chiefly used in soups and stews; requires to be tied up for blanching. Pkg., 5c; oz., 35c; ¼ lb., 40c; lb., $1.40.

Green Curled—Very fine. Pkg., 5c; oz., 20c; lb., 75c.

Collards.

Georgia—Pkg., 5c; oz., 10c; lb., $1.00.
Narrowfat—Pkg., 5c; oz., 15c; lb., $1.00.

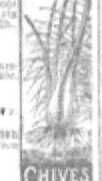

SALZER'S SPLENDID BEANS.

DWARF OR BUSH BEANS. NORTHERN GROWN.

1. Salzer's Golden Wax Bush Bean.

This bean during 1896 has again covered itself with glory and has earned the pre-eminent distinction of being the best Wax Bean in the world for general culture. It is planted with great confidence by all market gardeners and market farmers as one of the surest paying Wax Bean investments. Salzer's Earliest is much earlier and fills the want for a very early Wax Bean, but Salzer's Golden Wax fills the place of a general purpose Wax Bean. Our strain of Golden Wax has proven itself rust-proof. It is very bushy, thereby retaining moisture in the soil, so that the drought does not affect it. We heartily recommend this bean. Indeed, our three great Wax Beans, Salzer's Earliest, Salzer's Golden Wax and Salzer's Midsummer Wax, cannot be beaten the world over. We looked in vain while in Europe for a Wax Bean possessing more merit than any of the above three. It has been the means of making many a truck gardener rich, as we have gathered thousands from 5 to 20 bushels of our Wax Beans annually. It is the finest, most prolific, tenderest stringless Golden Wax Bean grown. It is very early, following Salzer's Earliest, of delicious flavor, and one of the best Wax Bush Beans in the market. Sells like hot cakes in green state. Splendid for family use, splendid for market, splendid for every purpose.

Price of Salzer's Golden Wax Bean.

Pkg., 10c: ½ pt., 20c; pt., 30c; qt., 35c; by express, pkg., 10c; pt., 20c; qt., 30c; pk., $1.00; bu., $3.90; 2 bu., $7.75.

S. SALZER'S RARE MIDSUMMER WAX BUSH BEAN NOVELTY—A WONDERFUL BEAN.

2. Salzer's Earliest Wax Bush Bean.

This bean has fairly leaped into popularity—enormous has been the demand for same since its introduction in 1892. For many years there has been a great call for an early Golden Wax Bean. With this in view we have been experimenting and originating new varieties, until to-day we believe we have the earliest Wax Bean in the world in Salzer's Earliest Wax Bean. This is a variety that will surely find a warm place in the hearts of market gardeners, who well know that the earlier they can get their Wax Beans in the market the handsomer their profit will be. This variety is extremely hardy. We have never seen them rust. It produces an extremely heavy crop, pods are very long, broad and showy, and not liable to blister.

Testimonials are received by the thousands and read.

Jno. Knoer, Minnesota: "Was ready for market 10 days ahead of other early wax beans."

Fred Willey, Indiana: My earliest Wax Beans were sold before my neighbors' were ripe. Your seeds are always ahead."

H. E. Green, Indiana: "One of the most profitable things that I planted the past year was the Earliest Wax Beans. They were ripe fully eight days ahead of my neighbors'. You remember I planted a bushel. They brought me over $280.00."

D. O. Flagg, Pa.: "The best paying crop that I had this year was the

Earliest Wax Beans. There was a big demand for them, and they were ready for market 10 days ahead of my neighbors', and brought in handsome profits."

J. Scheyer, Stillman, Ill.: "Salzer's Earliest Wax Beans I had in my market before other gardeners even thought of eating Wax Beans. Your seeds are the earliest and finest I have ever tried."

E. B. Pasch, Hatto, Tex.: "Salzer's Earliest Wax Bean is one of the finest Beans out I would not be without them. You may expect big orders. Salzer's seeds beat all."

It's the Bean for extreme early.

Price of Salzer's Earliest Wax Bean.

Large pkg., 10c; ½ pt., 20c; pt., 30c; qt., 35c, postpaid; by express or freight, pkg., 10c; pt., 20c; qt., 30c; pk., $1.25; bu., $4.00; 2 bu., $10.00.

3. Midsummer Wax Bush Bean.

Ten times as many beans were sold of this sort by us in 1896 as in 1895. That tells the story of its need and demand for a second early bean, ripening after Salzer's Earliest Wax and Salzer's Golden Wax, so that a succession of Wax Beans can be had for the market. This Bean fills a long felt want in this direction, whether for home use or market use. It produces an enormous crop of long, bright pods, brittle, clear, transparent color, and of exquisite quality. It is an ever-bearing as any Wax Bean can be, coming into use after our Golden Wax and continuing well stocked with large pods of a beautiful color, of tender quality, for a long period. Our experience with same proves it to be absolutely free from rust, and we have noticed in dry season that it withstands drought quite effectually. The dense foliage insures plenty of protection from the scorching midsummer sun, at the same time retaining abundant moisture around the roots, which keeps the plants continuously vigorous.

For private gardens it is especially valuable on account of the long duration of its bearing season. No better beans in the world than above three.

Price of Midsummer Wax Bean.

Pkg., 10c; pt., 20c; qt., 35c; postpaid; by freight, pk., $1.25; bu., $4.50.

SPECIAL PRICES.

1 package each above 3 great Beans, 28c, postpaid.
1 pint each above 3 great Beans, 75c, postpaid.
1 quart each above 3 great Beans, 90c by express.
1 peck each above 3 great Beans, $3.75 by express.

SALZER'S ROUND PODDED WAX BEAN.

This is what market gardeners have been waiting for for a long time. It has a round pod. The magnificent characteristics of this bean are small, dense foliage, enormous productiveness, roundness of pod and handsome appearance. The pods are of a clear, transparent color, good sized, remaining tender a long time; it is practically overbearing, free from rust, and solid, juicy and meaty to the center.

Pkg., 10c; pt., 20c; qt., 35c, postpaid; by express or freight, pk., $1.20; bu., $3.90.

We can also furnish Refugee Wax and Valentine Wax Beans. These are both round podded; extremely early; very fine, though not as good as Salzer's Round-Podded Wax. Pkg., 10c; pt., 20c; qt., 40c; pk., $1.20.

SALZER'S ROUND PODDED WAX.

Yosemite Mammoth Wax.

The pods frequently attain a length of 10 to 14 inches, with the thickness of a man's finger, and are nearly all solid pulp, the seeds being very small, when the pods are fit for use. The pods are a rich golden color, and are absolutely stringless, cooking tender and delicious. This is the coming Wax Bean for family or market purposes. It is enormously productive, as many as 50 of its monster pods having been counted on one bush. The plant is so large and vigorous, and the pods are so solid and pulpy, that they require a great deal of light and air to perfect them. We would again call attention to the necessity of planting this grand variety nearly twice as wide apart as ordinary Bush Beans. Pkg., 10c.; ½ lb., 20c.; pt., 35c.; qt., 65c.; pk., $1.50; bu., $5.00.

Prolific Black Wax.

Very productive, and one of the best varieties for early market. Pods, when fit for use, are of a beautiful, yellowish waxy color, fine quality, tender and delicious; very popular with market gardeners for snaps, nearly all the pods being fit for use at the same time, but it needs rich soil and good cultivation. An excellent sort for the private garden. This Bean is being much improved annually. It has been in our possession since 1884. Think of it! over 20 years, and each year we have endeavored to improve same. It is a splendid Bean, excellent for all purposes. Pkg., 10c.; ½ lb., 50c.; postpaid; by express or freight, qt., 25c.; ½ pk., 70c.; pk., $1.25; bu., $4.50.

Best of All Bush Bean (Green Pod).

This superb variety originated in Germany, and while it had been grown for some years around New Orleans, we offered it in the North for the first time in 1894. The pods are 6 inches long, very fleshy, succulent, stringless, and of rich flavor; they are produced early and abundantly. Altogether it is one of the most valuable green podded Beans for market or family use. Pkg., 10c.; pt., 20c.; qt., 35c.; ½ pk., $1.00; bu., $5.00.

BEST OF ALL BUSH BEANS.

Navy Beans.

Well known. Pkg., 5c.; pt., 10c.; by express, pk., 80c.; bu., $2.75.

There certainly is more better, and it has not failed to yield; all our gardeners. Pkg., 5c.; pt., 10c.; qt., postpaid, 25c.; by express, qt., 15c.; pk., 90c.; bu., $3.00.

Ne Plus Ultra.

A grand and distinct Bean. Sold only in packages and pints. Pkg., 10c.; pt., $1.

Boston Market Bean.

New, extra early, very delicious variety; long pods green and fine flavored. A Bean that will give you no end of rich pods, long, juicy and fine. Pkg., 10c.; pt., 25c., postpaid; by express, pk., $2.00.

SALZER'S SIX WEEKS. EARLIEST, FINEST, MOST PROLIFIC EARLY BEAN GROWN. RIPE 38 DAYS.

Salzer's Great Green Six Weeks' Bean.

Covered itself again with glory in 1895. The earliest Bean known; very prolific, hardy and full. Yellow seed. One of the best for family use in every respect, as also for early market. No trouble to sell $350.00 worth of Green Beans per acre of this variety. This Bean grows quick and sells quick; and the best of all is that everybody testing same is delighted with it that he would not get along without it at any price. It is a great boon for the market gardeners. Large, fine pods. Price of Salzer's Six Weeks' Bean! Pkg., 10c.; pt., 25c., postpaid; by express, pk., $2.00.

Low Prices.

The Prices of the 4 Following Wax Sorts are: by mail, free, pkg., 10c.; pt., 15c.; ½ lb., the; qt., 35c.; by express, pkg., 10c.; pt., 15c.; qt., 25c.; ½ pk., 40c.; pk., $1.00; bu., $3.75.

1. **White Wax**—Pods fair size, rich, tender and very prolific. Enjoys an enormous sale. Splendid for home use, either green or shelled.

2. **Ivory-Podded Wax**—A magnificent Wax Bean. Pkg., 10c.

3. **Wardwell's Kidney Wax**—Enormously productive. Pkg., 10c.

4. **Crystal White Wax**—Very quick growing and exceedingly productive. The pods are round, 5 to 6 inches long, nearly transparent.

Low-Priced Green-Podded Sorts.

Early Mohawk—Large, productive, dark colored variety; used in great quantities, fine for families. A green podded sort. Pkg., 5c.; pt., 15c.; qt., 25c.; pk., by express, 90c.

Refugee, or 1,000 to 1.

This is the great "Pickling Bush Bean." Pkg., 5c.; pt., 15c.; qt., 25c.; 90c.; bu., $3.00.

	Good for all uses. A splendid Shell Bean.
White Marrowfat.	Pkg., 5c.; pt., 10c.; ½c.; qt., 25c.; pk., 75c.; bu., $2.50.
Black Marrowfat.	

Salzer's Early Valentine.

One of the very best snap sorts, round, fleshy pods, which mature quickly and are of fastastic quality. This is the most popular of all green-podded Beans, both for the family and market gardener. We have always kept abreast of the improvements made in so important a variety, and have for some years past grown a strain that is repeated in actice earliness, cropness and handsome, round-podded appearance; in fact, so very choice is this strain of "Valentines" that one of our growers in his preference speaks of it as "Gilt Edged" and "Double Jointed." Pkg., 5c.; pt., 15c.; qt., postpaid, 25c.; by express, qt., 15c.; bu., $3.00.

SALZER'S EARLY VALENTINE BEAN.

FIELD BEANS—Very Profitable to Grow.

Salzer's White Wonder Field Bean.

SALZER'S WHITE WONDER FIELD BEAN

The grandest thing for a farm crop we have ever seen; side by side with any Bean known to us, it outyields it by fully one-third to one-half, making it a marvelous cropper. The pods are large and filled full with medium-sized pure white Beans. Extremely early; can be three weeks ahead of the Navy, and sold just at the time when Beans are rare. We consider it absolutely the finest, largest yielding, best selling field Bean known. Excellent for cooking and baking. Habit, dwarf, very bushy, and wonderfully full of pods. Just figure the profits on an acre yielding 30 to 50 bushels, at $2.50 per bushel. If you don't grow for market, get a pint or quart of the best Beans for home use. Over 10,000 farmers and citizens are planting this most wonderful of all White Beans. It's the yielder; nothing like it; so the world over. No Bean approaches it in yield, quality and readiness to find sale in the market. That's the universal verdict. It's a beauty and a quick seller in all markets.

PRICE OF WHITE WONDER.
Pkg., 10c.; pt., 30c.; qt., 50c., free, by mail; by express or freight, qt., 35c.; pk., $2.00; bu., $5.00.

Everbearing Farm Bean.

Most wonderful, largest, fodder Bean on earth. It's a sight worth seeing, a row of these giant Beans. Hogs relish them. Pkg., 10c.; pt., 30c.; qt., 50c., postpaid.

Salzer's Tree Bean.

This is a marvelous cropper and those not accustomed to fabulous yields scarcely credit the scores of bushels that an acre produces. It yields all the way from 30 to 100 bushels per acre. One customer writes: "From 1 pint of seed I grew 10 bushels. And another: "From 1 bushel of seed I grew 100 bushels." Pkg., 10c.; pt., 30c.; qt., 55c.; by express, pk., $1.00; bu., $3.25.

Salzer's White Wonder Field Bean.

Boston Favorite Bush Bean.

If you want a really good bean, Smith, try this one.

This is the great bean of Boston and the celebrated Boston Baked Beans which are known the world over on account of their richness and delicacy of flavor, are made from this bean. It resembles the Horticultural in habit of growth and color of pod with exception that the vine is stronger, more vigorous and the pods are larger and fill a bushel more quickly. It is an extremely prolific variety, one that can be planted any and everywhere with the assurance of success. The dry beans resemble the Horticultural bean except that they are somewhat larger and of better quality. It is the shell bean of New England, and no bean is more sought in the eastern markets and fetch fancier prices than the Boston Favorite bean. It can be planted any and everywhere and gives a rich harvest.

Price, Pkg., 10c; pt., 20c; qt., 35c, postpaid. **By express or freight** pt., 15c; qt., 20c; pk., 90c; bu., $2.90.

Henderson's Bush Lima Bean.

Magnificent dwarf-growing Limas; very early, of a delicious flavor, extremely productive, and should be planted in every garden in America. It's early, it's fine, it's just the thing for a family garden. It is wonderously prolific. A package or a pint will furnish sufficient for a good-sized family. It is one of those beans that can't be improved upon.

Pkg., 10c; pt., 25c; qt., 40c; pk., $1.75.

The Burpee Bush Lima.

This is a bush form of the well-known large White Lima Bean. It is very fixed in its bush character, growing to a uniform height of about 20 inches. While not so early as Henderson's Bush Lima, the larger size will commend it to many. The pods are the same size of the large Pole Limas and contain as many beans of the same delicious quality.

Pkg., 10c; ½ pt., 20c; pt., 30c; qt., 50c; pk., $2.00.

POLE BEANS.

Golden Butter Wax.—See Cut. A superb Pole Bean, growing rapidly, very productive; pods 1½ to 5 inches long; rich, golden yellow color; round, full and fleshy, entirely free from strings; the delight of the housewife. It is an ever-bearing Bean, bearing from early spring until late in the fall. Pkg., 10c; ½ pt., 20c; pt., 30c; qt., 50c; by express, pt., 20c; qt., 40c; pk., $1.35; bu., $5.00.

Salzer's Case Knife Pole Bean.—See Cut. The best white-seeded Pole bean; it is fine green sea Snap Bean, but is the best as a Shelled Bean; it is wonderfully early and remarkably prolific, outselling every Pole Bean grown except Salzer's Golden Butter. It is a great Bean for family and market use. Pkg., 10c; ½ pt., 20c; pt., 30c; qt., 50c; by express pkg., 10c; pt., 20c; qt., 35c; pk., 90c; bu., $1.50; bu., $5.00.

Salzer's Giant Black Wax.—This is a magnificent Bean, and the earliest of all Pole Beans; remarkably prolific and of delicious flavor. Pkg., 10c; ½ pt., 20c; pt., 30c; qt., 50c; by express, pk., $2.00.

Salzer's Improved Early Lima.—We have 10 years of cultivation succeeded in obtaining a Bean which ripens 10 days earlier than any Lima we have ever tried. Pkg., 10c; ½ pt., 20c; pt., 30c; qt., 75c; pk., $4.00.

The price of the following Pole Beans is: By mail, pkg., 10c; pt., 30c; qt., 50c; by express, pk., 90c; pt., 20c; qt., 35c; pk., $1.35; bu., $4.00.

Dreer's Lima—Early, very productive, superior quality.
King of the Garden—A splendid new Lima, growing rapidly and large. Beans often measuring 1 inch in length.
Scarlet Runner—The favorite Pole Bean of Europe.
Horticultural—Productive, large, round; for shelling or string beans.
Southern Prolific—Produces in clusters, excellent snap-short Beans in 50 days from germinating. The pods are very long, round and fleshy. Pkg., 10c; pt., 40c.
Yard Long—It is a Pole or Running Bean, with dark green foliage, and pods growing 3 feet and upward in length. Sold only in Packages. Pkg., 15c.
Broadwindsor—Greatly relished in England and Germany. Beans fully as large as a large Lima. Pkg., 10c; pt., 30c, postpaid.

Willing's Pride Pole Bean.

The most remarkable early Pole Bean that has ever come to our notice. A well-known seedman offered (for our full stock only a few bushels) a fabulous price, but we would not sell a novelty like this to a seedman for love or money, because our patrons must have the very best and this is the very best novelty that we know of. It is very early, ripens fit for market by August 1st in La Crosse, and bears pods often 14 inches long of delicious quality. It is the best Snap Pole Bean that we ever saw. For years Mr. Willing had a complete monopoly of this String Bean for picking in our town, and received fancy prices for it. This is certainly the greatest Pole Bean on the globe; we make no exception—no, not one!

Pkg., 15c; ¼ pt., 40c; pt., 60c; qt., 90c, postpaid.

Cornhill Pole Bean.

A great pole bean. It is the popular general purpose bean. It commonly planted with corn, hence the name. A quart or two planted in an acre of corn will give enough shell beans for the family all winter. It is a rapid climber, bears prolifically and of unusually fine quality. Price, pkg., 10c; qt., 35c; by express or freight, pk., 10c; qt., 35c; pk., $1.35; bu., $4.50.

Andalusia Pole.

A magnificent pole bean. Pods 8 inches long, broad thick, very solid and entirely stringless. Flavor rich, buttery. Price, pkg., 8c; ¼ pt., 20c; pt., 30c; qt., 50c. By express or freight, pt., 20c; qt., 30c; pk., $2.50.

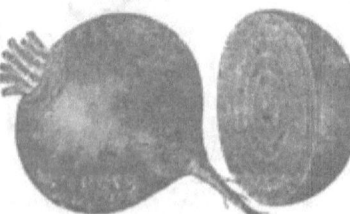

NEW BEET NOVELTY—SALZER'S INVINCIBLE

It is fair to say in the quintant of this description that, to our idea, this Beet combines more good qualities than any other round variety. In shape it is almost round, in size fully large enough to be extremely profitable and readily sought in all markets. The leaves are small and give the beet very close to the center of the path, while the root is very short and comes in right after our Red Beauty Beet. The flesh is of delicate texture, very rich, tender, sugary, and entirely free from fibre. It is one of the greatest novelties that we have been able to introduce.

The color of this beet is very remarkable. It is that deep, rich-red so greatly desired by market gardeners and for which customers are ready to pay fancy prices. The quality is superlative. We consider this the greatest beet novelty of the age and we are sure that customers purchasing some will be more than delighted and pleased with this magnificent acquisition.

Our favorite beets are the Salzer's Invincible, Salzer's Red Beauty, Best of All and Long Smooth Blood, for magnificent varieties, but the Invincible heads the list. A trial there is sure to please.

Pkg., 10c; oz., 30c; ¼ lb., 40c; ½ lb., 75c; lb., $1.40; 5 lbs., (sufficient for an acre) $6.00.

THE EARLIEST BEET NOVELTY — SALZER'S RED BEAUTY BEET

READY FOR TABLE IN 28 DAYS

1000 DOZ. BUNCHES PER ACRE @ 35c = $350.

Red Beauty.

Again, in 1898, among our 200,000 growers, Red Beauty proved itself positively the earliest Beet in the world. It is a perfect turnip-shaped, deep red, extremely early Beet, fit for table in only 28 days; of excellent flavor, good quality, having a delightful deep red color when cooked. Market gardeners are all pronounced in their hearty approbation of praise, saying: "It is the earliest, finest blood-red Beet in existence." The foregoing was written some years ago, and up to date, despite the constant efforts of seedsmen, they have not been able to produce a Beet which in beauty and earliness approaches Salzer's Red Beauty Beet, and we doubt whether any will ever be produced that is earlier than this, for we are constantly improving our own stock, and we think that the stock offered this year is better than ever before. In shape and general appearance and grand color are truly unapproachable; that i ts crimson so peculiar to Red Beauty Beet finds for it a rapid sale at fancy prices wherever offered. It is so perfect in all its requirements, so excellent in its flavor, so quick in its growth, so handsome in its appearance that everybody is "superlatively pleased" with same. Pkg., 10c; oz., 20c; ¼ lb., 35c; lb., $1.00; 5 lbs., $4.75.

300 Doz. Bunches
Best of All per acre at 35c.
$250.00.
That Pays.

SALZER'S BEST OF ALL.

A great acquisition; color outside is deep blood red; inside layers of blood red and light red alternately. When cooked are a beautiful dark red throughout, fine grained and unsurpassed in quality. At the age of "Eclipse" it is larger, while it continues to grow until late in the fall, attaining a large size, and making a good selling and eating Beet for winter. Now this Beet has been before the public but a couple of years, but the demand for same is something simply enormous. Everybody who has tested it will want it a second year. It is a great money maker, as its fine shape and size bring for it a most excellent prices wherever offered. Its flavor is superb, and in quality it is never found wanting. Indeed, Salzer's Red Beauty, Salzer's Best of All and Salzer's Long Smooth Blood Beets are the varieties you can bank on. They will never disappoint you. Pkg., 10c; oz., 15c; ¼ lb., 25c; lb., $1.25, postpaid.

SALZER'S BEST OF ALL BEET.

Spinach Beet.

Makes a great quantity of greens, in flavor very much resembling the beet Spinach. Good and wholesome for all summer use. Pkg., 10c; oz., 15c; ¼ lb., 35c

Early York Beet

This is a new strain of Turnip Beet, remarkably early, few inches, with very tender and sweet flesh. Its fine appearance, excellent color, splendid flavor, tender, juicy qualities recommend same to everybody. Pkg., No.j oz., 15c; ¼ lb., 30c; lb., $1.50.

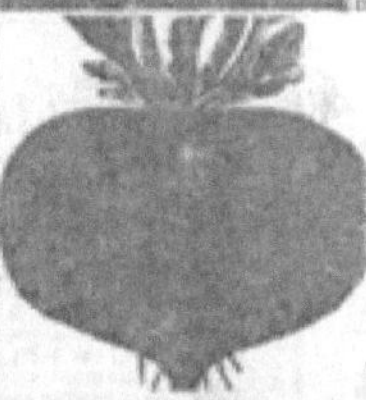

Edmunds' Beet.

It is of good size, very early, perfect in form, and of that deep rich blood color so much sought by gardeners. It commands a good price and a ready sale in all markets. It will produce fully 300 dozen bunches early Beets per acre, amounting to $100.00. Pkg., 5c; oz., 10c; ¼ lb., 30c; lb., 50c.

THE EDMUNDS' BEET.

ROYAL HALF LONG BEET

Dark Red Egyptian.

The earliest highly prized by market gardeners everywhere; size, about 3 inches, slightly flattened; skin dark red; flesh, fine, compact; texture, tender of superior flavor. Pkg., 5c; oz., 10c; ¼ lb., 30c; lb., 65c.

EGYPTIAN.

Improved Eclipse.

Intense dark red. We graved them with the Egyptian, and prefer Eclipse first, being larger Beets. Grow smoother, are globe-shaped, very early. For years this was the standard early variety, and like Dark Red Egyptian but had a tremendous sale and it is well worthy a place in every garden. Pkg., 5c; oz., 10c; lb., 50c.

ECLIPSE BEET.

Swiss Chard.

Cultivated for its leaves served as Asparagus. Pkg., 5c; oz., 20c.

SWISS CHARD.

Salzer's Royal Half Long Beet.

There is a great demand for a half long, medium size, early, fine quality, dark red table Beet, and this requirement our Royal Half Long Beet fully meets. It is one of those Beets — once planted, always planted. Pkg., 10c; oz., 20c; ¼ lb., 30c; lb., $1.00; 5 lbs., $4.00.

SALZER'S LONG SMOOTH BLOOD.

Salzer's Long Smooth Blood.

This is the finest Beet grown for fall and winter use. It is of deep red color, excellent flavor and enormous cropper, and keeps solid and fresh throughout the long winter. Cooks sweet, tender and crisp, and in every way may be considered the standard sort for the market and the home gardener. It must not be compared with the common Long Smooth Blood offered by many seedsmen at a low price. Its high grade was attained by long years of care and selection. We could introduce many thousand testimonials on our Red Beauty for extreme earliness; on our Best of All for large size and excellent quality as a round Beet; while more than 47,000 gardeners and citizens are ready to say that Salzer's Long Smooth Blood is the finest Beet of all late sorts — a regular money-maker. Each succeeding year adds thousands to its list of friends. Will you not be among them this season? Pkg., 10c; oz., 15c; ¼ lb., 25c; lb., 45c; 5 lbs. $3.00. ☞ NEW BEET NOVELTY—SALZER'S INVINCIBLE. SEE PAGE 36. ☜

Standard Table Beets.

CHEAP.

Standard seeds we can afford to sell lower than any firm in America; but when it comes to our great specialties in Beets, Beans, Corn, Carrots, Cabbages, etc., etc., we must get a fair price, to pay us for the tremendous care in growing and selecting the strains. Our great specialties cannot be supplied by any one but ourselves. If any seed man offers our specialties like Early Blood Radish, Lightning Cabbage, Red Beauty Beets, Scorcher Pea, etc., put him down as a "double-barreled fraud."

Early Blood Turnip—The standard early sort; good for both early and late use. Splendid in every and all particulars. Pkg., 3c; oz., 8c; ¼ lb., 18c; lb., 35c.

Bastian Extra Early—Probably one of the earliest varieties of Turnip Beet. It is of blood red color when boiled. Pkg., 3c; oz., 8c; ¼ lb., 15c; lb., 30c.

Dewing's Red Turnip—A fine variety of deep red color, and very early. Pkg., 3c; oz., 8c; ¼ lb., 15c; lb., 35c.

Early Bassano—Almost as early as the Egyptian; light color. Pkg., 3c; oz., 8c; ¼ lb., 16c; lb., 30c.

Giant Holstein Mangel.

A superior Mangel, long, red, of enormous size and excellent flavor. In the celebrated Holstein region (Europe) this splendid Mangel is used to the exclusion of all other sorts. It is eagerly eaten and relished by cattle, and returns a large yield of milk or fattening substance to stock. Think of 1,840 bushels per acre!

Pkg., 3c; oz., 10c; ¼ lb., 20c; lb., 35c; 5 lbs. (for 1 acre), $3.60; 10 lbs., $5.00.
By express: ¼ lb., 18c; lb., 46c; 10 lbs., $4.00.

MANGEL FOR STOCK.

No root crop is a better paying investment for farmers to grow than Mangel Wurzel. Sow in drills 14 inches apart and 3 inches in rows; now when ground is warm and moist. It will pay every farmer to plant an acre, as the yield is enormous. Feed after milking. A yield of 1,000 bushels per acre is common. Keeps well, and does cattle much good, as a change in food always does good.

Eiffel Tower Mangel.

1895 was a great year for Eiffel Tower Mangel. Is fairly covered itself with glory and called forth unanimous praise from thousands of farmers. Eiffel Tower stands way ahead of every Mangel yet tried. It is mammoth in size; a specimen, under favorable circumstances, having been grown

WEIGHING 101 POUNDS.

When we were overlooking the City of Paris, on the great Eiffel Tower, we thought of our great Eiffel Tower Mangel, and felt proud that we had named this grandest of Mangels after the big tower.

The Mangel is enormously, wonderfully prolific. Its yield is fabulous; 1,000 to 1,800 bushels is nothing uncommon on good soil. Its quality is of the highest order, and is greatly relished by all cattle, giving a wonderful flow of milk, and is an excellent food for fattening.

An Eiffel Tower, after which we have named this remarkable Mangel, is the most wonderful and tallest structure in the world, so is this Eiffel Tower Mangel the most marvelous prolific flesh and milk producing Mangel known on earth. "There," some one will say, "that's too strong!" Try the Mangel and you will say not half strong enough.

PRICE OF EIFFEL TOWER.
By mail: Pkg., 5c; oz., 10c; ¼ lb., 35c; lb., 60c; 5 lbs. (for 1 acre), $3.00; 10 lbs., $5.75.
By express: Pkg., 5c; oz., 10c; ¼ lb., 20c; lb., 34c; 5 lbs. (for 1 acre), $2.10; 10 lbs., $3.00.

Standard Mangels.

Price of the following 5 sorts:
By mail: Pkg., 4c; oz., 8c; ¼ lb., 18c; lb., 35c.
By express: Oz., 8c; ¼ lb., 10c; lb., 25c; 10 lbs., $2.25.

1. Red Mangel—Long red; very fine.
2. Yellow Globe—A good sort in every particular.
3. Red Globe—Large; of excellent quality.
4. Long Yellow—A long-growing sort. Highly prized and a large yielder.
5. Golden Tankard—Grows mainly above ground. Yields 1,000 bushels per acre. Very fine.

SUGAR MANGEL.

This class, although by far not so large a cropper as our unrivaled Eiffel Tower, has many excellent qualities. Its flesh is white and very sweet.

Sweet White—Largely grown for feeding purposes and for sugar. Pkg., 5c; oz., 10c; ¼ lb., 18c; lb., 35c.

Salzer's Jersey Sugar.

There has been among dairymen some slight objection to feeding Mangel Wurzel on account of a slight flavor that is retained in the milk. This we have endeavored to do away with, and we believe that our new Mangel, Jersey Sugar, fills the requirements completely. It is of enormous yielder, of fine, light white color, very sweet, and will produce an enormous flow of milk of the richest quality. Pkg., 10c; oz., 25c; ¼ lb., 70c; lb., $1.20; 5 lbs. (for 1 acre), $7.50, postpaid; by express, ¼ lb., 15c; 40c; 10 lbs., $4.00.

BEETS.

Vilmorin's Imperial—Under average conditions it has yielded 14 tons of roots to the acre, containing about 16 per cent. of sugar. Lb., by mail, postpaid, 40c; ¼ lb., 15c; oz., 8c; 10 lbs., by express, $2.00.

Klein-Wanzleben—This kind is cultivated on a larger scale than any other Sugar Beet. The root is conical, straight and even, quite large at the head and rapidly tapering. It is easy to dig, a heavy yielder, and contains from 15 to 16 per cent. of sugar. Lb., 40c; ¼ lb., 15c; oz., 8c; 5 lbs., by express, $2.00.

Salzer's German Sugar Beet.

Specially grown for us by a great Sugar Beet grower in Germany. The stock roots from which our seed was grown averaged 17 per cent. sugar. Pkg., 5c; oz., 10c; ¼ lb., 18c; lb., 40c; lb., by express, 30c; 5 lbs., $1.25.

Mixed Mangel Seed.

Every year there are hundreds of our customers who write us for mixed Mangel Seed, and we have concluded this season to meet their wishes, and have mixed of all the varieties that we have in excellent proportion. This mixture, we know, will at once become popular. It is cheap, and will surely give satisfaction. We can heartily indorse same. On our own farm the planting of mixed Mangels yielded over 700 bushels per acre. This mixture is unusually popular.

Price: Pkg., 3c; 2 pkgs., 5c; oz., 7c; ¼ lb., 10c; lb., 25c, postpaid; 2 lbs., 46c; 5 lbs. (sufficient for an acre), $1.10, by express, lb., 18c; 3 lbs. or more, 14c a pound.

SALZER'S LIGHTNING CABBAGE.

The most important crop among market gardeners and market farmers is Cabbage. Indeed, the failure of a Cabbage crop is a large item to their income. Failure in this depends largely upon the quality of seed used. America has the poet poor, been flooded with European grown Cabbage seed, from the fact that it is cheaper, and is sold at so a price or thereabout by some Illinois, Iowa, Minnesota and other cheap seedsmen who do not care for quality—just to sell Cabbage cheap. Our seed is all Northern grown, vigorous, full of life, and will produce fine, big heads everywhere.

We are going to, right in the start, make the broad sweeping statement that Salzer's Lightning Cabbage is absolutely the earliest, quickest-heading Cabbage on earth! Can we prove it? Yes. We introduced it in 1893, and since then the enormous amount of 1,087,000 packages have been planted, and thousands of reports have been sent us from these 1,087,000 growers, and every report says, in substance. It's the finest, heaviest, best selling, earliest Cabbage in the world—weeks ahead of other seedsmen's earliest sorts. There is no question about this, it has proven itself absolutely the earliest—it is the one Cabbage to plant for early.

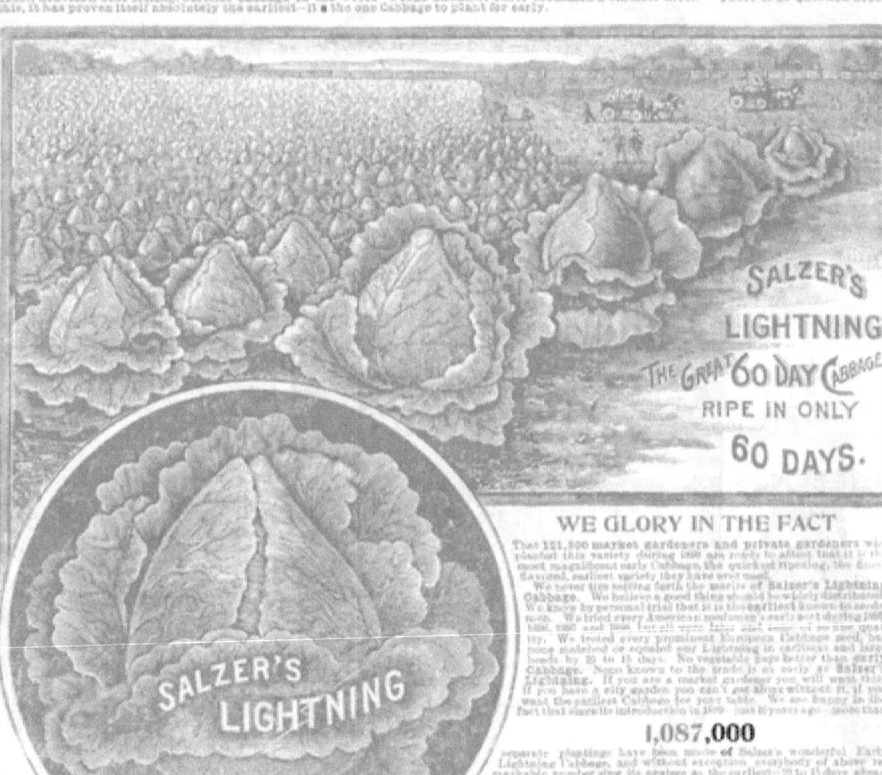

WE GLORY IN THE FACT

That 121,300 market gardeners and private gardeners who planted this variety during 1899 are ready to attest that it is the most magnificent early Cabbage, the quickest ripening, the finest flavored, earliest variety they have ever used.

We never tire setting forth the merits of Salzer's Lightning Cabbage. We believe a good thing should be widely distributed. We know by personal trial that it is the earliest known to seedsmen. We tried every American seedsman's early sort during 1895, 1896 and 1897, and beat them all ogee days after days—so as to sure quality. We tested every prominent European Cabbage seed, but matched or equaled our Lightning in earliness and large heads by 10 to 15 days. No vegetable pays better than early Cabbage. None known to the trade is as early as Salzer's Lightning. If you are a market gardener you will want this. If you have a city garden you can't get along without it. If you want the earliest Cabbage for your table. We are happy in the fact that since its introduction in 1899—just 10 years ago—more than

1,087,000

separate plantings have been made of Salzer's wonderful Early Lightning Cabbage, and without exception everybody of above remarkable number sing its praises as the earliest—10 to 15 days ahead of other seedsmen's earliest.

The Earliest Cabbage in the World!

And, therefore, it is, for the market gardener, the trucker, the ribbon, the farmer, yes, for everybody, a great money maker, for Salzer's Lightning Cabbage, coming in early, readily sells at $1.00 to $1.50 a dozen, and often far more.

Many prominent seedsmen have been after our Lightning Cabbage; they want the complete stock. Of course we would not part with it, for the BEST in the world in the seed line only is good enough for our customers. We offer no other seeds but the very best that we can grow or money can buy. Repeated tests show Salzer's Lightning ripe and sold before other seedsmen's early sorts are fit for the market. Try it for 1899, and have the earliest, best flavored Cabbage you ever had.

It Has Come to Stay and Make Happy Every Grower.

When we first offered this now matchless Cabbage, we had an idea of the tremendous hold it would take upon the affections of thousands of growers—upon those who use only one package annually for their own little garden, and upon the farmer and market gardener who use ½ pound, 1 pound and some 10 pounds or more. Every one, without exception, praises it as the earliest Cabbage grown, as the finest quality and surest yielding sort. Now, we could fill pages of this Catalogue with long letters from friends and patrons regarding this great Cabbage, but will append only a few.

Beat McPheeters,
Greenville, Ind.,
"I sold Salzer's Lightning Cabbage 45 days after sowing the seed. That is good enough.

Beats Him 10 Days Better.

Waverly, O., Jan. 26, '99.
Wm. Franke, Waverly, O., says:
"I sold Salzer's Lightning Cabbage 45 days after sowing the seed. That is good enough."

$10 for 15 Cents.

"I sold $10.00 worth from one package of seed, and had all I wanted for my family besides."
J. F. Angustin, Palmyra, Wis.

Price of Salzer's Lightning Cabbage Seed.

Pkg., 15c; 2 pkgs., 25c; ¼ oz., 35c; oz., 60c; ¼ lb., $2.00; ½ lb., $3.50; lb., $6.00, postpaid.   See, also, next page.

"Oh, for a Thousand Tongues to Sing!"

It would require 1,000 tongues, yes, 10,000, to set forth all the great qualities of our Lightning Cabbage! The extraordinary difference in the illustration between Salzer's Lightning and ordinary early Cabbage like Express, Etampes, etc. That's the way it acts. It is ahead every time. It is ripe and sold when other sorts come in. It is simply without an equal in earliness, ribbness, deliciousness of flavor and all the splendid qualities that go to make a good Cabbage.

It is the earliest Cabbage in the world, and 121,300 planters of 1898 will say so! We have great faith in Lightning as the earliest Cabbage in the world, and will pay at the rate of

$1,600.00 A POUND FOR A BETTER,

Finer, earlier Cabbage than the Lightning. Must be at least 5 days earlier. Lightning beats the world to-day.

10,000 Testimonials More Like This!

Sunset, Tex., Feb. 1, 1898.

"I have planted your Lightning Cabbage for 3 years, and I have had the earliest Cabbage in Sunset during that time. It's the earliest I ever saw."—E. E. McConnell.

H. J. Kay, Beaver, Neb.: "Your Lightning Cabbage is all you recommend, and your Giant Flat Dutch are great Cabbages. All my heads weigh at least 9 lbs."

T. Fanner, North Crandon, Wis.: "Your Lightning Cabbages are the finest I ever saw. They are 30 days earlier than any other sort grown in this county."

F. C. McClelland, Ottawa, Kan.: "Lightning Cabbage is the thing. Grows quicker and larger than any other early Cabbage, and every plant is sure to head."

E. Shepherd, Sunset, Tex.: "Your Lightning Cabbage is the earliest in the world."

The illustration shows you the way ordinary Cabbage, like Express, Etampes, Early York, all Head and other sorts use; earliest looks at the end of 40 days, showing nothing but frames, while Salzer's Northern Grown Lightning is headed and sold every time.

HEAR MR. AUGUST PRALLE, A LA CROSSE CO. GARDENER, TALK:

Mr. Salzer: "I wish to say this regards the justly far-famed Salzer's Lightning Cabbage: I grow, no doubt, as much very early Cabbage as anybody in this county. I have tried almost every seedsman's early sorts, but not one of them are as early as yours. Lightning. Indeed, there is not a single other seedsman's early sort as early as yours by fully 8 TO 15 DAYS,

And do you know these 8 to 15 days earlier sends big money for us market gardeners? It's the EARLIEST CABBAGE that makes for us the money, and SALZER'S LIGHTNING is the earliest, finest Cabbage in the world.

H. S. Garard, Jr., Huron, Ala., writes as follows: "Your Lightning, Ideal and Giant Flat Dutch Cabbages are three of the greatest Cabbages on earth. This is the third year that I received them, and I would willingly pay $1.00 per package for each rather than to miss them. Lightning is the earliest, finest cabbage in the world, and I have raised every other earliest sort that I could get. I have had fine, large heads, weighing from 8 to 10 pounds every day since the 12th day of May, for which I have been getting it to $3 cents a head, thank you a thousand times for the good you have done me by sending me such excellent seeds. Your cabbage seed was the means of raising the mortgage from my place.

Harriett Shingle, Whistler, Ind., says: "Your Giant Pea Tomatoes are immense. I love everything I promote. My neighbors laughed at me that I said I do for a package of Salzer's Lightning Cabbage Seed, but they were all glad to get plants from me because their seed did not come up which they bought elsewhere. It is the earliest cabbage in the world."

Jos. Grannison, Washington, N.J.: "Your Lightning Cabbage had a head to every plant set. The Abient is fool as good."

Thos. Robinson, Eureka, Ill.: "Your Lightning Cabbage is early enough for me."

C. A. Palmer, Lincoln, Neb., says: "Lightning Cabbage is big best money-maker. It beats all on earliest Cabbage.

And thus we could keep on and on, filling this catalogue with earnest, hearty, enthusiastic reports on our 3 great Cabbage, Lightning, Ideal and Giant Flat Dutch. They are prize winners everywhere. There is nothing like them. They are our great specialties. Any seedsman offering you these 3 sorts, or "just as good," you can tell him down and out. We sell these sorts only to our customers. In conclusion, we would say that if you wish the earliest Cabbage in the world, you must plant Salzer's Lightning. There is nothing quite so early, quite so fine or quite so good as Salzer's Lightning Cabbage, and we hope that you will try same, so that the number of our Lightning Cabbage customers will swell from 121,300 in 1898 to 156,000 in 1899!

Mr. August Pralle, the Great Cabbage Grower of La Crosse Co. Read his letter on Cabbage on this page.

Price of Salzer's Lightning Cabbage Seed.

Pkg., 15c; 2 pkgs., 25c; ¼ oz., 35c; oz., 60c; ¼ lb., $2.00; ½ lb., $3.50; lb., $6.50, postpaid.

SALZER'S IDEAL CABBAGE.

The earliest Cabbage in the world is Salzer's Lightning. The best, sweet heading Late Cabbage is Salzer's Giant Flat Dutch. "But what have you between?" we are so frequently asked. Up to the introduction there was no really high grade, high quality sort that we could offer. To meet this demand we have experimented for the past 5 years, until we have obtained what we desired, and now offer some under

Salzer's Ideal Cabbage.

Verily and truthfully the finest large, early or summer Cabbage in the wide world! That's strong, you think. Yes, it is a strong statement, but a statement we can prove every time.

What Are Its Claims?

Earliness! Ripe about as soon as Eastern seedsman's early sorts, with heads twice, yes, often three times, as large! When we were market gardening, years ago, if we could have had this Cabbage it would have been a fortune to us, because every market gardener needs just such a Cabbage, one that, as soon as Salzer's Lightning is ripe and on sale, will come with its noble-like heads of such beauty that they will sell quickly at $1.00 we doing. That's the price you will get for Salzer's Ideal!

Quality! Well, now, we do not know of a Cabbage so uniform in size, so beautiful in appearance and of such tender and excellent quality as Ideal. That is for a sound, early and summer sort.

New Carlisle, Ind., March 15, 1898.

Never too old to learn. I experimented in 1898 with other firms, bought 5¾ pounds of cabbage seed, received instead two ounces of Salzer. Instead of twenty. My neighbor bought two ounces of Salzer's Ideal Cabbage and set 2,300 plants, more than ½ more from one ounce! So much for Salzer.—John Wisner.

Let us sum up the matter: It is the earliest large Cabbage grown; it is the finest flavored summer Cabbage grown; it is the sure-heading summer variety known. More than 10,000 large, solid heads (ripe in this Northern country in July) can be grown to each acre, on account of its remarkably compact growth.

OUR THREE GREAT CABBAGE SORTS.

Salzer's Lightning for early, Ideal for second early, and Giant Flat Dutch for late, are the three sorts that we cannot conceive how we could in any way improve upon. They are unsurpassed in quality and sureness to head. Price of Salzer's Ideal: Pkg., 12c; 2 pkgs., 20c; ¼ oz., 30c; oz., 45c; ¼ lb., $1.30; lb., $4.25.

Price of Ideal: Pkg., 12c; ¼ oz., 30c; oz., 45c; ¼ lb., $1.30; lb., $4.05.

SALZER'S GIANT FLAT DUTCH

SURE SAFE SOLID

SUREST HEADER.

10,000 HEADS PER ACRE AT 5¢ $500 $500 PROFIT PER A.

NORTHERN GROWN SEED IS THE BEST

THE MOST WONDERFUL CABBAGE IN THE WORLD 9990 HEADS OUT OF 10,000!

10 POINTS IT IS DISTINGUISHED BY:

1. It's the Surest Heading Cabbage in the world.
2. Is the superior of all other Winter Cabbages.
3. Enormous solid heads, averaging 16 to 20 lbs.
4. Measuring 12 to 14 inches in diameter.
5. Specially grown heads often reach 50 lbs. each.
6. Interior creamy white, compact and crisp.
7. Unequaled for cooking or slicing; flavor especially fine.
8. It is the best winter keeper in forty states.
9. It has more friends than any other sort.
10. It is known to flourish on all soils.

ABSOLUTELY SURE HEADING— 999 OUT OF 1,000.

For sureness in heading and regularity in growth Salzer's Giant Flat Dutch certainly heads the list. No words of praise are too high for its merits. It forms every time, very large, solid heads, uniform in shape, color and handsome appearance. It has a very short stem, and at the same time it is a very compact grower. It forms few loose leaves which turn in from the head. Reports of 999 marketable heads from 1,000 plants set out are of daily occurrence. There are many magnificent strains of Cabbage offered in this catalogue, but we think we can safely say that Salzer's Giant Flat Dutch is equaled and surpassed by none.

PRICE OF SALZER'S GIANT FLAT DUTCH CABBAGE:
Pkg., 10c; 12 pkgs., $1.00; 100 pkgs., $7.50; ¼ oz., 20c; oz., 35c; ¼ lb., $1.25; lb., $4.00; 3 lbs., $7.00.

WE ARE PROUD OF SALZER'S GIANT FLAT DUTCH CABBAGE RECORD.

We can safely say that if you want the best late Cabbage you have ever grown, plant Giant Flat Dutch.

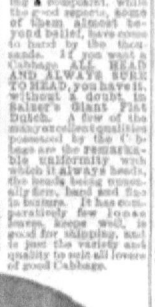

Hear Its Friends Talk.

1886—Keeps All Winter.
L. N. Homer, N. Y.: "No Cabbage ever kept so long for me as your Giant Flat Dutch. I sold 9,000 heads this spring, $186.00."

1887—Everybody Wants It.
C. C. Green, Pa.: "No trouble to sell your wonderful Giant Flat Dutch Cabbage. Everybody wants it and will pay a fancy price for it."

1888—Best Grown Since 1850.
W. J. Dunn, Ill.: "Have grown Cabbage since 1850, and I must say that Giant Flat Dutch is the very best."

1889—My Neighbors Envy Me.
Geo. Clark, Mich.: "My neighbors envy me because I have a more extensive and wonderful Cabbage, being your Giant Flat Dutch."

GIANT FLAT DUTCH LEADS ALL OTHERS.

No matter what Cabbage you have ever grown, for late Cabbage you will find by trying Salzer's Giant Flat Dutch that it will be superior to every other sort grown. There is reason for this. Our seed is grown with great care, and it costs us twice as much to grow our seed in the extreme North as it does to buy cheap seed grown on Long Island or imported from New York, or obtained in Washington and other Northwestern points. Our seed is grown from large selected heads with great care. We do not spare expense, labor nor time, to produce the best that can be had, and for this reason we cannot sell this wonderful Cabbage as cheap as some condemned sell other cheap imported stock. The imported Cabbage sometimes does well, but it often fails you; you never hear the word "fail" when you plant Salzer's Giant Flat Dutch Cabbage. We want you to try it this year, because we know it will give you great satisfaction.

1890—I take Prizes Every Time.
J. H. Meyer, Ky.: "I always take prizes on your Giant Flat Dutch Cabbage whenever I exhibit same."

1891—Superior in Quality.
Franz Schmidt, Ohio: "My customers always want Giant Flat Dutch Cabbage on account of its superior quality."

1892—Ahead of Any Other Sort.
F. Hyde, Ind.: "I have tried the 'ever held' Cabbage, offered by several members of Philadelphia at from $5 to $10 per pound. I would rather pay you $2.00 per package for your Giant Flat Dutch, because from every 1 lb. of seed I can sure to get 1 oz large, solid, fine heads, while from the Philadelphia seed I am never be sure of it."

1893—Never Has Failed Me.
Herm. Franze, Wis.: "I have grown Giant Flat Dutch Cabbage since 1888. It has never failed me, but has always produced large, fine heads."

SALZERS GIANT FLAT DUTCH. Look at Mr. Farmer Content!

He knows there is lots of money in Salzer's Cabbage. He plants no other. See the look of supreme content on his face! He has made lots of money on Salzer's Lightening, Ideal and Giant Flat Dutch Cabbages, and grew everyone to try them, for he knows THERE IS MONEY IN IT. We know there is lots of money for the market gardener and farmer who grows Salzer's Giant Flat Dutch Cabbage. It marches along as a conquering hero, excelling everything before it as a fall or winter Cabbage. Now, it does not matter whether you plant in the sunny South or in the cold North, wet East or dry West, everywhere Giant Flat Dutch does well and proves a winter.

1894—Made $500.00 Last Year.
F. A. Thomas, Ill.: "I made $500.00 on my Giant Flat Dutch Cabbage last year."

1895—Will Never Use Any Other.
C. F. Hill, Ia.: "Since I began using your Giant Flat Dutch Cabbage, I will use no other. It is the finest in the world."

1896—Never Saw Its Equal.
E. Frohnen, Mo.: "Your Giant Flat Dutch Cabbage wonderful. I have never seen its equal. My three acres are a solid worth saving. 30,000 big, solid, fine heads."

1897—Best I Ever Saw.
F. Kuss, Ia.: "Your Giant Flat Dutch Cabbage is the best I ever saw, and I have used Philadelphia seed for years."

1898—Every Plant Heads.
James Field, Ind.: "I planted one acre of Giant Flat Dutch Cabbage, and every plant made ship solid head."

FARMER CONTENT, WHO GROWS ONLY CABBAGE FROM SALZER'S SUPERLATIVE SEEDS.

PRICE OF SALZER'S GIANT FLAT DUTCH CABBAGE—Pkg., 10c; 12 pkg., $1.00; 100 pkg., $7.50; ¼ oz., 20c; oz., 35c; ¼ lb., $1.25; lb., $4.00; 2 lbs., $7.00.

We wish to repeat here, what we have said before, that for really fine vegetables, Cabbages, Onions, Peas, Radishes, etc., there is no seed superior, and but very little we say, very little, EQUAL to Salzer's Northern Grown.

Henderson's Autumn King.

Autumn King is an entirely distinct variety; best keeper we have ever seen; it produces enormous solid heads of that dark shade of green that is most desirable in a Cabbage, and has such small outer leaves that it can be planted much closer together than the ordinary late sorts, and can be relied upon to produce a greater weight of crop per acre than any other variety except Giant Flat Dutch. Of course, Giant Flat Dutch Cabbage cannot be beaten by any sort yet introduced. A distinctive feature of the Autumn King is the peculiarly crimped leaves, which not only add to its appearance, but enable it to be distinguished anywhere. Next to Giant Flat Dutch, it is unquestionably one of the best late sorts of to-day. It is certainly far ahead of the Surehead variety offered in Philadelphia.

Pkg., 10c; oz., 30c; ¼ lb., 60c; lb., $2.00.

AUTUMN KING CABBAGE.

BRAUNSCHWEIGER.

This is the celebrated Cabbage of Germany, and thousands upon thousands of acres are annually grown there to be made into Sauer Kraut, the favorite dish of the German, and not disregarded by the American. This Cabbage is particularly adapted for pickling; it forms a very large, fine-grained head. The flavor of this Cabbage is peculiarly pleasant. It is a variety that will give endless satisfaction, and we bespeak for it a trial. We wish you could have seen the huge fields of this splendid variety in Germany. It was well worth seeing, reminding us of the great fields one sees of our matchless Giant Flat Dutch in many parts of America. We are sure this sort will please you. Pkg., 10c; ¼ oz., 20c; oz., 35c; ¼ lb., $1.00; lb., $3.50.

SAY! We have greatly reduced the prices of standard seeds, offering them lower than any other responsible seedsman in America. We are the largest growers, hence our cut prices on standard sorts. Let us have your list to figure on. We will not be undersold.

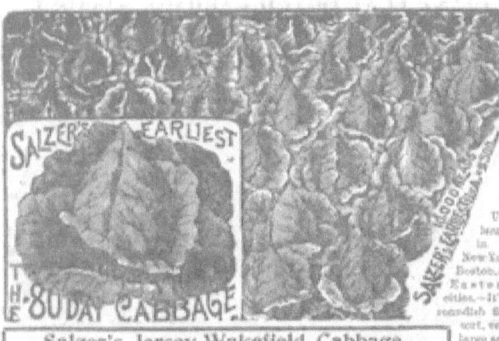

Salzer's Earliest Cabbage.

This Cabbage is brought forward to meet the wants of everybody. Recognizing the fact that a week earlier in the early Cabbage crop is from 25 to 50 per cent. more money in the market gardener's purse, our constant study and experimenting has been to introduce a Cabbage of fair size and extra early, and, next to Lightning, the earliest. Salzer's Earliest we unhesitatingly recommend as the very earliest, fully 12 days earlier than the Early York, Express, Etampe, etc. It is only a trifle later than Salzer's New Lightning. Small size hard heads, often weighing 9 pounds; fine in every particular. Pkg, 5c; oz., 25c; ¼ lb., 75c; lb., $2.00.

Henry Boehke, a market gardener near La Crosse, sold $200.00 worth of Salzer's Earliest Cabbage from 1½ acres of land. That pays!

Price Salzer's Earliest: Pkg., 5c; oz., 25c; ¼ lb., 75c; lb., $2.00.

EARLY SPRING CABBAGE.

EARLY SPRING CABBAGE.

Used largely in New York, Boston, and Eastern cities.—It's a roundish flat sort, very large and as early as the Wakefield. It is very uniform, round in shape, slightly flattened, very solid, even before the Cabbages attain their mature size. The flavor is excellent. On account of its shape, productiveness and solidity, it will prove a serious rival to the Wakefield. Gardeners cannot afford to be without this as it will be a "seller;" round cabbages receiving always the preference if offered in competition with pointed heads, while its compact form and good quality is esteemed for private gardens.

Lb., $3.00; ¼ lb., 90c; oz., 30c; ½ oz., 20c; pkg., 10c.

Salzer's Jersey Wakefield Cabbage.

This is one of the very best, most satisfactory early Cabbage for general crop we know of. Salzer's New Lightning GETS THERE in 60 days; hardy, solid, best, medium size; Salzer's Earliest, or 80-day, never fails to be on time, while our Extra Early Jersey Wakefield follows closely, and is a larger head. Our plan is to plant ⅓ Salzer's Lightning, ⅓ Salzer's Earliest or 80-Day, and ⅓ Extra Early Jersey Wakefield and Northern grown Cabbage seed; our customers will find, produce 25 per cent. more heads, and are fully one week earlier than Eastern stock. Our Jersey Wakefield is especially fine, all grown from selected heads. Our friends will find it far superior to any offered in America.

Pkg., 5c; oz., 20c; ¼ lb., 50c; lb., $1.75.

⅓ Common Jersey Wakefield—Pkg., 5c; oz., 10c; ¼ lb., 35c; lb., $1.10.

Short Stem Drumhead—A magnificent late cabbage, doing well everywhere. Pkg., 5c; oz., 40c; ¼ lb., 75c; lb., $2.50.

New Wonderful—All-the-Year-Round Cabbage. Pkg., 10c; oz., 50c.

All Head Early—Pkg., 20c; oz., 30c; ¼ lb., $1.00.

Shortstem Drumhead.

The Lupton.

This Cabbage was sent us by Eastern Seedman with great encomiums. It has just many of the claims. It is a fine loose cabbage, but we think a thousand miles behind our peerless Giant Flat Dutch. However the Lupton is worthy a trial.

Pkg., 10c; ½ oz., 10c; oz., 30c; lb., $2.00.

PHILADELPHIA STRAIN OF GENUINE SUREHEAD CABBAGE. Pkg., 10c.

SALZER'S
New Bridgeport Mammoth Cabbage.

Salzer's New Bridgeport Market—This is a new strain of Mammoth Drumhead Cabbage. It makes a large, round, solid, firm head which seldom bursts, and sells at advanced prices. The seed of this sort is scarce, and has often sold as high as $12.00 per pound in the Bridgeport Cabbage districts. To get the genuine seed of this wonderful new strain, buy of us. Pkg., 10c; 3 pkgs., 25c; ½ oz., 25c; oz., 40c; ¼ lb., $1.00; lb., $3.50.

PA—"I guess you are right, my son, it is too bad that he planted Salzer's Northern Grown seeds, as I advised him, he could now sell from 8,000 to 10,000 heads per acre at good prices."

Genuine **Surehead** Cabbage.

This is the celebrated strain of Surehead Cabbage offered by the seedsmen of Philadelphia. It is a very choice variety of late Flat Dutch Cabbage, but not equal to Salzer's Giant Flat Dutch, in all qualities that go to make up good late Cabbage. This stock is obtained from the same growers that all the prominent houses in Philadelphia obtain their Genuine Surehead from. It is a A No. 1 in every respect. Price of Surehead: Pkg., 10c; oz., 20c; ¼ lb., 40c; lb., $2.50.

One package each, 20 different kinds of Cabbage seed, our selection, postpaid, only 75c; 5 different sorts, our selection, 20c.

DUTCH WINTER OR HOLLANDER.

For several years past Cabbages have been imported from Holland and sold in the American market at prices nearly double those obtained for the product of our own gardens. Through our connection with the largest seed growers in Holland, we have obtained a supply of the genuine seed, and offer it at such a price as to bring it within the reach of all. The heads of this valuable sort are of medium size, averaging a weight of 8 pounds, are very solid and deep, and of a fine white color, making them entirely distinct from any other strain. Their quality is superior, and they keep better than any other sort, the heads being just as solid and perfect when taken up in the spring as when they were put away in the fall. No cabbage will sell beside it, even if offered at half the price. For sureness in heading and regularity in growth certainly this heads the list. No words of praise are too high for its merits. It forms every time very large, very hard, solid heads, uniform in shape, color and handsome appearance. It has a very short stem and at the same time is a very compact grower. It forms few loose leaves, which turn in from the head. Reports of 98 marketable heads from 100 plants set are of frequent occurrence. There are many magnificent strains of Cabbage offered in this catalogue, but I think I can safely say that this sort is equaled only by Salzer's Great Giant Flat Dutch. The illustration is an excellent representation of an average head of this variety. I can safely say that if you want the best Cabbage you have ever grown, plant Salzer's Giant Flat Dutch and Dutch Winter or Hollander the coming season. You will not be disappointed. This is grown in large quantities by the Cabbage growers near Racine, Chicago, La Crosse, St. Louis, etc. Lb., $3.00; ¼ lb., 90c; oz., 30c; ½ oz., 20c; pkg., 10c.

THE SUREHEADING DUTCH WINTER.

STANDARD CABBAGE SEEDS—LOW PRICES.

There are the finest strains of standard varieties of Cabbage in the world—are right up to Chicago's, Philadelphia's, New York's, Minneapolis' and St. Paul's very best strains. We offer them at very low prices. We wish it distinctly understood that no responsible seedsman is to undersell us. Let us have your list to figure on. We grow more seeds than all the seedsmen in Illinois, Iowa and Minnesota put together, and can surely save you money on large orders.

Red Dutch—This is the well-known small red pickling Cabbage, with very solid heads. Oz., 15c; ¼ lb., 50c; lb., $1.50.

Giant Red Dutch—This superior Red Dutch Cabbage is largely grown for its excellent pickling and fine cooking qualities. Pkg., 10c; oz., 20c; ¼ lb., 60c; lb., $2.00.

Green Globe Savoy—A fine Cabbage; small but solid heads; in every respect the Cabbage for family use. Pkg., 5c; oz., 15c; ¼ lb., 35c; lb., $1.25.

Mammoth Globe Savoy—Much larger than above; excelling it in all particulars. Large quantities of this are grown by gardeners. Style of head changeable from globe to flat. Pkg., 10c; oz., 20c; ¼ lb., 50c; lb., $1.70.

Late Flat Dutch Cabbage.

The standard late Cabbage; extra strain. Better than most seedsmen's best, because it's Northern grown! Pkg., 5c; oz., 10c; ¼ lb., 35c; lb., $1.10.

Premium Flat Dutch—Extensively grown; large and excellent for winter. Pkg., 5c; oz., 10c; ¼ lb., 35c; lb., $1.35.

Marblehead Mammoth—Largest Cabbage in the world; heads have been grown weighing 60 lbs. Pkg., 5c; oz., 15c; ¼ lb., 35c; lb., $1.50.

Early York—This has for years been the favorite. Very early sort; small heads; excellent flavor; good header. Pkg., 5c; oz., 15c; ¼ lb., 25c; lb., 90c.

Large York—Larger but later than the Early York; very fine. Pkg., 5c; oz., 8c; ¼ lb., 25c; lb., 90c.

Early Winningstadt—One of the very best early for general use; splendid in every way; much liked by gardeners as an excellent early Cabbage. Pkg., 5c; oz., 15c; ¼ lb., 45c; lb., $1.50.

Early Flat Dutch—The second early Cabbage; largely grown about New York and Boston; good size heads. Pkg., 5c; oz., 10c; lb., $1.10.

LATE FLAT DUTCH.

German Filderkraut—Well known to German growers; extra stock. Pkg., 5c; oz., 15c; ¼ lb., 45c; lb., $1.50.

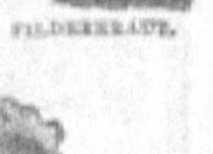

FILDERKRAUT.

IF YOU DESIRE SEEDS.

In large quantities, $5.00 worth or more, please send us your list to estimate on. We are the largest growers and can save you money.

The New 103 Cabbage, or Hundred Weight.

"This certifies that I sold to John A. Salzer Seed Co. my complete stock of my new colossal Cabbage 103, at $50.00 a pound. I call it 103, because I raised a head which, with leaves, weighed 103 pounds. JOHN KATTAN."

We urge all to test this wonderful sort. It is late and delights in a rich soil. Pkg., 15c; 2 pkgs., 25c.

5 Good Second Early Cabbages.

Standard Low-Priced Sorts.

1. **Salzer's Improved Market**—One of the very best second early Cabbages grown. It ripens next to Wakefield, while it is nearly double its weight. We brought it forward to meet the wants of our market, while we were extensively engaged as market gardeners. It is a sure header, and sells at high prices. Pkg., 5c; oz., 20c; ¼ lb., 60c; lb., $2.00.
2. **Excelsior Cabbage**—A very superior second early Cabbage; large full solid heads. Pkg., 5c; oz., 15c; ¼ lb., 35c.
3. **Henderson's Genuine Succession, or "All the Year Round"**—Planted early, it forms a good second early; planted later, it makes a fine summer sort; while planted late it gives large, fine, solid heads for winter use. Pkg., 5c; oz., 15c; lb., $1.90.
4. **Fottler's Imp. Brunswick**—An excellent second early. Pkg., 5c; oz., 15c; ¼ lb., 35c; lb., $1.90.
5. **All Season's Cabbage**—The best Cabbage; good for early, good for summer and good for late use. Pkg., 5c; oz., 20c; lb., $2.25.

1 package each above 5 sorts, 15c.

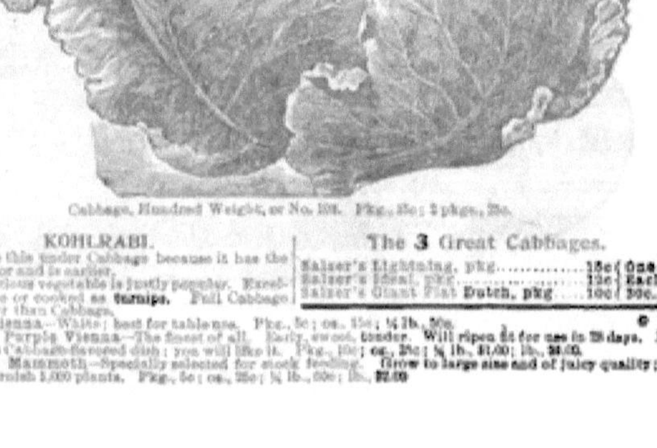

Cabbage, Hundred Weight, or No. 103. Pkg., 15c; 2 pkgs., 25c.

KOHLRABI.

We place this under Cabbage because it has the Cabbage flavor and is earlier.

This delicious vegetable is justly popular. Excellent for soups or cooked as turnips. Full Cabbage flavor; earlier than Cabbage.

Early Vienna—White; best for table use. Pkg., 5c; oz., 15c; ¼ lb., 50c.

Salzer's Purple Vienna—The finest of all. Early, sweet, tender. Will ripen it for use in 28 days. It is a delicious Cabbage-flavored dish; you will like it. Pkg., 10c; oz., 25c; ¼ lb., $1.00; lb., $3.00.

Salzer's Mammoth—Specially selected for stock feeding. Grow to large size and of juicy quality; 1 ounce will furnish 1,000 plants. Pkg., 5c; oz., 25c; ¼ lb., 60c; lb., $2.00

The 3 Great Cabbages.

Salzer's Lightning, pkg	15c	One Each, 30c.
Salzer's Ideal, pkg	12c	
Salzer's Giant Flat Dutch, pkg	10c	

SURE-HEADING CAULIFLOWERS.

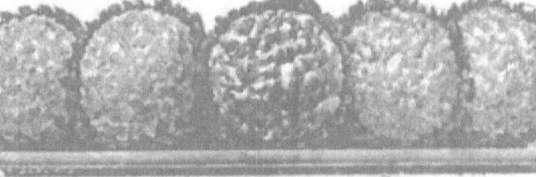

Salzer's Surehead Cauliflower.

We challenge the world to produce a finer, handsom or earlier Cauliflower than our New Earliest Sureha It will surpass in earliness the Snowball and every other kno variety. Whether for forcing or open ground, planted early late, it is the surest header of all. Very dwarf and compact growth like the Snowball, it can be planted very close, 16 inches each way, and is particularly desirable for forcing un glass. In our trial grounds every plant produced a supe head that surpassed every other variety in earline size and quality.

A Few Testimonials Only:

A. G. Ebert, Io.: "Never before had such a beautiful Ca liflower. Surehead is sure..."

Fred. Grock, Wis.: "I made $10.00 on the one ounce Su head Cauliflower. Every head was fine..."

G. G. Kennedy, Ind.: "Best and finest Cauliflower I ever ra..."

Salzer's Earliest Surehead

Is unquestionably the largest as well as the best of all Ca flowers. Market gardeners once having seen it, will plant other. We want to introduce it everywhere, hence our freezely low price. Price: Pkg. 10c.; 2 pkgs., $1.00; ½ oz., $2 ½ oz., $2.75; oz., $2.00; ¼ lb., $9.00.

Salzer's New Fancy Blue Ribbon Cauliflower.

SALZER'S NEW FANCY BLUE RIBBON. PKG., 25c.

Said to be the finest Cauliflower in existence. Heads fine shaped, pure white, very early and quality simply unsurpassed. It is the richest, rarest Cauliflower known, a gem in every respect, golden cut for the grower who wants the choicest regardless of cost. Package, 25c; 3 Packages for

La Crosse Early Favorite.

Growing side by side with Henderson's Snowball, La Crosse Early Favorite was decidedly the finest in appearance, earliest to yield, with largest number of sure heads; indeed it is the finest in every respect we have ever looked. Next to our magnificent Early Surehead, this is certainly the best sort to plant. Pkg. 10c; 3 pkgs., 25c; ¼ oz., $1.00; ½ oz., $1.75; oz., $3.00.

Snowball—Largely grown in the East. Very fine, and many customers prefer the Henderson strain of Snowball Cauliflower. It is grown in Denmark, and where ours our customers will like it. Pkg. 10c; ¼ oz., $1.50; oz., $5.00.

Erfurt Early Dwarf—This is the celebrated Cauliflower so largely grown in Erfurt. Early, fine, and sure to head. Pkg. 10c; oz., $5.00.

SNOWBALL. PKG., 10c. Early Paris—One of the earliest; small heads; quick grower. Pkg. 10c; oz., 75c.

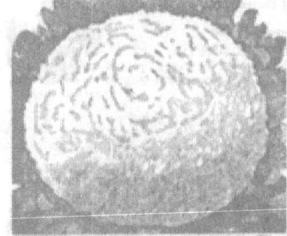

Extra Early Danish Snowball

Has grown invariably a sure head er. The flower head is of very fine grain, dense growth, while the plant has a very short stem dandelion colored leaves. While we are aware that prices are of little consideration in choice of this critical seed, it cannot be denied that if equal quality may be obtained, a moderate reduction in price is not to be despised. Pkg. 10c; oz., $2.00; ¼ lb., $5.00.

SALZER'S MIDSUMMER. PKG., 10c; 2 PKGS., 25c.

Salzer's Midsummer Cauliflower.

There has been for years a need for a second early Cauliflower, one with larger heads ripening right after our peerless Salzer's Earliest or Salzer's Blue Ribbon or the Snowball. Now in our Midsummer we believe we have just the thing gardeners are looking for, a sort that will bear a trial and when once grown, will be always used. Pkg. 10c; 2 pkgs., 25c; ¼ oz., 75c; oz., $1.50; ½ lb., $5.00.

Autumn Giant Cauliflower.

A gorgeous fall sort, with a fine heads; very large, and compact. Always head by market gardeners. Always best grown. Pkg. 10c; oz., $1.25; ½ lb., $5.00.

THE AUTUMN GIANT. PKG., 10c.

A BRAND NEW CUCUMBER.

Salzer's New Morning Star Cucumber

We delight in introducing new things, especially when these new vegetables are really superior in each and every respect over older sorts. That gives pleasure! Well, now, in Salzer's new Morning Star Cucumber we have a new Cucumber that's worth having, that brings joy to the grower and profit to planter! Next to Salzer's Earliest this is the most profitable to grow. It is very shapely, holding its rich green color throughout its entire long length, wh is very straight, smooth and symmetrical. It is one of those rare Cucumbers, both in shape, size and quality one so rarely finds, and we are confident if once grow once you will never be without them. It is splendidly adapted for the market gardener's planting—It's a Cucumber that pays. Pkg. 10c; 20c; ¼ lb., 30c; lb., $1.25; 4 lbs., $4.00.

SALZER'S EARLIEST CUCUMBER.

SALZER'S EARLIEST CUCUMBER is universally acknowledged by seedsmen, by market gardeners, by private planters, whether for gardens or acre cultivation, to be without a peer, the earliest, finest table variety in the world. Over 32,000 customers planted this in 1897, and all pronounced it the earliest, finest Cucumber in existence.

SALZERS EARLIEST CUCUMBER.

Talk about Cucumbers. We are positive that there is nothing in America, nothing in the wide world in the Cucumber line that will so quickly make money for the market gardener, citizen or farmer as Salzer's Earliest Cucumber.

We have just introduced it in remarkable early variety, and shrewd, judging from hundreds of reports, it is all perfect and uniform in growth, with beautiful, nice sized Cucumbers—but the size which sell—all perfect. We cannot too strongly recommend same. Although not as large as Salzer's Perfection, or Improved Long Green, yet it is so early—way ahead of every other sort except the Small Early Market—that it cannot but count. This variety is so early, so prolific, of such a fine quality, it is a bonanza, and the price is so low that everybody can enjoy an early Cucumber.

It is certainly the earliest Cucumber in the world. A Cucumber especially adapted for the hot-bed or early garden culture, as it sets quickly and produces beautiful Cucumbers quick in their growth, prolific. It is a great bonanza for market gardeners, a single hot-bed often yielding from $25.00 to $50.00 worth, according to your market. We have time and time again received $1.20 and $1.50 a dozen for these great early beauties, and we know that every market gardener who will carefully grow them in their hot-beds, or in some sheltered location outside will make lots and lots of money out of them.

What Gardeners Who Use Salzer's Earliest Say:

Frank Clark, Milwaukee: "Your Earliest Cucumber is a bonanza to market gardeners."

Wm. Goode, St. Paul: "I made more money out of 1 lb. Earliest Cucumber than out of anything else."

Henry Johns, Iowa: "It is the earliest Cucumber I ever tasted. Mine were the first in the market, and quickly sold at $1.50 per dozen."

Mrs. Fred Hall, Brooklyn: "I bought 1 oz. for my own use. They proved so very early and so prolific that I sold my surplus for $21.00 to my neighbors, because they were weeks ahead of theirs."

If we were to have but these Cucumbers, they would be Salzer's Earliest, Salzer's White Snow and Salzer's Long Giant, and then, of course, we would have a pickling Cucumber, and nothing in the wide, wide world equals Salzer's Prolific Pickle for this purpose.

If you have ever grown a finer Cucumber than Salzer's Earliest, that will make you more money and etc., we want to know it.

Price of Salzer's Earliest Cucumber.
Pkg., 10c: oz., 20c; ¼ lb., 50c; lb., $1.25; 4 lbs., $4.50.

SALZER'S GREAT JAPANESE CLIMBING CUCUMBER. It is a wonderful Cucumber. Pkg., 10c | oz. 20c.

Salzer's Perfection Cucumber.

hot-bed forcing, for early in the open ground, or, in fact, for any purpose whatever, is the best of all. We have never seen a strain so uniform in size, color and evenness, so complete in all the requirements that go to make a good Cucumber, as our Perfection. Indeed, the fact of its combining every good quality, its ready and quick sale in our market at double the common sort prices, its fine appearance and its remarkable enduring productiveness, lead us to give it the name of Perfection. We can heartily recommend same to all who desire a first-class Cucumber, profitable to the market gardener. Fr. W. Oberts, a Cucumber grower, sold $50.00 worth of Cucumbers from ½ lb. of seed. Don't fail! Pkg., 10c; oz., 20c; ¼ lb., 50c; lb., $1.00; 4 lbs., $3.75; by express, 10c less per lb.

Price of Salzer's Perfection Cucumber. Pkg., 10c: oz. 20c: ¼ lb., 50c; lb., $1.00, postpaid.

Salzer's New Everbearing.

We desire to call special attention to this unique variety. It is of small size, very early, enormously productive, and valuable as a green pickle. The peculiar merit of this novelty is that the vines continue to flower and produce fruit until killed by frost, whether the ripe Cucumbers are picked off or not, differing in this respect from all other sorts in cultivation. The ones that exhibits at the same time Cucumbers in every stage of growth, the small ones being perfect in shape, of a fine green color, and just the size for pickle, but to season. In our novels last summer all the market gardeners who visited us had planted Everbearing, were delighted with it. Pkg., 10c; oz., ½ lb.; ¼ lb., 40c; lb., $1.25.

Bismarck Cucumber.

Originated on the estate of Germany's Iron Chancellor, Bismarck. It is unsurpassed in excellence. Stock scarce. Pkg., 10c oz., long green Cucumbers. ¼ lb., 60c; lb., $1.25.

Salzer's Market Garden Cucumber.

A beautiful Cucumber, every one of which is fit for market trade. It grows very long, is very productive, matures very early, is handsome in appearance and desirable in color, and a great favorite wherever tried. It is the greatest outdoor Cucumber known, and is sure to please. Pkg., 10c; oz., 20c; ¼ lb., 40c; lb., $1.25; 4 lbs., $4.00.

None Such Cucumber.

Offered for the first time last year. It became at once popular as one of the finest long green Cucumbers. Pkg., 10c; oz., 20c; ¼ lb., 50c; lb., $1.25.

See Page 47 for Pickling and Other Sorts. Also for Mixed Cucumber Seed.

SALZER'S JAPANESE CLIMBING CUCUMBER. PKT 10 ¢ POSTPAID

The Salzer Japanese Climbing Cucumber is the greatest Cucumber novelty since Pharaoh forbid the Israelites this most delicious vegetable. This new Cucumber is a strong and vigorous grower, vines attaining nearly twice the length of common varieties, and may be grown on fences, poles or trellises, thus saving much valuable space in small gardens or in market gardens where land is dear. It is estimated that with this Cucumber the product of a given area can be increased threefold. The fruits are 10 to 12 inches in length, of a fine green color; the flesh is thick and firm, never bitter, and fine for pickling as well as slicing. It is very prolific, and the fruits being raised well above the ground, never suffer from wet weather or insects, vines are proof against mildews, and continue bearing until late in the fall. Pkg., 10c; oz., 20c; ¼ lb., $1.50.

Giant Peru.

They are fit to eat at any stage. The flesh is very white, very clear, peculiarly crisp, tender and brittle. Pkg., 10c; ¼ lb., 30c; lb., $1.25.

West India Gherkins.

A novel little Cucumber, grown mostly for show and pickles. Pkg., 5c; oz., 20c.

GIANT PERU. PKG. 10c

SNAKE. PKG., 10c.

IMPROVED LONG GREEN.

A Fine Cucumber.

This variety seems to have taken the lead all through the world as the great variety to plant for a general crop. Grown in every civilized country, and we know of no sort that we would more heartily recommend for general garden culture than this. Of course, our Salzer's Earliest, White Snow, Long Giant, Prolific and Japanese Climber are magnificent varieties, and should be planted everywhere as a trial, and will do well everywhere as a general crop, but our Improved Long Green seems to have captured the hearts of everybody for this purpose. It is safe to say that more seed is planted of this sterling variety than of any five other standard sorts. Next to Salzer's Perfection and Market Garden, it is without the very best to plant for all purposes. It is a splendid forcing Cucumber, as well as for general crop. One of the best selling Cucumbers in the market. Long, smooth, fine flesh, but few seeds. Grows from 10 to 12 inches long. It is the Cucumber you want for home and market. Enormously productive. Pkg., 5c; oz., 10c; ¼ lb., 20c; lb., 60c; 5 lbs., $3.00.

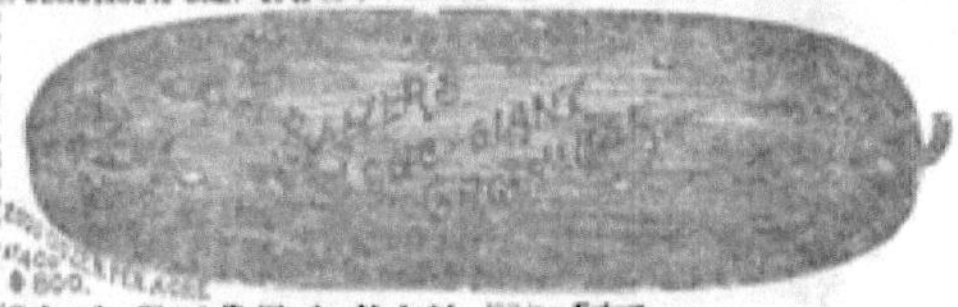

Salzer's Long Giant Cucumber.

This variety certainly surpasses all other grown varieties in its giant length and great beauty. It is positively the handsomest green Cucumber that we have ever seen, often measuring 15 inches long; very uniform in size, while the quality is all that can be asked for. It is extremely crisp and brittle and appetizing, with but few seeds, while its yield is something astonishing. A market gardener of our acquaintance reported 1,000 dozen per acre of fine, salable Cucumbers. Pkg., 15c; oz., 30c; ¼ lb., 90c; lb., $3.00, postpaid.

Salzer's Giant Tallby's Hybrid. White Spine.

On our ground it cropped enormously and every Cucumber was long, smooth, and fit for market, some measuring 15 inches in length, and bringing fully 50 per cent. higher prices than common sorts. Pkg., 10c; oz., 20c; ¼ lb., 45c; lb., $1.25.

SNAKE.

Have you seen this Cucumber as long as 4 feet, coiled up like a snake. Singular and remarkable curiosity. It is good for food, but is grown more on account of its oddity. Pkg., 10c; oz., 25c.

MIXED CUCUMBER SEED, all sorts and kinds. Pkg., 10c; oz., 15c; ¼ lb., 50c; lb., 90c, postpaid.

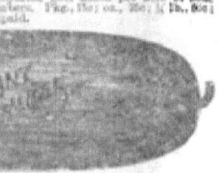

SALZER'S CUC. GIANT GROWN. PKG. 15c.

THE PRINCE OF CUCUMBERS.

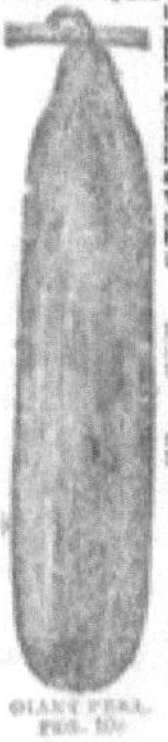

8 Cheap Cucumbers.

Price of following 8 sorts: Pkg. 5c., 10c; ¼ lb., 25c; lb., 40c; by express.

1. **Early Market**—The very earliest Cucumbers; good for forcing; 4 to 5 inches.
2. **Green's Prolific**—One of the best pickling sorts known; small, crisp, productive.
3. **Boston Pickling**—Fine pickler.
4. **White German**—This is the handsomest early variety known; is large and very productive; the white color is peculiarly clear.
5. **Nichol's Medium**—Henderson's favorite.
6. **White Pearl**—Fine white variety.
7. **White Erfurt Spine**—Wonderfully prolific; a good, early, long Cucumber, largely grown as a pickler. Improved.
8. **Long Green Sophisticate**—A good pickler; sells rapidly, and is of excellent taste.

SALZER'S PROLIFIC PICKLE.

For several years we have made Cucumbers for pickles a study, testing and originating new sorts for this purpose, until today we think we have perfection in Salzer's Prolific Pickle. It is fine in form, solid and thick in texture, excelled in quality, and combines all the elements necessary to make a good pickle. It is commonly productive, cropping from 300 to 400 bushels, with ease, per acre. The past summer we spent much time in meutering and greatly improving our Prolific Pickle, and we are sure our patrons will have the best offered in America. Indeed, as a large pickle grower who saw our strain says, "Salzer, your Prolific Pickle is perfection; don't try to improve it, it can't be done."

Price of Prolific Pickle.

Pkg., 10c; oz., 15c; ¼ lb., 20c; lb., $1.10; 5 lbs., $5.00. By express, ¼ lb., 20c; lb., 90c; 5 lbs., $4.50.

SALZER'S PROLIFIC PICKLE

400 BUS. R. A. $400. EACH

PICKLES 400 5 GALK. ACR

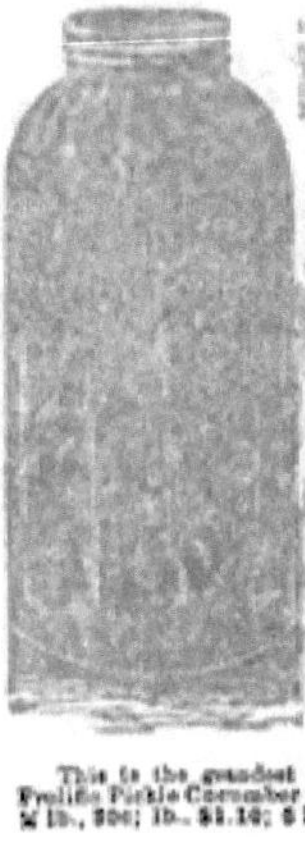

PRICE OF SALZER'S PROLIFIC PICKLE CUCUMBER.

This is the grandest of all pickling Cucumbers, ones that will delight and please every grower, no matter how critical he or she may be. The Salzer Prolific Pickle Cucumber will surely "fill the bill" and give great satisfaction. We offer same at a very low price, as follows: By mail, pkg., 10c; oz., 15c; ¼ lb., 30c; lb., $1.10; 5 lbs., $5.00. By Express, pkg., 10c; oz., 15c; ¼ lb., 20c; lb., $1.00; 5 lbs., $4.50.

CARROTS.

ok at these figures and say it does
pay to plant Carrots! Only use
ur needs.
oz. Salzer's Forcer...@ 30c, = $150.00
oz. First of All,......@ 35c, = 175.00
oz. Danvers Yellow..@ 25c, = 25.00
　　　Total, $350.00
That pays, does it not?

Danvers Yellow Carrot.

(Danvers Half Long.)

magnificent semi-stump-rooted Carrot
of orange shade and most excellent
er. Much sought, and always sells at
y prices in all markets. Valuable for
uses. It is of a rich, dark orange
t, and all the roots are wonderfully
oth and handsome. Last year it was
of the most popular Carrots in my
le list, telling in very large quanti-
Our seed is carefully grown. Our
at even 25c a bushel, if you get as
l yields as you do from our seeds, always pay. Pkg., 5c; oz., 10c; ¼ lb., 25c; lb., 20c; 4 lbs., $3.25.

Oxheart or Guerande.

magnificent Carrot for general culture. Indeed, by many considered the best of all. Intermediate, as to length, between
avers Yellow and the Shorthorn. It is thicker at the neck than the latter, and carries its thickness well down toward
ottom. With us it yielded at the rate of 35 tons to the acre, all marketable. Every Carrot can be pulled easily by hand;
igging is necessary. Pkg., 5c; oz., 10c; ¼ lb., 25c lb., 20c.

Salzer's First of All Carrot.

This Carrot has had a tremendous sale the past two years on account
of its extreme earliness and beauty. Gardeners all over America are
ordering it largely and find it very profitable. We believe this to be
the earliest Carrot in cultivation.

Well, now, there is a great deal of money to be made in market gardening out of Carrots. We know of school children planting ¼ lb. of
Salzer's First of All Carrot and selling $5.00 to $10.00 worth of earliest
Carrots in bunches before school in the morning. There is reason for
this. Everybody craves a Carrot in the extreme early spring, and this
is the time when Salzer's First of All Carrot is ready to tempt the appe-
tites of all. It is a worthy saying that the early bird catches the worm,
and that's just what's the matter with the early market gardeners. The
party that has the earliest vegetables makes the money; so if you want
to make the money, you should plant Salzer's Earliest Cucumber,
Salzer's Self-Blanching Celery, Salzer's Earliest Wax Beans, Salzer's
Red Beauty Beet, Lightning Cabbage, Telephone Corn, Earliest Lettuce,
Earliest Ripe Muskmelon, Fourth of July Watermelon, King of the
Earliest Onion, and so on through the list of Salzer's earliest vegetables. They will never go back on you, but will be the means of making
lots of money for you, if you plant a plenty.
Price of Salzer's First of All Carrot: Pkg., 10c; oz., 15c; ¼ lb.,
50c; lb., $1.50.

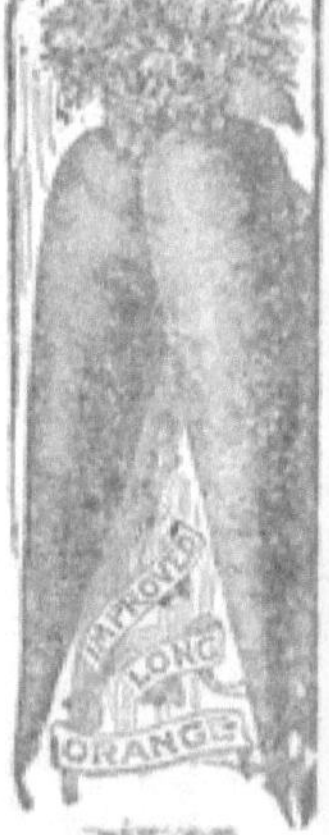

Salzer's Improved Long Orange Table Carrot.

This is the standard Carrot for table use, and especially for winter.
It is enormously productive, yielding as high as 29 TONS per
acre, and is of delicious flavor. An ounce of seed is sufficient for a
winter's supply for a family. No better Carrot can be found for all
purposes than this. We consider it the best strain of Long Orange
Carrot in the market. It is exceptionally smooth and fine. It will please you. Pkg., 10c;
oz., 15c; ¼ lb., 35c; lb., 25c.

Salzer's Midsummer Carrot.

This variety deserves general culture. In addition to its ripening in midsummer, it equals, if indeed it does not surpass, every
other variety in shape, yield and quality. Specimens have been
grown 6 inches in diameter, and of the very best table quality imaginable. Cannot be too strongly recommended. It is enormously productive, a single ounce of seed furnishing bushels of
Carrots. This Carrot really seeks no equal. It is so fine and of
such excellent qualities that it is hard to beat. It is exceedingly
productive and of a quality you are sure to like. It grows fully
as much weight as you serve as the ordinary varieties, and
as the roots grow much more above the ground, it is much easier
to gather the crop. This grand variety is sure to suit every one
who grows it. It cannot be too strongly indorsed. Pkg., 20c; oz.,
20c; ¼ lb., 30c; lb., $1.00; 3 lbs., $2.75.

Early Shorthorn.

Known favorably by all growers.
Considered by many the best early
table variety. Flesh fine grained
in color deep orange; has small
tops. Grows well in shallow soil.
Matures 8 to 10 days sooner than
Long Orange. Pkg., 5c; oz., 10c; ¼
lb., 20c; lb., 70c.

Chantenay.

A magnificent English Carrot grown in that
country in great quantities for fall use. Pkg.,
10c; oz., 15c; ¼ lb., 35c; lb., 90c.

ctar of
ngels.
page 25.

Standard Carrots—Low Prices.

lzer's French Forcer
or Forcing.

se of the earliest of all Car-
. It is very sweet and early;
mild sort. It is not nearly
arge as Salzer's First of All.
it is a great beauty and very
ty. This Carrot has enjoyed
unprecedented, almost bewil-
ng the little beauty. It is so
et Carrot for extreme early.
., 4c; oz., 10c; ¼ lb., 20c; lb.

Early Scarlet Horn.
(Pointed.)

An early imported sort of excellent merit.
This sort is grown quite extensively about
Boston and other Eastern markets. It is
really a valuable sort. Pkg., 5c; oz., 9c; ¼
lb., 15c; lb., 50c.

Scarlet Nantes.

A splendid half-long, stump-rooted sort.
Increasing in value and popularity. Pkg.,
5c; oz., 8c; ¼ lb., 15c; lb., 50c.

Salzer's Long Orange beats the world. Pkg., 10c; lb., 80c.

Carrots for Stock.

Carrots are excellent
for feeding to stock.
Horses relish them and
fatten on one feed of
Carrots daily. The yield
is so heavy that an
acre will keep your
horses fat and healthy
all winter.

Norman Belgian.

A yellow sort, grow-
ing to large size, and of
the finest flavor for
stock. We cannot too
strongly recommend to you to try
this Carrot. It is great
for stock. Have you a
harvest home, and you
desire to have him look
bright and feel gay,
feed him with Carrots
even a day during
winter. One ounce of
Norman Belgian will
furnish enough food.
Pkg., 5c; oz., 10c; ¼
lb., 25c; lb., 45c; by express, 10 lbs., $4.25.

Long White Belgian

A white Carrot which
has become the stand-

and for stock. It is very sweet and
gives excellent results as a stock
food. Pkg., 5c; oz., 10c; lb., 45c.

California Mammoth.

Very large; yields 100 tons per
acre. Pkg., 5c; oz., 10c; ¼ lb., 25c;
lb., 45c; 10 lbs., $4.00.

Mastodon.

Carefully selected Carrot. It is
grand for stock and very prolific.
Pkg., 5c; oz., 10c; ¼ lb., 30c; ¼ lb.,
50c; lb., 60c; 5 lbs., $2.50, postpaid.

MASTODON. PKG., 5c; OZ., 10c.

SALZER'S · SELF=BLANCHER · CELERY.

There is no Celery equaling it in taste, richness of color, perfection in blanching and earliness. In our home kitchen garden this variety
tender, delicious, crisp, brittle Celery, without any hoeing, completely blanching itself. It is preeminently the sort to grow and also for home
market or for shipping. The demand the last 3 years for this magnificent Celery has been something remarkable, no mushroom. Last year introduced
before. Almost every order seemed to want Salzer's Self-Blancher, until we sold almost every grain of seed, and everybody grew the finest Celery the
raw seen. Now we are sure that there is no self-blanching Celery ahead of Salzer's Self-Blancher. You will like it. It is early, crisp, tender—absolutely the

MONEY IN CELERY.

An acre contains 20,000 Salzer's Self-Blancher Celery,
10,000, or 1,500 dozen, @ 50c per dozen.................$750.00
15,000, later, @ 2c a piece...............................300.00

Now, the total cost of seed, labor, rent, etc., need
not exceed $100 per acre, which would give you the
handsome profit of $650.00 per acre.

This can only be made by Salzer's Early
Self-Blancher Celery, because it is the earliest.
Bunches being remarkably stocky and wonderfully strong grower, is very heavy, perfectly solid, of
a delicious, sweet flavor, and with all these points
is a wonderful keeper. One would think that
these would be a sufficient number of good qualities,
but to all these is added THE WONDERFUL
QUALITY OF SELF-BLANCHING to a very remarkable extent. Without banking up, or any
covering to speak of, even the outer ribs become of a yellowish white color, the heart being
large, solid, and of a beautiful golden-yellow.

Where the market is near, no crop pays
better than Celery, as it is in constant demand
from early June throughout fall and winter.
Salzer's Self-Blancher is a variety that
really should be called "All Season's Celery,"
from the fact that it is good in June, it is good
in July, and good throughout the year. It
keeps well, sells rapidly. It is handsome in
the extreme.

PRICE OF SALZER'S SELF-BLANCHER.
Pkg., 10c; 3 pkgs., 25c; ¼ oz., 30c; oz., 60c;
¼ lb., $1.50; lb., $5.00.

1. New Rose Celery.

A magnificent new Celery. The
color is a beautiful shade of new
of exceptional fine flavor, solid,
crisp and tender, and has proved
itself entirely free from stringi-
ness. It is a splendid variety for
late use. It keeps well and
blanches well. It is one of those
varieties that will certainly please
the private grower, while we recommend it to the market gardener
a small seedling of this is a novelty, for there are many families
who will be delighted to purchase
same. Pkg., 10c; oz., 25c; ¼ lb.,
50c; lb., $2.50.

2. Golden Self-Blanching.

A Grand Novelty.

The beautiful appearance of the
plant, with its close habit, compact growth, and straight vigorous stalks, is indescribable. The
ribs are perfectly golden green,
brittle and of delicious flavor,
surpassed by no other variety.
This has the decided merit of being self-blanching. When it bank-
bar up or any covering whatever, even the outer ribs become of a handsome, fresh, yellowish white color. The heart is large, solid, and of a
beautiful, rich, golden-yellow color, extremely early, and of the richest
flavor. Pkg., 10c; oz., 20c; oz., 35c; ¼ lb., 75c; lb., $2.50.

3. New Giant Pascal.

This has proved to be as great an addition to our list as the Golden
Self-Blanching. As it is an off-spring of the latter, it partakes of its
noble flavor, and has no bitter taste at all. The crisp stalks are of a
stalks are very large, thick, solid and not stringy, and naturally
tender and crisp, blanching like plant, and when desired can be blanched
lengthwise. The leafy green the outer stalks will average 2 inches
in width, and are fully as thick as a man's finger, and is well shown in
the illustration of a stalk of Giant Pascal, reduced in size. It blanches
very easily, and after a few days' earthing up, is perfectly blanched and
a beautiful white appearance. Pkg., 10c; oz., 25c; ¼ lb., 75c; lb.,

6. Well Known Celeries.

1. Crawford's Half
Dwarf—one of the
best. Pkg., 10c; oz., 15c.
2. Dwarf White
Solid—Excellent va-
riety. Pkg., 5c; oz., 20c;
¼ lb., 60c.
3. Seymour's Su-
perb White—One of
the finest large Celery
sorts. Pkg., 5c; oz., 25c.

4. Dwarf Gol-
Heart—Heart
golden-yellow, c
and very c
Pkg., 10c; oz.
5. Salzer's Gl
Celery—the
Celery known.
20c.
6. Crimson Ce
—Beautiful red c
Pkg., 10c; oz.

Turnip-Rooted Celery.

Turnip-Rooted—Well-known. Pkg., 5c;
10c; lb., $1.40.

Finest German—Pkg., 5c; oz., 20c; lb., 2
New Apple Rooted—Pkg., 5c; oz., 20c; lb.

Salzer's Turnip Celery.

Our Northern-grown Celery tests 99 heavy p
to the 100 planted; all are large, solid, ten
remarkably well-flavored bulbs. This is
immensely superior to the common Tur
Rooted Celery. The stock is carefully raise
Geo. Terp says: "From the 1 ounce or
sold $20.00 worth of roots."

John Benn, Milwaukee: "I bought ⅓ lb. t
zer's Turnip Celery and sold $9.00 worth,
roots were very fine."

Now we know that there is lots of money to
made by growing Salzer's Turnip Celery. T
try it for 1899 and be happy.

Price: Pkg., 10c; oz., 20c; ¼ lb., 60c; lb., $

4. Giant Golden Heart.

Mr. Robert Purvis found in his
dwarf Golden Heart Celery a few
plants of larger growth. These he
carefully set aside and grew their
produce on old seasons, thinking out
for seed only the thickest, tallest
plants. The result of this we now
have in our Giant Golden Heart, fully
equal in quality to the original
stock, far more productive, solid and
of best, true Celery. Another quality is its excellent keeping habit.
It thus cannot be excelled if the best
Celery for winter storage, for market
or for the private planter. Lb. $2.50; ½
lb., 75 cts., 30c [¼ oz. 20c]; pkg., 10c.

while it has the decided merit of being self-blanching. Without banking up or any covering whatever, even the outer ribs become of a handsome, fresh, yellowish-white color. The heart is large, solid, and of a
beautiful, rich, golden-yellow color, extremely early, and of the richest
flavor. Pkg., 10c; oz., 20c; oz., 35c; ¼ lb., 75c; lb., $2.50.

One package each of the 6 Best Celeries, 25c.

White Plume Celery.

The great objection to growing Celery for family use has been the trouble experi-
ienced in blanching it. Blanch by tying the plant and drawing up a little soil, when
the work of blanching is accomplished. Pkg., 10c; oz., 20c; ¼ lb., 70c; lb., $2.60.

Boston Market.

The great favorite in the Boston markets. It is early, very solid, white, of mild,
delicious flavor. Oz., 30c; ¼ lb., 60c; lb., $1.95.

White Walnut.

So called because of its rich, walnut-like flavor.   The stalks are solid and heavy,
of dwarf, compact growth.   Pkg., 30c; oz., 20c; ¼ lb., 75c.

CHAMPIGNONS OR MUSHROOMS.

The demand for Mushroom spawn among private growers and gardeners for growing in cel-
chs, etc., has increased with us such 100 in the past year over 500 per cent. Everybody is trying to
most delicious of all edible fungi. One booklet, "How Mushrooms Grow," is mailed you on rec
of 10c. The Mushroom is a delicious edible fungus, of a white color, changing to lev
when old. The gills are loose, of a pinkish and changing to livid color. It produces
seed, but instead a white, fibrous substance in broken threads called spawn. Can be grown in cell
and out-of-the-way places.

CULTURE OF THE MUSHROOM.

Our Booklet 10c; or mailed free with each order of 75c worth of spawn, tells all about
Price, lb., by mail, 30c; 4 lbs., $1.00; by express, 20c; 5 lbs., 75c; 10 lbs., $1.25.

A BED OF SALZER'S MUSHROOM.

SALZER'S FIRST-OF-ALL SWEET CORN.

For years, as our friends well know, we have boomed the Telephone Corn to the exclusion of all other sorts as the earliest variety in cultivation. We now take pleasure, however, in offering them a variety that is even earlier than the Telephone. This is a bold statement, but it is made with due deliberation, after careful tests by several hundred of our customers the past season. First-of-All has proven itself, in this test, 4 days, and in some cases a week earlier, than the Telephone. It will be found an especial boon to all market gardeners. Ears often 8 inches long, though the average length is but 5 to 6 inches. It is a magnificent Corn and will be a great bonanza to all who plant it.

THE SUBSTANCE OF THE WHOLE MATTER IS THIS:

Salzer's First-of-All Corn is the first of all to ripen no matter where you plant same. No matter alongside of which earliest Sweet Corn you test same you will always find that Salzer's First-of-All gets there quicker than any other variety known. Now there are thousands and thousands of customers who tried this Corn in 1896 and there was not one but what had the earliest Corn. It cannot be too highly recommended. Please note low prices: Pkg., 10c; pt., 20c; qt., 40c; postpaid; by freight, qt., 25c; pk., $1.25; bu., $3.75.

Salzer's Telephone Sweet Corn.

Next to "First-of-All" this is the earliest variety grown. The ears are of fair size, a size in great demand in the market. Quite a quantity of this Corn was distributed among large market gardeners, and one illustration truthfully depicts its merits as an extremely early sort. It creates a demand for itself in every market where once tried.

Your grocers, your market buyers, your family customers cry for it; everybody once going to for early will want no other. The kernel is white, the stalks short, the ears fair sized, the yield large, and its extreme earliness remarkable. It is the Corn to grow for private use, or for sale by the market gardener. Note our low price for this remarkable novelty.

By mail; Pkg. 10c; ½ pt., 15c; pt., 20c; qt., 40c; postpaid.
By freight or express: Pkg. 10c; pt., 20c; qt., 25c; pk., $1.00; bu., $3.00.

Northern Pedigree Sweet Corn.

Side by side with No Plus Ultra, Amber Cream, Early Minnesota, and Early La Crosse, it proved 4 days ahead of Early La Crosse, and from 7 to 12 days ahead of other sorts. Stalks dwarf, ears small, well developed, full and deliciously sweet. The drift of hundreds of testimonials received: "Had Sweet Corn from Salzer's Northern Pedigree ahead of my neighbors." Good sized ear and of the most delicious sweetness. By mail: Pkg. 10c; pt., 20c; qt. 30c; by express; Pkg., 10c; pt., 20c; qt., 25c; pk., $1.25; bu., $3.00.

New Early Champion Sweet Corn.

Produces ears 12 inches long in 60 days. This new variety is, without question, the earliest large Sweet Corn yet introduced, being only a few days later than the first early small sorts. Ears nearly as large as the Evergreen; pure white kernels, with medium sized white cob; very sweet, tender and full of milk, yielding from 2 to 3 ears to the stalk. Pkg. 10c; pt., 20c; qt., 25c; pk., 75c; bu., $2.50.

RICH, SWEET, TENDER.
Pkg., 10c; qt., 8c.

Corn—Country Gentleman.

This is used largely in the East, where it is called the finest of all Sweet Corn for private table. It is also known as Zigzag Corn, on account of the peculiar arrangement of its kernels. It is rather late, but is of a delicious quality, ripening 6 days before Evergreen Corn, and will delight the most fastidious epicure. Pkg., 10c; pt., 20c; qt., 35c; pk., $1.00; bu., $3.50.

Extra Early Adams.

This Corn is a splendid early variety, though not as early as the Telephone, Early La Crosse and these varieties, yet it follows these so closely with great large ears that it is one of the most profitable varieties that can be grown, on account of earliness and fine shape of ears; not sweet. Pkg., 10c; pt., 20c; qt., 30c; pk., $1.00; bu., $2.75.

Stowell's Evergreen Sweet Corn.

There is no Sweet Corn more generally and largely planted than the Evergreen. Now, our straw is vastly superior to the bulk offered. It has been carefully grown for seed and is sure to give great satisfaction. The ears are very large—we have seen them 10 to 12 inches long, usually very sweet, and will outsell the common varieties of late Sweet Corn two to one. You will like it because it will give satisfaction. Pkg. 10c; pt., 20c; qt., 30c; postpaid; by express, pkg. 10c; pt., 20c; pk., 60c; bu., $2.25.

Black Mexican.

This variety is always scarce. It is of excellent quality, medium late, and on account of its novel appearance is sure to be taking. Pkg., 10c; pt., 20c; qt., 30c; pk., $1.00; bu., $9.00.

PRICES OF FOLLOWING 8 SORTS:

By express, pkg., 5c; pt., 12½; qt., 17c; pk., 60c; bu., $2.25; by mail, pkg., 5c; pt., 15c; qt., 28c.

1. Perry's Hybrid (Ballard's Early)—Also known under Chicago Market. It is a fine sort; very sweet; a good second early; large, fine ears.
2. Early Minnesota—One of the best varieties for second early; splendid in all particulars.
3. Early Marblehead—Fine flavor and very sweet.
4. Moore's Concord—Largest and best second early.
5. Cory—A splendid, very early Sweet Corn; rich in flavor.
6. Mammoth Sugar—A large sort, very sweet; later than Evergreen.
7. Egyptian Sweet—Late, ears large and flavor rich and sweet.
8. Ricort Canner—A superb sort for canning, ripening 2 weeks before Egyptian.

☞ We can also supply at 5c a package, 15c a pint, 30c a quart and 90c a peck, the following: Early Adams, Burlington, Tom Thumb, Shaker's Early Triumph, None-Such, Excelsior and other standard Corn sorts.

La Crosse Early Sweet Corn.

Next to Salzer's Telephone and Salzer's Northern Pedigree, no Sweet Corn excels this in earliness and productiveness. Fine, large Kernels, deliciously sweet, of medium size ears. For illustration see above. Pkg., 10c; pt., 20c; qt., 30c; by express, pt., 20c; qt., 60c; pk., $1.25; bu., $3.00.

POP CORN.

Salzer's Silver Ball—With a vaster surrounding productiveness of this delicious taste, and pops readily and evenly. It is the Corn for everybody to plant. A package will be sufficient for family use. Give the boys on the farm an acre to plant Pop Corn for the market. It pays. Pkg., 10c; pt., 15c; qt., 40c; by express, pt., 15c; qt., 25c; $1.00.

White Rice—One of the finest, most prolific Pop Corns grown; largely planted. Very good. Pkg., 10c; pt., postpaid; by express, pt., 20c; qt., $1.00.

Queen's Golden—A splendid sort. Above all is its exceeding tenderness when popped, together with its delicious and delicate taste; splendid for all purposes. By mail, pkg., 10c; pt., 20c; qt., 30c; by express, pk., $1.00.

Amber Colored Pop Corn.

A new, rare, exquisitely beautiful Pop Corn, popping to perfection. Large amber colored ears. Pkg., 10c; ½ pt., 20c; qt., 35c, postpaid.

1. THE GERMAN COFFEE BERRY.

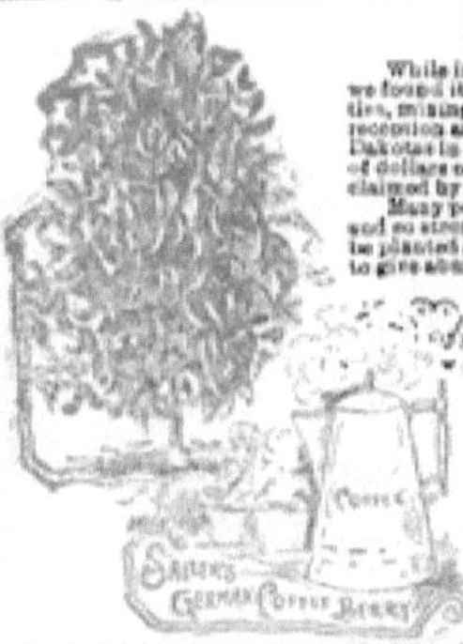

While in Germany in 1894 we took great pains to look up our great German Coffee Berry, and, to our surprise and pleasure, we found it used in almost all hotels and restaurants in Switzerland, Germany, Holland and France. They used large quantities, mixing it with Rio and other genuine Coffee, and we predict that no novelty offered in years will meet with such a hearty reception as the German Coffee Berry. It is the poor man's friend and the rich man's delight; ripening in Wisconsin and the Dakotas in 4½ months. It is wonderfully productive, and is destined to save the American housekeepers and farmers millions of dollars each year. It is certainly the best berry to mix in with other Coffee we ever saw; half and half will produce a drink claimed by many to be equal to a good cup of Rio.

Many people really prefer this Coffee to any other, and their testimonials are so hearty and so strong that it leaves no doubt but what it is a rare novelty and fine berry. It should be planted early, carefully cultivated, and set the plants about 2 feet apart, each way so as to give abundant room to spread and grow and bear abundantly. Give it room and sun and not too rich soil. You will be surprised at the great quantity you can grow from a package or ounce of seed.

☞ This Coffee must not be confounded with other dealers' Domestic or German Coffee Berry. ☜

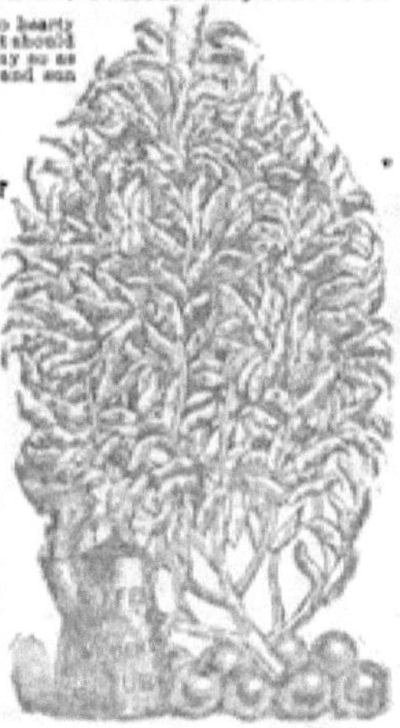

A FEW TESTIMONIALS.

"I made a cup of coffee out of the roasted berries you sent me, and I found it much better than coffee generally sold here."

"I like your coffee better than that which costs me 35c per pound."

"I ground, steeped and drank your new coffee and found it equal to any genuine coffee I ever drank."

"We consider your new coffee more delicious than the genuine coffee."

"Your new coffee is as good as any store coffee I ever tasted."

"Your coffee is a marvel. Its flavor is excellent."

"Raised 15 pounds of splendid coffee from the package you sent. Like it as well as genuine coffee."

"Your coffee Berry has come to stay. It makes excellent coffee."

Frank Winters, Iowa: "Now, as regards that Coffee Berry. I like it. I like the flavor and I think it is a great novelty."

James Clinton, Minn.: "The coffee Berry did splendidly. I am using it now, and it gives a healthy beverage."

Gordon Cole, Ind.: "In these hard times your Coffee Berry comes into full play. The ½ lb. gave me 50 lbs. I sold 25 lbs. to my neighbors for coffee. All like it."

S. Y. Harris, Mo.: "Wonderful, indeed, mixed with Rio half-and-half. Can't praise it enough. Like it as well as store coffee."

Willis Ross, Ohio: "The German Coffee Berry is a coffee berry, producing, to my taste, fully as good coffee as Arbuckle's package coffee. I like it."

Mrs. E. M. Brosius, Neb.: "I like your new coffee better than Arbuckle's package coffee."

"Last year I bought of you 1 pound of Coffee Berry; I planted it carefully and raised 180 pounds. This has kept me in coffee a year, and I sold 50 pounds to my neighbors for coffee, getting good price for same. I like the coffee very much."

Mrs. Mary West, Mich.: "Your Coffee Berry can't be beat. I have given it a fair trial. My boarders all like it and praise it."

W. J. Doll, Texas: "We drank some of your coffee, and I can truthfully say that it is a good substitute and tastes as well as coffee for which we pay 37½c per lb."

"Your new coffee is a great success. It is far better than the coffee sold here at 3½ pounds for $1.00. We can grow yours at a couple of cents per pound."

Opelousas, La., July 20, 1896. "Dear Sirs: I wish to inform you that I have made a trial of your German Coffee Berry, and that I find it all that one can desire. It is as good as the best straight coffee."—Jos. A. Bloch.

RIPENED AT LA CROSSE, Sept. 10, '98.

Thus we could keep on and introduce hundreds who have tested the Coffee Berry.

PRICE OF THE GREAT GERMAN COFFEE BERRY.

Pkg., 15c; oz., 30c; 2 oz., 50c; ¼ lb., 75c; lb., $2.00, postpaid. Full culture directions with each package.

☞ Should you wish to taste the bean, we will send a few (parched) upon receipt of 5c postage.

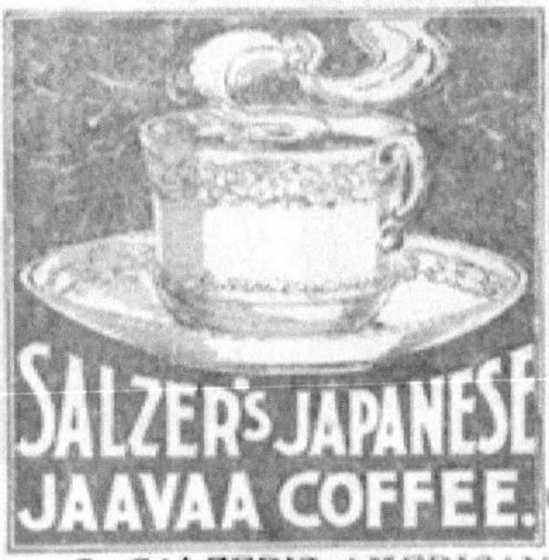

2. SALZER'S JAPANESE JAAVAA COFFEE.

All right: These two coffees with Chicory are immense. I've tried them.

Travelers in Corea and Japan, and missionaries on duty in those countries, have long referred to a berry that was used in these countries as a coffee substitute. It has been grown somewhat in the United States. Customers have written us regarding this coffee. Some call it Idaho Coffee, the Colorado Coffee, the California Java, and Domestic Coffee Berry. Some years ago a customer living in Texas, right near the border of Old Mexico, wrote us of his Japanese Jaavaa Coffee, and that it was known under the name of Old Mexico. We obtained a supply of seed, have grown it here in the North, and find that in some respect it is superior to our great German Coffee Berry, and we offer it as a fit companion to this most remarkable novelty in the coffee substitute line. The berry is larger, is different shaped, and the growth of the plant is somewhat different than the German Coffee Berry. We predict for this a tremendous sale and more that where once tried it will be tried again and again. It is certainly a healthier drink than genuine coffee, and we are sure that those using same will not regret it. We would like a report on this Japanese Jaavaa Coffee from all customers purchasing the seed this year. We believe it will completely revolutionize coffee-drinking in America. We have made a special price to such customers as wish to try both the great German Coffee Berry and our Japanese Jaavaa, of but 25c for the two packages. At this low price we hope that there will be a general trial of the bean all over America. Both our great German Coffee Berry and the Japanese Jaavaa ripened thoroughly at La Crosse this season and produced heavily.

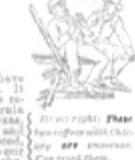

PRICE OF THE JAPANESE JAAVAA COFFEE.

Pkg., 15c; oz., 25c; 2 oz., 40c; ¼ lb., 60c; lb., $2.00, postpaid.

☞ 1 PKG. EACH, GERMAN COFFEE, JAPANESE JAAVAA COFFEE AND SALZER'S CHICORY 30c; 1 OZ. EACH, 50c. ☜

3. SALZER'S AMERICAN CHICORY.

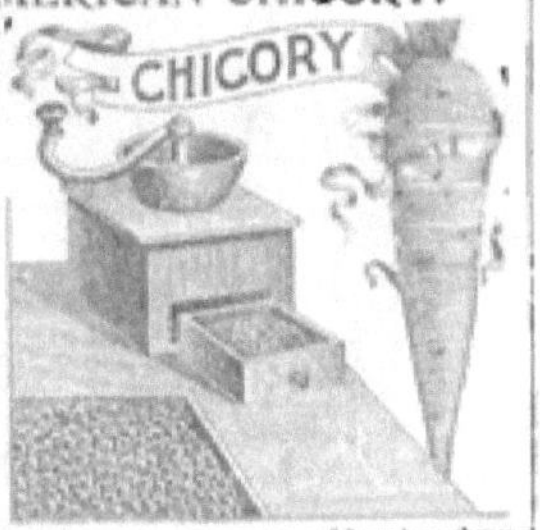

Here is the thing that you are looking for, just the root or substance needed to add extra flavor, substance, body, quality, richness, deliciousness, strength, and health to your coffee—whether you use Salzer's German Coffee Berry, Salzer Japanese Jaavaa, or whether you use the XXX store coffee or Java and Mocha or Rio—no matter which—Salzer's American Chicory will in the minds of chemists, doctors and others add strength and richness and quality and health!

Mrs. RORRER, a great American authority on cooking, says: "Chicory does more than make coffee delicious it purifies it, makes it healthful. I use four ounces or more to each pound of coffee."

Chicory neutralizes the bad effects of coffee, rendering it perfectly harmless to old and young. Reduces the price fully ½ and improves the flavor of coffee and imparts to it wholesome and beneficial qualities. Full directions as how to use, grow, etc., with each package. It's a thing you will surely want to try. It will pay! Pkg., 15c; oz., 30c; ¼ lb., 75c.

THIS MAGNIFICENT SEWING MACHINE

—Fully described in rear of this catalogue—is offered

FREE,

absolutely free, to the lady or gentleman who will sell

300 Packages at 15c. Per Package...

of either or all of the following

3 Great Coffee Plants...

1. The Great German Coffee Berry.
2. The Japanese Jaavaa Coffee.
3. The Salzer Coffee Chicory.

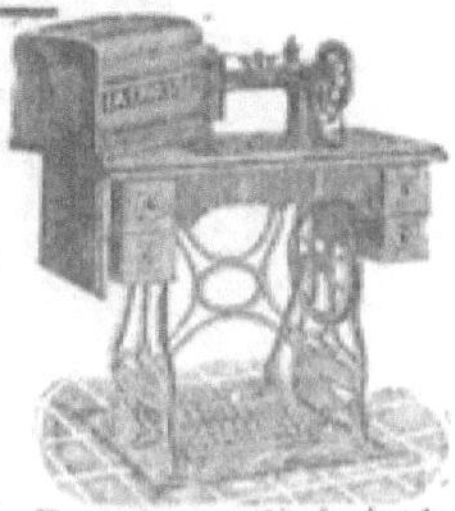

That is if your combined orders for above 3 Great Coffee Plants amount to 300 packages in all, and you remit $45.00 we will send you free one La Crosse Sewing Machine.

☞ ONE PACKAGE EACH OF ABOVE 3 GREAT COFFEE PLANTS, 30c; 1 OZ. EACH, 50c. ☜

HERBS, ETC.

The following medicinal Herbs are so well known that they need no special description. We urge all to plant some. What is more helpful to babe than Fennel tea! And just think of the good Sage tea. Anise and all the other sorts, too. You will want some, if not for medicinal purposes, then for flavoring. The package of mixed Herbs for 10c is very popular.

☞ **Price for all Herbs, except** as noted. pkg. 5c; oz. 25c.

Anise, Pkg., 5c.
Balm, Oz., 20c.
Borage, Pkg., 5c.
Bene, Pkg., 5c.
Belladonna, Pkg., 5c
Bornet, Pkg., 5c.
Hoarhound, Pkg.,5c
Henbane, Pkg., 5c.
Hyssop, Oz., 20c
Lavender, Pkg., 5c.
Parslane, Pkg., 5c.
Rue Saffron, Pkg., 5c
Tansy, Pkg., 5c.
Wormwood, Oz., 20c
Hop Seed, Pkg., 15c

Cardoon, Pkg., 5c.
Caraway, Pkg., 5c.
Catnip, Pkg., 5c.
Chervil, Pkg., 5c.
Coriander, Pkg., 5c
Dill, Pkg., 5c.
Sorrel, Pkg., 5c.
Sweet Basil, Pkg., 5c
Sweet Fennel, 5c.
Summer Savory,
    Pkg., 5c.
Thyme, Pkg., 5c.
Tarragon, Pkg., 5c.
Sweet Marjoram, 5c.
Rosemary, Oz., 20c.

SAGE.

A few ounces of Sage will plant enough for 300 bunches of dry leaves. At La Crosse it retails at 5c a bunch. This is a splendid thing for the school boy or school girl to plant in a corner of the garden, taking good care of same, and in fall tie in bunches and sell to their neighbors for flavoring or tea. An ounce of seed will furnish enough plants to sell $10.00 or $15.00 worth of dried leaves in our market.

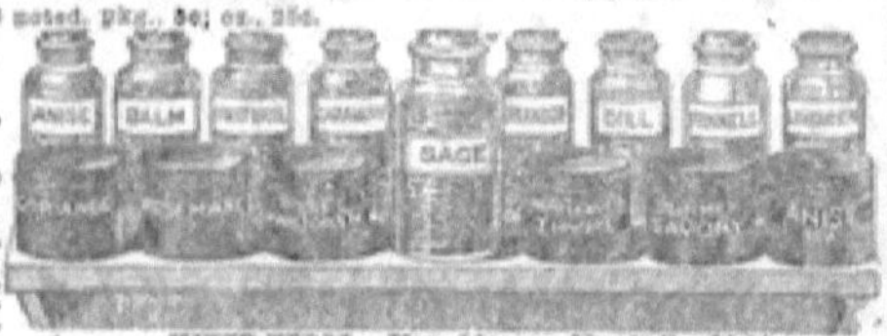

Common Sage— Pkg., 5c; oz., 30c; lb., $1.25.

Salzer's Giant— Nothing we ever sold gave more general satisfaction than our Giant Sage. It is a very profitable plant to grow. Very large and fine. Pkg., 10c; oz., 50c; ¼ lb., $1.50; lb., $2.00.

THREE FINE THINGS.

CHIVES   SALZER'S GIANT

☞ **New Javan Coffee. "See page 54.**

MIXED HERBS. Pkg., 10c; oz., 30c; ¼ lb., $1.00.

No other mixture of seeds that we have for sale has given such tremendous satisfaction as our mixed herbs and mixed peppers. Indeed, our mixture of herbs is immensely popular, as you get seeds of all sorts carefully mixed for just 10c a package. There are just thousands upon thousands of our lady friends and gardeners using the mixed herbs for their kitchen garden. A package usually will produce enough plants for any use varying desired for flavoring or medicinal purposes.

Price of Mixed Herbs: Pkg. 10c; oz., 30c; ¼ l., $1.00.

LEEK.

Splendid for flavoring soups, etc. Treat same as Onion; both leaves and bulbs are used. In fall plant a few in sand in cellar for winter use.

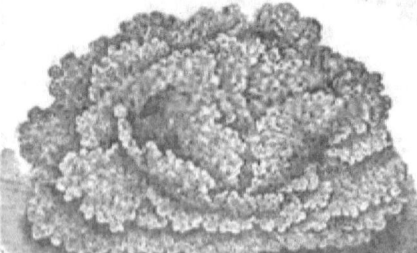

SALZER'S LARGE ROUEN

NEW WINTER.

New Winter Flag— Very fine. Pkg., 5c; oz., 30c; lb., $1.00.

Broad London Flag— Much used. Pkg., 5c; oz., 30c; ¼ lb., 40c; lb., $1.15.

Salzer's Large Rouen Leek. The finest, most prolific and profitable of all. Grows in enormous quantities in France and Germany. Splendid for flavoring. Pkg., 10c; oz., 30c; lb., $3.00.

1. Chives.

We cannot too strongly recommend the growing of a few dozen Chives; when once planted they live forever. A few plants taken in the house and placed in the cellar will, as soon as brought to light, sprout and bear an abundance of greens for salads, of strong onion flavor. Per pkg. 10c; per 100, $1.00.

2. Horseradish.

This splendid appetizer cannot be overestimated. It is an appetizer in every respect. Twenty-five will be sufficient for a small family. The roots grow and increase rapidly in size, and bear abundantly with each succeeding year. Plant in a corner of the yard where you wish it to grow, and it will repay you many times, as you can begin digging the next year. They increase and bear heartily. 6 for 20c; 12 for 35c; 25 for 70c; 100 for $2.75, postpaid.

3. Pieplant Root.

Nearly everybody is fond of Pieplant pie, or the same prepared in almost any way, as sauce, etc. Well, a dozen or two plants planted in a corner of your garden next to your Chives and Horseradish will give you an great abundance of this delicious plant. It is healthful, an excellent appetizer, a great tonic. This and Horseradish will keep your system strong and healthy. 3 for 20c; 6 for 50c; 12 for 75c, postpaid; 100, by express $5.00.

Okra or Gumbo.

Largely grown in Southern states. Its long pods are used in some. The Plant when warm.

Early Dwarf— Very fine. Pkg., 5c; oz., 10c; ¼ lb., 20c.

Long Green— Excellent. Pkg., 5c; oz., 10c; ¼ lb., 15c.

Mustard.

Excellent for salad. White or brown. Pkg., 5c; oz., 10c; lb., 50c.

Martinia.

For pickles. Pkg., 5c; oz., 30c.

Nasturtium.

The seeds, while young and green, are pickled and used as capers.

Tall— Pkg., 5c; oz., ¼ lb., 30c.

Dwarf— Pkg., 5c; oz., 10c; ¼ lb., 50c.

Cotton Seed.

Pkg., 5c; oz., 20c; ¼ lb., 25c; lb., 50c.

For Birds, Etc.

Hemp—For birds. Lb., 25c; by mail, 50c.

Rape—For birds. Oz., 5c; lb., by mail, 60c.

Rape—English, for salad. Oz., 10c; lb., by mail, 60c.

Garlic.

In great demand among the Italian, French and some American people for flavoring soups, sausages, etc.

Common Garlic Sets— ¼ lb., 15c; lb., 50c; 10 lbs., by express, $2.00.

Italian— Very prolific. ¼ lb., 20c; lb., 55c; 5 lbs., $2.25; by express $3.75.

Mushrooms.

(See Page 49.)

With our new culture on Mushrooms—A little booklet costing 10c, or which is sent free with each $1.00 order of Mushroom Spawn—it is made easy to grow Mushrooms. Lb., 20c; 4 lbs., $1.00, postpaid.

MUSHROOM. *See also page 49.*

---

2 NEW HEAD LETTUCES. 1 Pkg. of Each, 25 Cents.

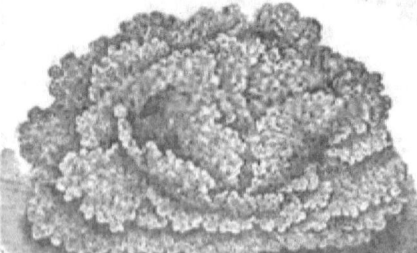

SALZER'S COLOSSAL HEAD

We have no hesitancy in saying that its superiors you can't find. These may appear to be strongcomplicated, but did I think your customer this season planting this Lettuce will willingly acknowledge the above to be correct. The branching leaves are of a bright light green color, slightly curled, while the inner leaves, which form the head, present a white appearance, and are as tender as if blanched. It forms a very large head, at times attaining a weight of 15½ lbs. When eaten it has a rich, nutty flavor, and is almost absolutely free from any strong or bitter taste. It resists wonderfully well Summer heat and drought, and is in every way the sort for the market or family gardener. NO PRAISE IS TOO HIGH FOR ITS MERITS. Pkg., 15c; oz., 30c; ¼ lb., 80c; lb., $3.00. ☞ One pkg., each 25c.

KAISER WILHELM

KAISER WILHELM—Over in Germany there are some 50,000,000 people who believe that the best Lettuce in the world is grown in that Kingdom. We agree with them that Kaiser Wilhelm head Lettuce is a big head variety—almost as "big-headed" as the present Kaiser appears to some Americans; but, setting all fun aside, this is a magnificent head of creamy white, pretty deliciously flavored Lettuce, sure to please, both on account of its size and quality. Pkg., 15c; oz., 40c; ¼ lb., 30c.

SALZER'S EARLIEST LETTUCE.

Now, then, we have learned a thing or two about Lettuce in the 20 years of our gardening experience, and we think we are perfectly safe when we say that Salzer's Earliest Lettuce is the earliest in the world, that we are saying something no man can contradict. It is indeed a remarkable Lettuce, grown quickly, beautiful color and shape, and will stake more money for the market gardener whether he sows seed in a hot bed or any sheltered position outside than any other Lettuce we know of. We have vindicated numbers of testimonials from market gardeners, from citizens and farmers, praising the merits of this Earliest Lettuce. It is the Lettuce for early; it is the Lettuce for general crop; indeed, it is fine all the time. We do not know how we could improve upon for an early lettuce, go the world over.

This variety we obtained from one of our customers in Germany, who pronounced it the earliest Lettuce grown in that country. Then we sent it to the market gardeners in Boston, who reported: "Earliest ever seen here." We then distributed it in Philadelphia, New York and other centers, and all united in calling it the "earliest of all." It is earlier than the Early Summer or Tennis Ball, or any lettuce known to us. Pkg., 15c; oz., 30c; ¼ lb., $1.00; lb., $2.75.

New Lettuce, Heavy Weight.

Grand Rapids Forcing.

The Best Sort for Shipping.

This grand new forcing variety stands more neglect in the way of water or ventilation, will grow greater weight on the same ground, and will stand longer after matures, than the loose-leaved Simpson. It is of handsome appearance, and not apt to rot, and will keep from wilting longer while exposed for sale than any other sort. Pkg., 5c; oz., 15c; ¼ lb., 35c; lb., $1.00.

Kaiser Wilhelm—A grand head variety. Pkg., 10c; oz., 40c; ¼ lb., $1.00.

Salzer's Sunlight Lettuce—A Great Novelty.

This is a decided novelty, which we are sure of once tried, will never be wanting in your garden. The Lettuce is a great beauty, very hand somely curved and fringed leaves, solid fine-shaped heads, very attractive, of white, silvery color. The variety is delicious, crisp and juicy, and of marvelous richness. To solve to run to seed. This sort has won for itself very many friends. It is of such excellent quality that it cannot fail to please the most critical. Pkg., 15c; oz., 30c; ¼ lb., 30c; lb., $1.50.

Golden Ball.

This novelty was obtained in Russia. It is of distinct color, a delicate golden yellow, retaining the same beautiful color to the center, which enhances its value. It is very crisp, tender, of excellent flavor, and is recommended for an early spring crop. It is long standing, remaining fit for eating a long time. Pkg., 15c; oz., ¼ lb., 35c; lb., $1.00, postpaid.

SALZER'S IMPROVED HANSON

EARLY SIMPSON — **SALZER'S PEER OF ALL**

A GRAND TRIO.

25cts 25cts

EARLY MEDIUM LATE

ONLY 25 CTS. FOR THE 3 PACKETS. — 3 PACKETS FOR ONLY 25 CTS.

Salzer's Early Simpson.

Greatly improved, one of the earliest of all Lettuce sorts, especially good for hot bed or hot-frame forcing, or for extremely early in the garden. Very crisp, yellow and tender. This and Salzer's Earliest we love very early. Delicious flavor, rich and curly. Pkg., 10c; oz., 20c; ¼ lb., 35c; lb., $1.00.

Improved Hanson Lettuce.

Unquestionably the very best medium late, hard-head Lettuce grown; indeed, we do not know of a superior in any respect. It forms a very large head, weighs as high as 5 pounds, sweet to the core, tender, crisp, and of the most delicious flavor imaginable. It resists summer droughts and heat to a wonderful degree, and is at all times ready for the table, with a toothy flavor, agreeable and pleasant to the taste. Pkg., 10c; oz., 25c; ¼ lb., 50c; lb., $1.00.

Peer of All Summer Lettuce.

This is a California novelty. The color of outer leaves is a beautiful even crimson. The head is enormous in size, and of excellent, delicious flavor. It withstands all sorts of dry and hot weather, and seems to flourish and store big heads under unfavorable circumstances. It is a grand novelty, and when once tried will become a standard, as it is the "Peer of All" Summer Cabbage Lettuce. Pkg., 10c; oz., 25c; ¼ lb., 50c; lb., $2.00.

1 PACKAGE EACH OF ABOVE—EARLY, MEDIUM, LATE—FOR ONLY 25c; 1 ounce of each 40c.

Mixed Lettuce Seeds—Very popular. It contains all sorts, colors, varieties and kinds, mixed, at but 10c a pkg.; 20c an oz.; ¼ lb., 50c; lb., $1.25.

All-Cream Lettuce.

This remarkable Lettuce does not head, but makes loose bunch of leaves, of superlatively fine quality. It should be in every garden. We have received hundreds of testimonials, all uniting in pronouncing it of extra flavor and remarkable for maintaining its high quality for an unusual length of time. It forms a beautiful plant, 10 to 12 inches high by 9 to 10 inches across; the leaves grow upright, the upper part of the outer leaves turning outward very gracefully, and are handsomely wrinkled. The edges of the outer leaves are of a glossy, reddish bronze, very ornamental and fresh in appearance; within, the leaves are almost white and wonderfully crisp and tender. It grows very quickly; is ready to cut early, and remains for weeks. It is the cream of all sorts. Pkg. 10c; oz. 20c; ¼ lb. 70c; lb. $2.50.

3 Big Head Lettuces for 20 cts.

1. New York Market ... Lettuce

Is a new and remarkable variety, one which is also remarkable for size and solidity of head, often measuring 16 inches in diameter, weighing 3 lbs. It blanches itself naturally, is crisp, very rich, oily, tender, and of excellent flavor and entirely free from bitterness. Pkg. 10c; ½ oz. 30c; oz. 50c; ¼ lb. 90c; lb. $2.50.

2. Salzer's German Butter.

We obtained this strain while in Europe in 1894, and it must not be compared with that offered by other dealers. It is Lettuce that we relished and rejoiced in almost all restaurants and hotels throughout Germany, and is served there never less than twice a day during the season, which seemed to last all summer. It is indeed a fine, buttery, green Lettuce, and we are sure that everybody growing same will be delighted therewith. This must not be confounded with the German Butter Lettuce that is usually sold. Pkg. 10c; oz. 20c; ¼ lb. $1.00; 2 lbs. $3.50.

3. Salzer's Prize Head.

This is one of the finest head Lettuces for all-year-round use in combination is splendid for family. Heads large, solid, tender, blanching perfectly, oily and buttery in look, surcoat of delicious flavor. Must not be confounded with the prize head Lettuce offered by other dealers. This is a finest. Pkg. 5c; oz. 15c; ¼ lb. 50c; lb. $1.35.

One package each of above 3 Big Head Lettuces, 20c.

One ounce each above 3 Big Head Lettuce, 50c.

ovelty.

NEW SUNSET. PKG. 10c.

VED LETTUCE. PKG. 10c.

Lettuces.

l for late fall and winter use mown. Oz. 15c; ¼ lb. 50c; no winter sort; good header h., 50c.

ttuce Sorts.

n standard Lettuce sorts, of these, we offer at only: ; ¼ lb. 30c; lb. 50c.
hich comes to us highly recPkg. 5c.
kg. 10c.
pular head varieties.
mall heads; one of the very ge., 5c.
, sweet and tender; a popuonce known for general use. is a fine cutting Lettuce.
Pkg. 5c.
fell known. Pkg. 5c.

Seed.

red. This is a fine combina$1.25.

GIANT HEAD LETTUCE NOVELTY—GERMAN BUTTER. PKG. 10c.

SALZER'S PRIZE HEAD. A GRAND LETTUCE FOR ALL PURPOSES. PKG. 5c; OZ. 15c.

MUSKMELONS.

Salzer's Melon seeds enjoy a high reputation among seedsmen and others for choice quality, excellence of flavor, strong, vigorous vitality and extra earliness. There is certainly no superior. Planting seed on edge assures quicker and surer growth. To ward off Bugs use Pyrethrum powder.

NEW MUSKMELON, NECTAR OF ANGELS.

It is the most remarkable earliest big Melon of the age. Its quality is superlati[ve], its earliness remarkable, its size enormous for its extreme earliness. This is t[he] Melon that market gardeners, market farmers and those who want to grow Melons f[or] money and profit are looking for; it is the thing for everybody to plant. Its ri[ch] quality, great beauty and wonderful earliness will place it at once in the front ran[k] as the best big early Muskmelon of the age. We are introducing same this year [by] giving away free sample packages, or, if not desired free, we sell same at the pric[e] found at the bottom of this article. Salzer Seed Co. warrant Nectar of Angels to [be] the biggest early Melon on earth!

FREE TO ALL MELON GROWERS.

We wish every Melon grower in America to test this variety, hence we make y[ou] the following offer: For each order of 25c worth of Melon seed you order from us yo[u] get free one package of Nectar of Angels: Thus if you order 25c worth you get fr[ee] one package, if you order 50c worth, 2 packages, if you order $1.00 worth you g[et] 4 packages and so on. If this Melon seed was sold at $1.00 per kernel, it would [be] cheap to get a start.

Price: Package, 15c; 1 oz., 40c; ¼ lb., $1.50; ½ lb., $2.50.

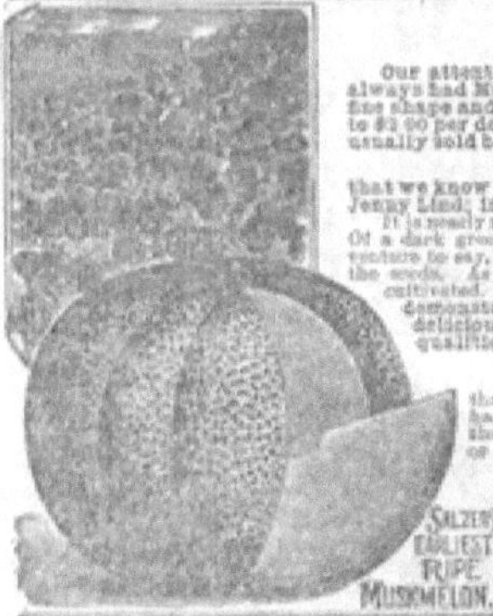

Muskmelon—Earliest Ripe.

Our attention was called to this Melon by a market gardener at La Crosse, who, for the past 4 years, h[as] always had Muskmelons from 8 to 14 days ahead of his neighbors. These Melons were of uniform size, fine shape and appearance, green-fleshed, extremely delicious, and sold readily in our market at from $1.[..] to $2.00 per dozen, the profit on an acre being something enormous, as all the melons were usually sold before the other sorts came into the market.

THIS IS THE EARLIEST GREEN-FLESHED MUSKMELON

that we know of, and it will be sure to create a sensation everywhere. It is ahead of the Jenny Lind; in fact, ahead of any Muskmelon that we know of.

It is nearly round, as may be seen by the cut, of good size, frequently weighing 9 to 11 pounds each. Of a dark green color outside, heavily netted, while inside they are of a rich orange color, and, we venture to say, with thicker flesh than any other variety in cultivation, there being scarcely room for the seeds. As to flavor, they take the lead of all, and are far ahead of everything else at present cultivated. It can be recommended alike for either home or market use, and has fully demonstrated that it deserves the name of EARLIEST RIPE. It surpasses all others in delicious flavor and unusual productiveness, beauty of form and desirable shipping qualities. It has positively demonstrated itself

AS THE EARLIEST MELON IN THE WORLD.

We sold upwards of 25,000 packages of this earliest Melon, and we know we have just that many thousand pleased, delighted, happy Melon growers, and each and everyone who has grown this earliest of all early Muskmelons, praised it ahead of other sorts. We know that this earliest of all early Melons will please everybody growing same, whether growing 1 or 2 hil[ls] or whether growing 20 or 50 or 80 acres.

> "Earliest Ripe is positively the Earliest Melon on Earth."
> So says J. Mauser, market gardener.

If you want to make money on earliest Melons, there is nothing in the wide world that yo[u] can plant that will give quicker returns than Salzer's Earliest Ripe Muskmelon, Salzer['s] Fourth of July and Salzer's Earliest Watermelon.

PRICE OF SALZER'S EARLIEST RIPE MUSKMELON:
Pkg., 10c; oz., 20c; ¼ lb., 50c; lb., $1.50; 3 lbs. (sufficient for 1 acre), $3.50.

3 RARE MELONS, 15c.

1. EARLY HACKENSACK MUSK—Delicious in flavor; un[ri]valed quality; splendid for market; wonderful in yield; pe[r]fection in all. Hard to beat for eating, shipping and selli[ng] qualities. Extremely early, large and prolific. Pkg., 5[c]; oz., 10c; ¼ lb., 25c; lb., 75c; 3 lbs., $1.70.

2. Acme—This is a splendid Melon, especially for shippin[g] purposes; growing to large size; of excellent flavor; goo[d] keeping qualities. Splendid for all purposes. Pkg., 5c; o[z.], 10c; ¼ lb., 20c; lb., 60c; 3 lbs., $1.70.

3. The Osage Melon—In 1886 simultaneously appeared i[n] our Western cities a Melon branded 'Osage,' of a mysteriou[s] delicious flavor. Its origin was unknown, its arrival shroude[d] in mystery, its sale rapid. Men would come and sample [a] Melon, buy one, and return within an hour for more, when th[e] supply was found to have mysteriously disappeared. It's th[e] greatest selling Melon on earth, salmon fleshed. Pkg., 10[c]; oz., 15c; ¼ lb., 30c; lb., $1.00.

One package of each, EARLY HACKENSACK, Acme an[d] THE OSAGE MELON, for only 15c.

Vine Peach or Mango Melon.

The Vine Peach, Vegetable Orange or Mango Melon resembles the Climbing Orange in taste and quality. Pkg., 10c; 3 pkgs., 25c.

Melon—Salzer's Mexican Banana

This is a Banana Melon, of a banana shape, banana flavor, banana color and banana quality; it resembles the banana in many respects, only that it is very much larger. Everybody who is fond of bananas will hail this Melon with delight, particularly so your little boy or girl. Give them the pleasure of growing it. Pkg., 15c; 2 pkgs., 25c; oz., 30c; ¼ lb., 50c; lb., $1.50.

MEXICAN BANANA MELON.

Persian Monarch.

A grand Melon; very large; of delicious quality; flesh almost salmon colored; meat juicy, thick and sweet. Pkg., 10c; oz., 20c; ¼ lb., 50c; lb., $1.50.

Climbing Orange.

The fruit is exact size, color and shape of an orange, of delicious scent. Pared and sliced and fried in butter they are delicious, being equal, if not superior, to Parsnips. For preserves and pies they are splendid, and for mangoes are considered superior to Peppers. Directions wit[h] each package. Pkg., 20c; 3 pkgs., 50c.

MELON PEACH. Pkg., 20c.

Pomegranate.

Similar to Vegetable Orange; of delicious flavor. Fin[e] for pickling. Pkg., 10c.

☞ With each 25c Melon order 1 package, with each $1.00 order 4 packages, Nectar of Angels, the earliest large Melon on Earth.☜

Montreal Market.

The fruit is very deep and regularly ribbed; skin green, densely netted; flesh remarkably thick, light green, melting, and of a delicious flavor. In every way one of the most desirable of all. Mssr. P. Schaubuhler, Dodge City, Kan., says: "Melons as big as half bushel. Just like boy pumpkins—soft, most thick, of the most delicious meat, flavor sweet and juicy." Pkg., 10c; oz., 20c; lb., $1.25.

The Princess.

Color, dark green; the flesh is of a rich salmon color, much thicker than other Muskmelons—and is sweet and luscious beyond description; very early and averages pounds in weight, often producing from 8 to 12 perfect Melons from a seed. Pkg., 5c; oz., 15c; ¼ lb., 20c; lb., 60c.

Rockyford Musk.

The melons of Rockyford, Colorado, are famed. We have two strains, a salmon colored and green fleshed.

Rockyford Salmon.
Rockyford Green Flesh.

{ Price, each sort, pkg., 10c; oz., 15c; ¼ lb., 60c; lb., $2.00.

MONTREAL MARKET. Pkg., 10c; oz., 20c; ¼ lb., 60c; lb., $1.25, 3 lbs., $3.50.

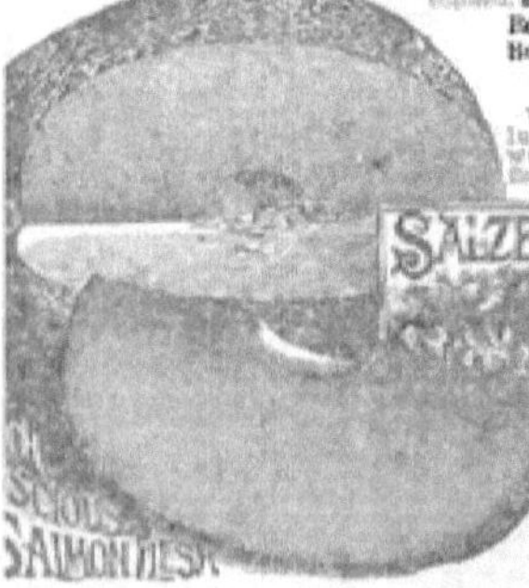

SALZER'S QUEEN OF ALL.

We pronounce Queen of All by all odds the sweetest, most delicious, luscious, richly-flavored, delicate but strongly scented Muskmelon we have ever eaten. The rich, aromatic flavor, the deep gold salmon flesh, solid but juicy, and general beauty and quality of this Queen of Melons is simply indescribable. The rind lustrous deep green, slightly netted, while its deep, thick, rich, salmon colored flesh is luscious, melting and delicious in the extreme. Price of Queen of All. Pkg., 15c; oz., 25c; ¼ lb., 50c; lb., $2.00.

Perfection Muskmelon.

Equally desirable and creditable to the planter of a dozen hills or the planter of tens of thousands. It has been planted by thousands of Melon growers in all sections of the country, and it has given one and all entire satisfaction. Pkg., 5c; oz., 10c; ¼ lb., 20c; lb., 60c.

QUEEN OF ALL, FIG., 25c.

PERFECTION MELON.

EMERALD GEM.

A very early and prolific variety, with a skin which, while it is ribbed, is perfectly smooth and of deep emerald-green color. The flesh, which is thicker than in most other Melons, is of a refined salmon color, exceedingly sweet and delicious. Pkg., 20c; oz., 20c; ¼ lb., 25c; lb., $1.00.

Well-known Muskmelon Sorts.

Price of the 12 Sorts. Pkg., 5c; oz., 10c; ¼ lb., 20c; lb., postpaid.

GREEN NUTMEG—Well known. It is a Melon for everybody, green flesh, thick, and of luscious quality.

WHITE JAPAN—Light skin, thick flesh, early and fine.

IMPROVED CASSABA—Pkg., 5c; oz., 10c.

SILVER-NETTED NUTMEG—Extremely early, nicely and nearly round, and of delicious flavor. Pkg., 5c.

BAY VIEW—Exquisite flavor, green flesh, spicy and very big. Pkg., 5c; oz., 10c.

LONG YELLOW CANTELOUPE—Pkg., 5c; oz., 10c.

ROUND YELLOW CANTELOUPE—Pkg., 5c; oz., 10c.

ORANGE CHRISTIANA—Pkg., 5c; oz., 10c; lb., 75c.

SKILLMAN'S NETTED—Pkg., 5c; oz., 10c; lb., 60c.

EXTRA EARLY CITRON OR NUTMEG—This is a very ly profitable variety to grow for market. In shape it is flat, medium in size, and heavily netted, a capital shipper, very popular.

ARABIAN SWEET MUSKMELON—One of the finest skinless ever introduced. It is very sweet flavored, odorous growth, very large and productive; a Melon for everybody.

JENNY LIND—It is astonishing that this, the most delicious small melon, is so little known. In the east it is so largely grown than any other variety, and thousands of thousands of baskets are annually shipped to New York and Philadelphia markets, where they always come with ready sale. It is one of the earliest. Pkg., 5c; oz., 10c; lb., 75c.

We can supply at above prices also the following: Newport, Irondequoit, Delmonico, Triumph, The Giant Banquet, Grand Rapids, Tip Top, etc., etc. We have sown 100 sorts. Write us for prices on large lots.

PINEAPPLE MUSKMELON.—(A Winter Muskmelon.) The quality is delicious, having a rich, spicy flavor that is not possessed by any other fruit. This and Salzer's Johnson's Christmas Watermelon cannot be excelled. Pkg., 10c; oz., 35c; ¼ lb., $1.00; lb., $3.00.

GOLDEN GEM.

Muskmelon of superlative quality. Pkg., 5c; oz., 20c; ¼ lb., 20c; lb., 75c.

WATERMELONS.

Cheap Standard Watermelon Seeds.

We offer here standard Melon seed at a very low price, because we are large growers ourselves. Hardeners tell us they are better in most cases than the best offered by others, because they are Northern grown.

Price of the following 6 sorts: Pkg., 3c; oz., 7c; ¼ lb., 13c; lb., 35c.

Kolb's Gem Early—Early production, medium size.

Cyclta—Very large, long striped.

Berliner, or Ice Cream—Very sweet and delicious.

Mountain Sweet—The old standard, one of the best.

Black Spanish—An odd, well-known variety.

Citron—For preserves.

We can also supply Cole's Early, the Boss, Cuban Queen, Green and Gold, Mammoth solid, Gray Monarch, Dixie and all other standard varieties of Watermelon, seeds at 5c per oz., ¼ lb. 20c. postpaid. Larger quantities, special prices.

Surprise.

Of round shape. Cream-colored skin of fair size, quite early and a good bearer; flesh salmon color, thick and of fine flavor; a good sort for family use. Oz., 10c; ¼ lb., 20c; lb., 75c.

No. 13, JENNY LIND.

MIXED MUSK MELON SEED.

PICKANINNY MUSKMELON.

We are sure that we have hit upon a popular method of distributing every known variety of Muskmelon seed. We grew last year a great many varieties, and have mixed same, and are offering them at a ridiculously low price, in order to give everybody an opportunity to grow dozens upon dozens of varieties.

Packages of over 200 seeds, 10c; 3 pkgs., 25c; oz., 15c; ¼ lb., 25c; lb., 65c; 5 lbs., $2.50.

Mixed Watermelon Seed.

We offered in a small way, as a premium, last year to several thousand of our customers, mixed Watermelon seeds. These were received and planted with a lively interest, and the reports on same were very flattering indeed, and we have concluded this season to offer same in a large way. These packages contain almost endless varieties of sorts in order to give our customers an opportunity to obtain the very best Melon sorts at a small cost. Of course, for a general crop we would recommend the planting of our Golden Kind Melon, Salzer's Earliest, Fourth of July, Wisconsin Hybrid, etc. In fact very Watermelon sorts on our list is A No. 1. Now, then, this mixture of Melon seed we are sure will please you. Pkg., 10c; 3 pkgs., 25c; oz., 15c; ¼ lb., 25c; lb., 60c.

1. SALZER'S EARLIEST WATERMELON.

There is nothing in the whole wide world quite so good, so luscious, so thoroughly refreshing on a hot July day, or, for that matter, any summer day, as cool, crisp, juicy, delicious Watermelon—one of those superb kinds that can be grown from our Northern-grown seed, all heart and core and but few seeds.

Salzer's Earliest Watermelon.

Absolutely the earliest Watermelon known. Sure to be first in the market. It is of the most delicious flavor, very juicy and sweet. It is pronounced by all who use it "absolutely the earliest," and very salable in the market. It is fit for market ordinarily on a hot July day, or, for that matter, any summer day, as half the time. Everybody should try this superb Melon. Splendid for family use, as a few vines will give you many early Melons. This is the Melon to plant when you are not sure of ripening. We always plant largely of this on that account. They have never failed us. Salzer's Earliest always ripened and brings first luscious Melons. It is a splendid Melon for every purpose—just the size for family use. We like it better each succeeding year, and that is what you want after using it.

Now, then, we have nothing to take back from the above, only to add that Salzer's Earliest still holds the proud, enviable solitary distinction of being absolutely the earliest Watermelon in the world, and its bigger brother, our matchless Fourth of July, is crowding it to the quick, coming in for second prize. In past years we paid out $300.00 in gold on these two Melons—trying to discover which was the earliest. Well, Salzer's Earliest always came in for first prize, but was closely followed by Fourth of July. We have increased Salzer Earliest fully one-half, so that it now bears just the size wanted for market—weighing 15 to 20 lbs. Nothing on the wide, wide, wide earth quite so early as Salzer's Earliest, the peer of all earliest Melons!

Price of Salzer's Earliest Watermelon: Pkg., 10c; oz., 20c; ¼ lb., 50c; 1 lb., $1.50; 2 lbs., $3.75; 5 lbs., $5.25. One package each, Nos. 1 and 2, 15c.

2. SALZER'S NEW FOURTH OF JULY WATERMELON.

There has been a great deal of speculation among seedsmen, and especially among market gardeners, as to whether a Watermelon could be produced that would ripen earlier and at the same time be larger than Salzer's Earliest, as Salzer's Earliest has had the enviable distinction for the past five years of being the earliest Watermelon in cultivation. Now, we think that in our new Fourth of July Melon we have solved this problem, and we are giving to the lovers of Watermelons a Melon as large again, of the most exquisite flavor and taste imaginable, which ripens several days ahead of our Earliest. This is a Melon that is bound to be popular at once.

First—On account of its magnificent quality. There is no Melon, not even the Wisconsin Hybrid, that is superior to it in quality.

Second—On account of its magnificent quality. There is no Melon, not even the Wisconsin Hybrid, that is superior to it in quality.

Third—On account of its size. It is just the size that will sell readily and daily at fancy prices during the early season of the Watermelon market.

When we sent forth this Melon under above description in 1895, we did so, believing that we had the very best thing in early large Watermelons extant, and the many excellent reports which came to us came during the past season fully confirm our belief. Just think of large, fine, luscious Melons, weighing all the way from 30 to 50 lbs., being raised in 45, 50, 52, 55, 58, 60, etc., days. That shows that this one of the crunchiest and positively the best early large Melon grown. We take hold, the past three years, $700.00 in gold in prizes on these two Melons, Salzer Earliest always being a couple of days earlier, but Fourth of July coming in a big, big second, with large luscious Melons. Don't try to get along without the above two early Melons.

Price of Fourth of July Melon: Pkg., 10c; oz., 20c; ¼ lb., 50c; 1 lb., $1.50; 2 lbs., $3.50; 5 lbs. (for 1 acre), $5.00.

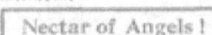

3. Wonderful Sugar Melon.

A new Watermelon; grows 18 inches long, rind yellowish green; shape, oblong. Very large, heavy, and of the sweetest flavor imaginable, hence the name. Pkg., 5c; oz., 10c; ¼ lb., 35c; 1 lb., 75c.

4. Salzer's White Rind Gem.

Here's a secret—don't tell any one. This is the finest Melon for family use extant. Sweet as honey, solid to the core; very juicy; flesh, crimson red. A rare novelty. Pkg., 20c; oz., 20c; ¼ lb., 40c; 1 lb., $1.25.

5. Sweet Heart.

Vine vigorous and productive, ripening early. Fruit large, oval, very heavy, uniformly mottled light and dark green. Flesh bright red, solid and very sweet. Immensely popular in hotels, restaurants and for private table. It is entirely distinct, very sweet, solid, large and early. Pkg., 5c; oz., 10c; ¼ lb., 25c; 1 lb., 60c, postpaid.

SWEET HEART WATERMELON.

Nectar of Angels!
Oh, look me up! Page 55.

6. SALZER'S GOLDEN RIND WATERMELON.

ABSOLUTELY NEW!

This is without question the greatest novelty of the age. There is nothing like it in the vegetable world, nor have we ever seen anything that is so perfect and unique a novelty as this. We paid $300.00 for a single Melon and were glad to get it, because it has always been our aim to give to our customers the finest of all rare vegetable novelties, and we believe that in our Golden Rind Watermelon we have a novelty pre-eminently distinct. It is the round Melon with a smooth beautiful golden rind, the flesh is deep crimson, solid but tender and delicious. It is a great shipping and keeping Melon. It will bear shipping farther than any other Watermelon that we know of. It is a great keeper, specimens having been kept until Christmas in perfection.

Now we wish to tell you a secret. There is no Melon that has ever created such a furore among seedsmen, among Melon growers and others as this, and if you buy seed this year we are sure that you will have a tremendous call for same the next season from your neighbors, for everybody seeing this odd, beautiful unique novelty growing in your garden will want same, no matter what the price, as there is a chance for you to make handsome money.

In 1897 and 1898 this Unique Watermelon Took 1200 First Prizes.

No matter where exhibited, it took first prize, for there is nothing in the Melon world like it in beauty, uniqueness, novelty and handsome appearance. The seed will go in 1899 like wildfire. Everybody will want it. Lots of customers write us they made from $5.00 to $25.00 selling the seed and selling Melons of this rare novelty to their neighbors. Now, you can do the same for 1899. Everybody, yes, everybody, seeing it wants to buy this great sensation of the age. Why, at the Interstate Fair a wealthy lady paid $1.00 for a single Golden Rind Melon, just to take it home! That's the thing. It creates a sensation everywhere. Try it for 1899.

Price: Pkg., 15c; 2 pkgs., 25c; ¼ oz., 40c; oz., 60c; ¼ lb., $3.25.

ABSOLUTELY NEW!

SALZER'S NEW GOLDEN RIND.

One package each of above 6 Wonderful Melons, postpaid, for 50c.
With each 25c order of Melon seed, you get free one package Nectar of Angels. See page 55.

THE TWO GREATEST WATERMELONS ON EARTH!

1. Wisconsin Hybrid Melon.

It is safe to say that 3,000,000 people tasted this grandest of all Watermelons during the past season, for we sold enough seed of same to the great Melon growers for the largest markets of America to raise at least 3,000,000 Melons. In addition to this, over 30,000 of our regular customers of 1892 are ready to attest that this is perfection in Watermelon. Our Wisconsin Hybrid is without a peer in the Watermelon field. It is the finest Melon we have ever grown—delicious flavor, splendid keeper, PEERLESS. It grows uniform in size, very heavy and solid, and is without doubt the best shipping Melon known.

TAKES HIGHEST HONORS WHEREVER EXHIBITED—113 LBS

LOADING WISCONSIN HYBRID FOR SHIPMENT

FIRST PRIZE WISCONSIN HYBRID 113 LBS

It brings 40 per cent higher price in any market than any other sort sold here. We have sampled and grown OVER 100 SORTS of Watermelon, but Wisconsin Hybrid stands immeasurably ahead of them all in all qualities that go to make up a GOOD MELON.

WE WANT TO TELL YOU A SECRET.

Lend us your ears, that is, the ear of the careful, shrewd, wide-awake, sharp, money-making melon growers. The secret is this, that the Wisconsin Hybrid Melon for quality, for richness of flavor, for fine appearance, for uniform big size, leads all other Melons in the world.

H. H. JACOBS, a La Crosse weekly gardener, brought one into our seed house in the early part of August weighing over 60 pounds, and it was positively the most luscious Melon we have ever eaten, and he said he had 1½ acres more of just such giants. Just figure the profit Mr. Jacobs made of 80c apiece. An acre will produce at least 3,000 of such giants. Now, then, be in the swim. While Salzer's Earliest and Fourth of July will pay you big money for earliest, Wisconsin Hybrid will pay you big money for a general crop.

PRICE OF WISCONSIN HYBRID: Pkg., 10c; 3 pkgs., 20c; oz., 25c; ¼ lb., 40c; lb., $1.50; by express, $1.40; 5 lbs., $5.00.

2. SALZER'S OH, MY!
The Greatest Watermelon on Earth.

OH, MY !

Salzer's Wisconsin Hybrid, that prince of Watermelons, which has had an unprecedented sale the past ten years, and whose equal many thought never could again be produced, must give way to our Salzer's Oh, My! Melon. This new Melon is a cross between the Wisconsin Hybrid and several other giant sorts, and attains the deliciousness so peculiar to the Wisconsin Hybrid, and which has been commented upon by thousands and thousands of growers of the Wisconsin Hybrid, and adds to same stronger shipping qualities and larger size. The color of the rind is one peculiar to its own—a very dark brownish green, but its great point of merit for the market garden trade is its uniform extreme size. We believe it to be the uniformly largest early Watermelon in existence to-day. In our latitude by September 1st melons of this variety will have attained the enormous weight of 50 to 95 pounds, and of a quality so rich that it seems to combine every good quality desirable in a Watermelon. It is extremely prolific; indeed, there is no other melon, excepting the Wisconsin Hybrid, that begins to approach it in prolificness. An acre will bear several thousand great Melons, weighing all the way from 30 to 90 pounds, and each fit to set before a king. We believe that in Salzer's

Oh, My! Watermelon and in Wisconsin Hybrid Melon we have the two great Watermelons of the age, and we heartily recommend same to everybody wishing be best that there is in Watermelons in the market or shipping trade. The two sorts are simply immense. They are unexcellable, of giant size, of richest quality, while the vines will remain green longer than of any other variety known to us.

PRICE OF OH, MY! MELON: Package, 10c; oz. 25c; ¼ lb., 45c; lb., $1.50; 5 lbs., $5.50.

1 ounce each of above 2 Great Melons, 35 cts.

City of Mexico Melon.

It is a remarkably productive Melon, from 10 to 17 large Melons being grown from a single kernel of seed. Its eating quality is superior. Its lusciousness is in the extreme. The flesh is of a rich red, solid to the core. It is of a beautiful appearance, and will stand shipping fully 1,000 miles, and sell like hot cakes on its arrival. Splendid for the North. Pkg., 15c; oz., 25c; ¼ lb., 40c; lb., $1.40.

Hungarian Honey.

This sweet-flavored Melon came originally from Hungary. Weigh from 10 to 15 pounds, each, and are almost round. Color of the skin is medium dark green, while the flesh is of a brilliant red color, and absolutely stringless. They ripen early; very productive. Pkg., 5c; oz., 10c; ¼ lb., 25c; lb., 75c.

Ironclad.

It is splendid in all respects; flesh solid, firm and of excellent flavor. It has been grown to weigh 100 pounds. Rind thin and hard. Pkg., 5c; oz., 10c, ¼ lb., 25c; lb., 75c.

Odelia.

This new sort has fairly leaped into popularity. Often weighing 50 pounds. Pkg., 5c; oz., 10c; lb., 75c.

HUNGARIAN HONEY MELON.

SALZERS NORTHERN GROWN

Salzer's Giant Sweet—The Giant of All Giant Melons!

Truly a wonderful Melon; yes, none that can beat it in size, weight and delicious eating qualities. We have grown them reaching enormous size —we will and mention the weight, because we want everybody to try and see the biggest one. It is the giant among Melons—for nothing exceeds it in size—and then the quality is simply delicious, luscious and melting. Just look at the dimensions of our Melon friends in the patch. Tough work to manage them. The largest Pkg., 15c; oz., 25c; ¼ lb., 50c; lb., $1.15.

THE GREAT DUKE JONES.
3. Kolb's Gem.—A Splendid shipper
4. Pride of Georgia.—This stands among children of large—bold and shoulders above
5. Green and Gold.—A great Melon no
6. Egyptian Red.—Grows so enormous
7. Scaly Bark.—A splendid shipper and tough rind which bears a great deal of rough
excellent flavor. Pkg., 5c; oz., 10c; ¼ lb.,
4. Seminole.—Oblong shape, very go
8. Florida's Favorite.—New; enormous large. Rind thin; color dark and light green

Rockyford Long Gr

This is the far-famed Long Green M. 10c; oz., 25c; ¼ lb., 50c; lb., $1.5.
Rockyford Oblong—Largely used in Rybold. Pkg., 5c; oz., 25c; ¼ lb.; 40c; lb
ger Mixed Melon seed, all sorts, ki

With each 25c Melon seed order, 1 package Nectar of Angels Melon free. See

---

BOTTOM ONION SETS

ONION SETS.

The cheapest way to raise Onions is from seed, but thousands of our custome
To these we say, buy a few sets. A quart or two is sufficient for a small family. The
make from 150 to 400 per acre from Bunch Onions, raised from bottom sets.

White Onion Sets—(Bottom.) Pt., 25c; qt., 35c; by express, qt., 30c; pk., $1.10; bu., $3.50. When one variety is exhausted, unless otherwise ordered, we ship another, Thus, if yellow were all gone, we would fill orders with white or red, etc.

Yellow Sets—(Bottom.)—By mail, pt., 25c; qt., 30c; by express, qt., 30c; pk., 90c; bu., $2.75.

Genuine Top, or Bottom Onion Sets—Produce the earliest large onions. Pt., 30c; qt., 40c, postpaid; by express, pk., 80c; bu., $1.50; bu., $2.50.

Red Wethersfield Sets—The great several purpose Onion, the best of all for big yield and keeps too when dry. Pt., 20c qt., 35c, postpaid. By freight, qt., 30c; pk., 80c; bu., $2.50.

For larger lots of Onion Sets, write for special low prices.

SALZER'S TOP ONIONS SETS
BOTTOM SETS

CHIVES—SCHNI

White Multiplier Onion Sets.

They are of a pure silvery white color, enormously productive, frequently producing as many as 20 bulbs in a single cluster from a single bulb planted; of excellent quality and also for bunching grows. Sets always rather large. Their keeping qualities are remarkable, having kept perfectly sound for a year; but their most important quality is **extreme earliness, being ready for market from 1 to 3 weeks ahead of other Onion sets.** Price, by mail, pt., 20c; qt., 35c; by freight or express, qt., 30c; ¼ pk., 65c; pk., $1.25; bu., $4.25.

THE WONDERFUL WHITE MULTIPLIER.

Yellow Multiplier.

A magnificent Onion. Produces Onions of excellent quality. Very early. Greatly like the White Multiplier only not in color. Qt., 35c, postpaid; by freight, qt., 30c; pk., $1.25; bu., $4.50.

SALZER'S IMPROVED RED WETHERSFIELD ONION.

The careful Onion grower knows that the Onion is one of the most important of culinary vegetables. They like a strong, deep and rich, loamy soil. The ground should be well dressed with well-rotted manure, trenched deeply. Sow as early as the ground is in working condition sow thinly. Draw drills 1 inches apart, and sow at the rate of 4 pounds to an acre. Keep the ground clear of weeds. There is only one really good seed onion for onion sowing, and that is Salzer's Northern Combine, illustrated and described on page 26 of this catalog. Should the stock of Onion seed become exhausted, we do not know why other seedsmen, fill pound orders at lowest market prices. Our stock of Onion seed is raised with peculiar care. None but the best Onions are selected for seed stock, and great care is exercised in the cultivation. We claim for it a quality superior to that offered by seedsmen, either grown in the North, is worth sixty-five pounds more to the purchaser—that is, if you want big crops of fine Onions. When stocks are exhausted, we fill at market prices.

This is our specialty. It is the grandest Red Onion for general crop grown. There is no seed equal to it in yield, in keeping qualities, in fine flavor, and for market. From every section of America come glowing letters of the success our customers had with this splendid Onion, sweeping every state and county fair before them. One raised from 1 ounce, 38 bushels; another, 200 bushels from 1 pound; a third, over 1,000 bushels per acre. These glorious yields gladden the heart, delight the eye and fill the purse, you can have by sowing Salzer's Northern-Grown Onion Seeds. It pays to sow Salzer's Improved Onion Seeds. Salzer's Improved Red Wethersfield is a splendid Onion; it grows large, solid, fine shape, excellent flavor, delightful color, is a remarkable keeper and an enormous yielder, just the Onion for the farmer, for everybody, the great general purpose Onion.

Now, Then! Salzer's Improved Red Wethersfield is one of the easiest to grow, is certainly one of the best keeping Onions, and is always of excellent quality. It is the greatest average big cropper among Onions.

1,213 Bushels Salzer's Red Wethersfield Onions Per Acre!

Is it possible that from an Onion the enormous yield of 1,213 bushels per acre can be expected? That's the question many American farmers and gardeners who have not used

OUR METHOD.

How I Grow 1,213 Bushels of Salzer's Improved Red Wethersfield Onions per acre will ask. Yes, it is not only possible, but you and every other planter, can realize this fond dream. You can grow on your own land 1213 bushels Salzer's Red Wethersfield Onions, the great general purpose Onion, by following our directions and by using Salzer Seeds. And you can grow this big crop, with but little investment, than you can grow an ordinary one of 104 bushels or so. Use Salzer's Seeds and Salzer's Methods. (Method sent with each package, colors or larger quantity ordered.) Onion seed, on account of the prolonged drouth, is not of so high germination as ordinarily, but care in the test. Why is Salzer's Improved Red Wethersfield Onion so superior, so possible, so high in quality? Simply by years of care and selection we have "bred it up" to the high standard, breed it up as carefully as the finest stock—the graded horse, or cow or sheep are bred up. It has taken years of pains and care and lots of money to do it—but the result is—the finest Red Onion in the wide, wide world.

IT'S THE GREAT MONEY MAKING ONION.

No Onion that we know will make you more money and do it easier than Salzer's Great Wethersfield. It's the great money maker because it is so heavy a yielder, and all Onions are so fine that they sell at good prices in all markets!

Thos. H. McCulloch, of Mason City, Iowa, under date of March 27th, writes: "Last season I sowed an acre of Onions with seed I purchased of you, the Yellow Globe Danvers and the Red Wethersfield,—and although the spring was late, wet and cold, still the seed germinated well, and I had a fine stand and good crop, and sold the crop in Chicago in November for $420.00 net."

It is without question that Salzer's Red Wethersfield Onion strain is the greatest cropping red Onion in America today, and we urge everybody to give it a test. The price is in the reach of all, how, and no such money can be made, that we look forward to the largest trade in this variety of Onion that we have ever had. The Onion is sure to please, easy to grow, sure to return a big yield, sure to sell quickly in any market, sure to keep long, and sure to please the housewife. When a seedsman tells you that his strain is "just as good," our experience shows it can be doubted just 50 per cent. Our Wisconsin grown strain beats the world! It would be cheap at three times the price.

Pkg., 10c; oz., 30c; ¼ lb., 90c; lb., $1.00; 4 lbs., $3.75. By express or freight, 10 cents a pound less.

Common Red Wethersfield as is offered by seedsmen as long as present stock lasts. Pkg., 30; oz., 7c; ¼ lb., 25c.

SEE REAR COVER FOR ILLUSTRATION OF SALZER'S IMPROVED RED WETHERSFIELD—THIS NOBLE ONION.

ONION SETS.
PAGE 59.

For Protection Please Read

TO PROTECT OURSELVES AND OUR PATRONS.

It is a fact that last year a goodly number of parties in Rockford, Chicago, Philadelphia, Minnesota and elsewhere offered cheap French and picked-up Chinese grown California Onion seed at low prices. Now this Onion seed was sent out in competition with our high-grade pedigree Wisconsin grown stocks. The result was that the low prices attracted some of our customers who bought their Onion seed from them.

Now, to protect ourselves we have purchased a small quantity from the same growers in France and California. In order to meet their low prices we are offering these at exact cost. The seed is sold for just what it is; no guarantee, of course. French and California grown, under the title, "Low-Priced Onion Seed."

THE CAREFUL ONION GROWER.

PLEASE READ AND NOTE THIS CAREFULLY.

All prices in this catalogue on Onion seed that do not call for **Low-Priced Onion Seed** are for our pedigree Onion seed stock, thus Salzer's King of the Earliest, Salzer's Autumn King, and others of our specialties, which no other seedsman has or can obtain from us, we have only the **PEDIGREE** stock, as we grow these ourselves, but of the common variety, such as Red Wethersfield, Yellow Globe Danvers, Flat Danvers, Silver King, Prizetaker, etc., we have a "Low-Priced Onion Seed" stock.

There is one big satisfaction when you buy these **Low-Priced Onion Seeds** of us, you get the best that France or these California growers produce, but for our own planting we would take Salzer's pedigree stock every time.

SALZER'S KING OF THE EARLIEST ONION.

We never tire in chanting the praises of this Onion. We believe we do a kindness to every patron and everybody whom we induce to purchase and plant this Onion, and put them on the track of making money. It was but yesterday that a good, bright gardener walked into our office and sincerely thanked us for advising and inducing him to sow Salzer's King of the Earliest Onion last spring, as also for the instruction and advice we gave him.

When we introduced this Onion 8 years ago, we had no idea it would spring so suddenly into popularity, for to-day there is no Onion grown in the North, or in the West or South, which is higher reputed than our King of the Earliest. After repeated and impartial trials this Onion has proved superior to all in **earliness and excellent qualities**, which stamps it absolutely the very earliest fine grade, fine quality, large red Onion grown. In our latitude it has frequently been ripe to sell by July 1st, when Onions invariably bring $1.00 to $2.00 per bushel, and that pays. The Onion matures quickly from seed, is of fine shape, beautiful rich red color, varying from globe to round flat, is of mild flavor, and ripens at a time when Onions command a high price. It is unquestionably the largest, handsomest, finest flavored, best shaped, finest keeping, most superior early red Onion ever introduced, and is an Onion that will sell on its merits in any market. It is the most profitable Onion in the world to grow.

If Any Seedsman or Merchant or Anybody Offers You an Onion

Just as good as Salzer's King of the Earliest, you can put him down for a trifler with the truth. Now, this is strong language, indeed, but it is the truth. There is no Onion offered in the world as good, and no seedsman has this type and cannot get it from us for love or money, because we must keep the best in the world for our own customers. We know that last year many seedsmen said they had an Onion just as early as our earliest (but they had not) and the result was a great many were defrauded by buying their cheap stock.

"HOW TO GROW 1,233 BU. PER ACRE" FREE, WITH EACH OZ. OR LARGER QUANTITY.

Price of King of the Earliest: Pkg., 10c; oz., 20c; ¼ lb., 50c; lb., $1.60; 4 lbs., $6.00, postpaid; by express, pkg., 10c; oz., 20c; ¼ lb., 45c; lb., $1.50; 4 lbs., $5.60.

Salzer's Wisconsin-Grown Pedigree Yellow Globe Danvers Onion Seed beats the world in yield.

Yellow Globe Danvers.

There are sections of New York State and the East where the Yellow Globe Danvers Onion is grown exclusively, and to which we usually ship several thousand pounds of Onion seed. Our strain is par excellence.

The Danvers Yellow Onions are known the world over as fine, great heavy cropping varieties.

This is a splendid yellow Onion. It is an enormous cropper, often yielding 800, 900, and even 1,000 bushels per acre with ordinary care, when the soil and climate are propitious. Now, this is profitable. The great value in the Danvers Yellow Globe is beauty of form, delightful flavor, splendid shipping and keeping qualities. Keep until new Onions arrive. A rapid seller in the market. It is an excellent family Onion. Each bulb is large, full and plump, all on account of our good climate, rich deep soil, and large, carefully selected Onion bulbs planted. Our stock of this magnificent Onion is indeed fine, all grown from selected bulbs, and will please the most critical market gardener's trade.

Salzer's Pedigree Stock: Pkg., 10c; oz., 20c; ¼ lb., 35c; lb., $1.25; 4 lbs., $4.75. By express, pkg., 10c; oz., 20c; ¼ lb., 30c; lb., $1.15; 4 lbs., $4.45.

Low-priced Onion Seed: Pkg., 5c; oz., 8c; ¼ lb., 20c; lb., 75c.

FLAT DANVERS ONION.

Flat Danvers Yellow Onion.

Many growers prefer this to the Globe Danvers, as ordinarily it is a very heavy cropper. It is a fine Onion, one you are sure to be pleased with, and the price is very low. Well known, a heavy yielder, a splendid keeper, beautiful appearance, and sells readily in all markets. Pkg., 5c; oz., 15c; ¼ lb., 30c; lb., $1.00; 4 lbs., $3.75.

LOW-PRICED ONION SEED (right up to Chicago and Minneapolis stocks): Pkg., 3c; oz., 7c; ¼ lb., 20c.

Prize Danvers.

A magnificent yellow Onion, flat to round, very prolific. Of it John L. Rath, Michigan, grew from 1 pound of seed 282 bushels, and says he might have had 300 bushels only it was too dry. C. L. Jansen, Missouri, grew from ¼ pound of seed, using our new method of "How to Grow 1,000 Bushels per Acre," 124 bushels and 10 pounds of fine large Onions. L. L. Larios, Wis., cropped 20½ bushels from 1 ounce seed, and E. C. Page, Penn., 24¼ bushels. J. C. Eldridge, Iowa, 22¼ bushels, and C. A. Hunt, Minn., 18¼ bushel, all from 1 ounce of seed!

Salzer's Pedigree Stock: Pkg., 5c; oz., 10c; ¼ lb., 30c; lb., $1.00; 4 lbs., $3.75; 10 lbs., by express, $8.00.

PRIZE DANVERS.

SALZER'S IMPROVED RED WETHERSFIELD, THE GREAT GENERAL PURPOSE ONION, AND HOW 1,218 BUSHELS CAN BE GROWN PER ACRE. SEE PAGE 60 AND REAR COVER.

3 GIANTS.

I. Salzer's Giant Silver King Onion.

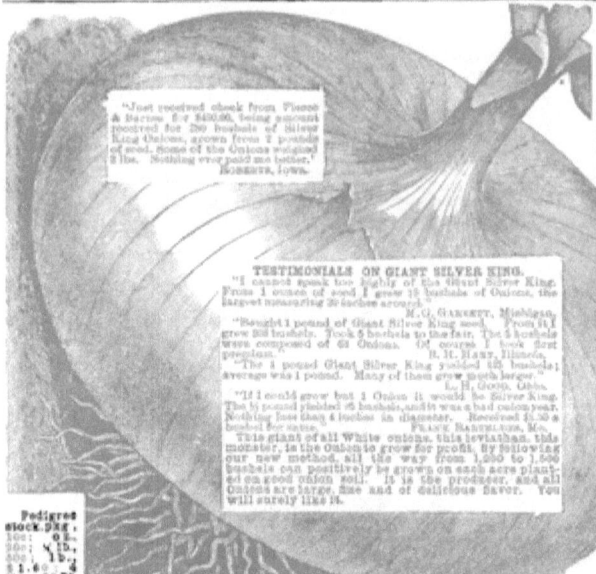

"Just received check from Pierce & Barrow for $450.00, being amount received for 260 bushels of Silver King Onions, grown from 7 pounds of seed. Some of the Onions weighed 2 lbs. Nothing ever paid me better."
ROBERTS, Iowa.

TESTIMONIALS ON GIANT SILVER KING.

"I cannot speak too highly of the Giant Silver King. From 1 ounce of seed I grew 18 bushels of Onions, the largest measuring 20 inches around."
H.G. GARKETT, Michigan.

"Bought 1 pound of Giant Silver King seed. From it I grew 300 bushels. Took 5 bushels to the fair. The 5 bushels were composed of 61 Onions. Of course I took first premium."
R.H. GLAZE, Illinois.

"The 1 pound Giant Silver King yielded 125 bushels; average was 1 pound. Many of them grew much larger."
L.H. GOOD, Ohio.

"If I could grow but 1 Onion it would be Silver King. The ½ pound yielded 95 bushels, and it was a bad onion year. Nothing less than 4 inches in diameter. Received $1.50 a bushel for same."
FRANK BAINBRIDGE, Ind.

This giant of all White onions, this leviathan, this monster, is the Onion to grow for profit. By following our new method, all the way from 1,200 to 1,500 bushels can positively be grown on each acre planted as good onion soil. It is the producer, and all Onions are large, fine and of delicious flavor. You will surely like it.

Pedigreed stock. Pkg.
1oz. . . . . 05.
2oz. . . . . 1oz.
4oz. . . . . ½
$1.60
1 lb. $5.75,
postpaid

With each succeeding year the popularity of this Onion increases, and it not only increases, but gardeners, farmers and truckmen grow more enthusiastic in its praise, and well they may, for this great Onion deserves every word of praise that can be spoken. Although we offered Silver King for the first time in 1896, we do not believe any other variety of vegetable, excepting our Giant Flat Dutch and Lightning Cabbage, has in ten years' time been more unanimously endorsed by one and all everywhere. We received thousands of letters and postals the past season, all containing words of the highest praise AS TO THE WONDERFUL SIZE, EARLY MATURITY AND QUALITY OF THIS NOW FAMOUS ONION, seed of which we have sold to tens of thousands of our customers. It grows larger than any other White Onion in cultivation. Bulbs are of attractive shape, flattened but thick through, as shown in illustration. Average diameter of onions from 5 to 7 inches; bulbs often attain weight of 2½ to 4 lbs. each. No other White Onion attains such mammoth size, nor will any other white variety grow uniformly so large. Skin is beautiful silvery white; flesh of particularly mild and pleasant flavor; so sweet and tender that it can be eaten raw like an apple. Every one desiring the largest and handsomest Onions of the finest flavor will be more than satisfied with the Silver King. Cannot be too highly recommended either for family use, exhibition at fairs and restaurants, or for sale in market, where the size and beauty will prove very striking. If you have not already sown Silver King, you should not neglect to sow it another year. It's the onion for everybody, but especially for the city garden. Over 100,000 gardeners found it to equal and surpass all the claims here in made. An ounce of Onion Seed, with our new method of culture, would give you 50 bu. Giant Silver King Onions.

PRICE OF THE GREAT GIANT SILVER KING ONION, HIGHEST GRADE—Pkg. 10c; oz. 20c; ¼ lb. 50c; lb. $1.60; 2 lbs. $3.00; 4 lbs. $5.75, postpaid; by express or freight, pkg. 10c; oz. 20c; ¼ lb. 45c; lb. $1.50; 2 lbs. $2.80; 4 lbs. $5.55.
LOW-PRICED SILVER KING ONION SEED: Pkg. 5c; oz. 15c; ¼ lb. 40c; lb. $1.25, postpaid.

2. Prizetaker Onions.

First offered in 1888, and it proved to be the greatest acquisition in years. The largest, handsomest, finest flavored most superior Yellow Globe Onion ever introduced. This simply magnificent Onion is certainly a wonder. There has never been an Onion in the United States that could equal it, and we believe it will supplant all other Yellow Globe Onions now in cultivation as soon as its sterling qualities are known, for it is certainly perfection. Of a clear, bright straw color, it always grows to a uniform shape, which is a perfect globe. It has a very small neck and always ripens up hard and fine, without any stiff necks. In market it attracts marked attention, and, although only offered to a limited extent, has always been picked out and selected at three times the price of any other sort on sale, either red, white or yellow. Produces 1,200 and more bushels per acre; keeping qualities are excellent, in spring the bulbs being apparently as firm and solid as when cut away in the fall.

1898 Produces an Onion Weighing 6 lbs. 5 oz.!

Can anything beat that? Farm and Fireside contained the following notice written by JOSEPH: "The King of all Onions. The greatest novelty in years, and the King of all Yellow Globe Onions. It is ahead of any domestic Onion I have ever seen, and finer than anything I ever expected to grow. If you want to see what the Onion looks like, go to the nearest fruit store and behold the Spanish Onion on sale at 5c or more a pound. There is no reason why the 'Prizetaker' should not take the place of the imported bulb, and be sold at a high price. The two varieties cannot be told apart. Here is a chance for the progressive Onion grower that he cannot afford to neglect, for there is money in it. The name 'Prizetaker,' although not very elegant, is, nevertheless, quite appropriately selected. Any fair, average specimen will take the prize at an exhibition against the finest specimens of other sorts. It is seldom, very seldom, that we come across a novelty that marks such a long step in advance in the culture of vegetables. Besides being a 'Prizetaker,' it will also prove to be a 'Pricetaker.'" A word to the wise is sufficient.

PRICE: Pkg. 10c; oz. 20c; ¼ lb. 50c; lb. $1.60; 2 lbs. $3.00; 4 lbs. $5.75; by express or freight, pkg. 10c; oz. 20c; ¼ lb. 35c; lb. $1.50; 2 lbs. $3.00; 4 lbs. $5.50.
LOW-PRICED ONION SEED OF PRIZETAKER ONION—Pkg. 5c; oz. 15c; ¼ lb. 40c; lb. $1.30.

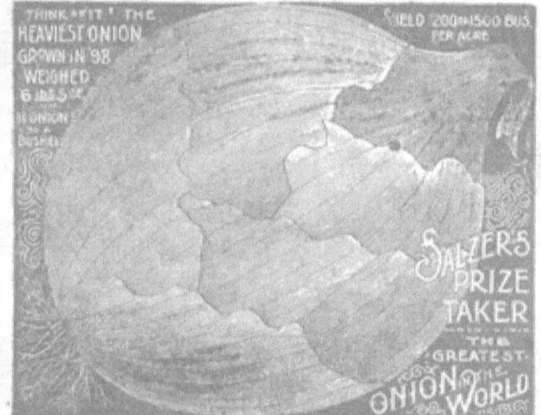

THINK OF IT! THE HEAVIEST ONION GROWN IN '98 WEIGHED 6 lbs 5 oz

YIELD 1200 to 1500 BUS PER ACRE

SALZER'S PRIZE TAKER THE GREATEST ONION in the WORLD

3. Salzer's Gladiator Onion.

This new variety is the largest and most popular Onion grown in Spain. It possesses the large size, mild flavor, excellent keeping and all other good qualities of the celebrated Prizetaker, but differs from that variety in its handsome skin, which, in contrast with its pure white, fine-grained flesh, attracts marked attention in market. We believe there is a great future here for this Onion, as, instead of the tops dying down or running to seed, as is the case with American varieties, it keeps on growing the entire season, thus attaining enormous weight and dimensions. A number of specimens sent by customers had attained a weight of 6 lbs. Pkg. 10c; oz. 20c; ¼ lb. 50c; lb. $2.00; 2 lbs. $3.00; 4 lbs. $5.75.

1 package each above 3 Giant Onions.				10c.
¼ ounce	"	"	3	"	45c.
¼ pound	"	"	3	"	$1.25.
	"	"	3	"	$4.50.

View of One of Salzer's **WHITE MILDNESS** Onion Fields, Growing Onion Bulbs for Seed Purposes.

New Onion—White Mildness.

Offered for the first time in 1896. This is the Onion to grow for your private garden or for high-grade, high-class, city customers, because they will pay you double the price for this handsome one, white, mild American variety of Onion. It originated with us in Wisconsin, keeps long and well indeed, we have kept tubers in handsome appearance for 12 months. It is very prolific, yielding 800 bushels to the acre. We know of no Onion that we can more heartily recommend for the kitchen garden than this.

It's an Onion for the epicure; its fine, rich quality commends itself to everyone who desires a rare deliciously flavored Onion. Its fine shape, beautiful color and delightful flavor stamp it as one of the very best.

Pkg., 10c; oz., 20c; ¼ lb., 75c; lb., $2.50; 4 lbs., $8.00. postpaid.

Onion Sets.
See Page 56.

White Globe.

A large, globe-shaped Onion, firm, fine-grained, of mild flavor, keeps well. This is one of the handsomest Onions grown. Of beautiful shape, clear white skin.
Pkg., 5c; oz., 30c; ¼ lb., 60c; lb., $2.25.

Extra Early Red Globe.

This variety matures early. It yields abundantly, is of mild flavor, and a good keeper, of medium size, deep red in color; very close grained, solid and heavy. Pkg., 5c; oz., 30c; ¼ lb., 50c; lb., $1.65.

Salzer's Autumn King Onion.

Salzer's Autumn King Onion is so beautiful as a picture—large, fine, roundish flat in shape, and enormously, yes, wonderously, productive. The Onion is large, just the size for general market, and just the size to produce the past year; the bushels per acre easily by following our new method of Onion culture, and 1,515 bushels on 1 acre. For fall it is superlative; indeed, it is one of the very best fall Onions we know of, and the fact that you can produce 1,515 bushels per acre with ease, combined with its beauty and quality, places it at once in the front rank of Yellow Onions.

Let Us Stop and Do a Little Reckoning.

Say you plant 2 acres of King of the Earliest and 5 acres Autumn King, let us see what they will do for you:

Two acres King of the Earliest Onion, at 600 bushels (new method), equals 1,200 bushels, or at a bushel, $1,200.00.

Five acres Autumn King, for late, 900 bushels (new method), equals 4,500 bushels, 6; but at a bushel, $1,800.00.

Or a total of $2,800.00 on 7 acres, and these 7 acres under our new method of Onion culture can be made to produce above yields anywhere.

Now, then, friend, here's a chance to make money for the coming year, and why not do it? We honestly believe that Onions will command a big price next fall. Your neighbor, and lots of your neighbors, are not going to plant Onions and that's your chance. Now, this is the time for you to plant plenty, and in planting plenty you will make money.

HOW TO GROW 1,215 BUSHELS OR MORE ONIONS PER ACRE.

These directions we think will positively give you 1,215 or more on each and every acre planted, if the season is favorable. These directions are sent with each ounce order or more of Autumn King Onion seed you buy.

Price of Salzer's Great Autumn King Onion.

Pkg., 10c; oz., 20c; ¼ lb., 35c; lb., $1.30; 4 lbs., $5.00; by express, lb., $1.20; 4 lbs., $4.60; 10 lbs., $10.00.

Late Red Globe.

This is the Standard Red Globe Onion. Not as prolific as Salzer's Red Wethersfield, but a fine Onion throughout. It is grown in the East in preference to Red Wethersfield. Yield is often 600 bushels per acre. Stock scarce. Pkg., 5c; oz., 30c; ¼ lb., 70c; lb., $2.50.

New Queen.

The earliest, finest of all white Onions. A perfect queen in the field of delicious flavor. Grows to 5 inches in diameter, sells rapidly in market; none earlier. It's a splendid Onion, sells well everywhere, is well liked by everybody, and succeeds splendidly in all soils and climes. Note the low price. Pkg., 5c; oz., 20c; ¼ lb., 75c; lb., $2.50.
LOW-PRICED NEW QUEEN—Pkg., 4c; oz., 15c; ¼ lb., 35c; lb., $1.25.

Salzer's 60-Day Onion.

A new white, small of early, gentle flavored Onion from Italy, ready to ripen enormously in 50 to 60 days. Watches all the handsome features of this early novelty. Try it. Pkg., 10c; oz., 25c; ¼ lb., 90c; lb., $3.00.

Italian Onions.

MAMMOTH POMPEII

Do well in every part of the United States. The following sorts grow the first year to 2 inches in diameter. If these bulbs are planted a second season they frequently reach the size of 6 inches.

Mammoth Pompeii—A wonderful Onion of enormous size and mild flavor. Pkg., 10c; oz., 30c; ¼ lb., 70c; lb., $2.25.

Giant Rocco—A splendid, large, globeshaped Onion; color bright; brown; readily produces Onions weighing 2 pounds from seed first year. Pkg., 5c; oz., 30c; ¼ lb., 60c; lb., $2.00.

Giant White Tripoli—Excellent variety, of mild flavor, rapid growth; almost 2 pounds from seed first year, and 4 pounds the second, Pkg., 5c; oz., 30c; ¼ lb., 60c; lb., $2.00.

Early White Naples—One of the earliest of the white Italian sorts. Pkg., 5c; oz., 25c; ¼ lb., 60c; lb., $2.25.

Marzajole—A capital keeper, large, beautiful white, flat-shaped, mild, fine flavor, big cropper. Pkg., 5c; oz., 30c; ¼ lb., 60c; lb., $2.25.

Giant Tripoli—A grand, deep red Italian Onion, of rapid growth, mild flavor, good keeping qualities and large yield; 1½ pounds grows from seed the first year, the second year growing to 4 pounds. Pkg., 5c; oz., 30c; ¼ lb., 75c; lb., $2.25.

SALZER'S PICKLING ONION

Salzer's Pickling Onion.

This is the finest of all white pickling Onions, growing rapidly, but remaining small, solid and of fine flavor. Three crops can be gathered for this purpose in one season. Pkg., 10c; oz., $1.50; 10 lbs., $12.50.

☞ THE GREAT GENERAL PURPOSE ONION IS FOUND ON REAR COVER AND ON PAGE 60. ☜

PARSNIPS.

Sow early in the spring, 15 inches apart, covering half an inch deep. They improve by frost, and can be left in the ground all winter. Five pounds seed to the acre.

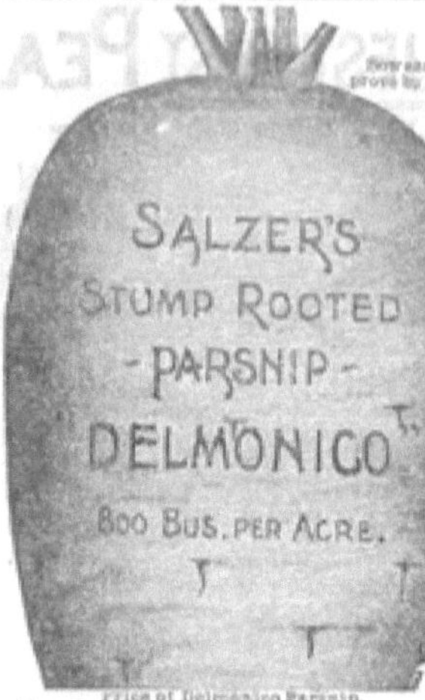

Salzer's Delmonico.

For many years the trade wished for a stump-rooted or half-long variety of Parsnip. We are pleased that our efforts have been crowned with success, and we offer this year our Delmonico Parsnip, believing it will be the most enormous, prolific and most profitable variety to grow. It is in a large measure a stump-rooted—just the thing the market gardener desires. It has very large roots, not long, while the flavor is all that can be wished for. They are easily watered, the roots being smooth, then very fine grade, and of excellent flavor. They are sure they will give great satisfaction to everybody that will try same. It is enormously productive and just the sort to give satisfaction.

HOW THEY LIKE DELMONICO.

Missouri—"Your Delmonico Parsnip paid me over $260.00

Ohio—"I planted 1 lb. Parsnips; sold half in the fall, the balance last spring. I paid $1.00 for the seed and received $98.00 back

New York—"Well, I am glad to write you that your Delmonico Parsnip yielded 800 lbs. per acre. I sold my crop for $260.00. Could have had more had I held till winter.

There is no doubt about it. Parsnips pay; especially Delmonico and Salzer's Crown. Try them.

Price of Delmonico Parsnip: Pkg., 10c; oz., 20c; ¼ lb., 50c; 1 lb., $1.00; 4 lbs., $3.00, postpaid.

Salzer's Crown Parsnip.

This is without doubt the finest, heaviest yielding, best flavored parsnip grown. It grows to a large size, is sugary, and is a relished article of food. The yield from 800 to 600 bus. per acre. Sow 4 to 5 lbs. of this sort per acre. Pkg., 5c; oz., 10c; ¼ lb., 20c; lb., 50c; 4 lbs., $2.00, postpaid.

Long Sugar—Splendid sort.

Student—Much liked; excellent flavor. For years this was the standard Parsnip, but now Delmonico and Salzer's Crown take the lead.

Price of Long Sugar or Student: Pkg., 5c; oz., 10c; ¼ lb., 15c; lb., 15c; 5 lbs., by express, $1.50.

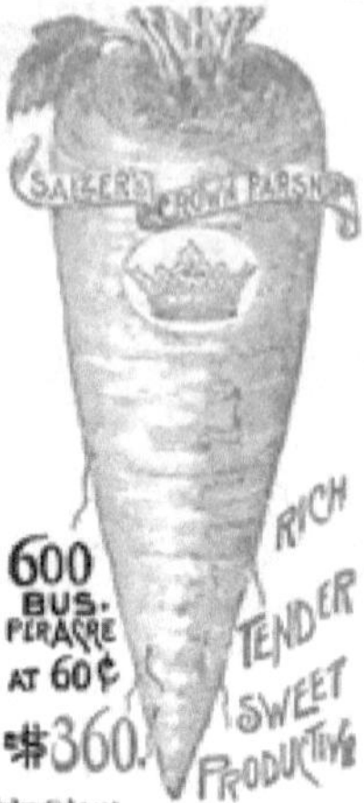

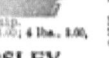

Price of Delmonico Parsnip. Pkg., 10c; oz., 20c; ¼ lb., 50c; lb., $1.00; 4 lbs., $3.00, postpaid; 50 lbs., by express, $6.00.

STUDENT PARSNIP.

PARSLEY.

A package of seeds will give enough plants to use all summer for soups, and garnishing for winter. Used in tremendous quantities for garnishing. No dish is quite perfect and artistic unless it contains a few sprigs of Double Moss Curled Parsley.

Moss Curled—Very fine and curled. Pkg., 5c; oz., 10c; ¼ lb., 20c; lb., 60c.

Fern Leaf—Pkg., 5c; oz., 10c; ¼ lb., 25c.

Plain—Excellent for sheep. Pkg., 5c; lb., 50c.

Turnip-Rooted—Pkg., 5c; oz., 10c; lb., $1.00.

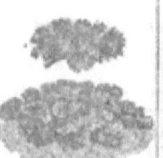

SALZER'S DOUBLE MOSS CURLED PARSLEY

MOSS CURLED PARSLEY.

Double Moss Curled. The handsomest of all finely curled. The Parsley for family use, on account of the fine-curled leaves and luxuriant growth. You will be sure to like it; this is used in enormous quantities. Nearly every order received from every customer is sure to call for one or more packages of this precious Parsley. It is always found in Mrs. Salzer's kitchen garden. It is unrivalled. Pkg., 10c; oz., 25c; ¼ lb., 50c; lb., $1.25.

Price: Pkg., 50c; oz., 25c; ¼ lb., 50c; lb., $1.25.

PEANUTS.

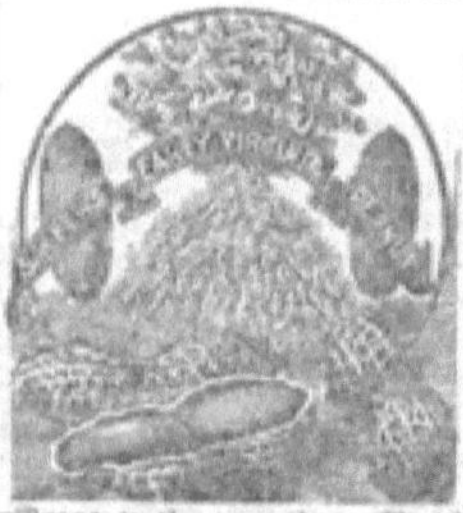

Early Virginia.

This remarkable variety combines the following good qualities, viz: earliness, size and prolificness. It does not require a rich soil. Its extreme earliness makes it a paying crop in the North. It ripened for us at La Crosse to perfection, yielding enormously. Now, it is the simplest thing, dear boys and girls, to grow Peanuts for the long winter months, and lots of fun besides, and an interest in the garden and on the farm. Pkg., 5c; pt., 35c; qt., 45c; 2 qts., 75c, postpaid.

New Spanish Peanut.

A new, very early and desirable variety, with upright foliage; planted by the end of April they ripen before Sept. 1st. It will pay to try them everywhere. Plant 2 inches deep, 10 inches in the row. Pkg., 20c; pt., 25c; qt., 40c, by mail.

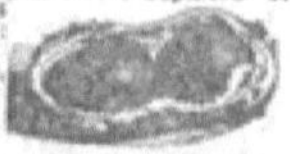

"Peanut Culture," a small booklet, 10c. Postpaid.

NEW SPANISH PEANUT.

Pieplant or Rhubarb Seed.

Nothing is easier to raise from seed than Pieplant. We have two splendid sorts:

Salzer's Giant. Very large, produces Pieplant the second year after seeding. Pkg., 10c; oz., 20c; ¼ lb., 75c; lb., $2.50.

Linnæus Rhubarb. A variety of Rhubarb that is in great demand, and is largely sold in the east. Pkg., 5c; oz., 10c; ¼ lb., 50c; lb., $1.50, postpaid. Pieplant roots.

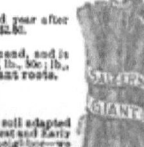

SALZER'S GIANT

SPLENDID PEAS.

The best paying crop for a market gardener is early peas. Seed is grown with unusual care (no suckers allowed to mature), on soil adapted to producing the best of Peas, and the result is there is no earlier Pea in America than Salzer's Scorcher, Salzer's Earliest and Best and Early May. There is more money in the early Peas—by early Peas we mean Peas ripened in the market just 8 to 10 days ahead of your neighbors—we say there is more money in such early Peas than in any other early vegetable grown on open land. Why, we have a gardener right here who made $500.00 last year from 1 acre of our Earliest and Best Peas—because they were just 8 days ahead of every other early sort about here. If that can be done on Earliest and Best, what will Salzer's Scorcher do—ripe in 30-30 days?

Dwarf Profusion Pea.

One of the earliest Peas with large pod. It grows rapidly, is very dwarf, is full of pods, and every pod is full of peas, ripening all at the same time. Pkg., 10c; ½ pt., 20c; pt., 30c; qt., 50c, postpaid; by express, pkg., 10c; pt., 15c; qt., 25c; pk., $2.50; bu., $4.75.

SALZER'S DWARF PROFUSION PEA

Notts' Excelsior.

A new extra early, extra dwarf, extra finely flavored, extra sweet kerneled, extra large podded Pea. It's taking the country by storm. Pkg., 10c; pt., 25c; qt., 40c, postpaid; by express, qt., 20c; pk., $1.25; bu., $4.00.

Salzer's Earliest and Best Pea.

This is our favorite early Pea; indeed, it is our first love. We consider it an old friend of ours, as it has been with us for the past 20 years. When we were market gardening in La Crosse, this Pea never disappointed us. It was always the first, the best, and the earliest in the La Crosse market, and many a dollar did we receive for its sale. We do not know of any Pea that is superior or would give the market gardener more profit and a greater sale than this variety. There is certainly no Pea offered by seedsmen to-day and we have tested them all that can equal it in earliness and uniformity of ripeness.

We do not remember, during 20 years, one instance when earlier Peas were ever brought into the La Crosse market than ours. We always offered the first, from the fact that our variety was fully 8 to 10 days ahead of the earliest. We have tried Landreth's Extra Early, Berpee's Extra Early, Henderson's First of All, Vick's Early, but all were behind our Earliest and Best. This Pea is early, growing from 18 to 20 inches high, a fine cropper, and of excellent flavor, and all who have tried it are emphatic in pronouncing it the very earliest, best favored Pea grown.

Of Course, Every Seedsman

Claims to have the earliest Pea—but the wide-awake gardener can't be thus fooled. For over 20 years this Pea was the earliest in the La Crosse market, and we keep right on improving it, and we challenge the world to produce an earlier, finer, more productive sort. (Of course, Salzer's Scorcher is earlier.) Frank Coburn, of Iowa, reports the enormous yield of 11,371 perfect pods from 1 pint of seed. Now, honestly, would you expect a Pea to be better? It is the Pea for early, for big yield and good quality.

We are shipping this to market gardeners in Philadelphia, New York, Chicago, Cleveland, St. Louis, St. Paul, Omaha, Kansas City, Detroit, Milwaukee, London, Liverpool, Paris, Berlin and other large cities, and when once used is grown to the exclusion of all "earliest" sorts by all market farmers and gardeners.

PLEASE NOTE THE LOW PRICE OF "EARLIEST AND BEST," GRANDEST OF ALL PEAS.

We have reduced the price of this Pea by the bushel, and hope thereby to introduce it into every market gardener's hands in America, for we believe that when they once try our Earliest and Best Pea, they will want no other for extremely early. Market gardeners have told us that they have secured from £50 to £60 bushels of green Peas per acre of this variety, selling them from £2.00 to £2.25 per bushel, as they are always earlier than their neighbors'. We urge everybody to try it.

By mail, pkg., 10c; ½ pt., 20c; pt., 30c; qt., 45c; by express, pkg., 10c; pt., 15c; qt., 30c; pk., $1.00; bu., $3.75; 5 bu., $17.50.

Salzer's Wonderful Dwarf Early May Pea.

This is a grand new blue dwarf wrinkled Pea. It is extremely dwarf, growing from 10 to 17 inches, and literally fills itself with large pods ripening evenly and of excellent flavor. It is very early—earlier than American Wonder,—testing in 45 days. When once tried, no other dwarf sort will be grown.

We know that all who try this Pea will agree with the words of a pleased patron by saying, "I do not exaggerate when I say that this is the very best dwarf Pea to grow in a family garden for the table that I ever saw. I congratulate you in placing a pea of its remarkable character before the American people, and I predict for it a bright future."

Its strong points are its delicious richness of flavor; its extreme earliness; its dwarf habit, needing no brushing, and its large-sized pod. We have sent out the past 6 years many thousand packages and to many thousand customers in America and Europe, and everywhere our customers are delighted with same. One of its distinctive features is its unusually regular habit of growth. It is of uniform bright, so smooth and level in its growth that a row resembles a well-kept hedge. It is also a magnificent variety for market gardeners to grow, as the pods are large, it fills up a bushel quickly, and brings a very fine price in market.

PRICE OF EARLY MAY PEA: By mail, pkg., 10c; ½ pt., 18c; pt., 30c; qt., 45c; pk., $3.25. By express, pkg., 10c; pt., 15c; qt., 30c; pk., $1.00; bu., $3.00; 2½ bu., $9.00.

SALZER'S "SCORCHER." THE EARLIEST PEA IN THE WORLD. READY FOR MARKET IN 30 DAYS.

SALZER'S "SCORCHER" READY TO PICK

OTHERS FIRST OF ALL ONLY IN BLOOM

SALZER'S SCORCHER PEA.

Stand aside; clear the track for the earliest Pea in the world! This is what the John A. Salzer Seed Co. have been after for years, and with this in view every earliest sort obtainable was tested and every improvement through hybridization and crossin : was made in order to attain these results, and to-day, w...

We Have Absolutely the Earliest Pea in the World in Salzer's Scorcher.

Now, if you will just stop to think what it really means to plant Peas to-day and have them ready and fit for eating in but 400 hours or 25 days you will quickly see the tremendous importance of this great improvement. Why, it is not more than ten years ago when it took Peas from 60 to 75 days to be fit for market. We took that record with Salzer's Earliest and Best and with Salzer's Early May, the two greatest early Peas grown in America the past five years, but in Salzer's Scorcher these two above-named magnificent varieties must take a back seat, they must clear the track, for Salzer's Scorcher is ahead of them in earliness. Now, we challenge the world, we challenge any and every seedsman in America, we challenge every market gardener or private gardener in America to produce a Pea as early as Salzer's Scorcher. We are positive that there is no Pea like it in America today. The ripening time of the first and most sorts, such as are offered by Philadelphia, New York, Chicago, St. Paul and Rockford seedsmen, is about 52 days. The average ripening time of Salzer's Scorcher Pea, tested by upwards of 500 customers in 1896, was a trifle over 34 days, or fully 18 days ahead of the earliest Peas that other seedsmen offer. There is not a dream of fancy, but a fact, a fact that you can demonstrate for yourself by planting a package or more of Salzer's Scorcher Pea. Here are a few of the 500 customers who tested this Pea in 1896, and above we give the result, the average of same being less than 34 days.

days....			days....		
Mrs. P. N. Pope..	De Quoin, Ill.		Chr. Schneerman,		Koehler, Pa.
J. W. Brueggeman..	New Bremen, Ohio.		Mrs. M. C. Small..		Halmerville, Ala.
J. Biselalli....	San Antonio, Tex.		Jacob Reed..		Eldorado, Kan.
John Berthold..	Partridge, Kan.		Ellis L. Crosby..		Manchester, Ia.
Henry Staehen..	Mt. Vernon, Ind.		Wm. Pease........		Rowe's Ferry, Va.
R. S. Scott.....	Pottsville, Ky.		M. Campbell........		Fountain Run, Ky.
May E. Lindsinger	Hemple, Mo.		Frank Hutchinson..		Thorntown, Ind.
F. R. Iverhart..	Mt. Carroll, Ill.		E. Johansson......		Wichita, Kan.

Now this Pea is the earliest in the world. The color is blue, the pod is large, of extremely beautiful appearance, full of large, fine peas, ripening quickly. This is the Pea to plant for money making. You can make three out of a quart of these Peas than you can out of a peck of such evenly varieties as other seedsmen sell, because these Peas will dress in the market about as soon as Southern Peas which are shipped North. We know that you will be delighted with this Pea in every respect. The flavor is superior, the quality cannot be beat, while in earliness it runs from 12 to 24 days ahead of any other seedsman's early. We recommend that you make a good planting of Salzer's Scorcher, then have Salzer's Earliest and Best for second, and Early May for third, and other sorts for later use. The fact is that Salzer's Scorcher Pea can be planted and sold before any other earliest Pea is fit for use, and Salzer's Earliest and Best can also be planted and sold before other seedsmen's early are ready. We leave it, for we make "earliest vegetables" our special specialty. The above illustration is a true and lifting one of this peerless Pea.

Price, by mail, pkg., 10c; ¼ pt., 25c; pt., 35c; qt., 45c; by express, pint, 30c; pt., 20c; qt., 35c; peck, $1.25. ¼ bu., $2.25; bu., $4.00; 2 bu., $7.00.

When writing to any of above-named parties, always inclose 2c stamp **for reply.**

SUGAR PEAS.

Over in Germany, and, in fact, in England and throughout Europe, no Pea is higher prized than the Sugar varieties. These are considered there, and, in fact, everywhere, when eaten tender, cooked, the greatest of delicacy. In the country districts of England it is served with a tender piece of Southdown mutton, and then served in a dish fit for a king. There is no Pea whose flavor equals the exquisiteness of the Sugar Peas. The pods and all are cooked, and the dish thus prepared needs no equal.

Dwarf Sugar.

One of the very best Sugar Peas grown. It is from 6 to 10 days earlier than the Tall or Mammoth Sugar Pea. Pkg., 20c; pt., 30c; qt., 50c, postpaid; by express, qt., 40c; pk., $2.00.

Tall or Mammoth Sugar Pea.

Salzer's Peas are the earliest in the world! Grows 3 to 5 feet tall, and bears immensely large, juicy pods of sweet, edible Peas, of the richest, most delicate flavor. Both Tall and Dwarf Sugar Peas are highly flavored. Pkg., 10c; pt., 30c; qt., 50c, postpaid; by express, pk., $2.00.

MARROWFAT PEAS.

We are often asked for a cheap, heavy bearing, arge summer and fall Pea. We always recommend the Marrowfats. thee the white or black-seed—both are good; yield abundantly; are very free from mildew, and are splendid for market, selling at good prices on account of their size and quality. For Canada Field Peas, see Farm Department.

Black-Eye Marrowfat—Pkg., 5c; qt., postpaid, 35c; by express or freight, qt., 15c; pk., 75c; bu., $2.00; 2 bu., $3.75.

White-Eye Marrowfat—Pkg., 5c; qt., postpaid, 35c; by express or freight, qt., 15c; pk., 75c; bu., $2.00; 2 bu., $3.75.

MAMMOTH SUGAR PEA.

A FIELD OF SHARPS QUEEN.

Sharps Queen.

This is a Pea of recent introduction, coming to us from England, where for many years Peas have been grown to such rare perfection. We have tested same for a number of years and find it A No. 1 in every respect. It follows Earliest and Best and Early May in ripening. It is of vigorous branching habit and grows from 2½ to 3 feet tall, pods are long and well filled with large Peas of excellent flavor. A most desirable Pea, and will be greatly appreciated by the market garden trade.

Price: Pkg. 20c; pt., 25c; qt., 40c, postpaid. By express, qt., 25c; pk., $1.25; bu., $4.25.

New Pea, Salzer's Midsummer.

This is a Pea that we have all been looking for for many years. It is one ripening at all times when Peas are scarce, that is before such varieties as Telephone, Stratagem, etc., ripen. It is a Pea attaining a height of fully 3 feet with long, well filled pods, of a delicious excellent quality, which are usually borne in pairs. It is a very healthy variety. Its vines grow robust, quickly, and are filled with magnificent pods. The beauty about these pods is that they are filled to the end with large peas and fill a bushel basket remarkably quick. We believe that Midsummer Pea will be hailed with great delight by all market gardeners and small planters on account of its rare quality and on account of its coming at a time when other Peas are scarce. We urge everybody to give same a trial. The vines measure 3 feet in height, are literally covered from top to bottom with handsome, well filled pods, which are usually filled with 10 to 12 very large Peas of superior flavor and rich quality, keeping in a good condition for a long time. This is a rare variety.

PRICE: Pkg., 10c; pt., 25c; qt., 50c, postpaid. By express, pt., 15c; qt., 30c; ½ pk., 75c; pk., $1.40; bu., $4.90.

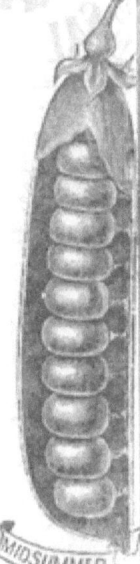

MIDSUMMER

FOUR FINE MAIN CROP PEAS.

TELEPHONE — THE BEST GENERAL CROP PEA IN THE WORLD

1. Telephone.
It is immensely productive of the finest quality and excellent sugary flavor vine strong, averaging 18 to 20 pods. The grandest tall Pea grown that close holding flavor of flat, tall pods from one kernel planted. It is very prolific and very fine for all purposes.
Price of Telephone Pea: Pkg., 10c; pt., 25c; qt. 40c.
By express, qt., 25c pk., $1.25; bu., $4.00.

2. Bliss Everbearing.
Late dwarf variety, of robust growth, forming sometimes as many as 10 branches from a single stalk; pods 3 to 4 inches long, containing 6 to 8 large wrinkled Peas, often half an inch in diameter, rich and marrowy. Continues remarkably in bearing, producing new blossoms after repeated picking until frost. Podded 3 bushels from ⅓ pint of seed. Pkg., 20c; 2 for 25c; pk., 35c; qt., 35c; pk., $1.15; bu., $5.00.

3. Horsford's Market Garden.
This is a wrinkled Pea grows from 15 to 20 inches high, is very stocky and requires no bushing. It is very sweet and extremely prolific, bearing pods always in pairs. On some plants over 150 pods have been counted.
Pkg., 10c; qt., 50c.
By express, qt., 25c; pk., $1.15; bu., $4.25.

4. Stratagem.
Vines about two feet in height, sturdy growth, bearing great pods from the ground to the tips. Very fine indeed.
Pkg., 10c; pt., 20c; qt., 50c.
By express, qt., 25c; pk., $1.50; bu., $6.00.

3 Early Dwarf Sorts.

THE WELL-KNOWN TOM THUMB.

Any of the following three Dwarf Early Sorts, by mail, pkg., 10c; pt., 20c; qt., 35c; by express, pt., 15c; qt., 20c; pk., $1.25; bu., $4.50.

1. Tom Thumb.—This is the best known Pea in the country; indeed for years it has been the standard early dwarf; smooth, even ripening Pea; is much sought for. Pkg., 10c.
2. American Wonder.—It is unquestionably one of the best for family use. It is a green, wrinkled Pea; large pods; very early; dwarf growth, and of delicious flavor. Pkg., 10c.
3. McLean's Little Gem.—It is very productive, has large, well-filled, thickly hanging pods of delicious Peas. Matures a week later than our Peerless Early May. Pkg., 10c.
Above 3 Dwarf Sorts Mixed.—The 3 sorts in one package, 10c; pt., 20c, by mail. By express, pk., mixed, $1.25.

HENDERSON'S HEROINE PEA.

Everyone who sees it wants it—seedsmen, market gardener and amateur. It is far superior to all other varieties of Peas, and it combines quantity and quality to a degree possessed by no other variety. The Heroine is a medium early, green wrinkled Pea, grows uniformly about 2½ feet high, and is literally covered with its long, heavy, pointed pods—in fact, so striking and distinct is this variety that it would be picked out at once in a field of 100 other varieties. The quality of this Pea is simply perfection—that rich, buttery, marrow-like flavor for which the Pea grown in the gardens of Old England are celebrated.
PRICE: Pkg., 10c; pt., 30c; qt., 50c; pk., $1.50; bu., $5.50.

CHEAP—Standard Peas.—CHEAP.

The price of the following 11 sorts by mail: Pkg., 5c; pt., 15c; qt., 25c; by express, pkg., 5c; pt., 20c; qt., 20c; pk., 80c; bu., $2.50.
1. Royal New Yorker.—Claimed to be the earliest.
2. Cleveland's Alaska.—Said to be one of the earliest Peas grown.
3. Improved Kent.—Is the finest second early Pea; pods unusually large and full, borne in great abundance; grows 2½ feet high.
4. Abundance.—Second early. Vines from 15 to 20 inches in height, sending out 6 or more branches from the root, each one heavily laden; pods long, containing long, wrinkled Peas of delicious flavor, $1.50.
5. Champion of England.—A superior late general crop sort.
6. Carter's First Crop.—One of the earliest.
7. McLean's Advancer.—Ripens 2 weeks earlier than the Champion of England; a magnificent wrinkled sort; productive; only 2½ feet high.
8. Blue Peter.—Dwarf, 10 inches, large pods; one of the earliest dwarf.
9. Prince of Wales.—The finest Pea grown for a general crop; wrinkled, branching habit.
10. Maud S.—Very fine and recommended by many as early.
11. First and Best.—Philadelphia, New York, Chicago, Rockford, St. Louis, St. Paul and other seedsmen's very earliest—about 6 to 15 days later than Salzer's Earliest and Best and Salzer's Scorcher.
We can supply another Pea sort at above prices, as we have all seedsmen's varieties in stock.

PEPPERS

Great quantities of Peppers are now used in the United States. We have hit on this plan of mixing all sorts together and selling at but 10c a package. This plan proved immensely popular last season. *See below.*

A PLANT OF RUBY KING PEPPER. THE FINEST PEPPER IN THE WORLD. PKG., 10C.

Ruby King—We hope all who grow red Peppers will try this splendid new variety. We recommend same heartily as the most profitable to grow for all purposes. It is unequaled, remarkably mild and pleasant to the taste, enormously productive, all its fruit handsome, frequently 6 inches long, producing from 15 to 25 large Peppers. Color, bright ruby red. Pkg., 10c; oz., 25c; ¼ lb., $1.00; lb., $3.00.

New Golden Dawn—In shape it resembles the Bull Nose, except that it is a little more pointed on the end; in color it is a beautiful gold en yellow. It is very sweet, not the slightest suspicion of a fiery flavor. Pkg., 10c; oz., 40c; ¼ lb., $1.50.

Long Red—Similar to the yellow, only bright red in color. Pkg., 5c; oz., 30c; ¼ lb., 75c.

Red Cranberry—Grow like Red Cranberries; very odd and fine. Pkg., 10c.

Red Chili—For pickling; small. Pkg., 5c; oz., 50c; lb., $2.00.

Cayenne—Long, fine. Pkg., 5c; oz., 30c; lb., $2.50.

Long Yellow—Of excellent flavor; good size and yield. Pkg., 5c; oz., 30c; ¼ lb., 75c.

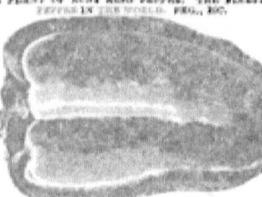

SALZER'S GIANT PEPPER. PKG., 20C.

This is the largest of all Peppers. Splendid for all purposes. Pkg., 20c; ½ oz., 20c; oz., 35c; ¼ lb., $1.00.

Mountain Sweet—Like above, only much larger. Pkg., 5c; oz., 25c; lb., $1.50.

Tobacco—A new Pepper novelty of translucent quality, richness and pungency. Pkg., 10c; oz., 50c.

Sweet Spanish—Mild flesh; early. Pkg., 5c; oz., 25c; lb., $3.00.

Red Cluster Pepper.

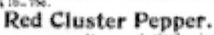

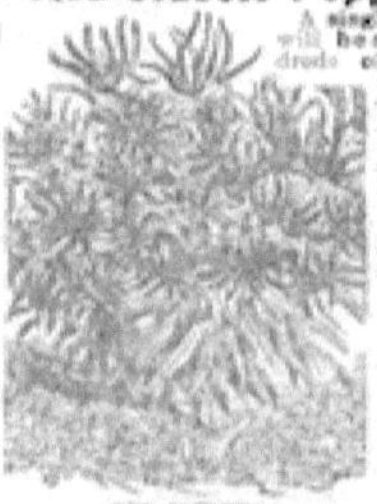

RED CLUSTER.

A single plant will bear hundreds of coral red colored; handsome little Peppers, which are very hot and pungent in flavor. Pkg., 10c; oz., 30c.

CAYENNE.

One of the very best. Pkg., 5c; oz., 30c; lb., $2.00.

Large Bell.

LARGE BELL.

Coral Gem.

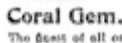

The finest of all ornamental Peppers; of sharp, pungent taste; 1,500 to 2,000 Peppers have been counted on one plant. Fine for pickling. Pkg., 10c.

MOUNTAIN SWEET PEPPER. OZ., 25C.

Mixed Pepper Seed.

All sorts carefully mixed. This gives you an opportunity of growing all varieties at a small expense. The mixture is par excellence. You will like it. Is immensely popular, for as thousands of our customers are ready to attest, you are sure to like this mixture of all kinds of Peppers, and watch the many Peppers how they grow. Pkg., 15c; oz., 60c; ¼ lb., $1.00.

New Celestial Pepper.

From China. Extremely ornamental. It is wondrously productive, 40 Peppers having been counted on a single branch. Until fully ripe they are of a delicate creamy yellow, then suddenly change to an intense, vivid scarlet. All carried upright. Pkg., 10c; oz., 40c.

Procopp's Giant.

A great Pepper. Almost as large as Ruby King, but not so large as Salzer's Giant. Pkg., 10c; ½ oz., 25c; oz., 40c; ¼ lb., $1.00.

PEPPER, PROCOPP'S GIANT. PKG., 10C.

RADISHES.

One of the most profitable crops to grow, for the market gardener and market farmer, as also for the private garden, is Radishes. There is no vegetable that is a better appetizer for breakfast than a fine, juicy Radish. In Europe these are served in restaurants with every meal, and enormous quantities are thus used. All that is required to bring them into constant demand in America is to furnish an early, good Radish. Our Northern-grown stock always produces the finest, best-eating Radishes.

2 Rare New Radishes.

EARLIEST SNOW WHITE ICE.   BLOOD RED SNOW WHITE TIPPED.

1.   Earliest Snow White Ice.

Here's the Radish that will bring you joy. Its par excellence in each and every respect. Its color is pure white, almost crystal, so clear and transparent. Its quality is superlative; it cannot be excelled except, perhaps, by Salzer's far-famed Early Bird Radish. It has a short top, is very rapid growing, fit for use in but 14 days, and sells at sight at an advanced price in all markets when once known.
Price: Pkg., 10c; oz., 20c; ¼ lb., 50c; 1 lb., $1.25.

2.   Blood Red Snow White Tip.

The Radish of your dream! It is beautiful in the extreme. It's lovely scarlet color points off to a pure white at the tip, giving it a delightful appearance. It's perfection itself when judged by quality and earliness. It's a producer. Each seed produces a fine, large, tender, juicy, delicious, very early Radish! These two new Radishes added to Salzer's famed Early Bird Radishes—all beautifully illustrated on rear of this catalogue—are three sorts hard to beat! Pkg., 10c; oz., 20c; ¼ lb., 50c; 1 lb., $1.25.

☞ One package each above two and Early Bird—in all 3 packages—for 20c; 1 ounce each, 35c; ¼ lb. each, $1.60.

NEW RADISH--SALZER'S EARLY BIRD.

Try the earliest
Radish in the
World.

"It is the early bird that catches the worm," goes the saying, and it is the market gardener who brings in the early vegetables to the market who catches the most money, or, in other words, makes the best profit out of his investment. For years in our market gardener trade, this was one of the main sources of income to us. In our new Radish, Salzer's Early Bird, we are sure we have the earliest Scarlet Globe Radish grown. The shape is regular, of rich scarlet color. The fruit is remarkably tender crisp and delicious, never becoming hollow or pithy. It is most desirable for forcing, being fit to pull in less time from sowing than any other turnip variety. It is alike valuable for out-door planting for spring, or in autumn, and will always command a good price throughout the year. It will not disappoint a single market gardener wherever it, but will be a source of genuine pleasure and profit. We know of none of our vegetables that will pay the market gardener better, and for the kitchen garden, than Salzer's Early Bird Radish. This is the earliest, the finest, the handsomest in shape of any early turnip Radish known to the trade at present.

READ EXTRACTS FROM LETTERS:

"From all my customers comes but one cry-'More Salzer's Early Bird Radishes!'" —S. F. Pittsburgh, Pa.

"Are fine Early Bird; or in days after planting. That's good enough."—Mrs. C. G. E. Evanston.

"My wife says the fine Radishes we are now using are 10-day Early Birds."—F. A. H., Nashville.

"Made more money on the 30 lbs. Early Bird Radish than on all others together, as I grow mainly Radishes for New York Market."—Geo. W., Long Island.

"Earliest, finest Radish I ever saw."—R. D. Columbus, O.

"Ripe and fit for use in 10 days."—H. Y. New York.

HERE'S A RED-HOT LETTER.

"To JOHN A. SALZER SEED CO. DEAR SIRS: That neighbor of a gardener, _____ in Illinois, advertises that his Radish was as early as your Early Bird. He is a liar! I got excited every time I think of it. The earliest? It is 12 days, (behind in earliness, and 10 years behind in quality of your Early Bird. I thought 1 lb. because he was so cheap, I do, but I lost both by it. His Radish was no good." R. T. Wis.

On our grounds at LaCrosse we had fine Radishes fit for the table (out-door grown) in 12 DAYS FROM PLANTING, and such fine Radishes, too!

Large, tender, delicious. Why, they are a month longer than Radishes need to grow in hot-beds 12 years ago in 21 days! Such Wonder! Improvements have been made in Radishes. We are sure none will be ahead of Salzer's Early Bird.

Now, the substance of the whole matter is this: If you are at all anxious, either as a market gardener or as a grower of Radishes for your own private table, to have Radishes from 6 to 12 days ahead of your neighbor, and if you are anxious to have the finest Radish that seed can produce, even under most adverse circumstances, then by all means plant Salzer's Early Bird. Its crisp, brittle flavor, as well as its remarkably good growth and fine color, alike recommend it. The color of the skin is a rich scarlet, while the flesh is pure white, of such mild flavor—always crisp, juicy, tender and delicious. As it has a very small, short top, it is equally valuable for forcing or open ground. In favorable weather maturing Radishes in about 6 days, and if we ate our Radishes in America as small as they do in France, this variety would produce Radishes fit for the table in 10 days. It is the Radish wonder.

Price of Salzer's Early Bird Radish: Pkg., 10c; 3 for 25c; oz. 20c; ¼ lb., 50c; lb. $1.35; 3 lbs., $3.00; 10 lbs., $9.00.

PRICE OF SALZER'S THREE GREAT EARLIEST RADISHES.

1 Package of Salzer's Famed Early Bird Radishes, 10c
1 Package of Salzer's Earliest Snow White Red, 10c
1 Package of Salzer's Blood Red, Snow White Tipped, 10c

The three packages to one address for 25c
1 ounce of each of these 3 sorts for 50c
¼ lb. of each of these 3 sorts for $1.00

SALZER'S EARLIEST WHITE RADISH.

We are very glad to be able to offer our customers this most remarkable white, olive-shaped Radish that we are fortunately able to secure in France, from one of the most prominent firms of French seed growers. This pure, white, olive-shaped Radish is earlier than any other Radish, red, white or any other color. When we state that good sized Radishes can be pulled in from 12 to 15 days from the sowing of the seed, all our friends will realize what a remarkable variety it must be. Has a small top, is solid, of crisp flavor, and in every other respect is a first class Radish. This is only the second year it has been offered in America, and seed is still scarce. Our friends, one and all, should not neglect to try it. Pkg., 10c; oz., 20c; ¼ lb., 50c; lb., $1.25.

SALZER'S EARLIEST WHITE RADISH, 10c.

Salzer's Earliest.

This is one of the earliest, finest, juiciest, tenderest, sweetest, best Radishes for early use grown. From 4 to 6 days ahead of the earliest varieties offered by Eastern seedsmen. Rich red in color. While this variety is not as early as the Early Bird, nor as fine, yet it has been before our customers so long that many of them prefer this to any of the earlier varieties offered by other seedsmen; indeed we believe it to be earlier than any turnip variety offered by other dealers. We have distributed over 100,000 packages of this variety and have yet to hear the first complaint on same, which proves that it must be A No. 1 in every respect. Pkg., 5c; oz., 10c; ¼ lb., 25c; lb., 90c.

All-Year Round.

Over 50,000 patrons who had sample packages agree that this by all odds the finest, sweetest, juiciest, tenderest, handsomest long white Radish grown. Grows very quickly, is crisp, and contains its excellent qualities throughout all weather, intense heat or cold. It is pure white, large size, a splendid early spring sort, a summer sort, a fall sort, a winter sort. No matter whether grown in the hotbed or in the open ground, it always turns out to be the best white Radish in existence. If you buy it once you will never, never, never go along without it. Pkg., 5c; oz., 10c; ¼ lb., 25c; lb., 90c.

SALZER'S EARLY ROSY MORN RADISH

Early Rosy Morn Radish.

A delicious Radish, splendid for all purposes on account of its earliness, its crispness and beauty; it sells readily and quickly in any market, and where once grown will be grown always. You are sure to like this seed. Pkg., 5c; oz., 10c; ¼ lb., 25c; lb., $1.35.

MIXED RADISH SEED—All sorts, kinds, colors and varieties. Pkg., 10c; oz., 15c; ¼ lb., 25c; lb. 75c.

SALZER'S · SPLENDID · RADISHES · FOR · ALL · THE · YEAR · ROUND

Erfurt Dark Red.

A superb new dark red early Radish for all purposes. At our market Radishes of this sort sold from 25 to 50 per cent. higher than any other sort. Crisp and tender. Pkg. 5c; oz. 10c; ½ lb. 30c; lb. 50c.

Salzer's 18 Day.

Our new 18 Day is a magnificent, deep scarlet, oblong to round shaped, tender, crisp, short-leaved, quick-growing, quick-selling variety, that is absolutely ahead of all others in earliness. Pkg. 10c; oz. 15c; ¼ lb. 60c; lb. $1.25; 5lbs. $5.00.

THE GREAT FORCING RADISH.
SALZER'S 18 DAY FORCING

Chartier's Radish.

Scarlet at top, shading to pure white at tip; very showy. Somewhat changeable in color and particular as to culture. Good at all stages. Samples grow to the length of 39 inches, crisp and tender. Pkg. 5c; oz. 10c; ¼ lb. 20c; lb. 35c.

Salzer's Long Scarlet.

Some 50,000 of our customers use this variety to their entire satisfaction. It has a bright red appearance, very brittle, crisp and tender; a splendid sort for market and family use. This is the great family Radish, and is A No. 1 for skipping purposes. The long Radishes, averaging 7 inches in length, made into bunches, have a very fine appearance and sell readily on account of the quality. The Salzer Long Scarlet Radish must not be confounded with many that are offered, because it is entirely different, the quality being so much better. The flavor is exceptionally fine. Sure to please the most critical taste. Pkg. 10c; oz. 15c; ¼lb. 30c; lb. 50c.

White Lady Finger.

A magnificent long, white fleshed, tender, crisp and delicious. Pkg. 5c; oz. 10c; ¼lb. 30c; lb. $1.00.

Early Sorts.

Prices of the following eight sorts, by mail, free: Pkg. 5c; oz., Pkg; ¼lb. 20c; lb. 40c; by express, pkg., 5c; oz., 10c; ¼ lb., 15c; lb. 40c.

1. Scarlet Turnip—Known the world over as the standard and early Scarlet Turnip Radish.
2. Wood's Early Frame—One of the very earliest.
3. French Breakfast—Olive shaped; red, white tip.
4. Scarlet Turnip—White tip. Red red. Very early.
5. Scarlet Olive—Very handsome dark red color.
6. Half Long Deep Scarlet—Splendid sorts.
7. Early White Olive Shaped—Very fine indeed.
8. Shepard—Long; very knobbed.

Any 3 Pkg's of these 8 sorts, 10c.

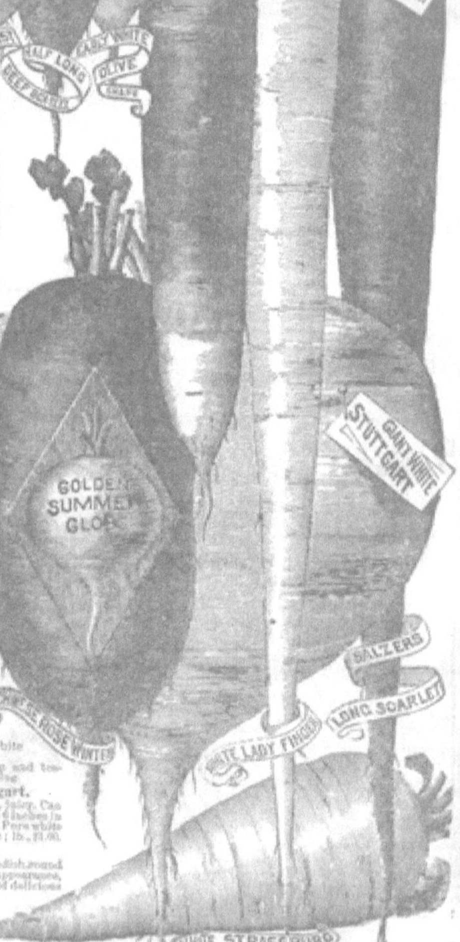

Summer Sorts.

The following Radishes, except when noted, by mail, free, Pkg., 5c; oz., 10c; ¼lb., 20c; lb., 40c.

Golden Summer Globe—directly prized for its excellent tender graphic.

White Turnip—A good white sort, largely grown.

Long White Naples—Crisp and tender. Good for summer planting.

Giant White Stuttgart.

Very large; bulb firm; firm, juicy. Can be used at any stage. Grows 4 inches in diameter. Splendid for family. Pure white. Pkg., 10c; ½ pkgs. lbs. oz., 30c; lb., $1.00.

Winter Sorts.

Alaska—A good winter Radish, round to oblong in shape, dark in appearance, while the flesh is pure white, of delicious flavor. It will keep in a cellar from fall to June. It will pay everybody to give it a trial. A package is sufficient for a family. Pkg., 10c; oz., 15c; ¼lb. 30c; lb. 50c.

Mammoth California—Mammoth tender white Winter Radish. If sown early, it is good for summer use. Pkg., 5c; oz., 10c; ¼lb. 30c; lb. 50c.

China Rose—Best sort of this magnificent rose colored, white flesh, Winter Radish. Pkg. 10c; oz., 15c; ¼lb. 30c; lb. 50c.

China White Winter—White color. Pkg., 5c; oz., 10c; ¼lb. 30c; lb. 50c.

Black Spanish Winter—Round sorts. Pkg., 5c; oz., 10c; ¼lb. 30c; lb. 50c.

Black Spanish Winter—Long sorts, Pkg., 5c; oz., 10c; ¼lb. 30c; lb. 50c.

Horseradish, Chives and Plants—Page 41.

White Strassburg—A white variety, very large and showy, half long in shape. It matures quickly, sometimes in six weeks, and holds its table qualities well. Pkg., 5c; oz., 10c; ¼lb. 30c; lb. 50c.

Mixed Radish Seeds—All sorts, kinds, colors and varieties, very popular. Pkg. 10c; oz., 15c; ¼lb. 25c; lb. 75c.

GOLDEN SUMMER GLOBE

SALZER'S SUPERIOR ALASKA 100 BU. PER A. WINTER RADISH

FREE!
Salzer's 50-Day the Earliest Tomato.

For 24 years there has never appeared a home-grown Tomato in our market earlier than ours. Indeed, our Tomatoes have always been from 10 to 25 days ahead of other growers, excepting, of course, when they used Salzer's earliest varieties. When market gardening, we always made our money on earliest Tomatoes, Cabbage, Radishes, Onions, Melons, Peas and Corn. Now, in this 50-Day the Earliest Tomato, we have something that is way ahead of Earliest of All, and that is saying a great deal. It was purchased from a gardener who demonstrated that the Tomato was earlier than our Earliest of All. Price, $1.00 per kernel for 500 kernels, making the snug sum of $500.00. Last spring we distributed a few of these kernels to customers who took great delight in same, and without exception praised them as the very earliest known. This year we are going to give a package of 50 kernels to each customer purchasing $1.00 worth or more goods providing he asks for it in his order. Positively no more than 1 package given to any party unless by purchasing. These 50 kernels originally cost $50.00, but we have grown a small stock of seed and take this method of introducing same to everybody, and we hope that each customer will make his order amount to at least $1.00, so he will get a chance to grow the finest of all fine Tomatoes and the earliest of all early Tomatoes. We are certain that it is ahead from 10 to 20 days in earliness of any other Tomato grown to-day.

LOOK AT THESE REPORTS.

Do you wish to make money? Well, sir, you can do it by planting 50-Day the Earliest Tomato. It's the greatest money maker in the world. Tomatoes in from 30 to 46 days! That's 50 days earlier than your neighbors, and that is when Tomatoes pay! Think of getting 100, or even so, a pound for hundreds of pounds, for ¼ ounce of seed will give 10,000 pounds of fine Tomatoes.

Here are a few reports from its friends who grew ripe Tomatoes in the time set opposite their names:

44 days, W. O. Liscn, Glosfer, Min.
46 days, David Ebner, Little Falls, Minn.
36 days, J. Murphy, Butler, Ind.
36 days, Wm. A. Coffey, Spooner, Ind.
40 days, Ferris Draye, Oakville, Ala.
50 days, Geo. U. Ross, Bloomington, Mo.

61 days, Lewis Hunt, Essex, Ohio.
52 days, Wm. Craig, Lamar, Mo.
55 days, W. W. Wallace, San Augustine, Tex.
65 days, Dora Noonan, Middleton, Wis.
56 days, S. J. Rinker, Urbena, Ohio.
66 days, Mary A. Lansbay, Lorامie, Ohio.

☞Read C. A. Palmer's letter on page 72.

This is no dream of fancy, but a fact. We know of a gardener in Milwaukee selling, from 1 acre of our Earliest Tomato, $50.00 worth of fruit before any of his neighbors had any in the market. This is a fact and can be proven by yourself if you will plant 50-Day the Earliest Tomato. Just plant a plenty; do not hesitate. It is sure to be the earliest, it is sure to be the finest, it is sure to bring the highest price in the market; and then everybody ordering $1.00 worth of vegetable seeds gets a package of this magnificent seed free.

FREE !

Now, we hope, that everybody will send in an order of $1.00 to obtain above package free. We have but a small quantity of seed for sale. It is not the largest Tomato, but it is surely the earliest. Why, gardeners tell us it was 20 days ahead of Atlantic Prize and such earliest sorts. Be sure and order $1.00 worth of vegetables and get the package free.

Price of Salzer's 50-Day the earliest Tomatoes. Pkg., 50 kernels, 25c; 3 pkgs., 50c; 7 pkgs., $1.00; ¼ oz. seed, $1.00; ¼ oz., $1.50; oz., $2.00.

SALZER'S NEW CANNING AND PRESERVING TOMATO.

PRICE PKG 20c

RED GRANITE

SALZER'S

TOMATO.

THE FINEST IN THE WORLD.

Tomato—Red Granite.

Here we have the greatest Tomato of the age for canners and market gardeners and private gardeners for pickling, canning and preserving. It's just the Tomato thousands have been looking for, just the Tomato wanted for canning, pickling, etc. Now we know that you will think that this is a strong statement to make, but when you once try this Tomato you will become convinced as to what we say. In this Tomato above all other Tomatoes that hold its intense color when canned or preserved. Its flesh is solid, peculiarly delicious, and will bear shipping a great distance. It is the best shipping Tomato that we have ever seen. While Salzer's 50-Day, the Earliest and Salzer's Earliest of All are way ahead of it in earliness, yet in quality, in those rare points that go to make up a perfect Tomato, we believe that Red Granite possesses more of them than all other varieties that we know of. If we were asked to select the best Tomato—best in regardless of Earliness—for in earliness Salzer's Earliest of All, Fifty Day and Salzer's La Crosse Seedling are about what just simply for quality—beefy, meaty quality, for uniform beauty of a high, scarlet which richness of color, for every day use whether as a fruit or as canned or preserved, we would universally take Salzer's new Red Granite! the king of all! It is large, smooth, and of a high, scarlet which richness of color is largely retained in canning and preserving. We heartily commend same, knowing it will give great satisfaction. We can only sell same in package, but our seed is scarce, but it would be cheap to buy this sort at ten times its price. Price of Red Granite: Pkg. 20c; 3 pkgs., 50c; ¼ oz., 75c; oz., $1.25.

SALZER'S EARLIEST OF ALL TOMATO.

Each succeeding season adds thousands of warm friends to this wonderful novelty, has stood the test of thousands of market gardeners, and in price gardens the past four seasons, and in each case carried off the palm of being absolutely the earliest. With us in the far North it has always been a strife to produce extremely early vegetables, such as will ripen and produce perfect fruit in a short time. In our Earliest of All, a beautifully colored, fine-fleshed Tomato, we have one ripe in 54 days under general conditions, and in 64 days under special care, stamping it the earliest of all sorts known. The size medium, perfectly smooth, and of delightful color and quality. We could fill ten pages with testimonials on this Earliest of All Tomato. Everybody who has tried it speaks of it only in highest praise. It cannot be excelled for earliness. It is ripe and sold at a high price in the market long before other sorts begin to ripen. This fact alone makes it extremely valuable to market gardeners and private families.

Salzer's Earliest of All is Positively the Greatest Tomato Novelty of the Century.

(We of course except the Fifty Days the Earliest, because that is earlier.) It is the only really first-class Tomato in America to-day—by early we mean 6 to 18 days ahead of any and all other sorts! We have so wonderfully improved Salzer's Earliest of All Tomato that it is way ahead in earliness and quality of some when first offered. Consequently it is with great pleasure we offer our customers this year a Tomato of such superlative merit in that quality, viz., earliness (which is really the most important quality of all, not alone to the market gardener, but the home gardener as well). We of course anticipate an enormous demand for seed of Salzer's Earliest of All, so would advise all our friends to favor us with early orders.

WHAT THE FRIENDS OF SALZER'S EARLIEST OF ALL TOMATO SAY.

Martin Hyer, La Crosse Co.: "On June 24th I had the first ripe Salzer's 'Earliest of All' tomatoes—that was exactly 15 days ahead of a Chicago earliest tomato and 21 days ahead of a Philadelphia earliest—Salzer's seeds proved the earliest with me and by all odds the finest."

C. A. Palmer, Lincoln, Neb.: "Your Fifty Days the Earliest Tomato and Lightning Cabbage are the greatest money makers I ever struck. I had tomatoes 30 days ahead of the best gardeners of this place, and beat them all on cabbage."

Frank Zacher, Jefferson, Mo.: "My Earliest of All Tomatoes were actually ripe before the earliest I got in Minneapolis showed a sign of ripening. I tell you, no seeds beat Salzer's."

J. Batcheldor, Quincy: "With me it proved the earliest by 12 days."

Fred. Walther, St. Paul: "Sold 24 bushels for $35.00. When my neighbors came in with ripe ones they got only $1.50 for their fruit."

F. Ogle, Ada, O.: "Your Earliest of All Tomato beat 10 noodsmen's earliest by 5 days."

Jerome Wing, Madison: "It is the earliest in the world, and at the same time the finest early Tomato I ever ate or saw."

A. C. Hirsch, Springfield: "Sixteen days ahead of Friend Newman. He gets his early Tomato seed in Chicago. After this he will use only Salzer's."

C. Wood, Pa.: "It is positively the earliest. Tried 16 seedsman's earliest, and each was 4 to 20 days later than yours."

H. Buda, N. J.: "Made $210.00 from the ¼ lb. Salzer's Earliest Tomato. How? Because it was sold 10 days before others came in."

Henry Schmidt, Detroit: "I told my neighbor your Tomatoes were the earliest and best. I cleared $300.00 on my patch because of earliness; he a trifle less than $90.00, because they were 2 weeks later."

Louis Knoll, Kan.: "My Tomatoes were ripe and sold before my neighbor's. He got his seed from New York; I from Salzer."

It is worthy a trial by everybody, especially for the home garden and market garden. It fills the bill fully for extreme earliness, beauty and deliciousness.

We never wrong praising this Tomato. We believe that since its introduction there are more market gardeners and market farmers throughout America who have made money out of same than out of any other variety that has been introduced for 50 years. In the above illustration Mrs. Gage is right. She knows what she has a good thing and does not hesitate to tell her neighbors so, and illustration, too, that Salzer keeps the earliest vegetable seeds.

Now, Salzer's Earliest of All Tomato is the very best early Tomato to grow for general crop, and while it is not as early as Fifty Days the Earliest, which we offer free this year, it certainly gets there quicker and earlier than any other Tomato in America to-day. You are sure to like it. We have greatly improved it for 1899, both in shape, yield, earliness and quality.

Price of Earliest of All Tomato: Pkg., 20c; 3 pkgs., 50c; 7 pkgs., $1.00; ½ oz., 30c; oz., 60c; ¼ lb., $2.00; lb., $6.00.

Salzer's Giant Tree Tomato.

We wish you could have seen a long trellis of Salzer's Giant Tree Tomato at La Crosse the past summer. It was a sight worth coming miles to see. There they stood, regular giant trees, ten feet tall, with a hundred pounds or more of great giant, luscious Tomatoes hanging on each vine. That was a sight; and such magnificent Tomatoes, too. Well, sir, we have seen the Salzer Giant Tree Tomato, grown for exhibition purposes, 16 feet tall! Regular climbing trees, and producing fruit of enormous size and delicious quality. One thing is certain, that fruit grown on such tall vines is not troubled by chickens or any other fowl bothering them. It is really a remarkable Tomato; remarkable in size, remarkable for its excellent quality and remarkable that it should grow like a tree. We offer it with great confidence, and believe that our friends will be highly delighted with same. We have seen fruit on the plant 6 feet tall, way out of reach of chickens, ducks, dogs, wet, soft weather, etc., etc., weighing 3¼ pounds, of a most delightful quality, round, rich, luscious. It must not be confounded with the Tree Tomato offered by a small firm in Minnesota and Illinois—this is a giant in size and great in quality. When once you grow it, it will always be found in your garden. Why, sir! fruit of Salzer's Giant Tree Tomato six inches in diameter and weighing 3¼ pounds is not uncommon, and such Tomatoes! Fit for kings. Luscious, meaty in the extreme.

Price of Salzer's Giant Tree Tomato: Pkg., 20c; 3 pkgs., 50c; oz., 60c.

SALZER'S GREAT GIANT TREE TOMATO. Fig. 250.
David Daniel Tucker's Directions—How to Grow Tree Tomatoes (worth their weight in gold), on each package of seed.

SALZER'S LA CROSSE SEEDLING.

In 1889, on trial grounds (where the year before we had tested many different Tomato seeds), we discovered, standing alone, upright and strong, heavily laden with rich, robust, reddish-tinted fruit, a Tomato full of unusual appearance and low growing habit. As it was a chance seedling we thought nothing of it that its luscious fruit should ripen by July 15th. But the following year, when on a patch of over 2 acres the ripening fruit appeared the first week in July, of unusual size, very handsome appearance and delicious flavor, fit for a king, our surprise and pleasure were great, and we wondered not that our head gardener, who had cared for and reared the seedling, exclaimed in wild delight, "Eureka, Eureka!" While Salzer's Earliest leads the world in early medium-sized fruit the La Crosse Seedling follows so closely upon its heels that we think in a year or two of careful selection it will outrival that sort in earliness. Has large, finely-flavored fruit, averaging in weight 12 to 14 ounces, while specimens on our ground this year weighed 18 ounces, the former being just the size so much sought in the market and for the home. Its strong stalks, upon which the fruit hangs closely, enable one to plant more per acre than of any other variety known to us. Its extremely prolific a single vine in our grounds yielding 108 pounds. This variety will be ripe and sold before sorts like Volunteer, Trophy, Livingston's Beauty, etc., show signs of ripening. The fruit is of a fine size, light purplish red in color, few seeds; ripens evenly, finest family variety ever introduced.

Price of La Crosse Seedling Reduced to:

Pkg. 15c; ¼ oz., 30c; oz., 60c; ¼ lb., $1.80.

There is nothing so sure as the rising of to-morrow's sun, Mr. Smith, and that is that Salzer's All Day the Earliest in the Earliest Tomato in America.

THE WONDERFUL LA CROSSE SEEDLING—GROWN BY 100,000 PEOPLE IN 1895.

THE FERRIS WHEEL TOMATO. THE FINEST. BEST OF ALL. FIT FOR A KING. TOMATO.

One pkg. each of Salzer's First Prize, La Crosse Seedling and Ferris Wheel, only 35c each.

Salzer's Ferris Wheel Tomato.

Tomatoes of this monster, this leviathan, this giant, have been grown weighing 5 lbs., and measuring almost 2 feet in circumference. We studied for an appropriate name and finally concluded to name it Ferris Wheel Tomato, in honor of one of the greatest inventions of the age. This Tomato possesses every good quality to be found in a Tomato. The vines are strong and vigorous, and easily bear their enormous weight of fruit, and when we come to giant size, weight, solidity, no other Tomato begins to approach it.

$5,000 IN GOLD.

to the party growing the heaviest Tomato above 5 lbs. during the season of 1896. We believe that with care a Tomato can be grown weighing 5 to 6 lbs., especially of this monster. Quality excellent. It ripens medium early, and is an A No. 1 variety for table use. We are sure that no Tomato offered within the last ten years will create such a sensation as this variety, and not only that, but this Tomato will give you better satisfaction as to quality and yield. Think of a 5 lb. and 6 foot in circumference. Why not have such Tomatoes? T. J. Schaffer, New Ashtabula, Pa., says:

Price of Ferris Wheel: Pkg., 20c; 3, 50c; ½ oz., 60c; oz., $1.00; ½ lb, $2.50; lb., $3.00.

NEW TOMATO—SALZER'S GOLDEN GLORY.

For many years there has been an inquiry for a first-class yellow Tomato, in every respect, equal to the many splendid red varieties that are grown, and in our effort to produce same we have tested every possible variety known. We now offer in Golden Glory what we believe to be by all odds the finest Yellow Tomato grown. We know that it will do credit in every respect to its golden name, and that it will at once leap into popularity, for we know that its excellent quality, its fine grain, its lusciousness, its large yield, and its power to withstand rot, will give it a place at once in every market gardener's field and in every city garden.

What Its Friends Say:

Mrs. Russell, Minn.: "Golden Glory pleased us very much. They are beautiful."

Mrs. Brown, N. Y.: "Golden Glory was my constant delight."

Mrs. Wheeler, Ia.: "They are admirably more people than any other fruit."

It is a variety of pre-eminent merit, of good substance, and especially excellent for slicing, the handsome golden yellow slices making a beautiful contrast with the red Tomato.

Price of Golden Glory Tomato: Pkg., 20c; 3 pkgs., 50c; ½ oz., 35c; oz., 60c.

Salzer's First Prize.

For years one of the best second early Tomatoes in existence. It has now given place to Salzer's Imperial. Pkg., 10c; oz., 30c; ½ lb., 75c.

SALZER'S WONDERFUL GOLDEN GLORY TOMATO. 20c.

The Morning Star.

Thousands of our patrons say this is the largest Tomato they have ever seen. They praise its quality, which is delicious in the extreme; they marvel at their size, their perfection of form and their enormous productiveness. Specimen Tomatoes weighed as high as 4½ lbs., while the average weight reported was more than 15 ounces. The fruit ripens evenly, color is of brilliant red, with very solid flesh of delicious flavor.

Pkg., 20c; 3 pkgs., 50c; ¼ oz., 40c; oz., 75c; ¼ lb., $2.00; lb., $7.50.

Free, see page 9.

Perfect Gem Tomato.

Thousands upon thousands of pleased patrons pronounce this the finest and best Tomato ever grown. Color, rich dark red. Remarkably solid, smooth and ripens evenly. It is almost an everbearing Tomato, bearing until killed by frost. It is a good shipper, does not crack an enormous yielder (so lbs. from one vine), and of the most delicious flavor. It certainly is the poor among Tomatoes. A good will convince everybody.

Pkg., 10c; ¼ oz., 25c; oz., 40c; ¼ lb., $1.25; lb., $4.00.

Red Currant.

Very fine for exhibition or to eat raw, as they are as small as a Red Cherry Currant. Pkg., 10c; oz., 25c.

Yellow Pear.

Very delicious for pickles or preserves, especially the latter. Pkg., 10c; oz., 25c.

Tomato—
Crimson Cushion.

A new race of Tomatoes, of very large size, smooth as an apple, uniform size, very prolific, very long bearing, an excellent keeper and of the finest quality. It has a deep red crimson colored color, is extremely thick and juicy, and but few seeds. It is one of the finest Tomatoes offered for years. Pkg., 10c; oz., 25c; ¼ lb., 75c.

Ponderosa Tomato.

Well known; of the Crimson Cushion type. Pkg., 10c; oz., 25c; ¼ lb., 75c.

CRIMSON CUSHION.   PKG., 10c.

RED CURRANT.

YELLOW PEAR.

FREE!
TO TOMATO GROWERS!

We have two new Tomatoes, upon which 10 years of careful improvement and work have been spent. We number them No. X and No. Z. We have a few thousand kernels of seeds which we are selling at 20c a parcel. We will give a package of 1 kernels to anybody ordering Tomato seed from us to the amount of $1.00. We wish this to fall only into the hands of Tomato growers who can appreciate a really grand thing, hence this special offer. A $2.00 order will get (both X and Z) 2 packages; a $1.00 Tomato seed order gets 1 package; a $3.00 Tomato seed order, 3 packages.
Price, per pkg., $1.00.

NEW IMPERIAL TOMATO.

Over this new acquisition Eastern seedsmen went fairly wild, claiming for it everything in the line of earliness, beauty and solidity of fruit. We have given it two years of careful trial, and now offer it for the first time. It is not nearly as early as our 50-Day the Earliest, it is 4 days behind Salzer's Earliest, but is the earliest Tomato otherwise that we know of. By this we mean that it is earlier than any of the other seedsmen's earliest sorts. We always make an exception of Salzer's 50-Day the Earliest and Salzer's Earliest Tomatoes, these two varieties being earlier by 8 to 10 days than any variety grown in America today. The fruit of the new Imperial Tomato is very large, is finely shaped, smooth and very thick, juicy, of beautiful color, and contains but very few seeds. It is an extremely prolific variety, plants yielding 1½ to 2 bushels of fruit during the season. We cordially recommend everybody to give it a trial. One seed is saved from only select fruit, and is very choice. Pkg., 20c; ½ oz., 30c; oz., 50c; ¼ lb., $1.50; lb., $5.00.

Sumatra Fig Tomato.

dried in sugar, like Figs, make excellent pies or tarts for winter use. Pkg., 20c; 3 pkgs., 50c.

How to make Figs out of the Sumatra Fig Tomato is described so clearly and fully on every packet of seed that any one can make them.

CALIFORNIA FIG.—a well-known Fig Tomato variety. Pkg., 20c.

2. Strawberry or Winter Cherry Tomato.

A dozen plants or more of this magnificent Strawberry Tomato should be found in every garden. They are especially the delight of the children, who eat this healthy, finely flavored luscious fruit with great relish. Prepared as preserves they are almost unequaled, in richness and delicacy of flavor, rivaling the Fig. Indeed, cake baked from the preserves of this Tomato seeks an equal. We are sure you will be delighted with same, either as a fruit to eat raw or as preserves.
Pkg., 20c; 2 pkgs., 50c; ½ oz., 650 oz., $1.00.

1 Package each above 4 Great Rarities, which includes Climbing Orange, only 50c.

4 GREAT RARITIES.
1. Sumatra Fig Tomato.

A beautiful and valuable variety of Tomato, used for making Figs. The plant grows in the form of a bush, 2 to 2½ feet high, literally covered with rich golden fruit. When 18 inches or 2 feet high, the plant should be staked or trellised to prevent its being broken down with the immense load of fruit.

IN 1895

it again covered itself with glory, and our lady friends are pleased in having stored away for winter use a good proportion of Fig Tomato preserves.

The beautiful Fig Tomatoes are about 1 inch in diameter and as even in size as if they had all been cast in one mould. The skin and flesh are a rich golden yellow, solid, thick-meated, with a flavor similar to other Tomatoes, but much sweeter and more palatable. For preserving or pickling they are perfectly delicious, and when canned or

NEW IMPERIAL TOMATO, ONE-HALF NATURAL SIZE.   PKG., 10c.

4. Climbing Orange.

A magnificent novelty, of rich flavor and delightful fragrance. See page 55 for the description. Pkg., 20c; 3 pkgs., 50c.

3. Salzer's New Improved Peach Tomato.

Imagine a Tomato that at first glance reminds you more of a fine, good sized Peach than anything else, and you have Improved Peach Tomato. The Improved Peach Tomato has a beautiful Peach-like color that resembles the delicate bloom of a Peach; it is twice as large as the old sort. Skin is exquisitely thin, and can be peeled like the skin of a Peach. We know of nothing that will attract the attention of visitors to your garden to so great an extent as a few vines of this Improved Peach Tomato, as it is astonishing how few people know that they are Tomatoes at first glance.
Pkg., 20c; 3 pkgs., 50c.

Salzer's Giant Peach Tomato.

A large, well-known sort. Pkg., 20c.

SQUASH.

It is a fact known to market gardeners that Northern-grown Squash, Melon, Cucumber, Cabbage and Onion seed is worth 50 per cent. more for large yield and for earliness than Eastern stock.

The price of the following 4 sorts is:
Pkg., 5c; oz., 10c; ¼ lb., 15c; lb., 45c, postpaid.

1. **White Bush**—Scalloped, early summer. The earliest of all.
2. **Yellow Bush**—Scalloped, early summer.
3. **Yellow Crook Neck**—Standard early.
4. **Pineapple**—This new variety has both skin and flesh of a pure creamy white color; good quality, flesh very thick and fine-grained.

THE FAXON.

Dunlaps Early Prolific.

No variety can compete with it for earliness. Its color is a brilliant orange red; quality excellent; a good keeper. Pkg., 10c; oz., 15c; lb., $1.00.

The Faxon Squash.

Can be used as very early, as medium and late, as it keeps all winter. Flesh deep orange yellow. Pkg., 5c; oz., 15c; ¼ lb., 40c; lb., $1.10, postpaid.

Red China—Rich orange yellow; fine, fine-grained, sweet, weighing 8 lbs. each; Pkg., 5c; oz., 15c; ¼ lb., 30c; lb., $1.00.

Boston Marrow—Fine, yellow for fall use. Pkg., 5c; oz., 15c; ¼ lb., 20c; lb., 60c.

Golden Custard Bush—Frequently grows 2 feet in diameter. Makes pies richer than custard. Pkg., 5c; oz., 20c; ¼ lb., 35c; lb., $1.00.

Pikes Peak—Splendid keeper. Its flesh is solid, thick, sweet and of a beautiful orange color. Pkg., 5c; ¼ lb., 15c; lb., 50c.

GOLDEN CUSTARD.

SALZER'S IMPROVED HUBBARD SQUASH.

SALZER'S IMPROVED HUBBARD
SALZER'S IMPROVED HUBBARD

THE GREAT HUBBARD SQUASH. Pkg., 10c; oz., 15c; lb., 75c.

Our Improved Hubbard **Squash is** the great Winter Squash of the century. It **is** the Squash that has **made** several market gardeners rich to our knowledge. There is fabulous money in 10 to 20 acres of this grand Squash. Our improved Hubbard is a careful selection of only the finest, most perfect fruit, and the result is uniform shape and size. The Hubbard is unquestionably the very best Winter Squash grown. Upward of 16,000 lbs. have been grown on an acre. The fruit is large, dry, fine-grained; flesh of excellent quality, and among **all** Squash the best keeper. A package furnishes enough for family use. We sell this seed largely in Chicago, where it is known as the best Hubbard in the world. Pkg., 10c; oz., 15c; ¼ lb., 25c; lb., 75c; 5 lbs. (sufficient for 1 acre), $3.00.

☞ We can furnish a cheap strain of Hubbard Squash, such as is offered in Chicago, Rockford, etc., at: Pkg., 5c; ¼ lb., 15c; lb., 45c.

Price of the following 9 sorts is: Pkg., 5c; oz., 10c; ¼ lb., 20c; lb., 60c.

1. **Bay State**—Color of skin blue-green, flesh deep bright golden yellow; attractive; sweet and tender; enormously productive; average weight, 12 lbs.
2. **Mammoth Bush**—An excellent large strain, earlier than the common stock; creamy white and average double in size; a prolific bearer; a splendid variety for Southern shippers.
3. **Perdhook**—A bright yellow, winter variety. The flesh is dry and sweet. Keeps sound until spring. Rapid, strong grower. Thick meat.
4. **Marble Head**—Flesh of lighter color than the Hubbard, while its combinations of sweetness, dryness and delicious flavor are really remarkable. *No. 4.*
5. **Essex Hybrid**—The finest-grained, sweetest, richest-flavored, best-keeping, thick, solid flesh variety grown.
6. **Putnam**—Fine-grained, sweet dry variety. *Sweet No. 6.*
7. **Perfect Gem** (*No. 7*)—Fine for summer and winter; creamy white color; thin skin, with fine-grained, deliciously flavored flesh.
8. **New Egg Plant**—So named from its peculiar fitness for cooking like Egg Plant; bushy.
9. **Cocoanut**—Small size, but remarkably heavy and very prolific; rich flavor.

MIXED SQUASH SEED—Many sorts and kinds. Pkg., 10c; oz., 15c; lb., 75c.

297 POUNDS
SALZERS GREAT CHILI
SQUASH
J.A. SALZER
LA CROSSE, WIS.

GREAT CHILI SQUASH.

HURRAH!

Here we have a Squash and a Pumpkin that for giant size can't be beat. We would like to see a Squash grown "bigger" than a Pumpkin. Which of the boys will do it and win the prize? $10.00 to the person growing the largest Pumpkin and $10.00 to the person growing the largest Squash. That is $20.00 you can make by growing a big Squash and Pumpkin.

Squash—Great Chili.

This is the Squash that is to beat the Pumpkin, and where is the boy who will raise the biggest Squash known? Specimens have been grown weighing 297 lbs. The largest in 1896 weighed 290 lbs., won by Johnnie Noll, Ill. Boys and girls alike compete for the prizes. Pkg., 10c; oz., **20c**; ¼ lb., 35c; lb., $1.10.

SALZER'S

Mammoth Pumpkin.

The heaviest **in** 1896 weighed 240 lbs. won by Gertie Holmes, Kansas. Just think of a field of these giants! It is the great prize-taker at fairs, etc. Give the boys and girls a chance growing them. $10.00 to the one growing the largest Pumpkin. Pkg., 10c; oz., 20c; ¼ lb., 35c; lb., **$1.10.**

IT PAYS TO BUY NORTHERN GROWN SEED
FIRST PRIZE
SALZER'S MAMMOTH PUMPKIN
301 lbs
SEED BOUGHT FROM
J.A. SALZER

SALZER'S MAMMOTH PUMPKIN. Pkg., 10c; oz., 20c; lb., $1.10.

Mixed Squash Seed.

Here we have hit it! All of above Squash varieties and many more sorts we have mixed and put up in large packages. We find this mixture very popular, just the thing to select for yourself after you see a great many sorts in all shapes, varieties, styles, oblong or round, flat or long, green, yellow, creamy, dark—yes, in endless colors and sorts growing, and from all these select the sorts best adapted to your soil and climate. Large pkg., 10c; oz., 15c; ¼ lb., 25c; lb., 75c; 5 lbs., $3.00.

Mixed Pumpkin Seed.

Lots and lots of Pumpkin Seed. Mixed all sorts and kinds; is fully described and shown on page 80, where we offer Pumpkin seed as a great premium to farmers! **Pkg., 10c., oz., 20c; ¼ lb., 50c; ½ lb., 75c; lb., $1.00.**

THE YANKEE PIE.

SALZER'S
YANKEE PIE
PUMPKIN

A splendid Pumpkin, produced **through** careful selection of the sugar varieties. We **are sure** that no Pumpkin ever introduced has given more genuine pleasure to our customers than this Yankee Pie. The Pumpkin is not large but is of a delightful quality, just the quality to make excellent pies, such good old-fashioned Pumpkin pies as "mother used **to** make." **We** know you will like them and know this variety will give you great satisfaction. It is extremely early, remarkably prolific, yielding **6** to 12 medium-sized Pumpkins to a vine; of **great** excellence. Flesh very thick, fine-grained, sweet, sugary, and of splendid quality for pies. It is the earliest pie Pumpkin we know of, and the best.

Pkg., **10c; oz., 15c; ¼ lb., 40c; lb., $1.25; 5 lbs., $6.00.**

New Japanese Pie Pumpkin.

This remarkable variety comes from Japan, and has proven a valuable addition to our pie and cooking Pumpkins. The flesh is very thick, and of a rich salmon color, nearly solid, the seed cavity being very small in one end of the Pumpkin; unusually fine-grained, dry and sweet, having much the same taste and appearance as Sweet Potatoes, making pies as rich without eggs as other varieties do with. Pkg., 10c; oz., 15c; ¼ lb., 40c; lb., $1.25.

Sweet Potato—Dry-grained, white and brittle, and of delicious taste. Claimed by some to be far ahead of Sweet Potato in flavor. Pkg., 10c; oz., 20c; lb., $1.50.

Large Cheese—This is a magnificent Pumpkin and is a tremendous yielder. We know it will give satisfaction, as the quality is superlative. It will surely please you. Pkg., 5c; oz., 10c; ¼ lb., 20c; lb., 50c, postpaid; 5 lbs. or more, by express, 25c per lb.

Connecticut Field—A standard field sort to be grown with grain, usually used for stock. Pkg., 5c; oz., 10c; ¼ lb., 15c; lb., 35c; 10 lbs. or more, 25c per lb.

Sugar Pumpkin—A splendid Pumpkin; large, handsome; excellent for pies. Pkg., 5c; oz., 10c; ¼ lb., 20c; lb., 50c; 5 lbs. or more, 25c per lb.

Cushaw—Well known. Oz., 10c; lb., 65c.

Mammoth Potiron—A giant Pumpkin, largely found in our Mission. Page 50. Pkg., 10c; oz., 20c; ¼ lb., 50c; lb., $1.15.

Golden Oblong—A well known sort. Pkg., 5c; oz., 10c; ¼ lb., 20c; lb., 60c.

Winter Luxury.

This we recommend as one of the best pie Pumpkins; an excellent keeper and enormously productive. It is very finely netted, and in color it is a golden russet. Pkg., 10c; oz., 25c; ¼ lb., 50c; lb., $1.50.

SALSIFY, or VEGETABLE OYSTER.

SALZER'S EARLY.

The soup and salad made therefrom have a delicious oyster flavor. Treat as Carrots, grow rapidly. No vegetable excels this for soups, that is if you are fond of the oyster. Can be stored in cellar for winter and you can have oyster soup without the expense of genuine oysters.

Salzer's Early—Roots mature early, are large and of fine flavor. Pkg., 10c; oz., 15c; ¼ lb., 50c; lb., $1.50.

Common Salsify—Pkg., 5c; oz., 10c; ¼ lb., 35c; lb., $1.25.

Scorzonera, or Black Oyster—Pkg., 5c; oz., 25c; lb., $2.25.

Sandwich Island—Very large, growing double the size of other sorts. Pkg., 10c; oz., 20c; ¼ lb., 50c; lb., $1.60.

SPINACH, SALZER's SAVOY.

DOUBLE THE YIELD OF OTHER SORTS PER ACRE

SPINACH.

A very important crop for market gardeners; is grown largely by the wide-awake gardener, for there is money in it. For early spring crop, sow in Sept. and cover with coarse straw in winter; for summer use sow in early spring successively until July.

Salzer's Savoy—This is the best spring, summer and fall Spinach we know of. It is very hardy to resist weather, grows quickly and refuses to seed to a remarkable degree. It is grown now by thousands of Spinach growers. On account of its shy seeding qualities the price is higher. Very fine; produces nearly twice the weight of crop. Pkg., 10c; oz., 15c; ¼ lb., 25c; lb., 50c; lb., by express, 50c; 10 lbs., $4.60.

Round Summer—The finest round summer variety; tender and sweet; largely grown. Pkg., 5c; oz., 10c; ¼ lb., 12c; lb., 30c; 10 lbs., $2.75.

Winter Prickly—A splendid fall and winter sort. Pkg., 5c; oz., 10c; ¼ lb., 12c; lb., 30c.

Long Standing—Stands long before running to seed; valuable on this account; tender and sweet. Pkg., 5c; oz., 10c; ¼ lb., 12c; lb., 30c; 10 lbs., $2.25.

Above sorts in 25 lb. lots, 15c per lb.

NEW VICTORIA.

NEW VICTORIA SPINACH.

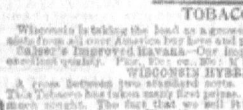

This new variety is distinguished for its exceedingly dark green color, and also for its very long standing qualities, being from 2 to 3 weeks later than the ordinary "long standing." The leaves are thick and spread out flat upon the ground. In our trials of Spinach last spring it outyielded every other variety, and at the same time stood longer before going to seed. Pkg., 5c; oz., 10c; ¼ lb., 15c; lb., 35c; by express, lb., 25c.

Pkg., 15c.

TOBACCO.

Wisconsin is taking the lead as a grower of fine Tobacco. Indeed, tobacconists from all over America buy here and pay fancy prices.

Salzer's Improved Havana—Our importation. Very fine, early and of excellent quality. Pkg., 10c; oz., 30c; ¼ lb., 80c; lb., $2.50.

WISCONSIN HYBRID. (See cut.)

A cross between two standard sorts. Is extremely early and of fine leaf. This Tobacco has taken many first prizes. It is very fine, early, and the leaf is much sought. The fact that we sell it largely in Virginia and Kentucky is proof of its excellence. Pkg., 10c; oz., 40c; ¼ lb., $1.00; lb., $3.00.

Connecticut Seed Leaf—Pkg., 5c; oz., 20c; lb., $2.00.

Kentucky Home—Pkg., 5c; oz., 20c; ¼ lb., 50c; lb., $1.75.

Missouri Leaf—Pkg., 5c; oz., 20c; ¼ lb., 50c; lb., $1.75.

PRINCE BISMARCK.

While in Germany we obtained Tobacco which is the favorite variety smoked by the great chancellor. It is early and of excellent quality. Stock scarce. This sort did splendidly the past summer in Wisconsin, Indiana, Illinois and the great West. It cures easily and is very fine. Pkg., 15c; ½ oz., 65c.

GENERAL GRANT.

The earliest of all Tobacco sorts. Pkg., 10c; oz., 30c; ¼ lb., 75c; lb., $2.75.

Cinnamon Scented—A fine Tobacco having the delightful cinnamon flavor. Pkg., 10c; oz., 25c; ¼ lb., 80c; lb., $3.00.

Yellow Oronoco—A splendid leaf Tobacco. Pkg., 10c; oz., 30c; lb., $2.50.

Yellow Pryor—A sterling sort; early. Pkg., 10c; oz., 30c; lb., $2.50.

White Burley—Greatly sought; early; large leaf. Pkg., 10c; oz., 25c.

Hyco—Has a great sale in the East. Pkg., 10c; oz., 25c; lb., $2.50.

TOBACCO MIXTURES.

All of above sorts mixed. This is a good way to select your sorts. Pkg., 10c; oz., 30c; lb., $2.50.

WISCONSIN HYBRID. PKG. 10c.

SALZER'S JUMBO SUNFLOWER.

Nothing should be more generally grown by the farmer than the Jumbo Sunflower. There is absolutely no waste to the crop. Every portion can be utilized. The seed is eagerly eaten by fowls, and they fatten thereon and lay more eggs than on any other food. It is relished by horses, and enables them to stand more work with less fatigue than if not fed therewith. Cattle, sheep, swine, etc., thrive and fatten thereon. The oil burns well, and 20 barrels can be made per acre. Outside of the feeding and health-giving properties of the Sunflower, comes their great value as fuel. Indeed, for treeless districts, nothing can excel it. On the cold, icy steppes and plains of Russia the Sunflower furnishes the inhabitants their only fuel. A correspondent of the Dakota Farmer says: "Having tried 'fuel,'

coal, wood and Sunflowers, I have settled upon the last named as the cheapest and best fuel for treeless Dakota. I grow one acre of them every year, and have plenty of fuel for one stove the year round, and use some in another stove besides. I plant same in hills, the same as corn (only the seeds to the hill), and cultivate the same as corn. I cut them when the seed, or top flower, is ripe, and let them lie on the ground two or three days. In this time I cut off all the seed heads, which are put into an open shed with a floor to it, the same as a cornerib. The stalks are then hauled home and packed into a common shed with a good roof on it." Nothing better for fattening cattle.

Price of Jumbo: By mail, pkg., 10c; oz., 15c; ¼ lb., 20c; lb., 45c; by express, pkg., 10c; oz., 20c; lb., 35c; 5 lbs. (for 1 acre), $1.50.
MAMMOTH RUSSIAN—Fine, large sort. Oz., 10c; lb., 30c; 10 lbs., by express, $1.50.

African Black Giant Sunflower Novelty.

Specimens have been grown measuring 9 feet in circumference. It is something wonderful. Now, this is the Giant, and it, with the Jumbo, is extremely profitable to grow. An acre is good to let hogs and cattle run in during summer for shade and nourishment, if not wanted for food. If you have a dozen chickens you will find it profitable to plant a package; if you have more plant an acre or a pound, as it is the healthiest food in the world for fowls! One grower in Nebraska writes: "Sowed rich. Have 20 acres in your Sunflower. This furnishes fuel, and food for lots of chickens, cattle, swine, horse and sheep. The proceeds will keep us alive until next crop." Pkg., 10c; oz., 15c; ¼ lb., 25c; lb., 50c; 5 lbs. (for 1 acre), $2.25.

White Beauty Sunflower.

After years of careful selection we are rewarded with a newly-bred Mammoth Single-head Sunflower with a massive white seeds, which, on account of the deficiency of the brown coloring matter in the outer covering of their hulls, are much superior to the darker sorts for stock and poultry food. Pkg., 10c; oz., 15c; lb., 60c, postpaid.

RUTABAGA.

Salzer's Rutabaga and Turnip seed enjoy an enormous sale on account of the sweet, juicy product of the crops. It will pay you to pay 20c to 30c a pound more for our seed than such as you buy in stores. Our seed produce big crops of fine, sweet, juicy, rich Rutabagas.

MAMMOTH RUSSIAN.

A new yellow Rutabaga of excellent qualities; enormous cropper; splendid for stock, the finest and largest of all; sweet, juicy, rich. It outyields such sorts as you buy in hardware stores, etc., three to one. It is the best Rutabaga for the farm for big crops of juicy Rutabagas in the world. No mistake, either! A magnificent Rutabaga, either for house use or for feeding to stock. Pkg., 10c; oz., 15c; ¼ lb., 20c; lb., 50c; by express, 100; per ½ lb., 25c; lb., 40c; 10 lbs., $3.00.

FIELD of SALZER'S MAMMOTH RUSSIAN RUTA BAGA.

THE GREATEST YIELDING EXCELLENT RUTABAGA KNOWN. PER., 30c.

New Rutabaga, All Gold.

Probably the very finest of Rutabagas for table use. It is not so large as our Mammoth Russian, found fully described above, but it makes up in quality. The flesh is of a beautiful golden yellow, of the choicest quality, and of excellent flavor and remarkable keeping quality. We distributed

10,000 TRIAL PACKAGES

all over the world where our patrons reside, and it is surprising how many hearty recommendations ALL GOLD receives. Of the hundreds, we select at random the following from Rev. David Forsythe, President of Amity College, Iowa: "You sent me a premium package of Rutabaga Seed—ALL GOLD—which I planted and grew. I think they are the sweetest and best I ever saw."

PRICE OF ALL GOLD RUTABAGA.
Pkg., 10c; oz., 20c; ¼ lb., 30c; lb., $1.00; 5 lbs., $4.50; 10 lbs., $7.50.

STANDARD RUTABAGA VARIETIES.

The following sorts are standard varieties here in America. They are all good, fine sorts for stock and home use, but if you want something really fine for the table, then by all means take either our Mammoth or our Great Mammoth Russian. These two last-named sorts are the peers of all. They are worth double any other sorts offered in America. Please remember this.

Price of the following 6 sorts: Pkg., 5c; 3 pkgs., 10c; oz., 5c; ¼ lb., 15c; lb., 35c; by express prepaid, lb., 30c.

1. White Sweet Russian—Best White Rutabaga. Excellent.
2. Laing's Purple Top—Popular sort; very productive; keeps well.
3. Skirving's Liverpool—A fine sort; firm, productive, splendid.
4. Carter's Imperial—A magnificent Rutabaga; largely used.
5. American Purple Top.
6. Sweet German Rutabaga—A splendid sort; well worth a trial.

MIXED RUTABAGA SEED.

There is a demand for mixed seeds, and especially so of Rutabagas. We have therefore gathered together the above sorts and several others we do not list, and made a great mixture. These many sorts give you an opportunity to test each kind and select for your next year's use. They are fine and of richest quality. Pkg., 10c; oz., 15c; ¼ lb., 25c; ½ lb., 50c; postpaid; by express, 1 lb., 40c; 10 lbs., $3.00.

ALL   GOLD.
Package.   10 Cents.

Salzer's Turnips are rich and juicy. (left margin)

Salzer's Turnips are rich and juicy. (right margin)

PRICES FOLLOWING 11 SORTS: Pkg., 3c; oz., 10c; ¼ lb., 15c; lb., 38c; by express, lb., 30c.

1. **Early Six Weeks**—About a week later than Early La Crosse.

2. **Early Purple Top Milan**—The bulb is flat and of medium size, very tender, sweet and white. It is an excellent keeper and sells rapidly in the market.

3. **Early White Flat Dutch**—Rapid growth, tender and sweet.

4. **Early White Strap Leaf**—This is the standard purple top turnip, growing to good size, excellent quality, sweet, juicy and tender; good for the kitchen or for stock.

5. **Purple Top Globe**—A superior variety much grown throughout Europe and America. It's splendid for stock and kitchen use.

6. **YELLOW ABERDEEN**—A sweet yellow Turnip, being particularly adapted to table use. It is in many places used in place of a Rutabaga, and sells quickly when its excellent qualities are known.

7. **Cow Horn**—Flesh white, grows rapidly, long; excellent for table use. It is in great demand among many stockmen who prefer this to any other variety except Milk Globe.

8. **Large White Globe**—The standard large globe; for home or stock. More used in all of this variety than any other sort except Salzer's Milk Globe. It's a great turnip and is in demand everywhere and sure to give great satisfaction.

9. **White Stone**—A superior early sort. Very fine for early fall.

10. **Orange Sweet**—Excellent variety.

11. **Yellowstone**—Much prized, fine appearance and sweet.

White Lily Turnip.

White Lily—A beautiful, medium large, round to oblong, pure white, tender, juicy, **sweet**, very early Turnip. One of the finest early table varieties **known.** Pkg., 10c; oz., 20c; ¼ lb., 50c; lb., $1.25.

Early La Crosse.

Unquestionably the very earliest turnip **grows**; a fine, pure **white** sort, purplish top, few leaves, of excellent flavor. This sort has taken every prize where exhibited for very early. **Pkg.,** 5c; oz., 30c; ¼ lb., 40c; lb., 75c; lb., by express, 65c.

MIXED TURNIP SEED.

Just the thing when you want but a package or an ounce of seed. All sorts and varieties, long, round, oblong, etc., of Turnip Seed in this mixture! Gives you an opportunity to test them all!

Pkg., 10c; oz., 15c; ¼ lb., 25c; 1 lb., 50c, postpaid.

Mixed Rutabaga Seed, same Price.

New White Egg Turnip.

Our seed has been grown with great pains, and we believe it will satisfy the most critical market gardener. The White Egg is one of the best for a private garden, and meets with a ready sale in all large markets. In our estimation it fills a little short of leading markets. All in all it is one of the most useful Turnips of the list. Pkg., 5c; oz., 10c; ¼ lb., 20c; lb., 70c.

Salzer's Milk Turnip.

Well there are upward of 50,000 people who have grown this great turnip the past ten years, and never a complaint and nothing but words of praise. You surely will join the procession if you but try this grand, juicy, tender turnip!

Here you have the best white Turnip for winter use grown. It is globe-shaped, grows very large, of delicious flavor, sweet, juicy, white flesh, solid texture—in a word, it is perfection. Just the Turnip to grow for stock and to store for your kitchen. It is an enormous cropper, and sells well in the market. Pkg., 10c; oz., 20c; ¼ lb., 25c; lb., 75c; by express, pkg., 10c; oz., 19c; ¼ lb., 20c; lb., 60c; 10 lbs., $5.00.

800 BUS. PER ACRE. OF RICH MILK-PRODUCING FOOD

SWEET! TENDER! JUICY! NUTRITIOUS!

SALZER'S MILK TURNIP.

800 BUS PER ACRE.

PRICE BY MAIL

Pkg., 5c; mail, free, 10c; oz., 15c; ¼ lb., 20c; lb., 75c; 10 lbs., $5.00. This is the greatest eating Turnip for winter use in the world!

PRICE BY EXPRESS

Pkg., by express, 10c; oz., 15c; ¼ lb., 20c; lb., 65c; 10 lbs., $5.00; 100 lbs., $40.00.

☞ It is well to remember, that the finest Turnip for fall and winter use, for either table or stock, is Salzer's peerless Milk Turnip. ☜

Salzer's Superior Northern-Grown Farm-Seeds

We are American Headquarters for Farm Seeds, growing more Barley, Buckwheat, Corn, Oats, Wheat, Flax, Potatoes, Grass and Clover Seeds, etc., than all Western seedsmen combined. This we do in the extreme North, ... and controlling large farms in Wisconsin, North and South Dakota. An illustration of one of our great farms is given below where on Gov. Sheldon and Lieut. Gov. Harried are visiting same.

We have, by actual test, learned that our Seed Wheat, Barley, Corn, Grasses and Clovers, Oats and Potatoes, etc taken from our farms and removed to Iowa, Ohio, New York, Nebraska, Kansas, Illinois and other states increase the yield fully 50 per cent.; yes, oftentimes more than doubled the yields!

RIGHT HERE

We want to say that we delight in doing business with the farmer; he knows what he wants and takes care o what he buys in the line of seeds, and to him above all others, and to his lively interest in our behalf, our enormou increased business is due. We now have the largest business of its kind in the world, but we must not rest unti every farmer in our great land plants Salzer's seeds, gets big crops and is happy.

With the liberal support and hearty co-operation of the farmer, we shall, in the future as in the past, urge onward in th fields of new seed tests and experiments, believing that if we can get a new sort to produce two bushels where one formerl grew, we are doing the farmers a great good. Our success in this line has been signal, and the farmer stands by us, fo our seed business is the largest in the world. We believe we have introduced new Oats, Barley, Corn, Potatoes, Buck wheat, Rutabagas, etc., that have increased the average yield largely; yes, often doubled it.

HOW DO WE SHIP FARM SEEDS?

By Freight.

All Farm Seeds, Potatoes and Tools, from page 79 on, are sent by cheap freight, customers paying charges. In all cases we get the lowest obtainable freight rates for our customers. In all cases we use our judgment in forwarding seeds, etc., at lowest cost to our patrons.

CHEAP FREIGHT.

The freight charges at the time of writing would be, on 100 lbs., to points in:

Iowa, Minnesota, Wisconsin, Illinois, Michigan, Indiana..$0.25—$0.35
Missouri, Ohio, Kansas, Nebraska, the Dakotas, about... .40— .75
New York, New Jersey, Pennsylvania, Connecticut, Georgia and Eastern states, about................... .50— .90
Texas, Louisiana, Florida, New Mexico, about.......... .75— 1.50
California, Washington and Oregon................. 1.00— 2.00

At such low rates it will pay you to order our Northern-grown heavy-cropping seeds. They double yields and give glorious crops.

By Express.

It often happens that you can send by express, at slight advance of the Express on a 25-lb. package, instead of by freight. In doing this the customer gets goods quicker. In all cases we use our judgment in forwarding.

This illustration is to show ex-Gov. C. H. Sheldon, Lieut. Gov. Chas. N. Harried, State Auditor J. R. Hipple, Land Commissioner J. L. Lockhart, Prof. J. H. Sheppard of Brookings College, Congressman J. A. Pickler, together with Senator Geo. Schlund, Senator J. W. Orcutt, Hon. R. C. Walcott, Hon. W. C. Kiser, Hon. S. R. Gold, Hon. C. E. Cambers, Hon. L. G. Taylor, Hon. K. E. Chilcott, Hon. L. C. Corbett, Hon. F. D. Adams, Hon. Ben B. Hoover, Hon. F. D. Hinds, and many thousand others, who viewed our trial grounds and farms in Dakota the past season, on railroads reduced rates from all parts of the state to this farm, in order that the farmers and others might profit thereby. Prominent newspapers throughout America have had descriptions of this farm, such as the Chicago Daily Inter-Ocean, the Tribune, Herald, Farm, Field and Stockman, Minneapolis Journal, the Post Pioneer Press, Dakota Farmer, together with almost every paper published in the state of South Dakota, many of the officers having visited same and reported thereon. Our Exhibition car was visited by more than 200,000 people during the Trans-Mississippi Fair at Omaha.

The Magnificent Appearance

Of Wheat, Barley, Oats, Potatoes, Corn and Grasses, together with hundreds of varieties of vegetable and berry plants, was universally commended upon. Indeed, we have hardly ever seen any crops that looked better anywhere. While in Dakota recently we saw fine Oat and Wheat fields, but we are sure that our yield on the Dakota farm was almost double the yield of the European farms, and we are glad that we can offer to our customers this year such a magnificent strain of seeds.

Ex-Gov. Sheldon, State Officials and Others Visiting Our Trial Farm.

Of Tremendous Interest

to thousands of visitors were our immense Potato fields, in wonderful vigor and beauty, farmers and other estimating the yields of some of the varieties as high as 700 bushels per acre on a large acreage. We belie they have the yield too high; for Potatoes were not so large a crop as many imagined last year. After all, if you plant Salzer's Potatoes it pays you, even if yo get 12%, cents a bushel. Why, the editor of the Rural New Yorker had from Salzer's Earliest Potato (besides being the earliest of all the varieties he tested) yield of 450 bu. per acre. Now, take this at 12½c a bushel, comes $56.00 per acre, 50 acres $2,500.00. What cro pays you better; Mr. Farmer?

In addition to the above named 1,000 acres, our company owns and controls other lands in the Dakotas, an large tracts in Minnesota and Wisconsin, for the production of Salzer's far-famed Northern-grown seeds. Ou crops have been unusually fine, quality high, and we are prepared to please every customer who will favor u with his order.

PREMIUMS.

We want to make it an object for you to see your neighbor, and have him order seeds with you, so that yo can send in large orders, and thus receive the seeds at reduced prices, as you will notice the greater the numb of bushels the cheaper the price. Thus, with the Big Four Oats, 1 bushel costs $1.50, 25 bushels $22.00, a scale of $33.50 on 25 bushels.

In addition to getting seeds cheaper by having large orders, we give the following premiums: Premium are only sent with your order when you ask for same. On all farm seed orders netting $10.00 or over we allo you to select any of the following eight premiums: Suppose your order is for $25.00, you could then select, you chose, a No. A1 Bell for the first $25.00, or any of the other premiums for the balance, $80.00. You need o select only of one variety, but of as many of the following as the amount of your order entitles you to, In addition, we always aim to throw in extra seeds.

1. The Bell.

It would do your heart good to read the hundreds of testimonials and hearty indorsements received, especially from the farmers' wives, on our bell premium. It is just the thing they want, as it is a great saving time and many a step to the good housewife. It is a great convenience. Every farmhouse will find a be to call their help quickly a great advantage. Here is a Premium Bell that you can get with little effort who else-required can be heard a full mile. An hour spent with your neighbors soliciting orders for our Farm an Vegetable Seeds gives you the Bell.

OUR PREMIUM BELL

Premiums only sent with order when you ask for same.

Order netting $25.00—No. A1 Bell, weight 40 pounds............$5.00 } These Bells are sent only whe
Order netting $30.00—No. A3 Bell, weight 75 pounds............ 7.50 } farmers request same, otherwis
Order netting $50.00—No. A4 Bell, weight 104 pounds.......... 25.00 } we make our own selection.

2. The La Crosse Sewing Machine.

This Sewing Machine is made for us in large quantities; is simple in construction, light running, easily managed, and warranted for 10 years. It is unique and attractive in style, and elegantly finished. It is listed everywhere at $55.00, but our contract with the manufactory is so large that we can afford to sell them for the strikingly low price of $17.50 cash with order, or if our customers will send us an order for $100.00 worth of Seeds, Plants, Tools, etc., taken at random from our catalogue, we will forward this machine free. The easiest way to get the machine and make your good wife happy is to see your neighbors and take orders for $100.00 worth of Seeds, Plants, Tools, etc. You have no idea how easy it is to get up a large order if you will make up your mind to do so. Has used with great satisfaction by Mrs. Salzer, and will surely please. Cash price, only $17.50.

3. Early Russian Millet.

(See page 95.)

Of this Millet we give the following:
On a $3.00 order we give 1 lb., cost $0.25
On a 5.00 order we give 5 lbs., cost ...... .50
On a 8.00 order we give 10 lbs., cost 1.00
On a 10.00 order we give 15 lbs., cost 1.50
On a 15.00 order we give 35 lbs., cost 2.25
On a 25.00 order we give 50 lbs., cost 4.00

4. Bismarck Hog Food.

This wonderful Pea (See page 82) we give as premiums as follows on your orders:
A $5.00 Farm Seed order gets 1 pk. $0.75
A 7.00 Farm Seed order gets 2 pk. 1.25
A 10.00 Farm Seed order gets 3 pk. 1.75
A 12.00 Farm Seed order gets 4 pk. 2.00
A 18.00 Farm Seed order gets 5 pk. 3.25

5. The McKinley Rocker.

THE McKINLEY ROCKER.
Our cash price, $3.66.

This splendidly built rattan-chair we give free with each order for $25.00 worth of Plants, Trees, Vegetable seeds, etc. The chair is worth $6.00 in any market. Our cash price, $3.66.

Salzer's Magnificent Pumpkins.

1. SALZER'S SILVER KING BARLEY.

The Egyptians claim the distinction of having first used Barley as a cereal. This we know—that it has been cultivated for many years. We really wonder what those great builders of the pyramids and the sphinxes, those dwellers on the fertile lands of the Nile, would really think if they could see our magnificent new Silver King Barley. Why, we believe that this new Barley of ours is so far ahead of the Barley that was grown 4,000 years ago as the telegraph is faster than the old mode of carrying news by carrier. We are going to start right in here, in the description of this Barley, in making what may seem to some a bold statement, namely, that there is no six-rowed Barley in the world that can approach it in yields, in the many good qualities and great excellency. Now, we know that you will say that this is a strong statement; but, sir, if you will use this Barley, and if you will give it a fair trial, as 1,000 of our customers have this past season, you will say, as they do, that it is not half strong enough. We are sure of this, for we know a little about Barley having introduced several of the very best varieties that are now in the trade in America, but our Silver King towers head and shoulders above them.

It is the Barley to grow in the North; it is the Barley to grow in the South; it is the Barley to grow in the East, and it is the Barley to grow in the West. It will do well everywhere and will return yields that will astonish you.

It's the Yielder. It's the finest bearded six-rowed Barley in existence, very early, ripe in June, of fine color. After Barley is cut you can get a crop of Early Russian Millet or Early Fodder Corn from same land.

In 1897 and 1898

The yield throughout America of Silver King Barley was simply astonishing,—almost fabulous. Here are a few of the growers:—

1. L. D. Nichols, Worthington, Iowa: "The Barley, I think, will yield 85 bushels per acre. It was too dry."

2. C. H. Mather, Colony, Kan.: "The Barley was very fine. Will yield 90 bushels per acre."

3. F. H. Hossler, Hamburg, Tenn.: "The Barley turned out very well. I think in a favorable season it will yield from 90 to 100 bushels per acre."

4. Wm. Powell, Linton, Ind.: "Your new **Barley is** very fine. It will yield 100 bushels per acre."

5. P. A. Stryker, Eaton, Ohio: "Your Barley is a hummer; 150 bushels per acre can be raised from same."

6. W. B. Peterson, Muscoda, Wis.: "Your Barley did splendidly. It is all right. It will yield 90 bushels per acre."

7. Mr. Andrew Boschert, brother of ex-Register of Deeds Boschert, says: "There has been Barley grown on my farm for over a quarter of a century, but I have never grown any that has been so wonderfully prolific as your Silver King Barley which I grew for you. One field in particular threshed out 80 bushels per acre, while another field went at the rate of 80 bushels per acre. This I think immense, especially when I took no special pains with same any further than to have the land clean and free from weeds. Common Barley, such as Manshury and Scotch, yielded at the rate of 35 to 40 bushels per acre. I think you have a bonanza in this wonderful new barley."

8. Nick Kutschelt, Arcadia, Wis.: "I raised 119 bushels and 3 pecks from 1 acre of your Silver King Barley the past season. It is the finest Barley I ever saw."

Read this Sworn Statement of Mr. John Breider.

9. "John Breider, Peter Wenner, Mike Casper and Christian Casper do each and severally solemnly swear that John Breider, living at Mishicott, Manitowoc County, Wisconsin, grew on one measured acre, containing 43,560 square feet, 173 bushels of 50 pounds per bushel, of Salzer's Silver King Barley the past season; that same was threshed by Princel & Ronaller, whose oath as to the correctness of above is hereunto appended. Subscribed and sworn to by John Breider. Christian Casper, Mike Casper, Peter Wenner.

"We, Mathias Princel and Frank Ronaller, owners of the threshing machine, do solemnly swear that we threshed for John Breider, of Mishicott, Manitowoc County, Wisconsin, 173 bushels of 50 pounds to the bushel, of Salzer's Silver King Barley, grown from 1 acre.—Mathias Princel, Frank Ronaller. Subscribed and sworn to before me this 19th day of October, A. D. 1896.—Bruno Miller, Justice of the Peace.

$100 IN GOLD

Mr. Breider won

Growing 173 bushels per acre.

PRICE OF SALZER'S GREAT SILVER KING **BARLEY.**
Pkg., 10c; lb., 30c; postpaid; by freight, pk., 60c; ½ bu., $1.00; bu., $1.85; 2½ bu., $3.00; 10 bu., $11.50; 30 bu., $30.00.

2. Highland Chief (Two-Rowed.)

A splendid Barley, though not so prolific and heavy-yielding as the Manshury, and far behind the Silver King; but is a fine, large, splendid-kerneled variety, and one that we are sure will please you.
Pkg., 10c; bu., $1.35; 2 bu., $2.25; 10 bu., $9.00.

3. Salzer's Manshury Barley.

No Barley, since its introduction, ever so gained so prolific a sale as Salzer's Manshury. The heads are very long, filled with plump kernels; straw is strong. It is six-rowed, and yields from 60 to 80 bushels per acre. Next to our Silver King Barley, this is the best to grow for a general crop. There are hundreds of farmers who think there is no Barley in the wide world that equals this. It is very prolific to boot, easy to thresh, no waste to please, usually has a excellent color and is eagerly purchased by maltsters. Prof. Henry, of Wisconsin's Agricultural College, in his report says: "The Manshury still heads the list in productiveness."
DAKOTA SEED—Pkg., 5c; by freight, pk., 50c; bu., $1.00; 2½ bu., $3.00; 10 bu., $9.50.

4. Salzer's Giant White Hulless Barley.

Our stock of the Giant White Hulless, as also the Black Hulless Barley, is short this year owing to an almost entire failure of the crop. In addition to this, the White Hulless is mixed with the common six-rowed Barley, though the black is quite pure. We make this announcement so that all purchasing seed will know beforehand just what they are getting of these two sorts this year. It is no detriment to be mixed, as far as feeding qualities are concerned, and what we say here of the White Hulless is applicable also, to the Black Barley. Both of these sorts furnish magnificent food for hogs and cattle; it makes the growing of hogs possible in the extreme north, Dakota, Montana and other states where corn growing is not profitable. Indeed to grow both of these two Barleys and feed them alongside of corn is one of the greatest things that the farmer can do, for the nutritious and feeding value of these two varieties of Barley are simply immense, and we urge every farmer having hogs or cattle to sow a few acres of these two Barleys for stock feeding purposes. The yield averages ordinarily 40 to 80 bushels per acre.
Price of Giant White Hulless Barley: Pkg., 10c; lb., 30c; postpaid, pk., 70c; bu., $3.00; 2½ bu., $5.50.

5. Black Hulless Barley.

BLACK HULLESS BARLEY.

What we have said of the excellencies of White Hulless Barley is applicable also to the Black Hulless Barley. Both sorts are splendid for stock feeding.
Price of Black Hulless Barley: Pkg. 10c; lb., 30c; postpaid, 40c; bu., $3.00; 2½ bu., $5.50.

FREE.

With each 1 bushel order of any of our 3 great Barley sorts we give 1 lb.; with each 2½ bu. order 5 lbs., with each 10 bu. order 20 lbs. of our Earliest Russian Millet. Five pounds is sufficient for one-half acre and will give you 3 tons of hay. It's wonderfully prolific and can be sown on same land after barley is taken off, and gives a big crop same year. For description see page 95.

6. SALZER'S GREAT BEARDLESS BARLEY.

It is positively the greatest Barley on earth. Now, while Salzer's Silver King Barley has the proud distinction of being the greatest yielder, the finest, plumpest-kerneled Bearded Barley on earth, we claim for Salzer's New Beardless Barley the same distinction under the beardless varieties. Two years ago we first introduced the Beardless Barley, and this we quickly takes up by a number of seedsmen and sent out under high-sounding names. We then did not push the Beardless Barley because we had it not perfected; but to-day, in our Salzer's Beardless Barley we have positively the greatest Barley on earth. It is just the Barley that you have been looking for, Mr. Farmer. We know it, because we have farmed for so many years, and have often been so annoyed and vexed in harvesting the common varieties of Barley that were covered with long, sharp, sticky beards! Now, that is all done away with, and thousands of farmers who tried Salzer's Beardless Barley for the first time in 1895 were more than delighted and pleased with the results. Not only were they astonished at the great yields and fine quality, but also—the best of all—the nuisance of "the sticky old beards" was done away with entirely. Now, that is just what you have been looking for, Mr. Farmer, and

Hogs Fatten and are Healthy and Happy on Beardless Barley.

Price: Pkg., 10c, postpaid; by freight, pk., 45c; bu., $1.25; 2½ bu., $3.00; 10 bu., $11.00.

7. Success Barley.

A beardless variety offered by quite a number of firms. It is fine in every respect, but we do not consider it so strong, healthy and prolific as our Salzer's Beardless Barley. Pkg., 10c; bu., $1.25; 2 bu., $2.25.

8. Dakota Silver Beardless Barley.

This, no doubt, is the Success Barley introduced by us some years ago and renamed by a seedsman. It is not as good or as prolific as Salzer's Beardless, though it is a beardless variety. Our stock was obtained from parties who were let by a certain seed company who offered them big prices for their products and then failed to come up to the mark.

Price: Pkg., 10c; lb., 35c; by freight, pk., 50c; bu., $1.00; 2½ bu., $2.50; 10 bu., $9.50.

FREE.

With each order for one bushel of our eight Barley sorts we give free one pound of Earliest Russian Millet, worth 25c; with each 2½-bushel order five pounds, worth 50c; with each 5-bushel order 10 pounds, worth $1.00; with each 10-bushel order 25 pounds; with each 20-bushel order 50 pounds of our Earliest Russian Millet. For description, see page 93.

New Japanese Buckwheat.

There is probably no cereal of recent production that has grown so fast in public favor. It is the most wondrously prolific, hardy Buckwheat known. Its yield bears on to the fabulous, as 60 bu. per acre is common, while it frequently yields as high as 80 and even 100 bu. It is a long bloomer, the kernel more than double the size of other varieties, of excellent flavor, and splendid for buckwheat flour.

John Tumbull, of Houston county, Minn., says: "I sowed 1¾ bu. of Japanese Buckwheat and harvested 132 bu."

Thousands of other farmers report yields of 50 to 100 bu. from 1 bu. of seed sown. It is the most marvelous cropper in the world.

Pkg., 5c/lb., postpaid, 30c; pk., by freight, 50c; bu. $1.50; 2½ bu., $3.00.

New Calcutta Buckwheat.

This variety comes from India, and rivals the celebrated Japanese Buckwheat in productiveness and yield, while in beauty it is far ahead of any other sort. Its kernels are smooth and fine, and it is in great demand as a milling Buckwheat. Every miller will want it. Pkg., 10c; lb., postpaid, 30c; by freight, pk., $2.00; 2½ bu., $3.75.

Common Buckwheat—Pk., 35c; bu., $1.25.

Silver Hull—Its advantage is, it blooms longer, matures sooner. Grain of a beautiful light gray color, while hull is thin. Exceptionally fine for bees. Flour of unusual richness. Pkg., 5c; lb., 25c; pk., 45c; bu., $1.50; 2½ bu., $3.50.

Russian Flax.

Growing Flax, even in a small way, pays. Our Russian Flax yields from 22 to 34 bushels per acre, and this, at a low price of only 60c a bushel, would pay. Pkg., 5c; lb., 30c; 4 lbs., $1.00, postpaid; by freight, pk., 50c; bu., $1.50; 2½ bu., $3.50.

Bismarck's Hog Food Pea.

Germany feeds her hogs Sand Vetch, Spurry and Giant Incarnat Clover; but the fattest flesh-and-blood producer—the fattest hog—is produced by peas and barley. That from Chancellor Bismarck, had a great estate; his hogs were always the secret and the envy of all, and we finally found. His was a rare food—a great Pea—that was used—a secret for years. It is said that from a single pod of this Pea our stocks has developed and grown until we offer it as a premium, (see page 88) and for sale. It is a great field Pea, so fat and rich as a Marrowfat, but more healthy and prolific, while the Pea itself is smaller. You will want this; it is immense. Given as a premium (see page 88). Price: Pkg., 7½c; ¼ bu., $1.25; 8 pks., $1.75; 1 bu., $2.00; 2 bu., $3.75.

Green Scotchman.

This Pea, above all others, should be planted by the farmer and stock grower. It is tremendously prolific, and is, indeed, a magnificent sort, a very hardy and vigorous grower, doing well in almost all climes, yielding all the way from 25 to 40 bu. of fine Peas per acre. We earnestly urge all farmer customers to give Green Scotchman a thorough trial. Hogs can be turned into the field and fed, just as they are ripening, and they will consume not only the Pea, but also most of the vines; or they can be turned into the field when ripe. They are great fatteners. These Peas sell at fancy prices in dry or green state for eating. Pkg., 5c; pk., 50c; ½ bu., $1.15; 2½ bu., $2.75.

White Hundredfold Pea.

This remarkable white field Pea is the result of careful selection, and is probably the heaviest yielding white field Pea, next to Bismarck's Hog Food Pea, known in the world to-day. It will yield all the way from 25 to 40 bu. per acre. Price, including sacks, pk., 50c; bu., $1.15; 2½ bu., $2.75.

Canada Field Pea.

Well known. Price: Bu., $1.50; 2½ bu., including sacks, $2.00; 10 bu., $8.25. When stock is exhausted will fill at La Crosse market price.

SALZER'S PROLIFIC COW PEA.

The Cow Pea has proven to be one of the greatest fertilizers of the age, and we doubt not—if we make the statement that it is richer in fertilizing matter, more lasting, more beneficial, a greater soil improver, and a better soil enricher than the fertilizer drawn out from the barnyard—that many of our farmer friends will feel like challenging this statement; but nevertheless, gentlemen, it is a fact. It will take longer to enrich a thoroughly worn-out piece of land to fertilize from the barnyard than by sowing a plenty of Cow Peas and plowing them under. You can put two very ordinary crops of Cow Peas on the same piece of land in one season by sowing them early in spring, after frosts are over, broadcast, at the rate of 90 pounds per acre, or in drills 2 inches apart, and, when these have attained the height of thirty inches plow them under; or sow a second crop at the same rate. This latter crop is ready either to plow under the first of October or to cut for food, or to let the cattle graze upon the same, and then replow the field before frost. The next season this land is fit for Corn, Potatoes, Oats or Wheat crop.

Pkg., 10c; lb., postpaid, 25c; by freight, 15 lbs., 90c; 25 lbs., $1.35; 50 lbs., $2.50; 100 lbs., $4.50.

Clay-Colored, Red Ripper or Whip-poor-will Cow Peas (well known), each sort—Pkg., 5c; 15 lbs., 75c; 25 lbs., $1.15; 50 lbs., $2.00;

NORTHERN GROWN SEED CORN

We wish particularly to emphasize this point, that Northern-grown seed is of untold value to the farmer, especially should Jack Frost visit the West in 1899, as early as he did in 1897. We hold that Corn ripening thoroughly in the Dakotas and Wisconsin, will grow with more vigor, be earlier, return larger crops, and in each and every particular be superior to Corn grown in other states. This point alone should make our Corn cheap at double the price asked. Rather pay $70.00 per bushel for Salzer's Northern-Grown Corn than take chances on Southern and Eastern Corn, even as a gift. Why, we bought some Iowa Early Dent Corn last spring, and it failed to ripen at La Crosse, in Northern Iowa, and Southern Minnesota. Such Corn is DEAR AS A GIFT!

FOUR GREAT FODDER PLANTS.

Probably the four most prolific fodder plants grown. Of each plant 10 lbs. per acre, in drills or rows, and then watch the enormous quantity of rich fodder it will produce. Cultivate like corn.

1. Kaffir Corn.

The average height is 5 feet. It is used as green fodder, and as such is eagerly eaten by all cattle, hogs, etc., while the seed (50 to 80 bushels per acre) makes an excellent fattener.

2. Milo Maize Corn.

The farmer is fairly wild over this. It will produce more rich green fodder than any other sort except Teosinte. It grows well where Amber Cane succeeds. The seed is an excellent fattener, and is relished by all cattle, hogs, etc.

3. The Jerusalem Corn.

Belongs to the non-saccharine sorghums, and was brought a few years since from the arid plains of Palestine.

4. Branching Doura Corn.

Yields from 5 to 10 stalks from one seed.

KAFFIR CORN.

WISCONSIN AMBER SUGAR CANE.

We often wonder how it comes that this magnificent plant is so greatly neglected as a fodder plant. Have you ever tried it, Mr. Farmer?

AS A PASTURE PLANT.

SEED REQUIRED AND HOW TO CULTIVATE.

EARLY AMBER SUGAR CANE.

BROOM CORN.

Wisconsin Evergreen—

California Golden—

Early Japanese—

EARLY ORANGE CANE.

Salzer's Great Brazilian Flour Corn.

One of the greatest novelties ever introduced. Originated in Brazil, where it constitutes the principal food of the inhabitants. It is truly a marvelous plant.

Price of Brazilian Flour Corn.

WISCONSIN EARLIEST WHITE DENT FIELD CORN.

This is the earliest large-eared Yellowish White Dent Corn.

SALZER'S SUPERIOR FODDER CORN

FEEDING IN GREEN STATE

$4000 LBS PER ACRE

for IDEAL CORN PLANTED

Ideal, 75c.

ing, right along, that rich quality is one... the same time, looking for a root-containing rich ... tive quality. For the purpose we wanted a rapid-growing, early, ... jointed, tall corn with a great abundance of leaves and tender stalk, rich, juicy, sweet, sugary flesh in the stalk, with a tendency to mature several ears, so a Corn of this nature furnishes more tons of green fodder per acre, and almost fool to the termination that common Corn gives. This is what we were after. A Corn succeeds even in the North, good ears, fine, hard-jointed stock and a prodigal supply of leaves,—and this we obtain, by careful selection, in Salzer's Fodder or Ensilage Corn. It is immeasurably ahead of the E. & W. Corn-sinensis, it outstrips that sort in yield and twice in quality. It will furnish more dry matter, more nourishment than any other ensilage Corn known.

See This, Oh Friend of Good Fodder!

Chas. E. Brands, Trevedell, Kenosha county, Wis., says: "The Salzer's Superior Fodder Corn that I got from you last spring is truly a great and wonderful Corn. I planted it the latter part of June, and some of it nearly ripened before the early frosts. There are two big ears on almost every stalk, and if it had been planted earlier there would have been magnificent Corn thoroughly ripened."

"Racine, Wis., Sept. 14—Out on my farm we planted nearly five acres of your Salzer's Superior Fodder Corn, and it is a sight. From one square rod we cut and bound 450 lbs. and this, I believe, is at the rate of 36 tons (72,000 lbs.) per acre—C. C. Beebe.

That is the way thousands of farmers feel about our Superior Fodder Corn, which certainly has no equal in the United States as a great food producer. Of course Salzer's Earliest Ripe is earlier by several weeks. Finds some of both—that's the way to do. The seed is so cheap.

Mr. Frank Riley, Iowa county, reports the following boats:

Red Cob Fodder Corn (from Nebraska)	20,000 lbs. per acre
R. & W. (obtained from Philadelphia)	25,000 " " "
Giant Fodder (from Iowa)	37,000 " " "
Salzer's Superior Fodder Corn	54,000 " " "

He says: "Salzer's Superior Fodder is certainly worth three times as much as R. & W., when big ears, full ears, and lots of them, together with the enormous quantity of leafy fodder is considered. Salzer's Superior Fodder Corn is positively worth double in nutritive value of any I ever saw. I have grown this Fodder Corn is simply peerless for very, very early."

Ten Thousand More Like It!

Mr. Riley's experiment is one of ten thousand. Wherever our Salzer's Fodder Corn was tested last year astonishing reports come of its excellent yield and nutritive quality. This is a hard shot if farmers—if our great and glorious United States would each plant 5 acres of Salzer's Fodder Corn, 5 acres to Salzer's Superior Millet, 5 acres Giant Spurry, 5 acres Superior Seed Vetch and 15 acres to Salzer's Alfalfa or Lucerne, they could make over $300,000,000 worth more cattle than they are now doing. Why not have these 30 acres net you $3,000 a year? How surely the $1,000 would make the chances in your home you and your good wife have long coveted to pay! Why not try it!

DON'T BE FOOLED by mendacious and others offering you the R. & W. or other sorts as "just as good." They are not. That's the way they will talk. Don't believe it. There is only one high grade, high quality, big yielding, nutritious sort, one that beats them all 50 per cent., yes, 100 per cent. and even more! That's the sort you want to plant, and that kind is Salzer's Fodder or Ensilage Corn.

Price of Salzer's Superior Fodder Corn: Pkg. 10c; by freight, pk., 50c; bu., $1.35; 2 bu., $2.00; 10 bu., $9.00.

SALZER'S EARLIEST RIPE.

This Corn has leaped with one wild bound into popularity and nothing that we have or sold has given such great satisfaction. Everywhere throughout the United States have Salzer's Earliest Ripe Fodder Corn was planted, is surprised and delighted of pleased and astonished the grower. It was ripe in 85 days and furnished magnificent eating Corn just at a time when farmers were short of Corn. If you plant this early, will have fine Seeding Corn by July, when you can reckon ears and have good Fodder Corn in September too. This is the most wonderful Corn in the world. It would take J. C. Webster's dictionary to fully describe its many merits, that is, if you are in the oat business, and if you are in the business to make money.

Our customers would be surprised if we told them how many thousand bushels of Salzer's Superior Fodder Corn are annually planted by our farmer friends. It has gotten to so that no Scotchman farmer—that is, a farmer up for the times, who is wide-awake—wants to go by without planting from 5 to 15 acres to Fodder Corn. Fodder Corn is one of the cheapest things that can be grown on the farm and one of the very best paying ones. We sometimes grow very largely of Fodder Corn, being anxious in preference to hay, if want the hay market is reasonably high we dispose of our hay and use fodder; because the fodder can be grown for about one-fifth what hay costs and another thing, if you cut such rich, luxuriant fodder as we offer, it is almost as good, yes, many farmers say better, as the very best hay, that is, for cattle.

Now for years there has been a call for an extremely early Fodder Corn, and in order meet this demand, we have been experimenting and improving, and testing and breeding and crossing varieties of Corn, until to-day we have

The Most Perfect, Earliest, Rich Fodder Corn in Existence.

This Corn will ripen out ears inside of 80 days after planting, and usually from 10 to 3 feet on the stalk. The foliage is probably 5 feet high, very leafy and heavy, and contains tremendous amount of nutritious matter. Of course this is not as pretty as or as good as Superior Fodder Corn, but it has the advantage over any and every other Fodder corn in the world to-day by its being 80 days earlier. The farmer can easily figure out a great profit in having a Fodder Corn extremely early, having it come all the time when pasturage is short, and he can then feed this rich, luxuriant Salzer's Earliest Ripe Fodder Corn.

We could furnish 5,000 testimonials of farmers who used Earliest Ripe the past two years; all are loud in their great praises. Remember both Early Ripe and Superior Fodder have Salzer's warranty to please. Says J. E. New, Webb, Minn.: "I just can't get along without your Earliest Ripe Fodder Corn. It is the finest thing I ever saw; and your Early Grey White Dent can't be beaten. I can't say too much for your corns." H. T. Lovejoy, Red Wing, Minn., says: "Grew 3 magnificent crops of Early Ripe Fodder from the same field the first season."

Another thing, if this Corn is desired for winter fodder, it can be planted early; it can be cut months ahead of frost, and can be stored away in frost or as shown, and will keep all winter. Thresh it down before your busy fall work comes on. We believe Salzer's Earliest Fodder Corn worthy of a thorough, extensive trial impartial test on every farm in the land, and we state unqualifiedly, and believe that there is nothing that if not the presence of [...] for profit generously of it.

You will send us its charm if you send us this for a Fodder Corn.

PRICE OF SALZER'S EARLIEST RIPE FODDER CORN: Pkg. 10c; qt., 40c; by freight, pk., 50c; bu., $1.50; 2 bu., $2.50; 10 bu., $14.00.

SALZER'S EARLIEST RIPE FODDER CORN.

Friends, 80 bu. ripe ears 80 days after planting!

QUEEN OF THE NORTH CORN.

For years we have experimented, and tested the scores of sorts offered by seedsmen, in search of truly superior Corn—one troubled, to fully withstand the rigor of our climate, the combining earliness, productiveness, fair size in ear and length of kernel in a golden whole; and this we have finally found in our superb Queen of the North, unquestionably one of the earliest, finest and most productive deep-grained Yellow Dent Corn grown. Grows to the height of 6 to 8 feet; very frequently bearing two well developed ears, with kernels closely set (so if wedged) on a thin cob, kernels very long and thin, beautiful golden-orange color. It is the finest appearing shelled Corn we have ever seen.

One Hundred Bushels Shelled Corn Per Acre.

It is decidedly the Corn for a general crop, especially in Wisconsin, Minnesota and the Dakotas—weighs more than any other Corn we know of. Seventy pounds of Corn on cobs when shelled weigh 61 to 63 pounds, leaving the cobs to weigh only 9 pounds.

Our seed of this is carefully grown, and we can safely say that no early Yellow Dent Corn offered in America can get up to it in earliness and big yields. For the past 10 years it has never failed on account of early frosts. IT WAS AHEAD of frost every time. Its solid ears are ripe weeks before! Look out for Nebraska and Iowa Seed Corn. We bought some in 1897 and it failed to get ripe in Wisconsin, Minnesota or Northern Iowa. Use only Wisconsin grown!

Lots of Money in It for You, Mr. Farmer!

Suppose, in the states of Wisconsin, Minnesota and the Dakotas, where early Corn is needed, the farmers had all planted Salzer's Peerless Queen of the North, an extremely early, heavy-cropping Yellow Dent. See the difference! These states planted

  2,231,734 acres to Corn, and received $4,203,000.00 bu., or about 21½ bu. per acre.
Now, had these broad acres been planted to Queen of the North, the result would have been:
  2,231,734 acres at only 45 bu. per acre (it has often cropped 75, 90 and 100) .... 104,390,330 bu.
  Deduct grown as above, ... 64,393,600 bu.

  40,727,360 bu. @ only 80c=$32,218,184.00]   A difference of .... 40,722,240 bu.
Just think of it, Farmer, and then act; act in the right direction, and plant Queen of the North for 1898.
Why, if you only plant 20 acres, it makes a difference of over 840 bushels.

PRICE OF SALZER'S QUEEN OF THE NORTH CORN:
By mail, pkg. 10c; qt. 35c; by express, qt. 20c; pk. 50c; bu. $1.50; 2½ bu. $3.00; 5 bu. $5.50; 10 bu. $10.00.

Salzer's King of the Earliest.

A peerless Yellow Dent Corn, resembling the far-famed Salzer's Queen of the North. It's early, a fine, full cob, and has been known to yield 120 bushels of Corn on ears per acre! It's a Corn for extreme early, though not so popular and early as Salzer's celebrated Queen of the North.

Price of King of the Earliest Corn:
Pkg. 10c; qt. 35c, postpaid; by freight, qt. 20c; pk. 50c; bu. $1.75; 2½ bu. $3.50; 5 bu. $6.00.

Early Huron Dent Corn.

This is sold by Philadelphia and other seedsmen as their earliest Yellow Dent Corn. Now, it is not as early as Queen of the North, but we have secured it from the introducer, Mr. Clark, who grows same for the Philadelphia seedsmen. Pkg. 10c; by freight, pk. 60c; ½ bu. 90c; bu. $1.50.

SALZER'S EARLY GIANT WHITE DENT CORN.

What Queen of the North Corn is among the earliest varieties of Yellow Dent Corn, namely head and shoulders above them all, Salzer's Early Giant White Dent Corn is among the white sorts. It is the most natural producing Corn that we have ever seen. By this we mean that it most produces and ripens Corn. It grows so easily and naturally as a weed and it produces without fail from one to three great big ears of Corn to each kernel planted. In addition to this it is always ahead of frost no matter how early and ready it comes to. This past season our Salzer's Early Giant White Dent Corn ripened for us at La Crosse thirty days ahead of the frost, and frost came the middle of September this year!

Salzer's Early Giant White Dent Corn is a magnificent corn to plant for a general crop; indeed we have farmers who plant no other. The Hon. J. C. Easton, who owns several score of farms, pronounces this the very best white Corn in existence. Governor Hoffman thinks there is nothing like it for heavy yields, fine quality and for sure ripening. Out in Dakota it ripened perfectly during the past cool season and wherever tried our Early

Giant White Dent Corn has proven the victor.

Right here in La Crosse, an Eight-Acre Patch the Past Summer Yielded 1,100 Bushels of Magnificent Ears.

It is really a Corn "to tie to," as the farmer says, and we earnestly urge everybody to give it a trial, no matter where you plant, whether in Dakota or down in Texas, as it is a Corn that will do magnificently everywhere. The ears are large, handsome, well shaped, large grains of white to satin white color (our artist we think has kernels too narrow and deep, borne on stalks growing to medium size, very heavy, with few suckers, producing from one to three splendid heavy ears to each stalk.

The highest report of yield that we have had comes from a customer in Iowa, who reports 213 bushels of shelled Corn from one single measured acre. We recommend this Corn because it grows as naturally as a weed. It must produce. That's its mission and for this reason we unhesitatingly indorse the same. It has never failed us. It has always borne heavily and it yield was all that we could expect from same. We close this description with a letter from Mr. Layton Yancy.

Mr. Layton Yancy, Waverly, Mo., writes regarding this Corn: "Your Early Giant White Dent Corn made a splendid yield, considering the unfavorable season. Was ready to crib almost 90 days before our home-grown seed. It has—most all of it—been spoken for for seed." Now, then, the way to make money is to follow Mr. Layton Yancy's example. Plant new varieties of seed Corn, Oats, Potatoes, Grasses, etc., and sell them to your neighbors for seed.

PRICE OF SALZER'S EARLY GIANT WHITE DENT CORN: Pkg. 10c; lb. 25c, postpaid; by freight, pk. 60c; ½ bu. $1.00; bu. $1.50; 2½ bu. $3.50; 10 bu. $12.50.

Iowa takes the prize on Giant White Dent with a yield of 213 Bushels Shelled Corn per Acre.

THE NEW LEAMING.

The new Leaming Corn is a grand strain. As we now have it, it is the earliest Yellow Dent Corn in cultivation, next to the Queen of the North. The Queen of the North is a smaller cobbed, earlier variety, which is followed closely by the Leaming. This strain ripened at La Crosse the past season by September 20th, ahead of Jack Frost every time. It is not a hard Corn, but sweet and nutritious, making excellent feed and the finest meal. The ears are large and handsome, with deep, large grain, of deep orange color, and small, red cob. The stalks grow to medium size (fine large), with few suckers, tapering gradually from root to top, producing two good ears to each stalk. Husks and shells easily. One hundred and thirty bushels shelled Corn to the acre are common on good Corn ground, with good, but not extra, cultivation. It is also adapted to a greater variety of soils than any other varieties, producing successfully on all light or gravelly land, where other varieties would not thrive. Hon. J. C. Easton, the great railroad magnate, owning and operating many farms, says: "Your new Leaming is the finest, earliest, heaviest yielding Yellow Dent I ever saw. Why, there were ears 12 inches long—fine, full, heavy."

I. H. Loschenge, Areaville, Ill.:—"New Leaming Corn will yield 75 bu. per acre. Common Corn, 60."

Now, then, we cannot say too much in favor of our strain of New Leaming Corn. It is odd different in all good qualities from it parent that many of our farmer friends tell us that we are too modest in nothing forth its claims, having been crossed with early and later Yellow Dent sorts, with a type quite uniform, very large ears, with equal cobs and deep kernels. Think of this magnificent Corn ripening on our lands in Minnesota, 100 miles north of La Crosse, and bearing at the rate of over

100 Bushels per Acre on 25 Acres—2,575 Bushels.

and then got ahead of the first September frost! It's a wonderful Corn—wonderful in all of its makeup. We have seen ear after ear measuring from 10 to 14 inches long, filled to the top with heavy, golden grain. It is difficult to believe that such handsome Corn can be grown in Western Wisconsin, South Dakota and Central Minnesota on account of the climate, but the field of 25 acres was the finest patch of even, large-eared, uniform-sized Corn that we ever saw. Like it? Of course you will. It's wonderful. It's hardy, it's early, it's ahead of Jack Frost here every time. It's a tremendous yielder, it's a producer of magnificent ears, it's the Corn to plant for profit, it's the moneymaker. Do try a bushel or more for 1898. PRICE OF NEW LEAMING: Pkg. 10c; pt. 20c; qt. 35c, postpaid; by freight: pkg. 10c; pt. 15c; qt. 30c; pk. 80c; bu. $1.25; bag (2 bu.), $2.25; 5 bu. $5.50; 10 bu. $10.00.

Salzer's Golden Triumph Corn.

Golden Triumph is Extremely Early.

STATE OF PENNSYLVANIA. } ss.
COUNTY OF BRADFORD,

JUST READ THIS AFFIDAVIT FROM MR. WALTERS.

PRICE OF GOLDEN TRIUMPH CORN.

Pkg., 10c; lb., 25c; 3 lbs., $1.00, postpaid; by freight, pk., 60c; ½ bu., $1.00; bu., $1.75; 2½ bu., $4.00; 10 bu., $15.00.

CLARK'S EARLY MASTODON CORN—YELLOW DENT.

Pkg., 10c; lb., 25c; 5 lbs., $1.00, postpaid; by freight, pk., 50c; bu., $1.40; 2 bu., $2.25; 10 bu., $15.00.

Iowa Gold Mine.

Iowa "Silver Mine" Dent Corn.

CHESTER COUNTY MAMMOTH YELLOW DENT

MAMMOTH WHITE DENT CORN

CHAMPION WHITE PEARL

Salzer's New White Cap Yellow Dent Corn.

NOW, MR. FARMER,

HERE ARE TWO LETTERS:

Price: Pkg., 10c; lb., 35c; postpaid; by express, pk., 60c; ½ bu., 90c; bu., $1.50; 2½ bu., $3.00.

GOLDEN I. X. L. YELLOW DENT CORN.

This great Yellow Dent Corn we sent out for the first time last spring under Salzer's Nameless Bounty, and a prize of $150.00 was offered for the most suitable name, which was awarded to Frank G. Watkins, who named it in this space, for the splendid name Salzer's Golden I. X. L. The idea of the committee, no doubt, was that, judging from the many excellent reports sent us to the quality of this corn, and the magnificent testimonials as to its yield, that it excelled all other known varieties of Yellow Dent, and judging from the hearty recommendation that farmers gave unto this Corn, it surely is well named, for this proud Corn can truly say "I Excel."

Fred Roberts, Annapolis, Mo., says: I must say that the yield is remarkable, fully twice as much as any other variety I ever tried—not a stalk with less than two good ears, and fully 60 per cent. with three or four ears; besides it is three weeks earlier than the usual kind planting here.

Silas W. Loomis, Petterville, Mich., who suggested the name Long Yellow Dent, says: Because the stalks grow long enough for fence-rails or hop-poles and the ears long enough for cord-wood, while the kernels are the longest ever seen by me. It is just the Corn the farmers have long been looking for, and it remained for Salzer's Seed Co. to furnish it. My only regret is that I did not plant a bushel of it.

$125.00 in Gold.

The following prizes were awarded and promptly paid to the winners:

1st prize, $35.00, W. A. Henson, Syracuse, N. Y. 27 lbs. from one acre
2nd prize, $25.00, Hans E. Lande, Kloristerville, Wis. 200 "   "   "
3rd prize, $15.00, Dora Besley, East Thetford, Mich. 200 "   "   "
4th prize, $10.00, W. A. Swingel, Ariel, Pa. 164 "   "   "

$25.00 in Gold for the Longest Ears.

1st prize, $10.00, W. L. Deneler, Bethany, Mo. 16 inches long
2nd prize, $7.50, John Martin, Parkerville, Mo. 16¼ "   "
3rd prize, $5.00, Salzer & Simonns, Brookville, Ohio. 15 "   "
4th prize, $2.50, Mrs. E. A. Coy, Springerton, Ill., and J. C. Barnett, Hickman, Ky. 14½ "   "

Above awards were made to the 1st, and the prize money promptly paid. We are sure that our customers who will plant Salzer's I. X. L. Corn for the coming season will be more than pleased and delighted with same. It is a enormous cropper, a grand, heavy-yielding, tremendously productive sort to plant. The only Corn that is its superior is Salzer's ALL GOLD, fully described on page 85. We urge farmers and others to give both of these corns names. Give it a trial.

PRICE OF SALZER'S GOLDEN I. X. L. CORN.
Pkg., 10c; lb., 35c; 3 lbs., $1.00, postpaid; by freight, pk., 60c; bu.
$1.75; 2½ bu., $4.00; 10 bu., $15.00.

Hickory King.

SMALLEST COB, LARGEST GRAIN, PURE WHITE DENT CORN.
So large are the grains and so extremely small the cob that on an ear broke a lb a half a single grain will almost completely cover the cob section, as shown by the illustration herewith. The stalks naturally bear two good ears each and occasionally three. The ears are uniformly well filled out, and it will make more shelled corn to a given bulk of ears than any other variety. Especially adapted for Southern corn states. It will not be amiss for Northern planters to test a package, and in a few years it will become acclimated, and that would be a great acquisition. By mail, pkg., 10c., 3 lbs. for 35c., postpaid; or by freight, pk., 60c; bu., $1.25; 7 bu., $6.00; 2½ bu., $3.00.

Minnesota King.

Almost an exact duplicate of Hickory King, only that the Corn is a beautiful yellow and much earlier, ripening perfectly in Minnesota, and yielding at the rate of 70 lbs. per acre. Pkg., 10c; qt., 25c, postpaid; by freight, pk., 60c; bu., $1.75.

FLINT CORN SORTS.

Salzer's South Dakota.

Ears large, long, of bright yellow color, kernels flinty size, thickly set; rows from 10 to 12 to a cob. Very productive, yielding 100 bushel baskets per acre. It is not uncommon to find 3 to 4 ears, 10 to 15 inches long, on one stalk. It matures early, and will be hailed with delight by our thousands of Dakota friends. A great point in its favor is that it has ripened at La Crosse, August 10th, fully 14 days ahead of the first slight frost. It is a magnificent sort, wonderfully prolific and very early; or, as a great field farmer said to us: "Salzer, your South Dakota Yellow Flint is not "Get there. Eli," but is there early and ripe waiting for Eli to get there!" Pkg., 10c; qt., 25c; by express, 20c; pk., 60c; bu., $1.50; 2½ bu., $3.00.

Salzer's North Dakota Flint Corn.

A magnificent variety of early White Flint Corn, with large ears, often 11 inches in length, solid kernels, with 8 to 9 rows to the cob, of a dark silver color. Price: pk., 60c; bu., $1.50.

PRICE OF THE FOLLOWING 7 SORTS:
Pkg., 10c; qt., 35c, postpaid; by freight, qt., 20c; pk., 60c; bu., $1.50; 2½ bu., $3.00.

1. Houghton's Silver White Flint.
This is a well-established variety, with uniform characteristics, including early maturity, medium size, both of stalk and ear.

2. Rideout or Mercer Flint.
Very early Yellow Flint.

3. Longyellow Field Flint.
Here is an 8-rowed Yellow Flint variety, the result of careful selection. The ears are from 10 to 16 inches long, 1¼ to 1½ inches in diameter. The cob is small, kernels large and hard. This Corn is well adapted to the Northwest, and is said to have produced 100 bushels of ears to the acre in Massachusetts.

4. Angel of Midnight Flint.
Begins to ripen August 5th, and is the earliest we have ever tried. Longest ears 14 inches, 8 rows, over 50 kernels in a row; kernels large, round, yellow, flat.

5. Squaw Flint Corn.
It was obtained from the Indians on the Sisseton reservation, where it never failed to ripen, and it was grown for us north of this reservation in South Dakota, yielding from 40 to 60 bushels Corn per acre. Early. It is as as though mixed, kernels often being white and black, etc.

6. Washakum Yellow Flint Corn.
Early; about 9 inches long; the kernel is long and deep, the color rich and glossy.

7. King Philip Corn.
This excellent colored Red Flint Corn is so well known that it needs no special description. It is an 8-rowed flint, from 8 to 12 inches long, and with good cultivation will yield 75 bushels per acre.

SALZER'S ALL GOLD or $3000·00 CORN

313 BUSHELS GROWN FROM ONE ACRE

ALL GOLD

or $3000·00 CORN

A WONDERFULL CROPPER

Salzer's New ALL GOLD or the $3,000 Corn.

The world does move and new crosses and hybridizations in the corn world have in the last ten years called forth the applause of the manufacturer and the wonder of our farmer who has taken pains to look into the matter. From a small yield of 33 bushels per acre, we have steadily progressed until the acre is now made to produce all the way from 80 to 313 bushels. Yes, sir! we say deliberately 313 bushels, for with Salzer's New Cross ALL GOLD it is possible for you, Mr. Farmer, to grow 313 bushels per acre. We know it. We were positive you can. There is no doubt about it. The vigor of this new corn, the great size of its ears, the enormous of the big ears and often three or four from each and every kernel planted makes this possible. Salzer's New ALL GOLD corn stands ready to completely revolutionize corn growing. It will make the careful farmer wonderfully rich. It's bound to do it! He can't help himself, wealth must come, providing he plants a plenty, therefore buy a bushel or two this year and experiment.

313 Bushels Per Acre.

How to grow 313 bushels per acre. It's easy. Take rich, deep, clean corn land. Place your rows four feet apart and one kernel of corn every 1½ inches in the row. If a kernel fails to come up, replant! This gives you over 11,000 hills of cornstalk to the hill at two pounds to the stalk; means over 313 bushels to the acre.

Give to ALL GOLD good, rich soil and one bushel seed planted on eight or nine acres is good for 1,500–2,400 bushels "sure as shooting!" Where a kernel fails to come up replant, so that the full number of stalks are on the acre. Now, so sure are we that this can be grown that we will give to the farmer growing the greatest amount of bushels, over

300 Bushels Per Acre, $100 in Gold.

We paid in 1898 $250.00 in prizes for the great I. X. L. Corn, a corn that is wonderful, but not nearly so remarkable, so prolific, so fine eared, so heavy, so golden, so rich and wealth producing as this new Salzer's All Gold. We are sure no corn you ever tried will please you better.

It's the Great $3,000 Corn.

At the rate of $3,000 per bushel was paid for the first start of this marvelously magnificent corn and we consider that cheap. We believe, Mr. Farmer, that if you paid us $100 a bushel for this corn you would be making money. Why, because it would pay you an immense yield, sure!

Take one bushel, cost $3.00, possible yield of 3 acres—2,100 bu.
Take one bushel common corn $0.30, possible yield of 3 acres—300 bu.

A difference in favor of All Gold of 1,700 bushels at 30 cts. a bushel of $525.00. We are not going to say much regards this corn this year. We have only two thousand bushels, but we advise you, Mr. Farmer, to do in the style to buy a bushel or more, get plenty, for your neighbors will want it for seed next year and will pay handsomely for it. It's the corn that will do its own talking next year. Then we will want 20,000 bushel seed to sell, for everybody who has seen this corn grow in 1899 will want it. It's a bonanza to every one growing it, as good as a gold mine. It's all gold, heavy, prolific. Buy plenty so you will have plenty to sell to your neighbors. It's the earliest big corn!

Look What Old Pennsylvania Produced!

M. M. Lother, East Troy, Pa., says: You were kind enough to send me a sample of your new $3,000 corn, sufficient to plant one acre. Pennsylvania is a splendid state for growing corn, and I am proud to report that I grew 300 bushels of the finest corn ever seen from the corn we planted. Your marvelous $3,000 corn, I believe it to be the greatest Yellow Dent Corn on earth, and it is sure to become a veritable gold mine to the farmer planting same largely. It is very early an enormous yielder, bearing two to three big ripe ears on a stalk.

It's the $3,000 Corn, It's the Corn You Will Want.

The corn that will make you money, will bring big crops of fine ears. It's the prize winner. Try it for 1899. The kernels are deep, long, reasonably large and are closely set on rather small cobs but making with the abundance of kernels a large, noble, heavy ear, just the kind of an ear that will fill a bushel basket quickly. It's so beautiful that the buyer always stands ready to pay a little more for ALL GOLD than any corn known to be. It's a beauty, a tremendously heavy yielder, a corn that is bound to be popular. It's early, right here in La Crosse, it was ripe Sept. 8, 1898, on the day we had our first frost the past season. It's only, very early for so big and noble an ear! Try it for 1899. Who wins the $100.00 for the biggest yield over 300 bushels. You can, no matter whether you live in Ia., Wis., Minn., Ill., Neb., Ka., or any other state. It's a yielder everywhere! Instead of asking $100 a bushel for it, it's surely worth that, we ask only 15 cents a very low price for this grand corn a arval.

PRICE OF SALZER'S ALL GOLD CORN.

Big Pkg., 15c; Pint, Postpaid, 30c; Quart, Postpaid, 50c.
By Freight, Pk., $1.00; ½ Bu., $1.70; Bu., $3.00; 2½ Bu., $6.50; 10 Bu., $25.
Farmers club together and buy ten bushels and get it for $2.50 a bushel.

SALZER'S GIANT SPURRY.

Our trip to Europe only the more favorably impressed us with the magnificent properties and splendid qualities and tremendous possibilities of Giant Spurry and Esparcette for the old, worn-out, poor, sandy defective, useless soils of America.

Dr. Hanley Stiles, of Lansing Mich., calls it the "Clover of sandy soils, yielding 7,700 lbs. per acre."

Swartz, a great agricultural writer of Germany, says that without Spurry the great Westland in Flanders, now the garden of Europe, would have been impossible.

Von Voght, another acknowledged authority, says: "It is better than Clover. Cows give more and better milk and finer butter, and in addition to this it improves the land in an extraordinary degree."

Dr. Kedzie, according to the Michigan Agricultural Station, says: "The Spurry has shown wonderful profectiveness. Its value as a manurial plant on light sands is pronounced. It seems to enrich the soil more rapidly than any other plant used.

Now then, the John A. Salzer Seed Co. has tested this for ten years, and can only add its endorsement to above. It is certainly the best plant to sow for hay or forage on stony or sandy soils to-day in the world. The seed germinates quickly; in forty days it is up; in sixty weeks it is ready to cut. It is an annual; should be sown in the spring. When sown for fertilizing, five 20 lbs. per acre; when sown for hay, 10 lbs. per acre. Indeed, after the third day cattle will leave the best Clover for it. Its luxuriance is astonishing.

Thousands Planted Giant Spurry.

The reports received from parties testing Giant Spurry are very gratifying indeed. Everybody pronounces it a tremendous hay producer, and by all odds the best green fertilizer.

J. J. Troutman, Pierce, Pa.: "Giant Spurry sown May 18th grew wonderfully fast."

John Thacker, Malvern, Ark.: Giant spurry grew about 2 feet high, yielding 3 tons per acre.

Chas Jennings, Deep River, Conn.: "The Giant Spurry grew 2 feet in height, and I cut two crops. Cattle seemed to like it."

Pennellville, N.Y.—When I received your catalogue, I thought that your claims were rather extravagant, but since I have tried your Giant Spurry I am ready to believe anything that you have to say about seeds. At present it is 30 inches high, and part that I cut is making a good second growth. J. H. Harris.

it very much. After getting second crop we grazed same."

Albert Frautzen, Grand Station, Mich.: "We had no rain from the time we sowed Giant Spurry until after harvested, yet it grew two feet tall and yielded 2 tons per acre. The second crop would have been heavier but we pastured that."

A. J. Florian, Thomaston, Conn.: "Giant Spurry did exceedingly well, growing 3 feet tall."

A. C. Clary, Dell, Wis.: "The yield of Giant Spurry was 4 tons per acre. When our partners dried up, we had Spurry for feed. The cows ate it with great relish."

Why Should you Plant Salzer's Giant Spurry?

First.—Because it is the most prolific fodder and hay plant for sandy soils, for worn-out soils, for poor and doubtful soils, known.

Second.—It flourishes on sandy, worn-out soils where no other plant flourishes, and returns big yields every time.

Third.—It comes next to the Clover as a fertilizer. Take the poorest soil on the worst soil that you can imagine and sow 20 lbs. of Salzer's Giant Spurry per acre and same. Do this two years and you will have a soil for Wheat, Oats and Potatoes.

Fourth.—The American Agriculturist and all prominent agricultural writers urge the planting of Spurry and Tvestaté.

Fifth.—Culture.—Prepare soil well. Harrow carefully. Sow for hay at the rate of 5 to 10 lbs. per acre. For fertilizing, sow at the rate of 20 lbs. per acre and plow under as soon as it is 18 inches tall. Test also sow two seedings a year for fertilizing.

Note.—There is positively no other seedsman in America who has the genuine Salzer's Giant Spurry, although some may use our illustrations and descriptions. We have sold seed to none except our farmer customers, hence other seedsmen's seed will not be the true Salzer's Giant Spurry, but more probably the common Spurry, which is 25 MILES BEHIND our matchless Giant Spurry. When you buy don't get fooled but buy the genuine of us.

PRICE OF SALZER'S TRUE GIANT SPURRY:
Oz., 10c; lb., 20c, postpaid; 10 lbs., $1.00, by freight, lb., 15c; 10 lbs. (for 1 acre), 90c; 50 lbs., $4.00; 100 lbs., $7.00.

SALZER'S PROLIFIC SPRING RYE

This magnificent Rye is of recent introduction, and it has proved, to many of our farmer customers, a better money-maker, a surer money-maker, a bigger money-maker and an easier money-maker than any other cereal planted, as good spring Rye brought as good a price as Wheat and yielded from 10 to 30 bushels per acre more. It is a magnificent sort. It can be used as a catch crop in case other winter crops fail. The price is seldom below 60c per bushel, while the yield rarely falls below 60 bushels per acre. We have but 2,000 bushels of this Rye on hand, and we request all our farmer customers who want the best thing in the cereal line to be had, to order early, as it is the early bird that catches the Rye as later on in the season it will surely be sold, and you cannot get any unless you order early. Our stock was grown on out stubble and a few Oats are occasionally seen in the seed; this is no detriment to the yield. Give it a trial for 1896. We are sure it will please you. It can be sown at the same time that spring wheat is sown, at the rate of about one and one-half bushels per acre.

As a Catch Crop,

We sowed some of our Sure-Cropping Prolific Spring Rye on Winter Wheat that had died out, waiting until almost May, and found it did splendidly. It gave us a yield of over 45 bushels per acre. It is one of the very best things to sow for a catch crop, as it always gives good yields.

PRICE—Pkg., 10c; lb., postpaid, 30c; by express or freight, pk., 60c; bu., $1.40; 2½ bu., $3.25.

WINTER WHEAT.

Will have these stock in fall. Write then for fall catalogue. All customers of this spring get same without writing, order now. As soon as stock is exhausted, we book orders and ship in fall of 1896, after wheat is harvested.

Martin Amber—Bush. Bu., $1.60; Pk. bu., $3.40
Mediterranean Hybrid—Bush. bu., $1.40; 2½ bu., $2.90.
Wisconsin Triumph—Bush. bu., $1.40; 2½ bu., $2.90.
Canadian Hybrid—Bush. bu., $1.40; 2½ bu., $3.00

As long as this season's Winter Wheat lasts, we can fill order in fall of 1896, after wheat is harvested.

Red Cross, Prize Taker and World's Fair Winter Wheat.

Bu., $1.50; 2½ bu., $3.50; 10 bu., $14.00.

SALZER'S ASSINIBOIA FIFE SPRING WHEAT.

This sort comes from the Assiniboia Valley, where it has been grown for years, always ripening and returning heavy yields. Indeed, the party from whom our seed stock was purchased assured us that his yield NEVER WAS LESS THAN 30 TO 40 BUSHELS PER ACRE, often reaching 50. In quality it is an extremely excellent milling wheat, possessing the properties of earliness and ENORMOUS PRODUCTIVENESS, resembling our American Hard Fife. Not absolutely pure, but absolutely big yielding. Our stock for 1896 this year is unusually fine. Pkg., 50c; pk., 50c; bu., $1.30; 2½ bu., $3.25; 10 bu., $12.50.

Salzer's Okanagan Valley Velvet Chaff Spring Wheat.

Velvet Chaff Wheat has long been in good repute throughout the wheat-growing states. In this we found a grower in the Okanagan Valley, B.C., who had a fine stock which he had grown for years, and gave yields like less than 35 and often 45 bushels per acre. We bought his whole stock. Pkg., 10c; lb., 30c; by freight, pk., 60c; bu., $1.50; 2½ bu., $3.50; 10 bu., $13.00.

Haynes' Pedigree Blue Stem.

Mr. Haynes took first prize at the World's Fair on this Wheat. So much has this Wheat been improved that it has increased the number of kernels abreast in the spikelet from three to four, with the fifth kernel commencing to make its appearance. The length of the head has increased one-third and the berry much improved in uniformity of color and handsome. In addition to this it is five days earlier than the common Blue Stem Wheat. This Wheat we know is A No. 1, and our farmer friends will do well to give it a thorough trial the coming season. We know they will like it, and we know it will pay them to pay double the price we ask for seed, in order to get the new stock.
Pkg., 10c; lb., 30c; postpaid; by freight, pk., 50c; ½ bu., 75c; bu., $1.50; 2½ bu., $3.50; 10 bu., $13.50.

FREE.

With each 1 bushel order or more of wheat you get free our grand and wonderful "Earliest Sunrise Millet." See description on page 94.

Farmers receive same Premiums on Assiniboia Fife, Okanagan and Haynes' Pedigree Blue Stem Spring Wheats as on Salzer's Marvel.—See under Free on Page 90.

THE GREATEST SPRING WHEAT IN THE WORLD.

SALZER'S MARVEL SPRING WHEAT

COMMON WHEAT ONLY 10 BU. P. ACRE

"How to Grow the Wheat" with each bushel order for Marvel Spring Wheat.

TAKE WISCONSIN.

NO MORE HARD TIMES.

TAKE 100 ACRES IN SALZER'S MARVEL WHEAT.

WE WARN YOU, SIR, THAT THE ONLY DANGER

FREE! FREE!

PRICE OF SALZER'S MARVEL SPRING WHEAT.

"Wonderful! This field of Salzer's Marvel Spring Wheat will surely go ... bushels per acre." That thrashing boss erred a trifle. It went a trifle over ... SALZER'S MARVEL SPRING WHEAT

Price:—By mail. pkg., 10c; lb., 35c; 3 lbs. $1.00; by freight or express, pk., 40c; ¼ bu., 65c; bu., $1.25; 2½ bu., $3.25; 5 bu., $5.90; 10 bu., $11.75; 20 bu., $23.25; 100 bu., $115.00—with Earliest Russian Millet thrown in free!

BIG FOUR OATS.

SHOWING THE 4 WHORLS.

Just Read What the Department of Agriculture at Washington, D. C., Has to Say Regards Salzer's Oats.

"Regarding your Oats, in my estimation, taken as a whole, for a large yield, this variety is better, than any other in the exhibit out of a lot of from 400 to 500 samples of all kinds of Oats."

SALZER'S BIG FOUR OAT

Look here, Smith, Big Four is the biggest yielder on earth.

TWO-FOOT LONG OATS.

The Oat Premium—A Tremendous Sensation — A Startling Novelty — A Wonderful Acquisition.

See Page 93.

250 Bushels Per Acre.

BIG FOUR

FIFTEEN SPLENDID POINTS.

First—New Blood.

Second—Stood the Test

Third—Earliness.

Fourth—Money.

Fifth—It is Bug-Proof.

Sixth—Withstands Drought.

Seventh—Strong Straw.

Eighth—Yield.

Ninth—Color.

Tenth—Quality.

Eleventh—Profit.

Twelfth—Quick Returns.

Thirteenth—Insurance.

Fourteenth—Cost.

Fifteenth—The Last Forty Bushels.

Just stop and do a little figuring, what profit it will bring to you to sow an Oat with so many rare good points.

PRICE OF SALZER'S NEW BIG FOUR WHITE OATS:

Pkg. 10c; lb. 35c; 3 lbs. 75c, postpaid; by freight pk. 50c; 1/2 bu., $1.00; bu., $1.50; 2 1/2 bu., $3.25; 5 bu., $6.75; 10 bu., $13.25; 20 bu., $22.50; 25 bu., $27.50.

SALZER'S BIG 4 OATS WONDER

VIEW ON JOHN A. SALZER SEED COMPANY'S FARMS, HARVESTING BIG FOUR OATS.

SALZER'S BIG FOUR WHITE OATS.

Let's Reason Together, Mr. Farmer.

Now we do not feel backward in pushing Big Four Oats, because we have had such hearty indorsements from thousands of farmers planting same the past season, and then with each order that you buy you get free that marvel of marvels, Salzer's Two Foot Long Oats. [illegible] Big Four Oats. [illegible] Salzer's Two Foot Long Oats. That is positively the wonder of wonders in Oats!

There is absolutely no risk in sowing this variety of Oats, and big money can be made out of it by wide-awake farmers. [illegible] will always complain of poor crops, low prices and hard times. [illegible] Oats, Corn, Potatoes, etc. [illegible] Just think of the thousands of dollars farmers have made throughout the United States on Salzer's Corn, seeds, on his Oats, Wheat, Barley, Potatoes, etc. [illegible] "more than good," as a pleased farmer expresses it.

Greatest Mortgage-Lifter in the World.

Seeding your land to this Oat would lift or pay the biggest mortgage you could possibly have on your farm, for it is the greatest cropper known! [illegible] from Maine to California and from Canada to Texas and some from foreign lands. Why, it is the Oat that takes everywhere, because it adapts itself so peculiarly to all soils and climes known! Try what you will, and you cannot beat the Big Four for yield and fine quality and good oatmeal.

250 Bushels per Acre.

We could introduce here several hundred farmers who tried these Oats in 1898, located in all parts of America, who had yields running all the way from [illegible] bushels per acre, but our space does not permit us to do so. [illegible] Big Four Oats. [illegible] Just read the letter of [illegible] on page [illegible] regarding Big Four Oats.

IT'S A SURE CURE FOR HARD TIMES.

The farmer reading the above description, together with the strong points in favor of Salzer's Big Four White Oats, must see in it a solution for hard times. No hard times can exist when the farmer gets two and three times as much [illegible] Salzer's Big Four White Oats would give [illegible] on 100 ACRES THERE WOULD BE A DIFFERENCE OF [illegible] BUSHELS, which would kill hard times [illegible] Salzer's Big Four White Oats? It is the most wonderful Oat in the world. [illegible] YES, WE KNOW, AS MUCH AS 250 BUSHELS PER ACRE CAN BE GROWN FROM THIS OAT WITH CAREFUL CULTIVATION. [illegible] We are moving with the speed of electricity everywhere; why not in the field of agriculture!

[illegible] We must introduce this picture. Just see the loaded money bags coming home from town. Well, [illegible] bushels [illegible] of the Big Four Oats at even [illegible] a bushel would be profitable! Do just try it for 1899, and be convinced [illegible] this Oat marvel is your friend and stands ready to make you rich.

Our Great Premium—SALZER'S TWO FOOT LONG OATS.

[illegible] is positively the greatest wonder in Oats on earth; a single head measuring 24¼ inches, or over two foot long, as affirmed to by the following honorable [illegible]

To whom it may concern:

[illegible] certifies that we were this day, Oct. [illegible], shown several heads of Salzer's NEW TWO FOOT LONG OATS by the JOHN A. SALZER SEED COMPANY, La Crosse, Wis., measuring respectively [illegible] inches long—more than two foot in length, surely entitling it to the name "Salzer's Two Foot Long [illegible]"

Hon. J. L. [illegible], Postmaster, La Crosse, Wis.	Wm. [illegible], Agent Southern Express, La Crosse, Wis.
C. L. V. Craft, Agent C. M. & St. P. Ry., La Crosse, Wis.	T. H. Lawrence, Agent American Express, La Crosse, Wis.
Wm. [illegible], Agent C. & N. W. Ry., La Crosse, Wis.	A. T. [illegible], Agent U. S. Express, La Crosse, Wis.
H. W. [illegible], Agent C. B. & Q. Ry., La Crosse, Wis.	Wm. [illegible], Agent Adams Express, La Crosse, Wis.
A. [illegible], Agent G. B. W. & St. P. Ry., La Crosse, Wis.	T. B. Lawrence, Agent Merchants' Dispatch Co., La Crosse, Wis.

[illegible] statement regarding this remarkable oats can easily be verified by addressing with stamp any of the above citizens of La Crosse. [illegible] It is worth $8.00 per pound, but we are going to give it free with each order for Big Four Oats under the following conditions:

We Give "Two Foot Long Oats" Free!

With each order for 1 peck we will give you free [illegible] of this oat marvel, worth [illegible]; with a 1 bushel order, 2 ounces worth $1.00; with a 2½ bushel order, [illegible]; with a 5 bushel order, [illegible]; with a 10 bushel order, 16 ounces, worth $8.00 and with 20 bushel order, [illegible]; with 25 bushel order, 40 ounces.

[illegible] this oats at $8.00 per pound is dirt cheap to get a start with. One pound properly planted as you would corn, is good for from 50 to 100 bushels of seed. [illegible] this Two Foot Long Oats growing will pay you a great price for seed stock next Fall. It will surely pay you to buy from 10 to 25 bushels of [illegible] Oats, in order to get from 16 to 40 ounces of the wonderful Two Foot Long Oats as a premium.

THE PRICE OF SALZER'S BIG FOUR WHITE OATS IS: Peck, 60c; bu., $1.50; 2½ bu., $3.25; 10 bu., $12.25; 20 bu., $22.50; 25 bu., $27.00.

SEVEN STANDARD OATS.

1. Salzer's Silver Mine Oats.

No Oat ever offered created such a sensation as Salzer's Silver Mine Oat, introduced 5 years ago. It no doubt was the greatest Oat ever introduced up to this time, but must now give way to our Big Four Oats, described and illustrated on pages 89, 90, 91. To say nothing of our Two Foot Long Oats, illustrated and briefly described on page 92. We have for years made Oats a great specialty of our business, and to show you what Silver Mine Oats can do for you, we introduce here three testimonials on same. It is a white Oat, strong, stiff straw, and we are sure you will be delighted with same.

Mr. F. U. Sinnett, Randalia, Ia., among others, writes: "Salzer's Silver Mine are the most wonderful Oats I have ever seen. I purchased of you 2½ bushels, which I sowed on 1 measured acre, and harvested 196 bushels and 15 pounds, only lacking 3 bushels and 17 pounds of the coveted 200 bushels. I am sure I would have gotten 200 bushels, yes, much more, but the season was so dry. People came for miles to see my beautiful Oats, and all pronounced them the finest they had ever seen."

Nick Kutschett, Arcadia, Wis., under date Sept. 21, 1896: "I raised 221 bushels and 30 pounds from 1 acre of the Silver Mine Oats the past season."

THE PRICE OF SALZER'S DAKOTA-GROWN SILVER MINE OAT is: Pkg., 10c; lb., 30c; 4 lbs., $1.00, postpaid; by freight, pk., 50c; bu., $1.10; 2½ bu., $2.50; 10 bu., $9.00; 20 bu., $17.50; 100 bu., $75.00.

Minnesota-Grown Silver Mine Oats.

We have a few hundred bushels light Silver Mine Oats. It grows well,—just as good as our Dakota-grown—98 kernels out of 100 in our test,—only it is light weight. We believe for seed it will give you bountiful yields. This is a good chance to get Silver Mine Oats at a very low price. As long as stock lasts we will sell at: Bushel, 75c; 2½ bu., $1.50; 10 bu., $4.50.

2. Salzer's Great Northern Oats.

This is one of **the** heaviest yielding varieties known. It has very strong stiff straw, does not lodge easily, with a comparatively soft shell, large kernels, and is relished by horses. We introduce herewith one letter to show you what our customers think of this Oat. Hundreds of letters equally as good on file.

Hon. I. D. O'Donnell, General Manager M. & M. Land Co., Montana, under date of July 15, 1895: "I notice by your catalogue that I have lost the first premium on Great Northern Oats by not sending in my report. I had intended all the fall to do it. I took the precaution at threshing and had plenty of witnesses as to yield. I had 162¾ bushels of Oats from the 2½ bushels of Great Northern Oats."

That tells the story: 162¾ bu. per acre on 100 acres, 16,250 bu., at 20c would net $3,250.00, or at the rate of $32.50 per acre. More than Wheat or Corn **pays** you. Just try Great Northern for 1899.

Price of Great Northern Oats: Pk., 50c; bu., $1.25; 2½ bu., $3.00.

3. Salzer's White Bonanza Oats.

Next to Silver Mine, this Oat has taken more premiums than any other variety known.

$500.00 IN GOLD.

In 1889 the *American Agriculturist* offered $500.00 in gold to the farmer raising the greatest number of bushels from one measured acre. It was won by W. R. Strickland, Albion, N. Y., who purchased of us 2½ bushels of White Bonanza Oats and sowed same on one acre,

yielding 134 bushels and 22 pounds.

Some 10,000 entered the contest, and the White Bonanza scooped them all.

PRICE OF WHITE BONANZA OATS:
Pkg., 5c; lb., postpaid, 30c; by freight, pk., 50c; bu., $1.25; 2½ bu., $3.00; 10 bu., $11.50.

4. White Superior Scotch Oats.

This Oat has great similarity to White Bonanza. There is this about it—it is a fine, plump Oat, with very strong straw. Pkg., 10c; lb., 35c, postpaid; by freight, pk., 40c; bu., $1.50; 2½ bu., $3.50.

5. Welcome Oats.

This has had a large sale. It is a very handsome White Oat, weighing from 40 to 50 lbs. per measured bushel, yielding all the way from 50 to 100 bushels per acre. Pk., 50c; bu., $1.00; 2½ bu., $2.50; 10 bu., $9.00.

6. Black Prolific Oats.

It is a grand Oat, which is with us absolutely rust proof, of great vigor and health. Our stock, like all Black Oats, runs into light shades. Pkg., 5c; pk., 50c; bu., $1.40; 2½ bu., $3.25; 10 bu., $12.00.

7. Improved White Russian Oats.

It is a wonderful stooler, 2,268 grains have been counted from one grain; yielding fully one-third more than common Russian White Oats. Seed this year is light. Pkg., 5c; pk., 50c; bu., $1.00; 2½ bu., $2.25; 10 bu., $8.00.

EARLIEST RUSSIAN MILLET.

Obtained by our representative in Western Russia, and there is nothing that we have ever offered that will so completely captivate farmers and stock growers as this EARLIEST RUSSIAN MILLET. It is positively the most remarkable, leafy, bushy, vigorous growing earliest Millet in the world, or as a farmer who obtained a bushel last year, and from same cropped fifteen tons of hay, and had lots of seed beside, said, It is surely worth its weight in gold to get a start with. The John A. Salzer Seed Co. warrants that every farmer will be delighted, and pleased, and astonished, and profited by sowing the EARLIEST RUSSIAN MILLET. It will make a magnificent crop of hay if sown immediately AFTER YOUR OATS OR BARLEY, OR RYE, OR WHEAT IS CUT, as it will ripen in from 60 to 80 days. For this reason we offer this Millet as a premium to our wheat and barley orders, and we hope thousands upon thousands will thoroughly try some the coming season. It is positively the Millet wonder, very, very, very leafy, prolific and exceptionally fine for hay and food; try it for 1899. You can get it free if you order barley or wheat, or also as a premium on a general seed order; see page 89. This Millet, like no other Millet, stands the hot, dry winds of the Dakotas, the burning prairies of Kansas and flourishes on the barren soils of Western Nebraska and Colorado. In fact, it grows where no other Millet grows. It would be cheap at ten times the price. Sow from 10 to 25 lbs. per acre.

Earliest Russian Millet.

E. B. Lovejoy, Red Wing, had 46 heads from 1 kernel of seed.

Price: 1 lb., 25c; 5 lbs., 60c; 10 lbs., $1.00; 25 lbs., $2.25; **50 lbs., $4.05; 100 lbs., $6.00.**

BROOM CORN, OR HOG MILLET.

A magnificent Millet, splendid for bird seed, but grander still for hog fattening. In such localities where Corn does not flourish, there is nothing in the wide, wide world that will give a greater yield than Hog Millet. This solves the problem as to the possibility of raising swine outside of the Corn belt. Hon. F. H. Smith, among others, says: "I had 31 hogs which I raised and fattened on Millet seed. They made an average weight of 324 lbs. on this food, and I fattened one hog that weighed 381 lbs. This hog gained, the last 30 days, 2½ lbs. per day." This is what Millet does. **Price, pkg., 5c; lb., 30c, postpaid; bu., by freight, $1.30; 2½ bu., $2.50.**

California Millet.

It is remarkably luxuriant. The growth is rapid, and hay cut therefrom of unusually excellent quality. It certainly is good for 5 tons of hay per acre. Pkg., 5c; lb., 25c, postpaid; by freight, pk., 75c; ½ bu., $1.50; bu., $2.50; 2½ bu., $5.00.

German Millet.

Cows, horses and other farm stock are exceedingly fond of it, eating it with much relish. Makes magnificent hay, and is very cheap, as it yields from 3 to 5 tons per acre. Salzer's Superior, pkg., 5c; lb., free by mail, 20c; by express, lb., 10c; bu., $1.10; 2½ bu., $2.50; 5 bu., $4.90. Prime to choice, bu., 90c; 2½ bu., $2.00.

Hungarian Grass.

Luxuriant, vigorous and leafy to an extreme barely imaginable. Unexcelled as a hay producer; all cattle relish it. Grown in enormous quantities in all states where grass is short. Can be sown as late as July. Pkg., 5c; pk., 30c; bu., $1.25; 2½ bu., $3.00; 5 bu., $5.90.

Siberian Millet, or Early Fortune.

This originated in Russia, although it has been named Siberian Millet. It is very prolific and bushy. Price: 1 lb., 20c; 4 lbs., $1.00, postpaid; by freight, 10 lbs., 50c; 50 lbs., $2.25.

Salzer's Dakota-Grown Common Millet.

We hold letters as follows:

"Mr. Salzer:—Last spring I sowed 5 bushels of your Dakota-grown Common Millet, 5 bushels received from St. Louis, and 5 from an Illinois seedsman. I did this to test the value of the different lots. I was a trifle prejudiced against you because I thought you talked loud in your catalogue about yield, etc., but I confess here that every word you say about yield is true. The 5 bushels from you gave me more fodder and hay by fully one-third than I received from any of the others, although I planted an acre more of each of the other kinds."

Salzer's Superior Common Millet, pk., 30c; bu., $1.25; 2½ bu., $2.90; 10 bu., $10.00.

Prime to **Choice** Common Millet, bu., 80c; 2½ **bu.**, $1.90.

SALZER'S SUPERIOR SAND VETCH.   (Vetch Sativa Improved.)

"SALZER'S SUPERIOR SAND VETCH"

Showing a plant of Salzer's Sand Vetch 11 feet long when 4 months old.

There was no patch more eagerly sought and more carefully noticed by thousands of farmers who visited our Dakota farms than our Superior Sand Vetch. It was worth coming miles and miles to see. It was sown in May, but soon covered the ground and kept on growing and blooming and blooming, surprising everybody. The yield must have been something like 1 tons per acre. We above you how rapidly it grows—we put a sample into our greenhouses, in pure sand, and in 7 days after sowing it was 10 inches tall, without a drop of moisture either in the sand or applied to it after sowing. This shows—

1. That it is a wonderful, rapid grower.
2. That it can get along without any moisture.
3. That it will grow despite adverse circumstances, as it thrives in the bare sand.
4. Among other good points we mention that it withstands cold. Sand Vetch can be sown in April and May and mown in fall, and the next spring, where sheltered, will come forth fresh and green and vigorous, and will form green herbage for cattle at once.
5. It is a tremendous yielder, producing all the way from 5 to 7 tons of the very best hay imaginable per acre.
6. While in Europe farmers told us they could not get along without Sand Vetch and Giant Spurry and Giant Incarnat Clover; that is, they would not attempt farming, as it would not pay them, their land being very expensive; but with above three articles, no matter how expensive the land, they can always make it pay. Now, here in America, no matter how poor the soil, these three items will enrich it and make it as fertile as the valley of the Nile; and no matter how rich the soil, these three articles will then enrich the farmer by sowing them, because the yield will be enormous and profitable in the extreme.
7. Quality. Salzer's Superior Sand Vetch makes the very best hay imaginable, with a quality equal, if not superior to any Clover hay that you ever fed.
8. Culture. It is a great seeder, therefore but 30 pounds are sown per acre, though some farmers in Europe sow more. If sown in rows it will soon cover the ground as a complete network, furnishing a tremendous amount of luxuriant fodder.
9. All agricultural colleges, all writers on agriculture, all practical farmers, recommend the growing of Sand Vetch. It is especially so in Europe. You cannot find an agriculturist there who would not recommend it, and it is also the case here in America by those who have given same a trial.
10. As a fertilizer it has but few equals, as it enriches the soil very quickly, and can be plowed under twice in a season.
11. When intended for hay Salzer's Sand Vetch should be left standing until the flowers have, for the most part, given way to the pods, and some of the seeds become well formed. The crop is then ready for the mower, and will yield according to the land, from 3 to 5 tons of hay per acre.
12. All summer long. You can have this excellent fodder plant, this excellent hay producer, all summer long, by sowing at different times. You can have pasturage from April until November by sowing two or three weeks apart, not only a little but a great abundance, as Sand Vetch produces heavily.
13. Don't fail to try it. If you do you will miss one of the great treats of your life time in farming, because we believe that our Sand Vetch will give you its that you have never had before. It will give crops such as you never have had before; and if your land is poor and you wish to enrich same, this will do it as quickly as anything you have ever tried.

James M. Stone, Forestville, N. Y., Oct. 9, has this magnificent testimonial on Salzer's Superior Sand Vetch: "Your Sand Vetch is immense. Took two plants to the Dunkirk Fair. It excited great curiosity. Standing on a chair and holding it by the roots as high as I could reach, the tops still dragged on the ground."

PRICE OF SALZER'S SUPERIOR SAND VETCH (quick growing):   Lb., 22c, postpaid; by freight, lb., 12c; 10 lbs., $1.00; 50 lbs., $4.50; 100 lbs., $6.50.

1. Velvet Bean.

This Bean is creating a great sensation in the South and Middle North. The planting that we had on our trial grounds at La Crosse surprised and startled us. We have some to believe that it is going to be one of the great green manure or fertilizing plants. It is tremendously prolific, vines running from 12 to 18 feet long. It is the bean to try everywhere. It, no doubt, will make as much green herbage as any plant grown. It is new, and we urge every farmer to give it a trial.

Pkg., 10c; pk., 35c; qt., 60c, postpaid; pk. of 15 lbs., $2.00; bu., $6.00.

2. Spelz.

What is it? It is neither corn, nor wheat, nor rye, nor barley. It is a combination of them, so to say. It is more like wheat than any of the others mentioned, but it is one of the greatest fodder producers in the wide, wide world. It is fed without threshing; no, not that, but it is fed with the hull, and in this way it yields all the way from 40 to 90 bushels per acre. It does unusually well in the Dakotas and Western Kansas, Nebraska, Iowa, etc. It will bear a trial everywhere. Sow 1 bushel per acre, and you will be surprised and delighted at its yield and at its feeding quality. The straw is exactly like wheat straw.

Pkg., 10c; lb., postpaid, 30c; by freight, 1 bu. of 60 lbs., $2.00.

4. Lathyrus Sylvestris Wagneri.

This plant is creating great excitement as a forage plant, especially in sandy, dry soils, as it sinks its roots 30 feet, and furnishes a great quantity of fodder, yielding as high as 10,000 lbs. per acre. It is a variety of Pea, formerly wild in Europe, and carefully cultivated and crossed. Thousands of acres have been planted in Europe, and here in America there are fully 10,000 farmers to whom we furnish the seed, and all who have tried it report good prospects and are sure it will prove a great acquisition as a fodder.

PLEASE READ THIS LETTER ON LATHYRUS:

Regarding Lathyrus, Conrad Doering, Cowlitz County, Washington, who has given it a thorough test here in America, says: "The Lathyrus is the earliest forage plant in spring, earlier than any grass we have, and all cattle eat it with great eagerness as soon as it springs from the ground. In the fall of the year, when all other fodder is dead, Lathyrus is green and keeps on sending forth new shoots. Cattle cannot be driven from the patch. They hate to leave the strength, giving, nourishing Lathyrus. It grows from 3½ to 4 feet tall, and does well on any kind of soil, even on very poor sandy soil."

Pkg., 10c; oz., 20c; ¼ lb., 50c; ½ lb., 75c; lb., $1.40; 10 lbs., $13.50.

3. Australian Salt Bush.
(Atriplex Semibaccatum.)

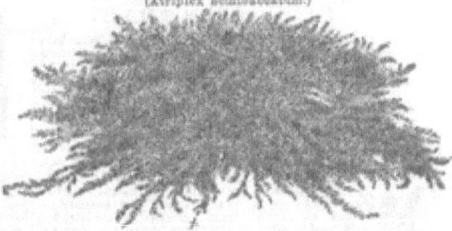

This forage plant, which was introduced a few years ago from Australia, has already been grown here with the very best of results, and we are continually hearing farmers speak of it in the highest terms, and the fact that a great many intend planting it very extensively this season speaks well for it.

The plants have a diffuse habit of growth, each one, when fully developed, covering an area of 8 or 4 feet in diameter. It is much relished by stock, and supplies the salt so necessary to their well being. The greatest recommendation, however, in the estimation of many farmers, is the fact that it will thrive better on alkali land than on any other. We are positively assured of the truth of this statement by farmers who have tried the experiment. We have seen specimens raised on alkali land, and cannot imagine anything more healthy looking or abundant. It is proved by analysis to be very nutritious, and contains, when dried, from 3 to 10 per cent. of salty matter. The yield is about twenty tons of green fodder per acre, which will make 5 tons of hay.

The plant is perennial; if intended for a grazing pasture it is better not to cut it the first year, but let the seed fall and thus form a sod. Prepare the land by plowing and harrowing as for other crops. The seed may be sown in beds or boxes and transplanted to from 3 to 4 feet apart, but it is better to sow it where it is to remain, either thinly broadcast in hills, taking care in all cases to cover the seed very lightly. Use one pound of seed to three-fourths of an acre broadcast or four ounces if transplanted. John A. Salzer Seed Co.'s Dakota test of this plant is satisfactory in the extreme.

Price: Pkg., 10c; oz., 50c; ¼ lb., $1.50; lb., $2.50, postpaid.

1 PACKAGE EACH ABOVE 4 GREAT FORAGE PLANTS FOR 25 CENTS.

Alfalfa, Bromus Inermis and Salt Bush.

The mixture of the following three great Grasses, Clovers and Forage Plants for dry, hot, high prairie soils, has proven itself extremely popular. Do splendidly in all Western States from Kansas, Iowa, Illinois, to Oregon. We have arranged two mixtures, which we sell at low prices.

Bromus Mixture—Composed of Alfalfa, Bromus Inermis and Salt Bush, 1 lb., postpaid, 30c; by freight, 21½c., for 1 acre, $2.50; 100 lbs., $12.50.

ALFALFA MIXTURE, FOR DRY SOIL.

Composed of suitable Grasses and Alfalfa Clover Bromus Inermis, etc., especially adapted for dry, hot soils. lb. (14 lbs.), $1.25; 100 lbs., $12.00.

RAPE--DWARF VICTORIA.

Our trip through a large farming district of England was a revelation, and Dwarf Victoria Rape the greatest revelation of all! We had been selling Dwarf Essex Rape for some years, but when we saw a large acreage of this, and the revenue to be obtained by feeding cattle and sheep therewith, our surprise knew no bounds, and we at once bought largely; and so give it a wide introduction we are not only offering it for sale, but are giving it as a premium. We wish we had room to print the hundreds of earnest, hearty letters our customers send us relating their wonderful success with Rape. Why, it makes our carts glad to no end of what great help we have been to farmers. Some write that Rape made them more food and more money than any one thing on the farm. No more poor mutton! Rape will make the poorest sheep fat and fine for market. Pamphlet on Rape—worth $500 to you—get it; costs only 2c postage.

SALZER'S DWARF VICTORIA RAPE — FOR CATTLE & SHEEP.

Rape as a Pasture.

Rape is unequaled as a pasture for sheep in the autumn; as a fattening food in the field it is without a rival in point of cheapness or effectiveness. The sheep that pasture upon it do the harvesting in the most effective manner and with but little cost to the owner. When Rape is established as a pasture the necessity for sending sheep and lambs to market in a bad condition will be removed. Cattle may also be pastured upon Rape, but through treading they destroy and waste it in a considerable degree. Because of this it is better to remove them to an adjoining pasture when they have satisfied their wants. The results are usually very satisfactory when they are pastured upon it in the day and fed fodlike the manner shod in the morning before going to the Rape pasture. This is an easy and economical way of making Christmas beef. Rape will keep a long time in early winter in heaps like shocks of hay. When thus put up at the approach of winter, it may be drawn and fed as desired.

What Does Rape Do in America?

Prof. Shaw, of Minnesota Agricultural College, reports on Rape: "On 14 acres Rape, after Winter Rye had been removed, 537 sheep and lambs were fastened thereon; 18 steers fed thereon for 10 days, and several acres were somless when winter set in.
. . . Further, 1 acre of Rape will pasture 10 to 15 lambs 5 to 3 months when Rye has preceded it. When sown above, it will pasture in head for two months. * * That the lowest average gain on lambs, fed on Rape alone, is 7 to 3 lbs. per month. There is a great need of Rape, especially in the fall of the year when the corn has been harvested, and just before the setting in of winter. Farmers are obliged to depend solely on their pastures to feed their stock. Now, after the pastures give out, they must begin feeding their hay. Dwarf Victoria Rape does away with all this and gives a luxuriant pasture and a tremendous yield during the months when same is so greatly needed. If sown in May, it grows rapidly, and can be cut or pastured the latter part of July. If sown the first half of July, it will come into fine play as a fodder in September. October and up to November.

Rape as a Catch Crop.

Rape is particularly adapted for being grown as a catch crop, as, like the turnip, it grows better late in the season. When a grain crop, therefore, has failed from any cause whatsoever, there is ample time to plow the land and to sow Rape upon it.

Of Superlative Value.

On our farms we sow Victoria Rape into last cultivation of Corn or on Oat and Wheat stubble, at the rate of 3 lbs. per acre. This gives a tremendous lot of good green fodder by fall, remaining until how fine. It is immense! It is the biggest yielder imaginable.

Culture of Rape.

This plant may be grown successfully in the following ways, viz.: 1. In the early spring to provide Pasture for sheep and swine. 2. In June or July on well-prepared land to provide pasture for sheep. 3. Along with grain, using 2 lbs. of seed per acre, to provide pasture for sheep and to get after harvest. 4. Along with peas, oats, clover seed, to provide pasture for sheep, and to get a "catch" of clover. 5. Along with corn drilled in broadcast to provide pasture for sheep. 6. In corn, sowing the seed with the last cultivation given to the corn. 7. Along with rye sown in August in sheep pasture. When Rape is sown broadcast, 5 lbs. of seed per acre will suffice. When sown in rows, say, 16 inches apart, and cultivated, from 1 to 3 lbs. will be enough. It is now being grown in the Northern and Middle States from the Atlantic to the Pacific. The day is not far distant when it will be grown extensively as a pasture for Swine in all the Northwest. Millions of sheep and lambs will be fattened on it in the United States. Our stock is the true Dwarf Essex, imported by us direct.
PRICE OF DWARF VICTORIA RAPE: Pkg., 10c; lb., by mail, 30c; by freight, 5 lbs., 81c; 15 lbs., $1.00; 50 lbs., $3.50; 100 lbs., $6.50.

Dwarf Essex Rape.

This is the only variety of Rape sold by ourselves in this country, and is highly recommended by agriculturists both in Europe and America, but it is always miles behind in yield, in length, leafy quality and in vigor of growth and hardiness to our splendid, yes, wonderful, Dwarf Victoria Rape. The Dwarf Essex we furnish at the following prices: Large pkg., 10c; lb., 30c, postpaid; by freight or express, 5 lbs., 15c; 10 lbs., 90c; 25 lbs., $1.65; 100 lbs., $5.00.

2. Salzer's Great Annual Fodder Plant, Teosinte.

"Shades of Egypt!" we hear some one ejaculating while he is looking at the illustrations of this most marvelous plant, and magnificent it is in every respect. It comes to us from the rich, fertile plains of the Nile, where travelers tell us its enormous yield of 500 tons of green fodder per acre is not uncommon. Does it want it in Egypt. What does it do in America? Almost equally as well. Give it a rich, warm, loamy soil and it will yield from 100 to 150 tons of green fodder per acre. It is simply marvelous. Down in Georgia, in Florida and North Carolina its yield is all the way from 100 to 200 tons of green fodder per acre. It grows to a height in three states of 16 feet, while a single kernel will produce from 90 to 100 stalks of the most nourishing green fodder imaginable. Our test in the North gives it an average yield of about 50 tons of green fodder per acre. On our own green lot at La Crosse, where the soil is sandy and warm, it yielded at the rate of fully 50 tons per acre, sending forth from 20 to 90 shoots from one kernel of seed. It was the most magnificent thing we had ever seen. We will call up a few farmers as witnesses:

Your annual Teosinte is an extra fodder producer. It grew 11 feet tall, and is splendid feed."—L. E. Cordova, Chicago, Ill.

Barbara Frye, Millersburg, Ohio: "All my seed that I got from you last year did splendidly. The Teosinte is excellent. It grew from 10 to 22 feet high, and from 5 to 50 sprouts from 1 kernel of seed."

Jos. A. Nottle, Caddo, Ky., says: "I am well pleased with Teosinte as a fodder plant. I grew from one kernel of seed 113 stocks, 16 feet high. That is immense."

C. K. Hawkins, Monticello, Iowa: "Wonderful! From 1 kernel of seed I grew 81 stalks of magnificent Teosinte."

Merritt Daniels, Arborville, Neb.: "Your Teosinte is grand. I have a great growth, 30 to 50 stalks from 1 kernel. Some hills planted to 2 kernels have 50 to 100 stalks. Horses, cattle and hogs eat it greedily, and will leave any other green fodder for it."

Culture of Teosinte.

We would advise sowing same in rows 3 feet apart, and the hills far enough apart to work. It wants plenty of sunshine and cultivation, and then it will grow so rapidly that it will soon cover a whole acre and look like a dense forest. It can be cut with a reaper and fed in the green state, or it can be dried and makes magnificent fodder for cattle during the long winter months. There are wonderful possibilities for our annual fodder plant, Teosinte, and we know that if you will give it a trial that it will more than pay you another year. Just try and grow this for your hogs. You will be surprised how they will relish it and what a tremendous amount of fodder and food you will get out of an acre for them.
Price: Pkg., 10c; oz., 20c; ¼ lb., 60c; ½ lb., 80c; lb., $1.40; 2 lbs., sufficient for 1 acre, $2.75; 10 lbs., $12.50.

☞ PAMPHLET ON RAPE—WORTH $500.00 TO YOU—GET IT; COSTS 2c STAMP! ☜

Salzer's Superior Grass and Clover Seeds.

SALZER'S RED OR JUNE CLOVER.

Salzer's Superior strain of seed is known all over America as the most wonderfully prolific in culture. It certainly beats St. Louis, Chicago, and Eastern Clover in yield, vigor, foliage and rich food matter from 30 to 50 per cent.

Why is Salzer's Clover so Superior.

The answer ex-Governor P. A. Hoffman, of Illinois, gives in a few words. He says: "Out of repeated tests made with Salzer's Superior Brand of Red or June Clover, never less than 99 kernels out of 100 grew, that is why I sow only Salzer's Grass and Clover Seeds."

Now, that is the experience of thousands and thousands of our customers all over America, and they write us that they would rather pay a little more for our Superior Northern-grown seed, and know that every kernel will grow, than to get inferior seeds from seedsmen who are not growers, and who, as a rule, buy from commission merchants who keep up scrubbing and everything that is offered. Now, our seed is carefully grown in the extreme North, is vigorous, and will grow every time. Being grown with good care in the far North, by us, for seed, is worth from $4 to $6 a bushel more than Chicago, Toledo, St. Louis, Minneapolis or Eastern seed for big yields. See the illustration—how vigorous, healthy and luxuriant!

La Crosse Prime or Merchant's Grade.

Merchants sell this grade largely out of their stores. It's not as clean and fine and pure as our Salzer's Superior Grade, hence the low price.

Price Salzer's Superior: Pkg., 5c; lb., 20c, postpaid; by freight, pk., $1.25; bu., $4.50; 2½ bu., $11.00; 100 lbs., $7.50.

Price La Crosse Prime or Merchant's Grade: Pk., $1.00, bu., $3.75; 2½, ..., $8.50; 100 lbs., $6.25.

WHITE DUTCH CLOVER.

A low, close growing species; sound, while heads; very fragrant; best adapted to moist soils, but does well on dry land; excellent for sowing with Blue Grass for pasture and lawn purposes. Sow in spring. Our seed is the hardy Wisconsin variety, very prolific. Our Wisconsin grade is a seed but mixed with Alsike, which is a decided advantage for pasture, meadows, etc., although we offer it at a lower price. For our own seeding we would take the Wisconsin-grown every time.

Price Salzer's Superior White Clover: Pkg., 10c; ½ lb., 20c; lb., 30c, postpaid; by freight, lb., 25c; pk., $1.50; bu., $5.00.

Price Wisconsin-grown White Clover: Pkg., 5c; ½ lb., 15c; lb., 25c, postpaid; by freight, lb., 15c; 10 lbs., $2.50; bu., $7.50.

SAND LUCERNE—This is a Lucerne Clover specially adapted for sandy soils. Largely used in Europe. Pkg., 10c; lb., 30c, postpaid; by freight, lb., 20c; ...

COMMON CRIMSON CLOVER—About 400 miles behind our Giant Incarnate Clover, which it resembles. Pkg., 5c; lb., 25c, postpaid; by freight, 10 lbs., 80c; bu., $2.50; 100 lbs., $3.00.

GENUINE ENGLISH CLOVER—This is the Red Clover of England and Scotland. Pkg., 10c; lb., 35c, postpaid; by freight, 10 lbs., $2.50; bu., $9.00.

BURR CLOVER—Claimed to be specially adapted for dry soils. Lb., 30c; ½ lb., $1.50.

YELLOW TREFOIL—Largely used in Europe. Pkg., 10c; lb., 30c, postpaid; by freight, pk., $2.50; bu., $8.00.

MAMMOTH RED CLOVER.

This is the clover that is used by farmers for a permanent hog pasture; it grows tall, and our Superior Strain of same is extremely leafy, bushy and of grand qualities. Two acres will furnish sufficient nourishment for 100 hogs all summer providing same can be divided off. There is no Mammoth Clover quite so good as Salzer's Superior Strain, and we again urge our customers who intend seeding to Grass, Clover or Timothy to use Salzer's Superior Brands in preference to any other offered by dealers, because these brands are grown for seed only, and we are the only seedsmen in America who grow their own seed. We warrant Salzer's Superior Brand to be of high germination. We will gladly mail you a sample to test upon receipt of 5c for postage.

W. R. S., in Country Gentleman, says of it: "It is known with us as the Mammoth or Sapling Clover. Its striking peculiarities are the immense growth it attains in rich, loamy soils, yielding much more bulk to the acre than Red or June Clover. It grows large on thin land, and takes well on all soils. As a fertilizer I think it surpasses all other grasses."

Price Salzer's Superior Brand: Pkg., 5c; lb., 25c, postpaid; by freight, pk., $1.25; bu., $4.50; 2½ bu., $11.00; 100 lbs., $7.00.

Price La Crosse Prime or Merchant's Grade: Pkg., 5c; lb., 25c, postpaid; by freight, pk., $1.20; bu., $3.45; 2½ bu., $9.50; 100 lbs., $6.85.

WHITE BOKHARA CLOVER.

This is a tall, shrub-like plant, growing to the height of 4 to 6 feet, with numerous extensive bearing numerous small white flowers of great fragrance during the whole season, which are continually sought by bees. Its the loveliest clover in the North, and vigorous. Pkg., 5c; lb., 50c; 50 lbs., $10.00; lb., postpaid, 60c.

MEXICAN HONEY PLANT.

A real honey wonder; good for bees. Pkg., 10c; oz., 40c.

JAPAN CLOVER—In great demand in the South, where it grows luxuriant. ½ Pkg., 10c; lb., 50c, postpaid; by freight, 10 lbs., $4.00. Teosinte—Read Page 90.

Salzer's Giant Incarnate, or German Mammoth Clover.

The glorious future of our Giant Incarnate Clover, this wonderful new Clover, can now be predicted with absolute safety. The year 1894 added to its ranks over 30,000 pleased farmers, who report the most glorious results obtained through the sowing of this, the grandest of all quick-growing Clovers! On the farms of Germany and France we saw it growing to the exclusion of almost everything else, except Giant Spurry and Sand Vetch, for hay! It is tremendously prolific. It is, indeed, one of the grandest Clovers known. It seems to stand alone as the great first-year cropper. Sown in April, it sprouts without delay, grows bushy and rank, yet of fine fiber, and is ready to cut and furnish an enormous crop of hay by July 10th. In the latitude of La Crosse it flourishes like a weed, thrives like one—yes, grows where other Clovers do but fairly well. It will make a wondrous growth the first season, and after this is cut, furnishes pasture. If sown in conjunction with grasses, it reveals its efforts to exceed them in growth and yield. This can be tested in our mixture for hogs, which for luxuriance of growth has few equals. It is an excellent variety for withstanding long and severe droughts. As a fertilizer it is of great merit on account of its strong roots and superabundance of foliage. On one of our farms the hog pasture mixture was cut twice, and furnished pasture in fall on which hogs fattened and gloried.

IF WE COULD INDUCE YOU to try our Giant Incarnate Clover this season, to sow liberally, that is 4 or 5 acres or more, sowing at the rate of 10 to 20 pounds per acre (20 lbs. is better than 10), we know that you would be so delighted and so thoroughly satisfied with the results that we would have your everlasting thanks for inducing you to try same. NOW, we have that you will give this magnificent Clover a thorough trial in 1895. Its yield in 1894 was 6¼ TONS dry hay per acre. That's astonishing, but that's the way it acts. Read Mr. Harborts's letter.

7

THE TWO GREATEST CLOVERS ON EARTH.

10,000 **Such** Testimonials.

A. J. Thompson, Neca, Wis.: "Giant *Incarnat* Clover sown April 20th, cut July 15th, making tons of fine hay, and is furnishing magnificent pasturage now.
John Bricken, Waterloo, Ill.: "Your Giant Incarnat Clover is now 5 feet tall. It will give me six or seven tons of hay to medium Red Clover. It is splendid.
L. H. Barge, Ragener, Mo.: "Your Giant Incarnat Clover and my Sand Vetch are all what your catalogue claims them to be.

Wm. Harberts, Little Rock, Iowa. "Your Giant Incarnat Clover is wonderful. From 10 pounds I had abundant pasturage all summer for 40 hogs, and I would advise every farmer to sow Giant Incarnat Clover for hogs. Why not do it for 1899, Mr. Farmer? Sow 10 lbs. per acre.
It is, Gerard, Dillburg, Kan.: "Your Giant Incarnat Clover seed, and all other seeds, received of you did very well. They are dandies.
Fred L. Pogt, Washington, D. C.: "The Giant Incarnat Clover Seed received from us was very satisfactory, and we received hay in abundance therefrom. Made hay six times from the same place where your seed was sown.
Peter Kryger, Leland, Idaho: "Your Giant Incarnat Clover did very well and all be best.
G. M. Schneider, Onion, Iowa: "I sowed Giant Incarnat Clover April 20th, why last I got 4 tons of hay per acre. It a grand.
C. L. Saxendale, Hennepin, Ill.: "I want to say in regard to the Giant Incarnat Clover, that it beats anything I ever saw. It is splendid for forage and splendid for pasture. Hogs and cattle eat it eagerly.
John Manston, Hamilton, Ill.: "Your Giant Incarnat Clover is simply immense. We have a magnificent crop."
D. A. Harper, Mt. Pleasant, Iowa: "Giant Incarnat Clover gave me tons of summer, although it was dry. Sown A. it 18th and is now 3 of tall."
Edward Erichson, Hampstead, Ill.: "I am well pleased with Giant Incarnat Clover. Single stalks make 35 tall heads.
Arthur B. Burgess, Cadillac, Mich.: "Your Giant Incarnat Clover and Sand Spurry are just what your catalogue claims them to be. I am more than delighted with same.
John T. Brody, Peterto Rapids, Minn.: "Your Giant Incarnat Clover is splendid. It grows 5½ feet tall. It is one of the greatest hog fatteners I have ever seen. Giant Spurry grew 3 feet tall."

Hear Mr. Hog Talk Hog Sense.

"I wish, Mr. Salzer, you could induce every farmer to sow some of your hog pasture mixture, which contains a large portion of Giant or Incarnat Clover, then we would not have to hunt around the pastures or a blade of grass, or root and squeal to get something to eat, but grow fat and strong and healthy, just as the farmer wants us to be when butchering time comes."

John A. Salzer Seed Co. considers that this most wonderful Clover for hogs, from the fact that within a few weeks after sowing it is ready with a luxuriant growth as it an enormous herbage. Indeed, there is no Clover or grass that we know of that will so quickly furnish fodder for hogs and cattle as this variety. It's urge every farmer throughout America to give this magnificent Clover a test. So have placed the price extremely low.

Culture and Price of Salzer's Giant Incarnat Clover.
Giant Incarnat Clover can be grown in spring or fall. The best time is spring. All the testimonials you read above are on Clover sown in spring, during the months of March, April or May, at the rate of 10 to 15 lbs. (as seed does not germinate too well) per acre. If sown in fall, sow the latter part of August or the early part of September.

PRICE OF SALZER'S GIANT INCARNAT OR PLAN MAMMOTH CLOVER.
Pkg., 10c; lb., 25c, postpaid, by freight, lb., 16c; 10 lbs., $1.00; 50 lbs., $3.50; 100 lbs., $6.75; 1 bushel bag (60 lbs.), $4.10.

Salzer's Giant Incarnat Clover, 24 days after sowing. Photographed from a single "bud. Just try 1 for 1899 and be happy.

Salzer's Alfalfa or Lucerne—Northern Grown.

A grand clover—the eternal clover of Europe and Mexico. Our attention thereto was first attracted in 1890 by a large patch near La Crosse holding its own through an unusually cold winter and spreading rapidly. Since then we have sold enough seed to Iowa, Wisconsin, Illinois, Minnesota, Missouri, Nebraska, Kansas, Indiana, Michigan, Ohio, Pennsylvania, New York, to sow 500,000 acres, and have the first complaint to hear its name. We say everyone is delighted therewith and reports great results. It will do well everywhere—that is can easily be acclimated, and we know if once on your farm you would not part with it for $100 per acre.

1. **As a Fertilizer.**—Down deep in the earth from 10 to 20 feet, sink the roots of this wonderfully vigorous Clover, searching for nourishment and bringing to the surface the chemicals and fertilizing natural stored deep in the earth for ages. The roots at the surface of well-developed plants are over 1 inch in diameter, spreading as shown in the illustration; they decay from the outside, a trifle each year, while the decayed matter is replaced with a stronger growth each year.

2. **Stands Drought.**—It makes the desert bloom as the rose—that is, on dry, barren, sandy soils, where no other plants live, the Lucern sprouts, sinks its roots deeply after moisture and nourishment, and—be and behold!—the barren, waste has been reclaimed—the land becomes rich and able to yield bountifully. Abundant illustrations are found on every sandy soil where tried; in the deserts of Utah, Colorado, etc., and on the sandy lands of every state where tried.

3. **Stands Wet.**—No matter how heavily it rains, how deep the snow falls, how wet the spring or winter, if your soil is well drained, it will flourish through it all and yield copious cuts of rich hay.

4. **It is Early.**—The first crop is in May, a second prodigal yield in July, a third in August, and no one allowing you to cut from 5 to 10 tons of nutritious hay per acre.

5. All horses, cows, pigs and sheep lick it and fatten very quickly thereon. It furnishes an extra amount of milk.

6. It is a great rock-miner, furnishing more good hay per year than any known Clover or Grass.

7. **ETERNAL CLOVER.**—Our wonderment was great when we saw enormous crops of this Clover growing in California, Colorado, Nebraska and other states. Farmers in the irrigated states told us that 10 tons was an average yield per acre. We asked a former Illinois farmer on the hay market in Denver: "What yield do you get from Alfalfa?" His reply: "This year, sir, I got over 12 tons per acre, and that land here."

9. **How to Test.**—We would try half a dozen spots on the farm, sow ing at the rate of 10 lbs. per acre. If it do s not succeed at one place it may at the other. No other has it succeeds, you can afford to let it grow, even if it is the very best sod on your farm.

10. **Northern-grown** seed.—To our knowledge we are the only growers of Northern-grown Alfalfa Seed in the world, and we urge upon our customers to give this seed the preference. We know it is worth $2.00 or $3.00 a bushel more than Clover sold in Chicago coming from Utah and Colorado. Just give it a trial and you will find what we say is true.

11. **Please Note.** You may be able to get Alfalfa Clover Seed cheaper of some others who are not growers, but—??? Rather pay a little more and get the hardy, vigorous Clover grown for seed, and seed only, by John A. Salzer Seed Co., La Crosse, Wis.

Culture of Salzer's Northern Prolific Alfalfa.
12. Sow with grain, or alone, at the rate of 10 to 15 lbs. per acre, bean sown. Have poor soil well plowed and harrowed. There will be a fair growth the first year, but you should not disturb this, even if plants are from 4 to 10 inches apart, but it looks all right for it; next year when you can cut all the way from 3 to 5 tons, and the following year still more, and so on for years. "It should be cut when in full bloom. A little old is better to cut when too young; when the bloom is ready to fall it need too late. Do not cut too soon at once; for if you allow a rain to fall on your hay after it is cut it will not be worth more than one-half the food. Do not let hungry cattle get on it while green, especially when wet, for it will bloat them, which is and to result in death. If you wish to pasture it, first feed your stock all they can eat well and then turn them on the green Lucerne, and no harm will come to them. It is the best thing in regard self weep-out land that I ever saw, and there is not a weed in this country this man stand before it."

PRICE OF SALZER'S SUPERIOR NORTHERN ALFALFA OR LUCERNE CLOVER.
By mail, pkg., 5c; lb., 25c; by express or freight, lb., 15c; 15 lbs. (for 1 acre), $1.50; (by mail, $3.50); bu., (60 lbs.), $6.00; 2½ bu., $14.75; 5 bu.,

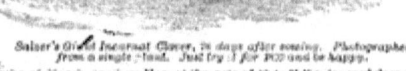

SALZER'S "SUPERIOR BRAND" WISCONSIN-GROWN ALSIKE CLOVER.

To tell you all the good qualities of this most excellent clover would fill a book, and then we would say, with the Queen of Sheba, "The half has not been told," for it is a Clover that is fairly leaping into popularity everywhere. It is almost doubt the most hardy of Clovers, resists the severest cold and extremes of drought and wet; heads round, flesh-colored; very sweet and fragrant; liked by bees; yields abundantly; excellent for hay or pasture; especially for lands liable to wash.

It is the hardiest Clover in the World.

Think of it—it does well in frozen Sweden, in ice-covered Norway; it flourishes on all soils of Canada. It is at home in Wisconsin, and laughs at 40 degrees below zero. It is unsusceptible to drought, moisture heat or anything that usually affects Clovers. Our seed is Wisconsin-grown by us, is thoroughly acclimated, and is worth, for luxuriant growth, $3.00 more a bushel than Chicago, St. Louis, Toledo and Eastern seed. Don't be put off by seedmen saying that theirs is just as hardy, vigorous and good as ours. It is not, by a long shot!

THE CANADA FARMER SAYS:

"The most prominent advantages of the Alsike Clover over the common red variety are that it does not heave out of the ground in the spring with the frost, and consequently can be sown on damp ground with good results. It makes finer and better hay, for the stalks are not so thick and woody as those of Red Clover."

Prof. Beal, the great authority on American grasses, says of the Alsike: "Alsike (like rather moist land, containing some clay. It is smoother and more delicate than Red Clover. The stems remain green after cutting. It stands dry weather and is not apt to winter-kill."

The Southern Planter says: "In the early spring sowed I pound on a quarter of an acre. It germinated well, and, like Red Clover, not only made a good stand, but in the following spring it came up well and on June 16th stood from 20 to 30 inches high."

Chas. —— Boonton,] "From the Alsike Clover I cut 2½ tons per acre, being 2 feet tall first cut."

Anna Olson, Rochester, Minn.] "The Alsike sown in April is now 2½ feet tall; very fine."

C. A. Guthrie, College Springs, Iowa.] "The Alsike (second crop this year) is now 2 feet high."

S. R. Irwin, Mechanicsburg, N. Y.] "The Alsike is very fine and large."

John J. Sass, Viroqua, ——.] "The Wisconsin Alsike did splendidly."

Jos. Pomeroy, Losterville, S. D.] "Wisconsin Alsike does well in this county."

Hans Kruse, Chelsea, Wis.] "The Wisconsin Alsike does splendidly. It is 3½ feet tall; good for 4 tons hay."

G. Osborn, Palmersburg, Ill.] "Have had good crops with Alsike and Alfalfa."

S. Pettygire, Rinard, Ill.] "The Wisconsin Alsike sown April 5 measured 4 feet in July."

LOOK AT THE ABOVE ILLUSTRATION!

That is the way Salzer's Alsike Clover acts. See the vigor it shows in its first week's growth, after the frost has left and the warmth appears; then look at the third week, and the luxuriance of the fourth, and the magnificent growth of the sixth week. It is peerless in every respect. But you must remember, in order to get this magnificent growth you must get the true Salzer's Wisconsin-Grown Alsike Clover. Now, no other seedsmen can offer you Salzer's Wisconsin-Grown Alsike, grown right here under our eyes, and we urge upon you, if you are going to make a trial, make it with the genuine article, and purchase same of the Salzer Seed Co.

THERE IS DANGER, SIR!

Providing you sow your land to Salzer's Extra Grass Mixtures and their magnificent Clover Sorts, that you will either have to build your barns larger to store your wonderful crops of hay, or have 100 to 200 tons to sell in the market. We will want you in time, if you do not work these glorious results, you must sow some other seedsman's Grass Seeds, for the Salzer Seed Co.'s Mixtures and Clovers are grown for seed only, and will return yields that will make your heart glad and surely fatten your bank account.

CULTURE OF ALSIKE CLOVER.

Sow 8 to 10 pounds per acre. The seed is very small. Have soil well prepared. Usually best to sow under cover of Spring grains. This patch can usually be pastured a little in the fall, while for seed purposes the first crop is taken. The first, second and third cuts will make magnificent hay. It prefers a moist soil, containing a trifle of clay, but stands dry weather splendidly. It attains its heaviest yield the third year. Salzer's Wisconsin-Grown Alsike seed is the winner everywhere. B Seed contains some Timothy, as this grass does splendidly when sown with Alsike.

PRICE OF SALZER'S SUPERIOR WISCONSIN-GROWN ALSIKE SEED.

By mail, pkg., 5c; lb., 30c; by freight, lb., 25c; bu., 60 lbs., $6.00; 2½ bu., $17.00; 100 lbs., **$11.50,**
B Alsike—Lb., 15c; pk., $1.50; lb., $5.50; 2½ bu., $13.50; 100 lbs. and each, $9.00.

1. ESPARCETTE—SAINFOIN—FOR SANDY, SUNNY SOILS.

We cannot speak in too strong words of praise in favor of Esparcette or Sainfoin Clover, as this plant produces such a superabundance of herbage, such a large quantity of excellent hay and so good a quality of pasture, that we heartily indorse same. It is sown and planted in tremendous quantities throughout Europe. We are sure that if once cultivated on your lands, you will not wish to get along without it. Much used in Europe, where there are many parts in which a farmer could not pay his rent without the use of this Clover, as it makes the poorest, sandiest land yield heavily the second year. It can be sown with Barley. It thrives on dry, chalky, sandy soil.

FOR SANDY SOILS.

Geo. Wilde, Mo.] "I bought 100 lbs. Esparcette of you and cut 5 tons magnificent hay."

Emil Berg, Iowa.] "Would not part with the Esparcette. It's splendid for cattle."

Franz Staate, Ill.] "Planted 50 lbs. Esparcette; yielded 2½ tons fine hay."

Herman Nebraska, Ohio.] "From the 100 lbs. I cropped 4 tons of elegant hay. Splendid for cows."

A New York agricultural writer says: "On the whole, it has done better with me than any of the Clovers I have sown this spring. Its analysis shows that, either in a green or dried state, it compares favorably with any of the Clovers in flesh-forming principles, and from the long period of its cultivation in Great Britain, and the high estimation it is held in for cultivation on the inferior soils already stated, its value as a hay crop (and no grass requires so little pains in curing as Sainfoin) cannot be overestimated. It is well worthy of a more extended trial than has yet been given it in this country."

Pkg., 5c; lb., postpaid, 25c; by express, 10 lbs., $1.00; 50 lbs., $4.50; 100 lbs., $7.75. Sow 20 to 40 lbs. per acre.

SERADELLA.

In Europe this is considered one of the most important hay plants for good, light soils. Its nutritive value is considered equal to that of Red Clover, while its produce is larger. It gives good results, except on land that is too heavy or too poor. On very light land it is considered best to sow it with Sheep's Fescue. Cattle like it, either as hay or green fodder. It is usually sown in spring—sometimes alone and sometimes under cover of Oats, Wheat or Rye, and furnishes, after the removal of the crop, a good cutting or pasturage. Pkg., 5c; lb., by mail, 25c; by freight, 10 lbs., $1.15; 100 lbs., $10.50.

GRASSES.

Grass is king, for no other product of the land returns such continual paying yields as the meadows and the pastures. The farmer having the best meadow today is the lucky man, for no crop pays better. Over 10,000 farmers, scattered all over America, tried our Extra Grass Mixtures last spring, and despite the exhausted severe drought, we have not had a single complaint, and thousands of complimentary letters, praising the great merit of our Extra Seeds have encouraged us in our efforts to supply the farmer with Live Northern-Grown Grass and Clover Seeds. The fact that we have had not one complaint as to our Grass and Clover Seeds must be proof to everyone that our grade is high, that our quality is superior, that our prices are right, and that our Northern-Grown Grass and Clover Seeds are the best to sow, are absolutely sure to grow, flourish and return a generous, heavy yield of Grass. Should stocks become exhausted, we will fill at market price.

Salzer's Dakota-Grown Timothy.

So well known that it needs no description. Our seed is Dakota-grown, and of an unusual vigor. Our patrons will be surprised at its strong growth and heavy cropping properties. It is certainly worth the more than common seed, or, as John Walworth, of Iowa, said: "I would rather pay $3 a bushel for your matchless, vigorous Timothy and $10.00 a bushel for your Red Clover, than $1.25 a bushel for Chicago or St. Louis Timothy, and $5.00 for their Clover, because your seed is so fine and of such unusual productiveness, and I get double as much from it."

Please read what we say regarding Clover Seed under prices for Red Clover. The same applies to our wondrously prolific, rich hay producing Timothy. We, if you wish common Timothy, such as is sold in Minneapolis, Des Moines, Chicago, Milwaukee,—seed grown by anyone and everywhere,—we sell same under Prime to Choice much cheaper than our matchless, prolific, carefully-grown Dakota Timothy.

PRICE OF TIMOTHY SEED.

Salzer's Superior.—Lb. by mail, 15c; by freight, lb., 8c; pk., 55c; bu., $1.65; 2½ bu., $3.95; 100 lbs., $3.15.

Prime Merchants Grade.—Pk., 50c; bu., $1.25; 2½ bu., $3.00; 100 lbs., $2.65.

Canadian Blue Grass.

(Poa Compressa.) The hardiest grass in cultivation; should not be confounded with the Kentucky Blue Grass. Canadian Blue Grass shoots the leaves very early. All grazing animals eat it greedily; cows find on it produce a very rich milk. It is especially relished by sheep. Its bluish-green stems retain their color after the seed is ripe. It shrinks less in drying than most other grasses. It is an excellent grass for dry, sandy, thin soils and banks, and for covering the surface of rocky soils.

Salzer's Superior.—Pkg., 5c; lb., postpaid, 20c; by freight, pk., 40c; bu., 1½ bu., $1.25; 100 lbs., $7.00.

Prime.—Bu., $1.25; 100 lbs., $6.00.

Red Top—Chaff Seed.

Sheep are particularly fond of this, either as grass or as hay. It is especially valuable for a permanent pasture, where grazing is continuous. It withstands our cold winters and flourishes almost everywhere. Fields should be well stocked with cattle, or they do not like Red Top if allowed to grow old or dry on the meadow. It would answer well to sow Red Top separately on moist land where old grass has run out or become mossy; on such places it would fill the soil with numerous roots and make it more passable. Also on moist, undrained soils, liable to occasional overflow, if cut early, it has a thick bottom and makes a heavy crop of second-hand hay. Sow 14 lbs. chaff per acre.

Lb., 12c; postpaid, 20c.
No. 1.—Salzer's Superior Chaff, Pk., 40c; bu., 80c; 100 lbs., $6.00.
No. 2.—Chaff Seed, Pk., 45c; bu., 75c; 100 lbs., $4.50.

Clear Red Top Seed.

This is the seed free from chaff, while the above seed contains chaff. One pound of this seed will go as far as 4 pounds of the chaff seed—it is usually sold by dealers. It is only within the last 2 or 3 years that mills have been made that will take Red Top from the chaff. Now, we earnestly advise everybody who wants Red Top Seed to buy the Clear or Fancy Seed, because he gets more for the money. It is always scarce and high priced, but 100 pounds will need more than 400 pounds of the other! It is a surely one of the very best grasses to sow for permanent sheep pasture.

Prime to Fancy.—Pkg., 5c; lb., 20c; postpaid; by freight, 14 lbs., $1.50; 100 lbs., $9.50.
Salzer's Superior.—Pkg., 10c; lb., 25c; postpaid; by freight, 14 lbs., $1.75; 50 lbs., $6.50; 100 lbs., $11.00.

Bermuda Grass.

It is a tender, delicate Grass, growing overand binding the most arid and loose land; grows luxuriantly in every kind of soil. It is the best Grass for the South grown; it furnishes rich, green, luxuriant pasture nine months of the year. It would be cheap at ten times the cost.

Pkg., 10c; oz., 30c; ¼ lb., $1.00; lb., $3.00; 5 lbs., $12.50, postpaid.

Kentucky Blue Grass.

It does well everywhere, from Maine to the Pacific coast, and from the Gulf to the frozen line of Northern Canada! It is surely well known.

Known the world over as the rich verdure decking the celebrated Blue Grass region of Kentucky. It is one of the very best grasses for dry meadow growth. The hay crop is of such excellent quality that all cattle relish it and fatten. It is readily eaten by cattle, it carries its verdure into winter longer than most other sorts of grasses, and in the early spring is out soon with its rich green. It makes exceedingly fine hay and is fit for cutting in early spring; indeed, this is the first plant that puts forth its leaves, and remains green of the season is favorable. Early in the fall it takes a second growth and flourishes vigorously until the ground freezes. Blue Grass makes the sweetest and best of hay. It should be cut as the seeds begin to ripen; sprout well and protected from rain and dews; on the second day stack and shelter it. Good Blue Grass is rare this year.

PRICE OF BLUE GRASS.

Salzer's Superior Kentucky Blue Grass.—Lb., postpaid, 25c; by freight, lb., 15c; pk., 55c; bu., $1.50; 100 lbs., $9.00.

Prime to Fancy Blue Grass (not our growth).—Lb., postpaid, 20c; by freight, lb., 12c; pk., 50c; bu., $1.25; 100 lbs., $7.00.

Salzer's Wonderful Orchard Grass.

The most valuable of all Grasses for either pastures or hay lands. Whether grown alone or in mixtures, it is immeasurably ahead of all other grasses. We consider it the very best of all Grass sorts to sow. It can be cut 3 weeks earlier than Timothy if sown alone, but we urge it being sown in a mixture with other grasses, as then it comes into grand play as the leader of all. It grows wonderfully luxuriant—furnishing, when sown alone, from 2 to 3 tons of hay per acre, and when sown under our Orchard Grass Mixture for rich soils, at the rate of 4 tons of hay per acre. If cut for hay, while other grasses are thinking about starting again, the Orchard Grass is already up, and furnishes rich, green herbage in lavish quantities. It's a splendid pasture grass, and is eagerly eaten and very nutritious. We list two grades. Great care should be exercised in buying Orchard Grass, as much is offered by seedsmen who are not growers that is mixed with Perennial Rye, etc.

"It is as Clover Bottom says: Know of no grass better adapted for Wisconsin and Illinois, and that deserves greater attention on the part of the American farmer, than Orchard Grass. It flourishes on any and all soils. It is extremely rich in herbage. The leaves are flat, vigorous, juicy, of a dark green color, and of great nourishing power. It has these excellent points to recommend it, it is extremely early, immeasptible to drought—indeed, it will flourish when other grasses dry out—and is enormously reproductive."

Salzer's Northern-Grown Superior Orchard Grass.—Lb., postpaid, 25c; by freight, lb., 20c; pk., 65c; bu., $2.10; 100 lbs., $13.75.

Prime to Choice (this is the grade usually sold by seed dealers).—Lb., postpaid, 20c; by freight, lb., 12c; pk., 50c; bu., $1.60; 100 lbs., $11.00.

Meadow Foxtail.

One of the most desirable of all Grasses for permanent pasture, being early and rapid in growth. It thrives best on rich, moist soils. Hardy and prolific, returning heavy crops. It stands in great repute among the farmers of England and Scotland, on account of its quick growth. It vegetates with extraordinary luxuriance, and is, therefore, both as a first crop and as after Grass, justly considered as holding the first place among the best Grasses, whether used as green fodder or made into hay; cattle are fond of it, though it is said to be best relished by cows than by any other stock.

Pkg., 5c; lb., 25c; bu., $3.25; 100 lbs., $23.00.

MEADOW FOXTAIL.

Meadow Soft Grass.

Holcus Lanatus—This is used in great quantities in some portions of Europe. Prof. Flasen of Mississippi quotes Hon. Wm. Lewis of Louisiana as having grown the grass with great satisfaction for many years, and calls it the best and most profitable grass for some lands. In Ireland it is largely used in pastures, entering almost all pasture and meadow mixtures.

Lb., 15c; bu. of 14 lbs., $2.00; 100 lbs., $13.00.

SALZER'S CELEBRATED LUXURIANT RYE GRASSES.

ENGLISH RYE GRASS.

(PERENNIAL RYE.)

Perhaps there is no Grass of the newer varieties that is being so largely sown all over America as English Rye, with the exception possibly of the Orchard Grass.

It is found to flourish on all kinds of soil, and grows under circumstances of different management on many upland situations, though firm and somewhat moist richlands are the most appropriate. It soon arrives at perfection, and produces, in the first year of growth, a good supply of early herbage, which is much liked by cattle.

Known as the best of all Rye Grasses, owing to its splendid qualities and large acreage in England of this superb Grass. It enriches on dry soils, though it prefers moist lands. It arrives at perfection rapidly and is eagerly eaten by cattle. Cut for hay immediately after blossom.

Salzer's Superior—Pkg., 5c; pk., 40c; bu., of 14 lbs., $1.75; 100 lbs., $5.50; lb., postpaid, 15c.
Common—14 lbs., $1.50; 100 lbs., $5.75.

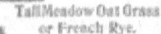

ITALIAN RYE GRASS.

It is a wonderfully rapid grower and returns heavy hay crops. Thrives nicely. Sow 20 lbs, per acre. It is particularly adapted for permanent pastures or meadows, where it thrives luxuriantly, bearing great quantities of nutritious hay. Compared with any of the varieties of Rye Grass, the Italian Rye Grass affords a stronger braid, arrives at maturity sooner, has a great abundance of foliage, which is broader and of a more lively green color, grows considerably taller, is more upright or less inclined to spread on the ground, its spikes are longer, and upon the whole produces a vast bulk of food, which is a nobler, and the greatest quantity of rich herb.

Salzer's Superior—Pkg., 5c; lb., 10c; pk., 50c; bu. of 14 lbs., $1.20; 100 lbs., $7.50.
Common Italian Rye Grass—lb., $1.00; 100 lbs., $6.00.

TALL MEADOW OAT GRASS or French Rye.

A magnificent Grass of rapid, luxuriant growth, growing on rich soil by June 10th to the height of 4 feet. Earlier than Timothy. Cut when in bloom. Can be cut three times, and does well with Orchard Grass and Red Clover. Does well if sown alone, or a mixture of 2 parts of Orchard Grass, 2 parts Tall Meadow Oat and 1 part either Red or Alsike Clover, will give excellent results, when sown this way, 25 lbs. per acre should be used. We believe the Oat Grass to be much more valuable than the Timothy, for the reason that it furnishes more hay and does not exhaust the ground so much. Can be fed as a pasture grass, all cattle relishing same. Tall Oat Grass vegetates with great luxuriance; it is very early, productive, and affords a plentiful aftermath. It is found most beneficial when retained in a close state of feeding. It makes good hay, is natural to sandy loams, but thrives best on strong, tenacious clays. "It possesses the advantages of rapid, quick and late growth for which the Tall Oat Grass is esteemed, tillers well, and is admirably calculated for a pasture Grass. I measured some on the 20th of June, when in blossom (where it should be cut for hay), and found it 4½ feet long. I have sown it in autumn and spring, with Clover, on a sandy loam, with good effect.

Salzer's Superior—Pkg., 5c; lb., 15c; bu., $1.30 100 lbs., $13.50.
Common Seed—lb., $3.75; 100 lbs., $12.00.

THREE SPLENDID FESCUE GRASSES.

I. MEADOW FESCUE.

This magnificent grass does exceedingly well in America. Indeed, our climate and soil seem to be particularly adapted for the growth. Does exceedingly well, especially in this section named further on in this sketch. A grass of great value, growing to the height of 4 feet and produces a great amount of hay per acre. For moist soils, and has no superior as a pasture grass sown with other grasses. How true and quick is remarkable in many respects. It serves on all soils, does splendidly on the prairies of Iowa and Nebraska, furnishing in all those where tried, especially Illinois, Wisconsin, Missouri, Indiana, Ohio, Michigan, New York, Pennsylvania and the South. Grows on wet or dry soils. When well grown you will wonder how you got along without it. Sowing alone, use 35 lbs. It is nutritious and excellent in all respects. Englishmen find it is receiving good attention. Dr. Stebler pronounces it one of the most magnificent grasses in culture. The great seedsman, Sutton, in England, calls it one of the most valuable, perhaps the most valuable of all good grasses that can be sown. It is a magnificent grass for permanent pasture, outlasting almost every other variety sown.

Lb., 12c; lb., $1.00; 100 lbs. $7.00.

2. SHEEP'S FESCUE.

Excellent for sheep pastures; is short and dense in growth, making it valuable for grass plots. This variety of grass is fast becoming indigenous to America through large range, and although it is not so tall a growing variety, nor as luxuriant a grower as Meadow Fescue, yet it does splendidly.

Lb., 15c; 100 lbs., $10.00; lb., $1.50.

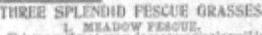

Hard Fescue, it is not an excellent sort to mix in with other grasses. It has a three tufted habit of growth; is short, with upright leaves. It is particularly relished by sheep, hence the name Sheep's Fescue. It is very largely cultivated, spread by its suckers for pasture, grows, as it will last almost a lifetime.

3. HARD FESCUE—This is a splendid grass, and may be classed among the very best native grasses for several purposes, as it will thrive on a great variety of soils and produce a great amount of fodder, and has the habit of resisting the effects of severe droughts in summer to a remarkable degree. Hence it is a splendid grass for dry, light soils. Well adapted for parks and pleasure grounds. Rapid growing; hardy; relished by cattle and sheep. Sow 20 lbs, per acre. Lb., 15c; lb., $1.50; 100 lbs., $10.00.

JOHNSON GRASS—A superb forage plant. Prevents from seed sown in spring. It is not hardy in North; hardy in South. Grows 5 to 10 tons of hay per acre in South. Sow 1½ lbs. per acre. Lb. 50c; postpaid, 25c; pk., by express, $1.30; bu., (75 lbs.), $4.00.

Salt Bush—A rare grass. See page 58. Tassels 114 stalks 14 feet high from one single kernel!

Water Meadow Grass—

This is a splendid pasture grass for wet situation. It is eagerly eaten. Sow 30 lbs. per acre. Pkg., 5c; lb., 30c; bu., $3.00; 100 lbs., $25.00.

Water Fescue—A grand grass for moist soils. Lb., 25c; bu., $2.50; 100 lbs., $17.00.

Floating Meadow—Grand for wet soil. Pkg., 5c; lb., 30c; 100 lbs., $25.00.

Water Spear—For wet soils. Pkg., 5c; lb., 25c; 100 lbs., $25.00.

Fowl Meadow—A splendid Grass of luxuriant growth and heavy hay yield. Excellent for mixtures. Grows 4 feet tall. Pkg., 5c; lb., 15c; 100 lbs., $10.00.

Rib Grass—Does well on dry soils, especially so in pastures and on barren soils. Relished by everything. Lasts years; grows 2 feet high. Pkg., 5c; lb., 20c; postpaid, 25c.

BROMUS INERMIS.

The Uncrowned King of the Deserts and Dry, Sandy Soils.

The most wonderful of Grasses for dry soils. It is a Grass for the desert, a Grass for drought-stricken countries, the Grass for Nebraska and the Dakotas, for Iowa, Kansas, Texas, Colorado, Montana; yes, for each and every state of the United States; in fact, say and everywhere where you are apt to have long sieges of dry weather; but one need not think that it does not do well on soil where there is plenty of moisture, for on such soils its magnificent, luxuriant growth comes into full play.

This Grass comes to us from Russia, and it does exceptionally well in our territory. It grows a tremendous crop, yielding all the way from 3 to 7 tons per acre, as you can cut same two or three times a year. It grows from 2 to 5 foot tall. In Dakota we obtained from one patch of five acres over 1,000 pounds of seed, in addition to four tons of excellent hay. Although the price of this Grass is a trifle high, it surely will pay everybody to plant same beautifully. Nothing that we had on our great South Dakota farms did better or pleased the public at large better as a Grass than our Bromus Inermis. It is the Grass for the Dakotas, for Kansas, Iowa, Nebraska, Montana, etc. It is very nourishing, equally as nourishing as Timothy or Orchard Grass. We recommend it for trial, and give it our unqualified endorsement. It is, indeed, a Grass invaluable for the dry and hot regions, on account of its drought-resisting qualities.

The Department of Agriculture has been experimenting with this Grass at its experimental stations in the arid regions. The Experimental Grass Station at Garden City, Kan., says: "We have grown Bromus Inermis successfully, and we think it is the coming grass for the arid regions of the West. It is green from the middle of March to about November." Prof. Shaw, of Minnesota, pertinently says: "This Grass cannot be obtained too soon by the farmers of the Northwest." It is the great Grass for hot dry climes and soils. It will grow on all kinds of soil, even on yellow sand, and is equally good for pasturing, curing into hay or cutting green. All kinds of stock eat it readily, and it is very rich in nutritive value. Perennial: 2 to 5 feet high, flowering in June and August.

The South Dakota Experiment Station, of Brookings, says:

This is this best Grass that has yet been tried at this station. When properly sown it catches well, giving a good end the first year; in favorable seasons a fair yield of hay may also be obtained. Up to the present the best results have been obtained by sowing plenty of seed on well prepared ground as early as possible in the spring. From two to two and one-half bushels should be sown, the acre, depending somewhat upon the season and condition of the soil. The forage, though coarse, is of excellent quality, and, under ordinary circumstances, a large amount of early spring and fall feed may be obtained, in addition to a good yield of hay. Thus far the grass has endured drought perfectly, and has never winter killed in the least.

It is a Tremendous Grower.

On our own fields where we have now cultivated same for the fourth year, the Bromus Inermis attains a height of 3 to 5 foot. It is extremely hardy and furnishes an immense amount of magnificent hay. When we were in Europe we were most remarkably impressed with the future of this Grass. In Russia, where same is at home, they put it three times for hay, and it is not so unusual thing to get nine tons of extremely nutritious hay per acre. In addition to this, good pasturing late in fall. Now, what it can do in Russia we are sure it can do even in a greater measure here in America, for we have soils that are peculiarly adapted to it. We have grown, in a small way, Bromus Inermis and Alfalfa clover together, and have made a mixture which we call our Bromual Mixture. This is composed of Alfalfa and Bromus properly mixed to give the very best results. There is not an agricultural college in Canada or America that has tested same but indorses it emphatically. You will do the same by giving it a trial, but by all means buy our Northern-grown seed, as we are the only seedsmen in America growing same.

If we were set on a 160-acre farm, and given a choice of but one thing to grow, to grow rich upon," we would unhesitatingly choose Bromus Inermis—the most remarkable Grass known to man today. This may be better Grasses, but as yet they are undiscovered! Why? Because Bromus Inermis is a sure grower, a sure yielder, and is sure money maker. It's said to all sense members; its grand Grass the best, and its hay, from 3 to 7 tons per acre, the very best nourishment that can be found.

In Dakota Bromus Inermis yielded for us in 1898 at the rate of 7 tons hay per acre.

PRICE OF BROMUS INERMIS.

Salzer's Splendid Dakota-Grown Seed.—Lb. 20c.; Postpaid, 25c; 14 lbs., by freight, $1.25; 100 lbs., $15.00; 250 lbs., $35.00.
No. 2 (as is sold by all other seedsmen, imported). Pkg., 10c; lb., $1.75; 100 lbs., $11.00 and; 250 lbs., $25.00.

Alfalfa, Bromus Inermis and Salt Bush

Are three great Grasses, Clovers and Forage plants for dry, hot, high prairie soils. Do splendidly in all Western States from Kansas, Iowa, Illinois, to Oregon. We have arranged two mixtures which we sell at low prices.

Bromual Mixture.—Composed of Alfalfa, Bromus, Sainfoin and Salt Bush. 1 lb., postpaid, 30c; by freight, 16 lbs., for 1 acre, $2.50; 100 lbs., $12.00.

Alfalfa Mixture for Dry Soils.—Composed of suitable Grasses and Alfalfa Clover, Bromus Inermis, etc.; especially adapted for dry, hot soils. Bu. (14 lbs.) $2.15; 100 lbs., $12.00.

| 1. RED FESCUE. | 2. SWEET VERNAL. | 3. WOOD MEADOW. | 4. CREEPING BENT. | 5. TALL FESCUE. | 6. FESCUE GRASS. | 7. ROUGH-STALKED MEADOW. | 8. DOGTAIL. | 9. YELLOW MEADOW. |

1. Red Fescue—Splendid for sowing on dry, sandy soil; hardy; excellent for this purpose. Lb., 30c; 100 lbs., $15.00.

2. Sweet Vernal—Fine for all pastures; imparts a sweet fragrance that is liked by all cattle. Rapid growth. Lb., 35c; 100 lbs., $18.00.

3. Wood Meadow—Well adapted for either pasture or pleasure grounds, having succulent and nutritious herbage; of early growth, and thriving well under trees. Pkg., 5c; lb., 25c; bu., $2.25; 100 lbs., $12.00.

4. Creeping Bent—Resembles Red Top. Does best on wet, marshy soils. Relished. Rapid growth. Lb., 30c; bu., $1.50; 100 lbs., $15.00.

5. Tall Fescue—Splendid on poor lands. Rapid and luxuriant growth. Greatly relished by all cattle. Lb., 30c; f. 25; 100 lbs., $16.00.

6. Fescue Grass—A native of Australia. Does well on any soil; thy soil, yielding two heavy crops a year. Much liked by cattle, which will eat over everything to get at it. Lb., 30c; 100 lbs., $24.00.

7. Rough Stalked Meadow—Valuable for pastures and meadows, particularly on damp soil and sheltered situations, producing a constant supply of nutritious herbage greatly liked by cattle. Pkg., 5c; lb., 30c; bu., $3.25; 100 lbs., $18.00.

8. Dogtail—Very valuable for dry lands and sheep pasture. Lb., 25c; bu., $2.50; 100 lbs., $25.00.

9. Yellow Oat—Good for dry pastures and meadows. Pkg., 5c; lb., 40c; 100 lbs., $40.00.

Grass and Clover Mixtures—What to Sow.

It is often difficult for our patrons to select proper Grasses and to mix them the same thoroughly for their use, and it thus comes that we are annually requested by thousands of our friends to select and mix for them soils adapted for their soil and climate. This, from our large experience in the culture, nature and requirements of grasses for pastures and meadows, we can often do more satisfactorily than they. When customers wish a luxuriant growth of either meadow or pasture, it will pay them every time to buy our Grass Mixtures. Our seeds are Northern-grown, and our farmer friends will be surprised to see the unusual Vigor, that this lends to them. Northern-grown seeds, when a strong growth is wanted for hay or pasture, usually return 50 per cent. more crop than Eastern stock. Our Grass Mixtures for pastures and meadows are composed of appropriate grasses in such quantities as are required to produce an even, healthy, vigorous, strong growth on the different soils, as is found under the following mixtures.

☞ For the pastures we want grasses to mature and bloom at different times, so that cattle find nourishment all the season; while for the meadows the opposite is preferable—all should bloom and ripen at the same time.

THOUSANDS OF PRAISES.

Ex-Governor Hoffmann of Illinois, one of the ablest practical agriculturists of America, says: "You no doubt remember my purchasing a lot of Grass seeds from you last year. The varieties included Orchard Grass, Tall Meadow Oat, English Rye, Meadow Fescue, Timothy, Clover, etc. to seed down a ten-acre lot to permanent meadow. The present foresummer was unfavorable to Grass, yet we cut on the 10 acres about 25 tons of splendid hay. The aftergrowth will furnish superior pasture during the fall."

An Iowa farmer says: "Your Grasses gave me the finest meadow in this state." A Michigan farmer: "The Orchard Grass Mixture is a beauty to behold; such a thick green I never saw before. Some of the blades are three feet high. The Alsike Clover is a wonderful grower." One from Illinois says: "The Giant Incarnat Clover is in full bloom. Such magnificence!" One from Indiana exclaims: "How can you clean your Clover and Grass so thoroughly." A Minnesota farmer is happy because he can cut three tons tame timent hay per acre from first cut of our Extra Grass Mixtures. A Texas Granger says his grass field is the wonder of all. A Tennessee husbandman is willing to proclaim to the world that Salzer's Extra Grass and Clover Mixtures are the best in the world.

H. B. Adams, Fairfield, Wash., October 1897.—Your Grass Mixture is all you claimed for it. It has made a strong, vigorous growth and gives promise of making a heavy yield of hay next season. It would pay for cutting even now.

A. McCoy, Bangorville, W. Va.—The Grass Mixture I ordered from you last spring did well. I think your Grass Mixtures beat anything in this country.

Henry Garvin, Holland, Wis., October, 1897.—The Clover and Grass Mixture that I bought from you last spring are in good standing, so are also all the other seeds I bought from you.

☞ Thus thousands of our farmer friends write us, and thus you will praise our Grasses if you will but use them in 1899. ☜

LAWN GRASS SEED.

It is the easiest thing in the world to grow a beautiful lawn. How often in our own city, as well as when away from home in other towns, do we find people spending from $10.00 to $15.00 worth of Lawn Grass Seed would do the work,—would do it better and give a thicker sward and a greater growth than any and you can find and put on anywhere. There is nothing that gives quicker growth and a thicker sod than Salzer's Superior Lawn Grass Mixture. It not only does well in the North, but it does well in the East, West, South and anywhere and everywhere.

Sown with Salzer's Superior Lawn Mixture. A quart of seed sows 30x35 feet, cost 30c, postpaid.

CULTURE OF LAWN GRASS.

For a lot 50x100, we would sow 10 quarts of Lawn Grass Seed; for an acre we would sow 50 pounds. It always pays to sow Lawn Grass thickly, in order to get a good growth at once. Prepare your soil well, sow the seed and cross the same firmly. With roller it aimning, attach two boards, 8x16 inches, to your feet, and "walk it down." A man can thoroughly press 30,000 square feet easily in one day.

Salzer's Superior Mixture contains a small sprinkling of White Clover. Qt., 30c; 4 qts., 70c; pk., $1.25; 10 qts., $1.75, all postpaid by express, qt., 25c; 10 qts., $1.50; pk., 85c; bu., $3.00; 50 lbs., $7.50; 100 lbs., $14.00.

Salzer's Superior Mixture Without White Clover—Qt., 25c; 4 qts., 75c; bu., $2.75; 50 lbs., $7.00; 100 lbs., $13.00.

LAWN MOWER.

To keep a lawn in fine trim, an easy-running grass-cutting Mower is essential. We believe we offer the very best, simplest, easiest-running Lawn Mower made. We use them on our lawn to our entire satisfaction, and would not part with our machine for a machine costing two or three times as much. A child can work ours and will do it gladly. We offer two popular sizes—one coming a 14-inch and the other a 16-inch swath. Each Mower, with wrench and crank, is carefully boxed, ready for use. This Lawn Mower is A No. 1, and will surely please, and is so cheap that it ought to find a home everywhere. Price: 14-inch, $3.50; 16-inch, $4.75.

OUR GREAT HOG PASTURE MIXTURES.

Here we have two great mixtures, one No. 11 and the other No. 25. We cannot say enough in praise of the same. No. 25 will give you quick results; indeed, we have seen some sown in the latter part of March that was fit for use in April. It is very luxuriant and of quick growth. The No. 11 is for permanent hog pasture mixture. Now, that is an excellent mixture of such Grasses as do well and are of permanent character.

PERMANENT HOG PASTURE.

No. 11. Specially selected for a permanent hog pasture on good, rich soils. We can heartily recommend this mixture. The Grasses contained therein are A No. 1. They are splendid for hog pasture. They sink their roots deeply, as a rule, and furnish a great abundance of herbage. We cannot too strongly recommend same for permanent pasture.

	PER ACRE.
English Blue	Alsike Clover,
Orchard Grass,	White Clover, } 15 lbs. at $20.34; $5.80
Mammoth Clover,	Timothy, } 50 lbs. ... 5.15
Rough-Stalked Meadow,	} 100 lbs. ... 11.00

No. 25.

This mixture for pasture is renowned. Salzer's Hog Pasture Mixture has stood the test for years, and the increased sales annually attest its popularity. The mixture we offer here comes into play the first year as that splendid Clover, Salzer's Giant Incarnat or German Mammoth (see pages 97 & 98), enters largely into its composition. We are sure that it will please everybody. It is very cheap. This mixture secures splendid feed in the first season,—yes, luxuriant pasturage.

2 lbs. Salzer's Giant Incarnat Clover,	
3 lbs. Salzer's Mammoth Clover,	} 14 lbs. (sufficient for 1
3 lbs. Salzer's English Rye Grass,	acre) $1.50
3 lbs. Salzer's Italian Rye Grass,	} 50 lbs. $5.00
2 lbs. Salzer's Creeping Bent Grass,	} 100 lbs. 8.50
1 lb. Timothy.	

☞ Bromeal Grass Mixture, see page 102.

SPECIALLY SELECTED EXTRA GRASS MIXTURES.

21. Orchard Grass Mixture.

This is the finest mixture that we make, the body of it being that peerless Grass for rich meadows and pastures—Orchard Grass. It is arranged specially for farmers who want the highest results, no matter at what price or expense.☞

ORCHARD GRASS.
English Rye,   Red Clover,
Italian Rye,   Timothy,
Sheep Fescue,   Tall Meadow Oat,
Meadow Foxtail,   Red Top,
Hard Fescue,   Alsike,
Sweet Vernal,   Canadian Blue Grass,
Bu. (14 lbs.), $2.50; 50 lbs., $8.50; 200 lbs., $28.00.

22. Alfalfa or Dry Mixture.

This is a mixture for dry, sandy soils, and is composed largely of Alfalfa Clovers. It is of rare quality and gives magnificent pastures and meadows.

Bu., $3.75; 100 lbs., $12.00.

33. ☞ Specially Selected Grasses for Sheep Pastures.—Bu. (14 lbs.), $1.85; 50 lbs., $6.00; 100 lbs., $9.00.

24. Grass Mixture for Sandy Soils.—Bu., $2.00; 100 lbs., $13.00.

25. Grass Mixture for Shady Places.—Bu., $2.00; 100 lbs., $15.00.

A Luxuriant Meadow—From Salzer's Mixture.

To get a magnificent stand of grass it is imperatively necessary to sow good Northern-Grown Seeds. Now, we were the first seedsmen in America to make a specialty of Northern-Grown Seeds. We now have scores of imitators, but none whose Grass and Clover Seeds equal ours in vitality and vigor of growth. Our Grass Mixture will be a source of constant pleasure and profit, and the fact that dozens of seedsmen imitate our mixture is proof that they are good.

We cannot too often urge upon you to be very careful in the purchase of your Grass and Clover Seeds, as so many seedsmen are forced (because they **do not** grow seed themselves) to buy Grass Seeds in common markets. We **leave** you to judge what can be so obtained. We are the only seedsmen in America making the growing of **Farm Seeds** a great specialty of our business.

VIEW OF OUR CELEBRATED LA CROSSE MEADOW, JULY 3ᵈ 94 YIELDING 6⅔ TON MAGNIFICENT HAY PER ACRE.

In order to have as magnificent a meadow as above illustrated, it is necessary to sow Salzer's Extra Grass and Clover Mixture. We would sow an average of 21 pounds per acre. These **Extra Grass and Clover** Mixtures are carefully selected to give the greatest possible results, and contain, among others, the following varieties, properly mixed:

EXTRA GRASS AND CLOVER MIXTURES FOR MEADOWS.

14. FOR RICH DRY SOILS.

Tall Meadow Oat,
Kentucky Blue,
Orchard Grass,
Meadow Foxtail,
English Blue,
Timothy,
Italian Rye,
Alsike Clover,
Red Clover,
English Rye.

Bu. (14 lbs.), $1.75; 50 lbs., $6.00; 100 lbs., $11.00;
200 lbs., $20.00.   Sow 14 to 21 lbs. per acre.

15. FOR RICH, MOIST SOILS.

Meadow Foxtail,
Meadow Fescue,
Rough-Stalked Meadow,
Orchard Grass,
English Blue,
Creeping Bent,
Alsike,
Hard Fescue,
Red Top,
Crested Dogstail.

Bu. (14 lbs.), $1.75; 50 lbs., $6.00; 100 lbs., $15.00;
200 lbs., $30.00.   Sow 14 to 21 lbs. per acre.

16. FOR MEADOW WET SOIL.

Creeping Bent,
Tall Fescue,
Red Top,
Rough-Stalked Meadow,
Fowl Meadow,
Timothy,
Alsike Clover,
Floating Meadow,
White Clover.

Bu. (14 lbs.), $1.75; 50 lbs., $6.00; 100 lbs., $11.00;
200 lbs., $20.00.   Sow 14 to 21 lbs. per acre.

OUR EXTRA MIXTURES FOR PASTURE CONTAIN:

17. FOR RICH, DRY SOILS.

Meadow Foxtail,
Orchard Grass,
Sweet Vernal,
Meadow Fescue,
Dogstail,
Timothy,
Blue Grass,
English Rye,
Italian Rye,
White Clover,
Red Clover,
Alsike.

Bu. (14 lbs.), $1.75; 50 lbs., $6.00; 100
lbs., $11.00; 200 lbs., $20.00.   Sow 14 to 21
lbs. per acre.

18. FOR RICH, MOIST SOILS.

Meadow Foxtail,
Hard Fescue,
Orchard Grass,
English Rye,
Italian Rye,
Wood Meadow,
Rough-Stalked Meadow,
Red Top,
Dogstail,
Tall Fescue,
Red Clover,
Alsike.

Bu. (14 lbs.), $1.75; 50 lbs., $6.00; 100 lbs.,
$11.00; 200 lbs., $20.00.   Sow 14 to 21 lbs. per
acre.

19. FOR WET SOILS.

Creeping Bent,
Red Top,
Fowl Meadow,
Floating Meadow,
Tall Fescue,
Rough-Stalked Meadow,
Timothy,
Alsike Clover.

Bu. (14 lbs.), $1.75; 50 lbs., $6.00; 100
lbs., $11.00; 200 lbs., $20.00.   Sow 14 to 21
lbs. per acre.

The **HOG PASTURE MIXTURES** on page 103 are worthy a trial. They give results. So do **SPURRY, SAND VETCH, LATHYRUS, VICTORIA RAPE, PUMPKINS, TEOSINTE, EARLIEST FODDER CORN**, etc. Please look up their descriptions.

Don't fail to sow a few acres of Salzer's Great Bromus Inermis Seed. See page 102.

LA CROSSE SEEDS.

Given free with each $15.00 order from this page and pages 102, 104 and 105.
See page 106.

Cheap Grass and Clover Seed Mixtures.

We are often advised by our farmer customers that they see offered Grass Seed Mixtures by seed merchants who are not growers but who go into the open market and buy up these Grass Seeds and sell same to the farmer trade at a lower price than we offer our Extra Grass Mixture, which are found fully illustrated and described on page 104 of our catalogue. Now, in order to meet the prices of these dealers, we have arranged the following mixtures. They are all composed of our best Grasses and we know that for the price they will give great satisfaction. Were we to use our own planting, we would in every case use our Extra Grass Mixtures, or our New Renovator or Quick Results Mixture, for we believe that these Mixtures are composed of Grasses in such proportions as will do well everywhere. In addition to this, our Extra Grass Mixtures give best results before the farmer public for many years and have given great satisfaction everywhere. These Mixtures can all be ordered by numbers. The prices, in all cases, are extremely low, and we hope to receive large orders for same.

Please bear in mind that these Cheap Mixtures on this page are better in quality and germination than the best mixture offered by many seedmen, for we believe we are the only seedmen in America who grow Grasses and Clovers for seed.

CHEAP CLOVER-GRASS MIXTURES FOR PASTURES AND MEADOWS.

GOOD, CHEAP GRASS SEEDERS.

To sow Grass Seeds economically and well, a good Seeder is absolutely necessary. We offer 4 splendid Seeders at very low prices.

Cahoon Hand Seeder.

Sows all kinds of Grain and Grass Seed, and, at a common walking gait, sows from 4 to 8 acres per hour, throwing Wheat, Rye and Barley 36 feet; Hemp, 26 feet; Oats, 33 feet, and Timothy 18 feet. The bag and hopper will hold about 22 quarts. Note the remarkably low price we are selling this splendid Seeder at. Also given free with a $30.00 order of Grass and Clover Mixture, found on pages 103, 104 and 105.

Price of Cahoon Seeder, only $2.75.

Thompson's Wheelbarrow Seeder.

A perfect Seeder. Complete machine, including wheelbarrow; weighs but 40 lbs. You simply push and it will do the rest. It runs itself. It is a remarkable machine. It takes a wide sweep. Forty acres can be sown in one day. It is especially adapted for sowing all kinds of Clover, Millet, Timothy, Flax and Grass Seeds. Full directions with each machine.

No. 1. Complete Clover and Grass seeder, with 14-foot hopper, $7.50 each; 2 machines for $14.50.

The Chicago Seeder.
Well known; does good work. Each, $1.75.

Little Giant Seeder.
Well known; like Cyclone. Each, $1.75.

Cyclone Seeder.

Similar to the Cahoon, though a cheaper make. Each, $1.75.

La Crosse Hand Seeder.
Here is the Seeder for rich or poor, splendid in all respects, doing its work perfectly. It will pay for itself in sowing 5 acres twice over. It was brought forward to meet the demand for a cheap, perfect Hand Seeder. Its great advantage is that it sows the ground three times in going over the field, leaving no possible chance of skipping. From 20 to 30 acres can be sown in a day if the seed is handy. Full directions accompany each machine. Also given as a premium with order of $12.00 for Grass and Clover Mixtures (pages 103, 104 and 105).

Price, $1.25; 3 for $3.50.

SALZER'S NORTHERN GROWN SEED POTATOES.

Wrote us one of the largest Illinois seedsmen who had seen our Dakota potato farm: "Let me congratulate you, Salzer, on the really only fine potato farm I ever saw in my life. You will surely get 500,000 bushels this year."

Nothing gives us more genuine pleasure and satisfaction than the wonderful, yes, marvelous, increase in our Seed Potato trade. Seedsmen who have visited our Seed Potato cellars marvel at the quantity of our choice stock, and wonder what we would do with all of it. We now have cellars having a capacity of over 60,000 bushels. The IMMENSE POPULARITY of our Potato is accounted for by their being GROWN IN THE EXTREME NORTH. There is reason in this—there is a world of difference between a Dakota Northern-grown Potato and an Eastern, or one grown along the shores of lakes. We have taken Potatoes from Michigan and New York and planted side by side with the same sorts from our Dakota farms, and NEVER got a two-thirds crop. While our Dakota sorts would give out by the hundreds of bushels per acre, Michigan and Eastern Potatoes would give us $50.00, and, now and then, an unusual yield of 100 bushels per acre. Now, our gardener or farmer friends, if you plant ¼ acre or 20 acres of Potatoes, it will pay you to buy your Seed stock from us; plant in it early varieties or great, glorious yielding varieties are what you are after. Why, we have hundreds of farmers who buy regularly from 3 to 20 barrels a year for their Seed, because it more than doubly pays them to do so. Think of 200, 300, 4, 5, 500 and 600 bushels per acre, and then compare the average yield you get!

Would You Believe It?

Wisconsin, with her 125,000 acres planted to potatoes, yielding 6,000,000 bushels, or 50 bushels per acre. Had these been planted to our Dakota-grown Potatoes, at only 200 bushels per acre, they would have yielded 25,200,000 bushels, or nearly FOUR TIMES AS MUCH! Are not these last of opportunities to the farmers? What did your Potatoes yield you in 1896? How did they compare with the extraordinary yield thousands of our customers had? Why not have them in 1897?

Customers in the South.

We begin shipping Potatoes to Texas, Alabama and the South the first of January, 1896. There is no Potato that does better in those states than our great Salzer's Earliest Six Weeks' and Salzer's Earliest, and for late Good Times, and we assure customers they will be delighted with them. We expect to ship 100 carloads of Seed Potatoes to Texas alone this year.

SECTIONAL VIEW OF J. A. SALZERS POTATO CELLARS LA CROSSE WIS.

Don't take Michigan Lake shore (watery) Seed Potatoes as a gift, when you can buy Salzer's heavy yielding Dakota-grown stock so cheaply.

SALZER'S COLOSSAL ARTICHOKE

It is, without question, the greatest root hog fattener in the world. Its yield is enormous, bordering on the fabulous. Farmers who have given them a thorough trial the past year report yields from 500 to 1,500 bushels per acre. Plant the Artichokes where you can allow them to remain, and your hogs, if turned into them, will grow fat and healthy, and will not know what sickness is. This is the universal verdict. They are the best hog food known, and are now attracting much attention on account of their great fattening properties, great productiveness, and the ease with which they may be grown. They need not be dug in the fall; as hogs should be turned in on them, and will help themselves in rooting for them. One sow will keep from 20 to 40 head in one tendollars from October until April, except when the ground is frozen too hard for them to root. They are also said to be preventative of cholera and other hog diseases; and they are so highly recommended for milch cows, increasing the yield of milk and at the same time improving their condition. If Artichoke stock becomes exhausted, we book the order and fill in fall 1896. One barrel will seed an acre, though we prefer 3 barrels 3 acres.

Lb. 35c; 3 lbs., $1.00, postpaid; by freight or express, pk., $1.00; bu., $1.50; bbl., $2.50; 3 bbls., $7.00.

SHOWING HOGS, FAT, HEALTHY AND HAPPY ON COLOSSAL ARTICHOKES.

SALZER'S EARLIEST SWEET POTATO PLANTS.

This Earliest Sweet Potato makes it possible for families relishing this most delicious vegetable to have them in their own garden before Southern Potatoes arrive.

CULTURE—Plant, in latitude of La Crosse, about May 15th; if very forward season, a little earlier. Plant 2 feet apart in rows, and rows 3 feet apart, in rich, well-worked, warm (sandy, if possible) soil. The plants or runners are planted, not the Potatoes. Orders will be filled when weather is warm enough to plant—about May 1st to 20th. For Southern States, earlier.

Plants, postpaid—Per 12 plants, 30c; 25 plants, 60c; 50, $1.20; 100, $2.00; 300, $5.00.
Salzer's Earliest Red—Lb., 40c; by freight, 12 lbs., $1.50; 50 lbs., $3.50; bbl., $5.00.

LOOK OUT FOR WATERY MICHIGAN POTATOES—THEY MAY BE CHEAPER, BUT OH, HOW POOR IN YIELD!

OUR FAMOUS PEACH BLOW PREMIUM POTATO.

THE FREE POTATO.

Salzer's Improved Peachblow.

Is there a young farmer who has not heard his father or mother speak of the famed Peachblow Potato of 25 and 30 years ago? It seems to have become extinct, but the old Peachblow was considered for years and years the very best Potato on earth.

We are happy to say that we have a small stock of the new Peachblow Potatoes, and in order to give it a very, very wide distribution, we shall give same as a premium with each barrel of Potatoes ordered of the following varieties:

Salzer's Earliest Potato at	$5.00 per bbl.
Salzer's Great Six Weeks Market Potato at	2.75 "
Salzer's President McKinley Potato at	4.00 "
Salzer's Free Silver Potato at	6.00 "
Salzer's King of the Earliest Potato at	6.00 "
Salzer's Extra Early Ohio at	7.50 "
Salzer's Maggie Murphy at	3.50 "
Salzer's Champion of the World Potato at	3.50 "
Salzer's Secretary Wilson Potato at	6.00 "
Salzer's Robust Potato at	4.00 "
Salzer's Earliest Potato Collection at	5.50 "
Salzer's Prize Potato Collection at	3.25 "
Salzer's Good Times Collection at	3.00 "

We would not hesitate a moment to pay the cost of a barrel of any of above varieties of Potatoes to obtain a pound of this rare Peachblow Potato. One pound properly handled will give you 150 pounds of seed to work from the next year. We have none for sale; only offer them as a premium to widely distribute this year.

SALZER'S EARLIEST POTATO.

The John A. Salzer Seed Company consider this Potato the earliest on earth. They warrant same to be the earliest. For the past ten years they have tested every seedsman's earliest sort, and especially so the past 5 years, every earliest variety offered by seedsmen in Michigan, Minnesota, Illinois, New York and other states, and have invariably found them from 5 to 15 days later than Salzer's extremely early, extremely fine Salzer's Earliest Potato. There are thousands upon thousands of market gardeners and market farmers who will fully corroborate what we say regards Salzer's Earliest Potato. There is positively no Potato in America today that can touch it in earliness by from 5 to 25 days.

The next earliest potato is Salzer's Six Weeks Market, and they come near number of other seedsmen's earliest sorts, but the two earliest potatoes in America are Salzer's Earliest and Salzer's Six Weeks' Market.

Take our word for it, no matter what seedsman or merchants will tell you, Salzer's Earliest is the earliest potato in the world. Insurance and Salzer's Earliest heads the list. That's the place for it. It has earned this proud distinction on account of its being the earliest in the world,—that is, the earliest introduced for general culture. Salzer's Earliest Yes, but it has ripened tubers fit to eat in but 30 days - 4 weeks. Who would have thought that possible ten years ago! Indeed, this is the earliest Potato in the world; at least seedsmen 5 to 15 days earlier alongside of over 30 seedsmen's earliest sorts. We do not think that for earliness, enormous productiveness and fine appearance, for strong, vigorous growth, excellent flavor and early ripening quality, any praise, no matter how strong, is too high for its merits. Salzer's Earliest is one of your weakly, dwarfish things; it is full of life, vigor and healthfulness, and as soon as planted sprouts quickly, apparently determined to get three weeks ahead of its relatives, and so it does. And, sir, it does it every time. It is the great Earliest Potato, and although it is being crowded by our Six Weeks, it still leads as the champion Early Potato of the world! No Potato ever introduced that gets there quicker, in finer form, sells more quickly than Salzer's Earliest. Its friends are legion. It is the seedling of celebrated Triumph or Bliss Beauty type, but is earlier than either and twice as prolific.

It is a Potato for Money Making.

Now every farmer and market gardener is in the business, not for the glory or pleasure alone, but for profit. They want to make money, and that is right. Now we know of no Potato to plant from which they can make quicker money and more money than from Salzer's Earliest. It is a Potato that has as yet found no equal in earliness with the one exception of Salzer's King of the Earliest. This latter Potato is earlier than Salzer's Earliest, but the rock is so scarce and the prices so high that but few will be able to plant it for general crops, that is, in large quantities. Its one price of Salzer's Earliest is low. Just think of it. Only $5.00 per barrel! There is no farmer in America that cannot afford to invest and plant from 5 to 20 acres.

Now the hearty crop was plastic and dorrepresented as found on the next page could be furnished by the hundred, but space forbids. We, however, will introduce one here, which goes to show how splendidly our Northern-grown Potatoes are adapted to all soils and all states, and which goes to prove that it will pay you to change your seed Potatoes every year and buy them from us, the Northern crop that you will get will double, aid more than double your crop.

Here is a letter from Curtis Coffeen, Tuscola County, Mich., who says as follows: "I could not give your Potatoes a fair trial on account of the great drought, but nevertheless, the 25 only seed Potatoes purchased from you are a grand success. Some of my neighbors lost their entire crop of their own seed on account of the dry weather while I have lost none, by baking or drying up in the ground, because your seed proved to be as hardy and so vigorous and so fine; all hardly lost a single hill. The tops are very thrifty. The potatoes large and smooth and of excellent in far superior quality for eating. There will be a tremendous crop despite the drought, which has been the worst ever known here.

It is just like that wide awake farmer, Martin J. —, Vineland, N. J., says: "I like your Earliest Potato and every word true of what you claimed in your catalogue for Salzer's Earliest. It is absolutely the earliest Potato we have ever tried. So it is with your Cabbage and other seeds which I have cultivated. The have always proven everything that you claim for same."

There is Absolutely no Risk.

There is no risk taken in planting this Potato. It is sure to grow. It is sure to be the earliest; it is sure to fetch in a lot of money because it sells at sight at a fancy price, and an any and every market on the globe. It is a beautiful Potato, and its bright, perfect color wins for it friends everywhere. It is a great yielder. For an early Potato there is nothing that exceeds it, and farmers can do no better than plant heavily of this variety for extreme early. We know you will like it, because it not only produces heavily, but it is so extremely early that it will fetch in loads of money. Why not try it for new and plant from to diseases? When your neighbor sees this Potato growing he will want to buy it from you for seed, and will pay you from $1.00 to $1.50 a bushel. This is the way you could make money.

THE EARLIEST POTATO IN THE WORLD

You can have Salzer's Earliest Potatoes for dinner 25 days ahead of your neighbor, unless he plants Salzer's Earliest too.

Salzer's Earliest Will Surely Make Money for You and Pay Your Debts.

Now we are just as sure of Salzer's Earliest being able to make money for you and to pay your obligations, if you so say, or, as we are sure that fourth of July or Christmas is coming, just supposing you waned and enough that here we fit times of Salzer's Earliest Potato. Just think of it! Suppose you should plant 5 acres and the yield would be, judge it very low, at but 100 bu. per acre, and you crop same in June and sell them at a second crop of $15.00 from 5 acres, and you would make the money inside of eight weeks. Now would not that pay you? You could plow the land and get a second crop of your Potatoes from the same soil just as easily as not. Now we want to make money as possible. We want to enable farmer prosperous, happy and rich, and we know of nothing that could make it quicker than Salzer's Earliest Potato. It is a money maker because it is the Earliest Potato for general crop ever introduced. We have never had half enough of these Potatoes, but we believe that this year our stock is large enough to supply all our demands.

On our farm in Dakota, on soil that was not irrigated, we had growing a large acreage of these Potatoes. Ex-Governor Sheldon and other state officials and prominent farmers and editors viewing the patch of this Potato were highly delighted with same. A single hill was dug, planted from 2 eyes, which contained the marvelous number of 30 well-developed Salzer's Earliest Potatoes (see cut next page), and every Potato as pretty as a picture and fit for a king.

Now this is the Potato we shall ask you to try, and we know that you will be delighted with same, otherwise we would not urge you to give it a trial. We have placed the price per barrel very low, and we will also add it to our Salzer's Earliest Collection in order to distribute the same the world over this coming spring.

Price of Salzer's Earliest Potato (see also page 105): Pk., 60c; bu., $2.00; bbl., $5.00; 3 bbls., $10.50.

SALZER'S EARLIEST POTATO FRIENDS ARE LEGION.

We have offered this magnificent Potato, this earliest among all early, for the past few years, and it has won friends by the thousands throughout the United States, Canada and Europe. It is the earliest Potato introduced, and takes a back seat for no other Potato except Salzer's King of the Earliest.

Fred Marvelin, City Point, Wis.: "Your Earliest are A No. 1 fine flavor. Am well pleased with them."

John Berger, New Washington, O.: "Your Earliest were fully two weeks ahead of the earliest Potatoes here."

F. M. Elston, Sciota, Ill.: "Your Salzer's Earliest is certainly the Earliest Potato in the world. It is fine. It will yield fully 400 bu. per acre. Your Early Six Weeks and Harvest King are grand."

Geo. Snape, Bay State, Minn.: "Your Earliest Potatoes are exceedingly good. There is no need of raising about them. They talk for themselves. They are the best Earliest I ever saw."

John Ily, Mt. Clare, Neb.: "Salzer's Earliest Potato withstood the drought. It is a good cropper and is the earliest I ever saw."

Mrs. Catharine Thoman, Ithaca, Mich.: "Salzer's Earliest Potato is the earliest Potato I ever saw."

I. J. Austen, Lake Fork, O.: "Salzer's Earliest Potato has proven to be an exceedingly fine Potato. It is extremely early and a great yielder. I can highly recommend them as first-class in every respect."

W. W. Dinwiddie, Taconis, Ia.: "Salzer's Earliest Potato was fit for use in 30 days. We have an excellent stand of Alfalfa Clover from your seed."

Heinrich Holz, Harrisburg, Ill.: "Your Earliest Potatoes are splendid; your Alfalfa Clover excellent."

Jacob Dietzman, Platteville, Wis.: The Salzer's Earliest Potatoes are wonderfully fine."

J. B. Satterlee, Manchester, Ia.: "I took first premium here on Salzer's Earliest and Six Weeks Potatoes. They are very fine."

John C. Dolan, Monroe, Wis.: "Salzer's Earliest Potatoes yielded at the rate of 450 bu. per acre, and it was no year for Potatoes here."

J. M. Scharf, S. Dak.: "Salzer's Earliest I ate in 30 days after planting."

A. E. Finn, Tex.: "It is the Potato for Texas. I'll for sale in 90 days."

Jule Toms, Miss.: Nothing like it ever seen here. Ready for the market in 30 to 45 days."

W. H. Horne, Fla.: "Salzer's Earliest is the finest Early Potato I ever saw."

G. A. Gordon, Ga.: "Like it immensely. It is as early as the earliest and kidges ahead."

Karl Mehr, Tex.: "Mail you a big tuber of Salzer's Earliest—40 days after planting—you see it would have been fit to dig 10 days ago."

The Editor of the Rural New Yorker—the great American Authority on Potatoes calls Salzer's Earliest Potato—the earliest of over 90 early varieties tested by him, yielding 464 bushels per acre!—That's the way it is always!—Salzer's Earliest is the Earliest!

Now, for 1899 We Challenge the World.

When we challenged the world last spring, offering $5.00 a pound for a potato, that... could... accepted the challenge? Did any win? No, not one; for all acknowledged gracefully, too—that no potato known to them exceeded in earliness Salzer's Earliest! We tried many sorts from our own potatoes what thought they had an earlier variety, but they all proved later. So, now again, we challenge the world to produce or show an earlier sort. We will pay $5.00 a pound for an earlier variety than Salzer's Earliest! ... Produce an earlier sort if you have one; we want it.

Now, Mr. Farmer and Gardener, we venture to say with great certainty and with great freedom that there never has been a farmer who has purchased Potatoes from us but has profited in increased yields on account of so purchasing. Just take Mr. Coffeen, who is the only man in his neighborhood who has grown a crop of potatoes. Why? Because he planted Salzer's Northern-grown, vigorous seed. Read the letter, page 97, from Curtis Coffeen.

It is a fact that no matter how bad the drought, how long you must wait for rain, how poor the weather, if you plant our vigorous Northern-grown seeds, you are almost sure of a big yield, at least that is the experience of tens of thousands of our customers. Now why not try it for 1899 and have a tremendous yield?

Price of Salzer's Earliest Potato: 1 lb., postpaid, 35c.; 3 lbs., $1.00; by freight, pk., 60c.; bu., $2.00; bbl., $3.60; 3 bbls., $10.50.

This is the Great Potato for Texas and the South.

It is the quickest growing Potato in America, and is especially adapted (as it... ... ...) produce finer and more potatoes than any sort or kind known in Texas. It is 50 per cent. better in yield than the old Triumph, which it resembles in form, being rose color roundish tubers, flesh a pinkish... and sells quickly everywhere. Women of Texas and the happy South, North, East or West, this is the Potato to plant and plant a lot of for very early! The price is ridiculously low. So... then... sent us 45... I, John Bell... for La... Bell... then it... Salzer has the genuine.

Salzer's Earliest and Salzer's Six Weeks grown thousands... from 30 to... by Jaye of... of Early Wichigan, Queen, Kfrom... and most American earliest sorts!

Salzer's Earliest Six-Weeks Market Potato.

It is without question that the Earliest Six-Weeks Market Potato, which we describe on this and the next page, is the greatest Potato of the age. It is ahead of Salzer's Earliest in quality and yield, but is not quite so early, but is 10 days earlier than Early Michigan, Bovee and such "claimed earliest sorts." There is another great advantage in planting Salzer's Earliest Six-Weeks Market in preference to any other earlier sort, and that is that it is always a reliable yielder. Salzer's Earliest Six-Weeks Market, which we call "earliest" because it is a great improvement on the common Six-Weeks Market, has never failed us to produce extremely early, very large tubered potatoes. A little later than Salzer's Earliest, but always sure.

It is the great general purpose potato of the world to-day. By this we mean that it is good, extremely early, $\&$ for market everywhere in six weeks and less than in even. It is good for midsummer, it is good for late summer, it is good for fall, and it is magnificent to put into winter quarters, where it will keep splendidly all winter and give you the finest flavored, best quality eating potatoes imaginable. We never can tire extolling the merits of Salzer's Earliest Six-Weeks Market Potato. There is really no potato that is its superior, and if we had but one Potato to plant, that would be the Potato every time. The yield the past season was astonishingly large, acre after acre yielding from 500 to 500 bushels per acre. It is a wonderful Potato in every respect.

Salzer's Six-Weeks Market Potato has had a magnificent run as the earliest Potato in America (with the one exception of Salzer's Earliest). The last named sort (Salzer's Earliest) is without a peer as the earliest Potato, but Salzer's Earliest Six-Weeks Market is of each excellent quality, of such ravenous earliness, that we gladly devote much space to it in our catalogue.

Market gardeners and all others who grow Potatoes! What could you afford to give for Potatoes that will produce fine, large, beautiful tubered stock from planting, when in two or more weeks ahead of any other kind, if you knew they would positively produce such? Yes "No"! Well, we will say to all who are fortunate enough to receive this catalogue that SALZER'S EARLIEST SIX-WEEKS MARKET WILL do all this. It is worth its weight in gold for a start of seed to many market gardeners, as such it may can get the fancy prices before other kindred sorts in market. We offer for your consideration the accompanying report from the originator, who has been a Potato grower all his life, and is now 52 years old, and from others whom full addresses are on file in our office. After reading these you cannot longer doubt that this is a most remarkable variety. This new Potato originated in Ohio in 1885, and we purchased of the originator the entire stock and right to introduce it. The originator says: "They have created such excitement in my neighborhood that I could sell the whole crop to my neighbors at a fancy price." Growers medium to large size, oblong to round shape, light, flesh-colored skin; white flesh; very smooth shape; eyes even with the surface; tubers grow close together in the hill. The potatoes begin to form when the vines are only 4 or 5 inches high. The tops and tubers grow woody, and at 6 weeks from planting are a fine marketable size, and reach maturity in 75 days. As a table Potato they are not excelled; even for late spring they keep sound and solid. They grow so rapidly and mature so early that the Potato bugs have no chance at all, making their crop, if planted early, before the young bugs become numerous; while for yield they are wonderful, considering their earliness.

Why, but yesterday Mr. Aug. Kahlwei, a La Crosse County farmer, received from us a check for $350.00 for Potatoes grown on less than 1 acre. He was proud to pay off the last mortgage on his farm and that is what you, Mr. Farmer, can positively do if you plant plenty of Salzer's Potatoes. There is nothing that will pay you better than Salzer's Earliest, see page 101, and Salzer's Earliest Six-Weeks Market. It is best for general market, best flavored, best early Potato we know of. In addition to this it is a potato you can sell every month of the year, because it has magnificent keeping qualities ahead of every other early variety.

Down in Texas and Alabama, in Florida and throughout the South

This potato is fairly captivating the hearts of all planters. It is crowding the Red Triumph and Stray Beauty varieties to the wall. Every planter who has once used Salzer's Earliest Six-Weeks Market will plant same in preference to every other known variety of Potatoes. They do this because Salzer's Earliest Six-Weeks Market will yield three times as much in Texas as Red Triumph; in addition, the Potatoes will have from 4 to 6 weeks longer in the South than above varieties. That is the Potato to plant for Texas and the Southern States; that is the Potato to bank on in those states; that is the Potato to bank on everywhere where you desire an extremely early, extremely fine, extreme good-keeping Potato. Salzer's Earliest Six-Weeks Market fills the bill every time. In 1897, 524 bushels; in 1898, 460 bushels earliest large potatoes.

Going home from market loaded with money—the result of planting Salzer's heavy-cropping Earliest Six-Weeks Market Potato.

EVERYBODY TELLS US

That we are the largest growers of Seed Potatoes in the world; that we handle thousands upon thousands of barrels more than any half dozen seedsmen combined. We believe this to be the case, as we make a great specialty of Seed Potatoes, and believe there is no firm in the world having a finer variety of heavy-cropping Potatoes than we. In the Earliest Six-Weeks there is more new blood, more new vigor than in any Potato, outside of Salzer's Earliest and Salzer's Wilson, offered in America to-day. We have given this Potato a thorough test all over America, and never was a Potato so eagerly sought after, or ever gave better satisfaction than this. There are scores and scores of customers who pronounce it the earliest Potato in the world, and not only the earliest but the best in the world.

Its strong points are these:
1st. It will yield three times as much as the Early Ohio, the Hebron or Rose.
2d. It is from 8 to 10 days earlier than either of those two varieties.
3d. We have never seen same blight or decay, as they are of unusual health.
4th. Its quality is unsurpassed by any sort grown. It is magnificent.

5th. It is very smooth, of a good shape, but comparatively few eyes.
6th. It is an excellent keeper, and, although caused by many the "earliest in the world," is also one of the best keepers in the world.
7th. It is one of the heaviest yielders for an early Potato that we know of.

The Originator Says about this Potato:

"Potatoes have been my favorite crop ever since I was a boy (am now 52 years old), and I always took great pleasure in seeing what good strong and large yields I could get, but never did I see a nicer Potato than this. I have raised a great many kinds, sent for the earliest in the catalogues, and have raised them from seed and got some very good ones, but none that came up to my ideal of a perfect Potato until I originated this. I have now discarded all others, and raise this for early, a main crop for market and hope one. This year has fully convinced me that I have at last produced the best early Potato in cultivation. I think it combines more good qualities than any other variety in the world. I have given it a fair trial and it has proven itself superior to all other varieties. Grown on a light clay soil, and without manure or fertilizer, they yielded at the rate of 250 bushels per acre, which can be increased with both it yielded 101 bushels this year, and in 1897, in South Dakota, 220 bushels earliest large Potatoes per acre.

Salzer's Earliest Six-Weeks Market Potato.

This Potato will revolutionize Potato growing from the fact that we have sent out many thousands of barrels throughout the United States. Before the introduction of Salzer's Earliest Six-Weeks the Early Ohio was the earliest potato, but Salzer's Earliest Six-Weeks is fully 20 to 30 days earlier than the Early Ohio. Now we know that Salzer's Earliest Six-Weeks Market is the best Potato to plant for early. Our plan would be to plant Salzer's Earliest Six-Weeks for early and Salzer's Lightning Express or Early Wisconsin for the second early. These two Potatoes are very different in shape and both cousin for the second early. Both are beautiful, both are early, both sell well on any and every market on the globe. Both are of fine quality and of fine appearance and are great yielders, and we heartily urge all our customers to give same a trial.

We hope you will give Salzer's Earliest Six-Weeks Market Potatoes a trial this year. It is the potato for Texas and the South, for the West, Northwest, North and East,—yes, for every section of our great Union.

Price of Salzer's Great Earliest Six-Weeks Potato: Pk., 60c.; bu., $1.50; bbl., $3.75; 2 bbls., $5.40; 5 bbls., $13.25; 10 bbls., and 10 lbs., Feachblow only $26.00.

Salzer's Earliest Six-Weeks Potato Resists **Every Drought.**

This Potato has a great record as a drought resister. That is, if you want a Potato for general crop, Salzer's **Earliest** is always ready as a rule before any drought comes, and is sold at a fancy price, **as** this Potato as a rule is not put into the cellars on account of its fancy price for early.

Now with Salzer's Six-Weeks Market you have the same thing, and if you do not want it for early, it will do splendidly **to put to your** cellars for late, as it is a great keeper. Indeed, the Six-Weeks Market Potato not only is an extra early Potato, but is a Potato that is good all **summer** and all fall through, and is fit for sale any time after 45 to 50 days from planting, although many of our customers bed Potatoes, as you will find by the testimonials, in **less time than above** We know you will like this Potato, its shape, its color, its size, its quality, its yield. In fact it is a perfect Potato in **every** respect.

Hear Salzer's Earliest Six-Weeks Market Potato's Friends **Talk.**

Andrew Follweiler, Tannersville, Pa., says: "Your Early Six-Weeks Market Potato is the grandest Potato I ever raised. Everybody is astonished who sees them. We raised 25 bu. from 1 bu. of seed, having some tubers weighing over 2 lbs."

R. C. Bush, Meridian, Miss.: "The Early Six-Weeks Potato is far superior to anything I have ever seen here for early Potatoes, and for table purposes they are unexcelled. My neighbors say they are the best they have ever eaten. It is a heavy producer."

Fred A. Hoener, Newark, Ill.: "Last spring I thought you told big stories about big Potatoes, but having tried a barrel of your Early Six-Weeks. I am ready to swallow almost anything you say. Every one here wants some of your Early Six-Weeks Market Potatoes."

N. Barbour, Belle Plaine, Wis., "Your Six-Weeks Market Potato is the earliest I have ever grown."

Geo. M. Harmon, Indian River, Mich., says: "The best potato I ever saw is Salzer's Six Weeks Market. If I can find a man that would pay an extra price for 1,000 bushels grown on one measured acre of Salzer's Six-Weeks Potatoes. I will grow them. I have some hills that would estimate over 2,000 bushels per acre.

Jackson Bower, Long Rapids, Mich.: "The Six-Weeks Market Potato we commenced to use 40 days after planting and used them all summer. There is no better potato.

Mrs. Hannah Treville, Midland, O. "We have just dug our Six-Weeks Market potatoes. They are very fine—are the earliest we have ever seen fine. W. Beardslee, Wichita, Kes. "We beg to report that the newer ordered of you last spring are all right, notably on the Six-Weeks Potatoes and Cabbage and Onion Seeds."

Hannah Anniversary, Junction City, Kan.: "Your Six-Weeks Potatoes were as large as walnuts in 35 days. If we would have had plenty of moisture, they would have been double the size."

Geo. A. Triplett, Ironwood, Mich. "The Six-Weeks Potatoes did splendidly. They will go 400 bu. per acre."

G. Lindemann, Paw Paw, Mich.: I planted two barrels Salzer's Six-Weeks. They are the grandest Potatoes I ever saw. They are pronounced the finest, earliest and best in this county by all who saw them. Will yield fully 200 bu."

R. Taylor, Ashland Co., Wis.: "One pound Early Six-Weeks Market Potato yielded 147 pounds of fine, sound, smooth tubers; produced marketable Potatoes in six weeks."

J. G. Kerr, Tenn.: "I had a load of your Six-Weeks Potatoes to Nashville in just 42 days after planting."

J. M. Schart, Brown Co., S. D. "Fit for table in 30 days. Nothing ever introduced like it."

R. G. Smith, Minn.: "Sold a load in Minneapolis market for $1.60 a bushel 48 days after planting."

J. F. Hoffman, Montcoro.: "It is the earliest Potato. Ripe in 6 weeks."

Geo. Koenig, Ill.: "It is the best Potatoes in 50 days—for a king."

W. D. Walker, Ind.: "40 days after planting I dug 1 peck from 1 hill."

F. G. Rose, Mass.: "It is the best Potato I ever saw; sold some 46 days after planting."

Joe Cannon, Iowa: "I would not believe it, but now I do, for I ate Six-Weeks 46 days after planting."

All Day Long.

We could keep on with testimonials and good words and praises on this Potato all day long. The above suffices to demonstrate to you that it is indeed the very earliest in the world and at the same time one of the very best early Potatoes that has ever been produced, and we accordingly recommend same to anybody and everybody who is in want of a really good Potato. Several prominent seedsmen are offering a Potato for Six-Weeks that is not genuine. To get the true Salzer's Six-Weeks Market buy only of us. Our stock is grown ahead of Michigan seed.

The successful Potato grower uses Salzer's Planter, Hill Sprinkler and Hill Quick Sprayer

It is the Great Mortgage-Lifting Potato.

That is, 10 acres of this early Potato, fit for market in 6 weeks, will bring, in nine out of ten markets in America, 80c a bushel, or for 10 acres, on an average yield of over 300 bushels per acre, $2,700.00! Now, that pays. That lifts the mortgage and buys lots of things you have long wanted! This great, early Potato, with our matchless Champion of the World for late, and then our wonderful Big Four Oats and our Extra Grass Mixtures, if generously planted by farmers in 1896, will positively prove a blessing, will positively make you money, yes, lift the old mortgage th at has bothered you so long. Look at the rank and file of the great farmers army who have used this Potato. Is there one who was not pleased? No, sir! Everybody praises its beauty, earliness and great money-making qualities. Let it do good work for you; let it make you rich and happy.

PRICE **OF** SALZER'S NORTHERN GROWN EARLIEST SIX-WEEKS POTATO.

3 lb., postpaid, 35c; 3 lbs., $1.00; by freight, pk., 60c; bu., $1.50; bbl., $2.75; 3 bbls., $5.40; 5 bbls., and 5 lbs., Peachblow only $12.25; 10 bbls., $25.00.

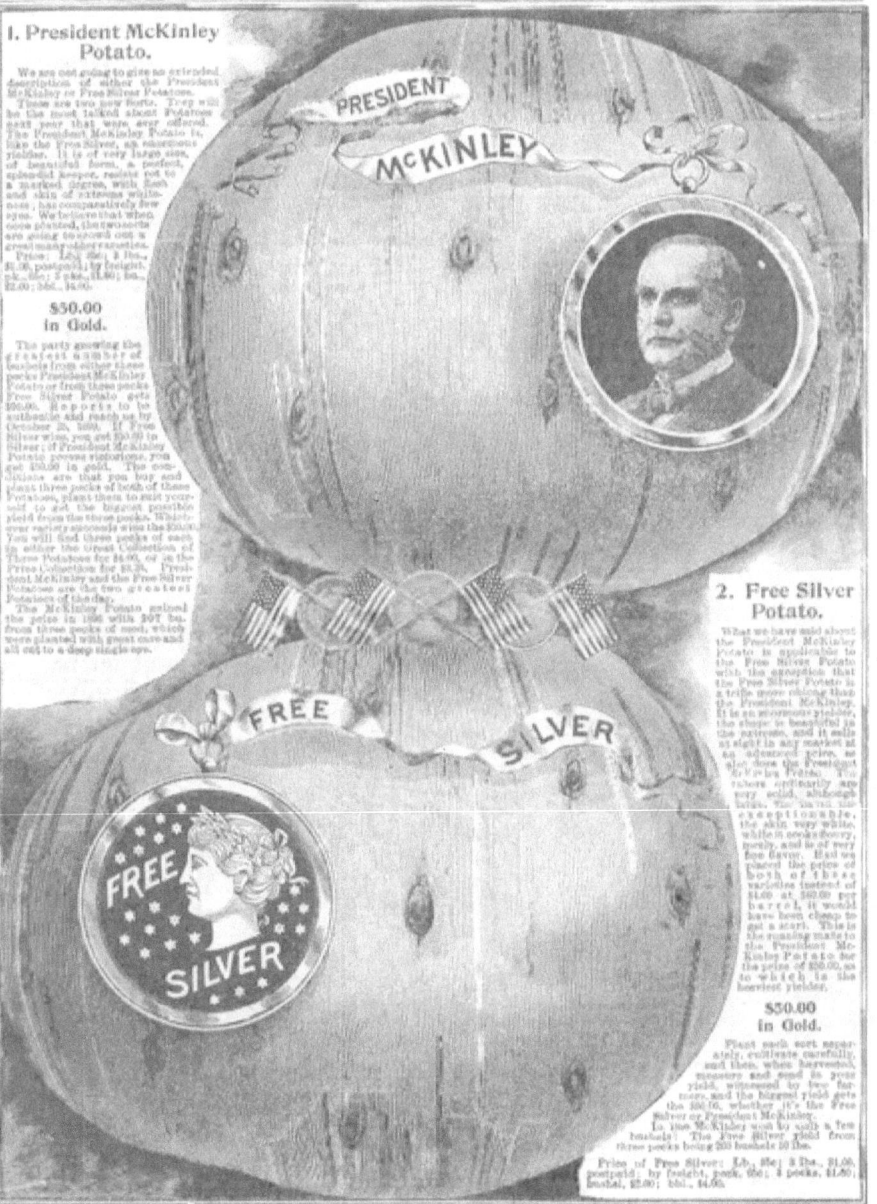

1. President McKinley Potato.

We are not going to give an extended description of either the President McKinley or Free Silver Potatoes. These are two new sorts. They will be the most talked about Potatoes next year that were ever offered. The President McKinley Potato is, like the Free Silver, an enormous yielder. It is of very large size, of beautiful form, a perfect, splendid keeper, resists rot to a marked degree, with flesh and skin of extreme whiteness, has comparatively few eyes. We believe that when once planted, the two sorts are going to exceed out a great many other varieties.

Price: Lb, 35c; 3 lbs., $1.00, postpaid; by freight, pk., 60c; 3 pks., $1.50; bu., $2.00; bbl., $4.00.

$50.00 in Gold.

The party growing the greatest number of bushels from either three pecks President McKinley Potato or from three pecks Free Silver Potato gets $50.00. Reports to be authentic and reach us by October 20, 1899. If Free Silver wins, you get $50.00 in Silver; if President McKinley Potato proves victorious, you get $50.00 in gold. The conclusions are that you buy and plant three pecks of both of these Potatoes, plant them to suit yourself to get the biggest possible yield from the three pecks. Whichever variety succeeds wins the $50.00. You will find three pecks of each in either the Great Collection of Three Potatoes for $4.00, or in the Prize Collection for $3.25. President McKinley and the Free Silver Potatoes are the two greatest Potatoes of the day.

The McKinley Potato gained the prize in 1896 with 207 bu. from three pecks of seed, which were planted with great care and all cut to a deep single eye.

2. Free Silver Potato.

What we have said about the President McKinley Potato is applicable to the Free Silver Potato with the exception that the Free Silver Potato is a trifle more oblong than the President McKinley. It is an enormous yielder, the shape is beautiful in the extreme, and it sells at sight in any market at an advanced price, as also does the President McKinley Potato. The tubers ordinarily are very solid, although some helps, too, be an exception able, the skin very white, while it cooks floury, mealy, and is of very fine flavor. Had we placed the price of both of these varieties instead of $1.00 at $50.00 per barrel, it would have been cheap to get a scarf. This is the running mate to the President McKinley Potato for the price of $50.00, as to which is the heaviest yielder.

$50.00 in Gold.

Plant each sort separately, cultivate carefully, and then, when harvested, measure and send in your yield, witnessed by two farmers, and the biggest yield gets the $50.00, whether it's the Free Silver or President McKinley.

In 1896 McKinley won by only a few bushels! The Free Silver yield from three pecks being 203 bushels 10 lbs.

Price of Free Silver: Lb., 35c; 3 lbs., $1.00, postpaid; by freight, peck, 60c; 3 pecks, $1.50; bushel, $2.00; bbl., $4.00.

151 3 Great Lots, down composed of 3 pks. McKinley, 3 pks. Free Silver 1, 3 pks. Champion of the World, for only $4.00.

SALZER'S NEW CHAMPION OF THE WORLD POTATO.

We are going to start in right here with a broad and bold assertion that this is the most remarkable Potato of the age. (We except our two new seedlings, President McKinley and Free Silver.) Now, you will say that this is pretty strong, and that it is contradictory; but it is not. We will tell you why we think this is the most remarkable late Potato of the age; and it is remarkable in so many respects that it is entitled to this distinction. In the first place it has a remarkable name, and, as its name would indicate, it is truly and honestly and surely the Champion of all Potatoes in the World. By this we mean, when it comes to yield, when it comes to plow out bushel after bushel, when it comes to quality, when it comes to beauty of appearance, when it comes to solid but delicious flesh, when it comes to excellent flavor and splendid keeping qualities, when it comes to fine-sized tubers and ready-selling properties, we must say that there is no Potato that is its equal, and that no Potato combines all of above magnificent qualities in one whole, except the Champion of the World, and for this reason we have named the same Champion of the World. Now we are going to make another broad assertion right here in the beginning of this description of Champion of the World Potato, and we shall deliberately say that it is the most prolific, heaviest-yielding, greatest producing Potato known in the world to-day. Now, we have underscored these words and printed them in bold-faced type so that each and every one may read them, for we believe that each and every word above is the truth and only the truth; and we are going to say right here, before we proceed further, that, although we have tested, in the last 20 years, possibly 5,000 different Potato sorts, there has never been one that has shown such remarkable yielding qualities and excellent habits as this one, and we frankly state that it is in our estimation, the greatest, the most wonderful, the most remarkable late Potato of the age. Champion of the World is a Potato beautiful in the extreme, in long to oblong, of handsome form, white skin, large size, lovely appearance, which aids to sell it in any market of the world at an advanced price over common varieties. It is very healthy, vigorous and an enormous cropper, yielding 1,687 bushels per acre.

Now when we say a test yield of 1,687 bushels per acre, there are a great many farmers who will shake their heads and say that it is absolutely impossible, but here is what the Rural New Yorker authorities have to say on potatoes: Uncle Sam's Potato yielded at the rate of 1,000 bushels per acre, and Sir Walter Raleigh Potatoes at the rate of 1,036 bushels per acre. Now this shows what can be done with new blood, and we believe in Salzer's McKinley, Salzer's Free Silver and Salzer's Champion of the World we have the greatest Potato on earth.

Price of Champion of the **World Potato:** Lb., 25c; 3 lbs., $1.00, postpaid; by **freight, pk., 60c; ¼ bu.,** $1.00; bu., $1.50; bbl., $3.50; 3 bbls., $9.00.

For $4.00
We send one barrel of these three general crop Potatoes, as follows: 3 pecks President McKinley, 3 pecks Free Silver and 3 pecks Champion of the World, and 1 pound State of Wisconsin, all for $4.00.

SALZER'S KING OF THE EARLIEST POTATO.

This Potato we offered in 1896 as a premium, and it has proven itself the earliest large Potato in the world. It is of the Early Ohio type, a seedling of the Early Six Weeks Market, which it resembles in every respect except that it is earlier. Everybody who tested same last year is delighted therewith, reporting same as ripening or as fit to eat in 28 to 35 days after planting. Mr. Jackson Brown, of Alpena County, Mich., says: "Your Potato beats anything I ever saw or heard of. King of the Earliest is the earliest. I planted mine May 25th, and dug Potatoes of good size the 25th of June; but I took great care of them, hence got such excellent results."

Think of it—Potatoes in less than 4 weeks. Is not this marvelous?

We have reduced the price of this Potato so as to place it within the reach of every farmer. Price: Lb., 25c; 3 lbs., $1.00, postpaid; by freight, pk., 60c; ¼ bu., $1.50; bu., $2.50; bbl., $6.00.

EXTRA EARLY OHIO—SPECIAL STOCK.

We have a limited stock of Wisconsin grown Extra Early Ohio Potatoes containing some seconds, hence the extremely low price. This has been bred up to earliness in ripening and to heavy yields. It is one of the very best Potatoes for a general crop imaginable. It is not so early as the Salzer's Earliest Six Weeks, but it is a beautiful Potato and one sure to give satisfaction for general early crop. We offer this at a remarkably low price. Price: Peck, 50c; bu., $1.50; bbl., $3.00.

BLISS OR RED TRIUMPH OR STRAY BEAUTY.

Well known the world over. About 20 days later than Salzer's Earliest, which is a seedling of Stray Beauty. Largely used in Texas and the South. Price: Lb., 40c; 3 lbs., $1.00; by freight, pk., 75c; bu., $1.50; bbl., $3.50.

STATE OF WISCONSIN.

Our great premium Potato of 1896—our stock very scarce. A great, large, white Potato. Peck, $1.20; bu., $3.50; bbl., $7.50.

UNCLE SAM.

A new white Potato to which the Rural New Yorker accredits a yield of 1,000 bu. per acre. Lb., 25c; 3 lbs., $1.00, postpaid; by freight, pk., $1.00; bu., $2.50; bbl., $5.00.

SIR WALTER RALEIGH.

A large white Potato which the Rural New Yorker gives a yield of 1,036 bu. per acre. Lb., 25c; 3 lbs., $1.00, postpaid; by freight, pk., $1.00; bu., $2.50; bbl., $5.00.

NINE STANDARD POTATOES.

Price each sort: Peck, 50c; bu., $1.25; bbl., $2.00.

No. 1. Salzer's Hundredfold, oblong to long, white.
No. 2. Burbank, well-known white sort.
No. 3. Salzer's Ironclad, a roundish snow-white Potato.
No. 4. American Wonder, a heavy yielding white sort.
No. 5. Rural New Yorker, known everywhere as a heavy yielding white Potato.
No. 6. Carman No. 1, a great beauty large white.
No. 7. Harvest King, a magnificent white sort.
No. 8. Algoma, very early, some 15 days later than Six Weeks.
No. 9. Early Michigan, about 20 days later than Six Weeks and yields less by half.

Price of above nine sorts each: Peck, 50c; bu., $1.25; bbl., $2.00.

For Only $1.20.

Customers often write us for a cheap Northern-grown Potato. We have a barrel of such Potatoes, as we may often have a large stock of this barrel Potatoes, all Northern-grown—good for big, heavy yields. We sell them for only $1.20 a bbl. Of course, if we were farming, we would rather pay a little more and get a barrel of Salzer's Earliest Six Weeks—or $4.00 for the great general crop Potato, or one of the other collections—but the $1.20 per bbl. are all right and will please.

Price: 1 bbl....................$1.20

Extra for bbl. and packing, .40 $1.50

We charge for barrel or packing only on the cheap collection of $1.20 a barrel. No the Potatoes only cost us $1.20, the barrel 25c; total only $1.50. In each case where you do not send the 25c for barreling, we either return the money or send only 90 lbs. Potatoes.

No. 1. Salzer's Earliest.

This is the earliest Potato in the world. Every variety is to be bountiful as a pasture. These to be variety that we know of maintains no handsome an appearance, that is so early early, rather than of it is the Potato that gives them in earliness quicker than any other variety on earth.

It is fully described on pages 107 and 108 of this catalogue.

We urge everybody describe the earliest potato on earth to try this sort.

Price, pk. 60c; bu, $1.00; barrel, $3.50; barrels, $10.50.

No. 2. Salzer's Six Weeks Market.

In quality this is the best, heaviest yielding, handsome earliest variety of the earliest Potato on earth. It comes into play about 8 days after Six Weeks Market and several weeks later than Salzer's Earliest, but it is a fine Potato's Potato that will bear a trial in every garden in the country. It keeps nearly good well. Is of fine flavor and rich succulence, and we are sure will please everybody, giving it a trial.

Price, peck, 60c; 5 pecks, $1.00; bu, $1.00; barrel, $3.50.

No. 3. Burpee's Extra Early.

This Potato is sent out with great realness by an Eastern seedsman, claiming for it to be the earliest good Potato. It is quite a little bit earlier than any of the other seedsman's very earliest sorts. This gives you an idea how very early Salzer's Six Weeks Market Potato is. It is an extremely early, choice, elegant variety.

It is fully described on pages 108 and 109 of this catalogue.

Price, peck, 60c; 5 pecks, $1.00; bu, $1.00; barrel, $3.50.

No. 5. Secretary Wilson Potato.

We introduced this great potato last year with the following.

We are not going to say anything about this great novelty this season. The Potato is going to do its talking next year. The Potato is without fault, without an earlier or more perfect potato in it. In every jeweled put on it. We are going to sell it and keeping properties as can be had. We know it will do it, due to the great secretary of agriculture, for whom we have named it. Perfectly, more than 15 pounds sold to any one party.

We secured $1.00 per lb., for each and every lb., of Secretary Wilson Potato sold last year, and we disposed of a great many lbs., and there is not a farmer who has tried some but what is delighted with the extraordinary success of Secretary Wilson Potato. This Potato is really an agricultural wonder, not only in yield, but in extreme earliness and extreme richness and delicacy of the eating qualities of this magnificent Potato. If we had only one Potato to choose, Secretary Wilson would be that one Potato, because it possesses every element that goes to make a really first class eating Potato. It is extremely early, ripening after Salzer's Six Weeks Market; it is extremely fine grained, extremely prolific and has keeping qualities in a remarkable degree. We have eaten Potatoes of Secretary Wilson 11 months of the year. We know greatly reduced the price of this Potato this year, and in order to secure widespread distribution we have introduced it in our most popular Salzer's Earliest Collection. Price, 1 lb., postpaid, 40c; 3 lbs., $1.00 peck, $1.00; bu, $3.50; bbl., $6.00.

NO. 4. Scharff's Early Dakota Potato.

Mr. Scharff speaks very strongly on the merits of his Potato. He is the introducer of this valuable sort, of which Scharff ing and yet his Potato proved on our farms fully 8 days later than Salzer's six weeks market. But it is a Potato that we urge everybody to try.

J. M. Scharff, Brown Co. S. D., has this to say regarding Scharff's Early Dakota Potato. It is positively the earliest Potato that I ever grew, it is fit for table use from five to ten days ahead of the Early Ohio, it is a better cooker, has an excellent flavor and is magnificent in every respect. It is not subject to any disease, I want the Potato on as follows:

1st. It is ten days earlier than the Early Ohio.
2nd. It is immensely superior in quality.
3rd. Less subject to scab or disease.
4th. Never or rarely hollow.
5th. It yields again as much.
6th. They keep much better than the Early Ohio, as they do not rot as easily, etc.
7th. I could cordially and heartily recommend anyone to say body that wants the earliest good Potato rate, deliciously flavored, enormously productive, extremely early Potato variety.

Price, pk., 60c; bu., $1.00; bbl., $4.00.

SALZER'S EARLIEST COLLECTION.

We know you will be surprised how we can sell this magnificent Earliest Potato collection composed of 5 of the grandest Potatoes on earth, separately packed in a barrel, for but $3.50, but we wish to give these Potatoes a widespread distribution, hence the low price. The collection contains:

$3.50

1 SALZER'S EARLIEST,	1 pk.	$1.50
2 SIX WEEKS,	"	1.50
3 EARLY DAKOTA,	"	1.00
4 BURPEE'S EARLY,	"	1.00
5 SECRETARY WILSON,	1 peck	1.00
Total		$6.00
And 1 lb. Peachblow free!		

FOR ONLY $3.50 PER BARREL!

In all 11 pecks, separately packed. Catalogue price of $6.00, we sell for but $3.50; 1 bbl., $3.50; 3 bbls., $10.00; 10 bbls., $27.50.

SALZER'S PRIZE COLLECTION

FREE SILVER

KING OF THE OHIOS

CHAMPION OF THE WORLD

PRES. McKINLEY

$50.00 PRIZES

SALZER'S PRIZE TAKER

THE POTATO MARVEL

2 BUSHELS PER ACRE

1. Salzer's New Champion of the World Potato.

This Potato is described more fully on page 112, and we request you to read the remarkable record made by this most remarkable late Potato.

Price: Lb., 40c; 3 lbs., $1.00, postpaid, by freight: ½ bu., 60c; bu., $2.00; bbl., $5.25.

2. King of Ohios.

This Potato originated in Dakota. It is a seedling of the old Ohio variety. It differs from that variety in so far that the King of Ohios is a medium early Potato, and is far more attractive than the Ohio varieties. It is not unusual for the King of Ohios to return a yield of from 400 to 600 bushels per acre. It is a magnificent Potato in every respect. The quality cannot be beat. It is even better than its parent, the Early Ohio, in keeping and cooking qualities. It sells quickly in any market, as it is of fine shape and the others of a very salable, attractive size. It is a Potato than is worth trying.

Price: Lb., 40c; 3 lbs., $1.00, postpaid; by freight, pk., 75c; bu., $1.00; bbl., $4.00.

3. Salzer's Prize Taker.

This Potato we introduced several years ago and it has had a remarkable run. It is more oblong than long, though our illustrations show it long; er than it really, as a rule, grows. It is a Potato, that if you have once planted same and put it into your cellars for winter use, you will want it a second time. You will want it right along. The flesh is pure white, floury, rich and delicious in flavor. Tubers are large and withstand drought exceedingly well. It is an extremely prolific, healthy variety. It is a Potato to bank on, as it never fails. Price, lb., 35c; 3 lbs., $1.00, postpaid; by freight, pk., 60c; bu., $1.75; bbl., $4.00.

4. Pres. McKinley Potato

This remarkable Potato is more fully described on page 111. We offer a prize on the McKinley and Free Silver Potatoes of $50.00, which will be paid to the variety which proves itself the heaviest yielder in 1896. You will find particulars in regard to this on page 111. It is a grand Potato, full of new life, new blood and new vigor. It will surely please. Price, lb., 35c; 3 lbs., $1.00, postpaid; by freight, pk., 60c; bu., $1.75; bbl., $4.00.

5. Free Silver, Potato.

A running mate of President McKinley Potato. It is grand in every respect. Large, white, flowery tubers. Wonder on the Free Silver and President McKinley Potatoes, a prize of $50.00, which will be paid to the variety which proves in 1896. You will find full particulars in regard to this on page 111. Price, lb., 35c; 3 lbs., $1.00, postpaid; by freight, pk., 60c; bu., $2.00; bbl., $4.00.

SALZER'S WONDERFUL PRIZE COLLECTION.

It is seldom, if ever that we have offered a collection of finer, newer blooded soils, of heavier croppers, of better flavored varieties than our matchless Salzer's Prize Collection. This collection is composed of that King of Potatoes—King of the Ohios, then that magnificent medium Potato, Prize Taker, and the very prolific Salzer's Champion of the World, while it contains three pecks each of the two greatest new Potatoes of the age, President McKinley and Free Silver. This is the required amount of President McKinley and Free Silver to plant to compete for the prize of $50.00.

This collection is composed of:

1 peck Champion of the World.
½ peck King of the Ohio.
1 peck Salzer's Prize Taker.
3 " President McKinley Potato.
3 " Free Silver Potato.

In all 11 pecks separately packed in 1 bbl., with 1 lb. of the great Peachblow thrown in as a Premium.

☞ Now this barrel is delivered free on cars here for but $3.25; 3 bbls., and 3 lbs. Peachblow Potato, $9.50.

1. Salzer's Earliest Six-Weeks Market.

This is the most remarkable of all our potatoes. There is

2. Salzer's World's Fair.

We cannot tell you how tremendous a sale Salzer's Earliest World's Fair Potato has had since its introduction by us in 1896—and no man who has planted this potato would part with it for a great deal. It's par excellence; it's the boss; it's indescribably good. Fine, large, noble

3. Carmen No. 3.

Named for the great editor, and a great Potato it is, honoring the great writer. Size is large, color white—more round oblong than long; of powerful vigor, unusual productiveness, yielding as reports so, over 1,000 bushels of

4. Salzer's Good Times Potato.

This collection is named after this Potato. With the election of Mr. McKinley as president, the farmers of America can certainly look for better times, as the protection idea of Mr. McKinley is what will set our mills going and furnish to the farmer a great home market at advanced prices. That's the way thousands of farmers feel. Now, this Good Times Potato is going to come in for its share of the credit among farmers in making good times. It is, like the Champion of the

POTATO EYES, POSTPAID, BY MAIL.

POTATO EYE CUTTER, 50c.

There are thousands of families living in cities and country who would like to grow a few Potatoes of our early Potatoes, or some of our magnificent, sterling new varieties, and who do not wish, on account of high express charges on a peck or bushel of seed, to buy this quantity. For these we have adopted a new plan of sending Potato Eyes by mail postpaid.

These are carefully packed with damp moss and we warrant them to arrive in good condition for growing, no matter how far away. In this way our customers can have the pleasure of trying our new varieties at little cost. In sending the eyes by mail there is nothing to pay for transportation, as we pay all postage. All orders for the South can be sent any time in the winter with safety. Orders for the North and West will be booked when received, and sent when spring opens or planting time arrives.

PRICE OF POTATO EYES POSTPAID.
The price of all our Potato Eyes:

Per 25,	Per 50,	Per 100,	Per 250,	Per 1000,
25c.	50c.	$1.10	$2.50	$9.50

Upon receipt of the Potato Eyes if too early to plant, put in moist earth and place in cool location without danger of freezing.

Positively no less than 50 furnished of one kind at above price. With careful culture, 30 eyes produce 5 bushels; 230 eyes, 25 bushels.

The Acme Potato Planter, 60c--3 for $1.50.

This is a wonderful invention. A great labor saver. Cheap as dirt. Anybody having from 1 to thirty acres of Potatoes to plant will find the Acme will do the work better, cheaper and quicker than any other machine made. We prefer it to the Aspinwall or any other potato planter, costing fifty times as much.

ANY MAN CAN PLANT TWO ACRES.
with perfect ease in a day. The secret of the Acme Potato Planter's work is that it makes the holes, drops and covers the seed at one operation.

PLANTS EASIER.
The erect position, the carrying of the seed on the shoulder, the ease with which it can be changed from one shoulder to the other, combine to relieve that part of farm work of much of its disagreeableness. "Almost as easy as walking!" is the remark of many who have used it. The weight of the planter is only 3½ pounds.

PLANTS BETTER THAN THE ASPINWALL!
It is very important in planting Potatoes, that they be placed in moist soil and covered before the soil dries out. This the Acme Planter does perfectly. Ordinarily the holes are made or furrows turned of a horse is used, and the soil exposed to the hot sun for the day. The soil soon dries. Next the Potatoes are dropped, and perhaps they are left to blister in the sun. They are then covered at an unequaled depths. The dry ground draws away moisture that may be left in the seed away from it, and the result is no crop. Moral: Use the Acme Hand Potato Planter and take no such chances, for it drops the seed into the moist soil and covers it at the same time. We urge you to give the Acme or the Salzer Planter a trial. They are gems of the first water.

You can make $10.00 in one day by selling the Acme Planter to your neighbors. Price, each, 60c.

The Farmers Praise the Acme Potato Planter.

Wm. T. Wane, Mo.: "Discarded my Aspinwall. It's no good when compared with the peerless Acme Planter, and then Aspinwall costs 45 times as much and not half so good."

Jacob Helena, La Crosse Co.: "Use only the Acme Planter. My 60 Aspinwall lies idle."

Dan Thiel, Iowa: "I grow 12 acres of Potatoes. With the Acme Planter, costing me $2c, I planted the lot in one week. Never had so fine a stand of Potatoes."

Price of the Acme Planter, each 60c; 3 for $1.50.   Planting Bags—to hold the seed—each, 60c; postpaid, 60c.

The Salzer Planter.
This is an improvement on the Acme, it costs more and is a better tool. In all respects it is similar to the Acme. The Salzer cannot be beat for a cheap, effective perfect Planter.

Price, 75c.

The Salzer Potato Planter. Greatest Planter on earth. Price only 75c.

The Hill Potato Sprinkler.
A machine for which thousands of farmers, as well as everyone, have long looked; one that is simple, effective, never out of order, easy to handle and does its work exceptionally well. One man can sprinkle two rows at a time, as shown in the illustration.

The reservoir can easily be strapped on the shoulder. One or both of the sides can be used at once, as desired. They are made of galvanized iron and brass will last a lifetime, with proper care, and save from 15 to 25 per cent. Paris Green. The price of same is so ridiculously low that we know every farmer ordering Potatoes will have one of these practical, splendid machines come along with his order. Price, only $2.75.

The Solid Comfort Bicycle.

We have entered into contract with one of the largest manufactories for a brand new 1899 model wheel, a wheel embodying every improvement of acknowledged merit, a wheel that we can sell for cash for but $19.95. It is the wheel of all wheels. We use the wheel ourselves. We are enabled to sell it at so low a price because we have taken the complete output.

Full description of this marvelously beautiful wheel, this serviceable wheel, will be sent upon receipt of a 1c stamp. We honestly believe that $5,000 of our customers will avail themselves of this opportunity to get this high grade, serviceable, easy riding, solid comfort wheel at so low a price. Order early, as there will be a great rush for this wheel.

Price, gentleman's wheel, cash with order... $19.95
Price, lady's wheel, cash with order... 19.99

KNIVES.

The farmer boy is entitled to the best knife out and here we have it in our Montana Favorite, a strong bright blade, just the knife for all purposes. It is indeed a great general purpose knife. Price, ebony handle, brass finish, German silver ends, 90c, postpaid; white handles, $1.15, postpaid; pearl handles, $1.35, postpaid.

More and different styles of knives are illustrated in our catalogue of implements, which is freely mailed on receipt of 1c postage.

Economy Kitchen Set.
The Economy Kitchen set is immensely popular, sells at sight, contains one splendid bread knife, one cake and one paring knife. Price 95c, postage 15c. The Christy Set 90c, postage 15c. The Buckeye Set 80c, postage 10c.

Farmer's Butcher Knives.
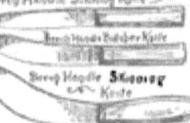

Bevely Handle Sticking Knife
Ebony Handle Butcher Knife
Beveled Handle Skinning Knife

6 inch butcher knife, 6 inch sticking and 6 inch skinning knife, the three knives needed during butchering time on every farm industrious. Quality A No. 1. 75c for the three knives postage, 15c.

Hog Ring and Pruning Knives, see page 137.

The Lusher Vegetable Slicer and Cabbage Cutter.

With six knives. A magnificent tool. It cannot be too strongly indorsed. It is made of the best material, tinned over to prevent rusting. Always carries a keen edge without sharpening. It is A No. 1 for slicing cabbage, apples, carrots, cucumbers, radishes, etc. Six slices are cut with every stroke of the hand, so that in a minute enough can be prepared for a large family. It is yours since we have found a tool so satisfactory, so great a labor saver, and of such great utility.

Price, 50c; postage, 10c.

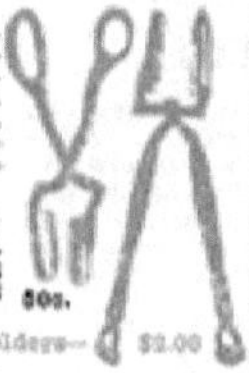

THE AVERY TRANSPLANTER.

Plants removed by it ready wilt, even though transplanted during the scorching heat. Small, single-hand size, each, 50c.; postpaid, 60c; two-hand size, for postions, $2.00

SCUFFLE HOES.

Very effective. 5½-inch, 30c; 7-inch, 40c; 9-inch, 50c; 10-inch, 70c.

Buttonhole Bouquet Holders—Each, by mail, 5c. $2.00

TRANS-PLANTING TROWELS,

Each, 45c; by mail, 50c.

GARDEN LINE REELS—Each, 65c; postpaid, 80c.

TREE PRUNER.

Eight-foot pole, $1.50; 10-foot pole, $1.65.

KNIVES.

Budding— Each, 80c; ivory handled, without ivory point, 90c.

Pruning—No. 1, 75c; No. 2, 85c; stag handle, extra large pruning, $1.25.

Asparagus—45c.

High Grade Pruning Shears. No. 1, 50c; No. 2, 75c, postpaid.

For vineyard and other pruning where an instrument that cuts well on the point is needed.

THE LEVIN PRUNER.

This is the best tool of all; works like a charm and is very cheap at that, each, 50c; No. D, 90c.

Strong Spring Pruning Shears.

A splendid shear. Item on collar, work. No. 1, 45c each; No. 2, 70c each.

GRAPE OR BOUQUET CLIPPER. Fine for picking bunches of grapes, fruits, flowers, etc. Each, postpaid, 50c.

GARDEN TOOLS.

Ladies' Favorite; 6 pieces. 70c; by mail, 90c.

THE OSBORNE WEEDER.

The cut explains itself. It is a great labor saver, $1.00.

MICROSCOPE.

By mail, 30c.

LANG'S WEEDER.

It is very conveniently used, and fits the hand so comfortably that the fingers are entirely free for use wherever necessary. Net price, 25c postpaid, 30c.

TURF EDGER.

With sole, 15c.

EXCELSIOR WEEDER.

Each, 15c; by mail 20c.

SCIENTIFIC CORN HUSKER.

The greatest little tool on earth.

"When" some one says, "it's strong enough, if you have any corn to husk, this little tool will do it better, quicker, and easier than any other husker we know of. Each, postpaid, 10c; 3 for 25c.

ROSS HUSKER.

Heavy leather combination mitt, protected by solid steel rivets. It is immensely popular. Price, each, postpaid, 25c; 3 for 60c.

ROSS CALF WRIST SUPPORTER.

This is an excellent support for the wrist in husking corn. Price, each, 20c; 3 for 50c.

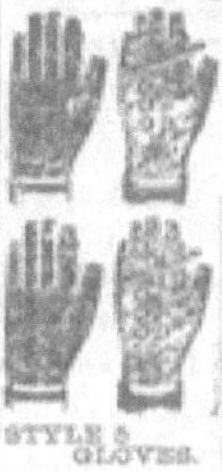

STYLE 4 GLOVES.

Calf split stock, tanned by water-proof firm process, well protected by leather and steel scallops, excellent for corn husking. Price, per pair, postpaid, 80c; 3 pair, $1.75.

STYLE 3 GLOVES.

This is all calf; the most popular Glove on the market; retails everywhere at 65c per pair; splendidly made. Price, postpaid, 50c; 3 pair, $1.35.

FAMILY POP CORN SHELLER.

A gem; a beauty; just the thing the boys and girls are looking for to shell popcorn, sweet corn, etc. shells it boxed in an hour. Price, postpaid, 25c.

THE LA CROSSE CORN SHELLER.

A boy or man, with one hour's practice can shell a bushel of corn in 3½ minutes. It is a magnificent machine throughout. We have never known one to get out of repair. In addition to that, it is sold at an exceedingly low price to place it within reach of everybody. We know of no sheller at twice this price that we would rather have than the La Crosse.

Each, 85c.

85c.

CYCLONE CORN SHELLER.

Very simple, very effective, with a little practice a boy or man can shell a bushel of corn in 4 minutes. Each $1.15.

THE BALL BEARING SHELLER.

The latest improvement in corn shellers. Each $2.15.

THE LA CROSSE SHELLER. Price, 85c.

CORN HOOK—Price, only 40c; postpaid, 65c.

THE HANDY HAMMER.

Wrench, nail and staple puller and wire splicer, 10 inches long, weight 1½ lbs., made of the best malleable iron, the most convenient tool ever invented, handy when ever a hammer or wrench is needed. A perfect tool for any use. The claw is pointed to pull tacks or staples or spring keys. The nail puller device is in front. The wrench is to use the claw and the wire splicer at the end of the handle makes a good splice; drive wire, avoids injury to the hands in splicing the barb or other wire. It is worth more than its cost for that alone. Price, only 25c, postpaid, 35c.

BOYNTON'S LIGHTNING PRUNING SAW.

Holes are provided in the handle for attaching to a pole with screws or bolts, to use in cutting higher branches. The Boynton teeth are used for the larger limbs, while the fine teeth are used for cutting the small limbs and twigs. Price, 16-inch, $1.50; 24-inch, $2.25. Only 50c.

THE GOPHER TRAP.

It is simple, but effective; if it is cheap, but sure to kill, and catches them by the dozen. Each, 60c; postpaid, $1 for $1.50.

MOLE TRAP.

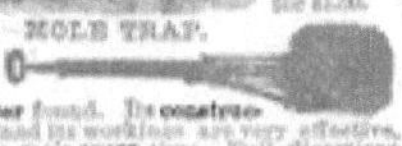

This is the only perfect Mole Trap that we have ever found. Its construction is simple, and its workings are very effective, as it catches the mole every time. Full directions regarding same with each machine sold. Each, $1.00; 3 for $2.50.

IMPERIAL EGG FOOD.

(Trade Mark.)

The finest food in the world to make hens lay and cure the many ills that fowl flesh is heir to, 40c; by mail, 50c; by freight, 10 lbs., $1.75; 100 lbs., $16.00.

FRESH EGGS

POULTRY

This preparation keeps eggs fresh for many months, indeed for years. A can is sufficient to preserve 50 eggs. Price, by express, can, 40c; 6 cans, $1.15; 12 cans, $1.50; by mail, postpaid, 1 can, 50c. Circular concerning same, if cheap.

OYSTER SHELLS.

Just the thing to keep poultry healthy, happy and busy laying. Price, per 10 lbs., 25c; per 50 lbs., $1.00; per 100 lbs., $1.50; 200 lbs., $2.50.

THE SANITARY.

The finest thing on earth for furnishing pure water for poultry, chickens, ducks. Price, 1 gallon, 40c; 3 gallons, 75c.

THE LEADER ALL-STEEL SCRAPER.

There is a big demand for scrapers. Hardly a prosperous farmer to be found but wants one. We have one of the best forms, ever made. No. 1 holds 2 cubic feet, and No. 2 holds 4 cubic feet. Price, No. 1, $1.50.

WAREHOUSE TRUCK.

This is so well known that it needs no description. Every farmer will want one, as the price is so very low. Each, $1.65.

POST-HOLE AUGER.

WAREHOUSE TRUCK. Each, $1.65.

Its adjustable center admits the passage of stones, and will make a post hole deep may also transport. Each, Post $1.25.

TROWELS—Fine Garden Trowels, strong and durable. Each, 10c; postpaid, 16c.

INSECT DESTROYERS.

Ideal Sprayers or Force Pumps.

The Aquarius.

THE IDEAL.

Scollay's Sprinkler.
The Very Best.

SCOLLAY'S SPRINKLER. Price, only $1.50.

THE AQUARIUS.

The Kill Quick Bug Exterminator

Price, only 50c.

For 10c

Lawn Fertilizers.

Garden Veg. Compound.

Walker's Excelsior Brand Fertilizer

Commercial Fertilizers.

	300 lbs.	1,000 lbs.	2,000 lbs.
Dissol'd Raw Bone	$3.25	$51.50	$10.00
Super Phosphate	3.00	11.00	21.00
Potato Grower	3.25	31.50	30.00
Truck Manure	3.00	22.00	42.00
Raw Bone Black	3.75	16.00	32.00
Corn Grower	3.00	14.00	27.00
Prairie Phosphate	3.75	13.00	25.00

A bag holds 200 lbs.   Price, fluctuate.

Insect Destroyers.

U. S. Bordeaux Mixture.

The Lenox Sprayer.

Acme Powder Gun.

Sulphur Bellows.

Combination Barrel and Box Cart.

Hand Cart, Only $4.98.

The Steel Barrel Cart.

THIS FINE STEEL CART, $3.75.

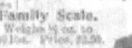
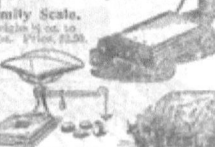

100 lbs. SHEEP FERTILIZER FOR LAWNS SALZER SEED CO. LA CROSSE

Sheep Manure for Lawns.

Platform Scales.

Family Scale.

Wagon Scales.

SALZER'S GREAT IDEAL CULTIVATOR.   Price, Fig. 1, $4.25.

This is the tool that has lived in our fancy and dreams for years. And we now shout and sing because we have found all those splendid qualities we have longed for. The cut fully shows the Ideal with our new Pattern Handle and Braces. These are absolutely new and the most effective and stiffest combination known, at once making the tool rigid, yet allowing adjustment of handles in height and otherwise.

It Expands by means of our entirely new expander, which at the same time is wonderfully simple, but very strong and quick. By means of this device the Cultivator can be expanded instantly, or reduced from 11 to 20 inches by a single move and without loosening any bolts. By putting bolts in outside holes of expander they can be expanded to 29 inches, a width greater than ordinary cultivators.

The Depth is under perfect control by means of a new lever wheel, and the new patented depth regulator, which are moved instantly in unison by a single lever, making one set work, standing the machine and relieving the operator.

It works like a charm. Quickly it can be changed to a PLAIN CULTIVATOR; 2d, to a furrow; 3d, reversed for hoeing; 4th, for shallow cultivation; and 5th, as the big illustration shows, ready for general duty.

The price of this great cultivator, as shown without the three extra sweeps arranged for shallow cultivation, is but $4.25; with the two 10-inch and one 12-inch sweeps, as shown above in Fig. 5, arranged for shallow cultivation, the price is complete, $4.75. The Cultivator is a marvel of beauty and utility. Of course, in expanding same as a plain cultivator, or for placing out for hoeing, it is just necessary to take off the expander or depth regulator. It is positively the greatest tool on earth for the price, as other dealers ask $7.50 to $9.00 for a cultivator far inferior. The two 10-inch and one 12-inch sweeps, 50c.

Price, as shown in the illustration: Fig. 1, only $4.25; with the 3 extra sweeps, as shown in Fig. 5, $4.75.
Price, complete as shown in all of the illustrations Figs. 1, 2, 3, 4 and 5 (with three extra wide cultivator sweeps), $4.75.

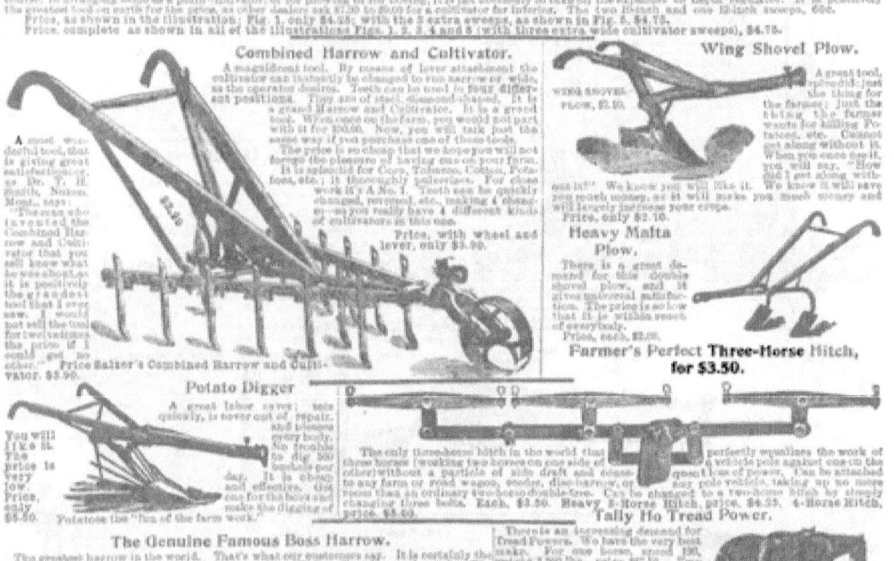

Combined Harrow and Cultivator.

A magnificent tool. By means of lever attachment the cultivator can instantly be changed to run harrow or wide, as the operator desires. Teeth can be used in four different positions. They are of steel, diamond-shaped. It is a grand Harrow and Cultivator. With one on the farm, you would not part with it for $20.00. Now, you will talk just the same way if you purchase one of these tools.

The price is so cheap that we hope you will not forego the pleasure of having one on your farm. It is splendid for Corn, Tobacco, Cotton, Potatoes, etc.; it thoroughly pulverizes. For close work it's a No. 1. Teeth can be quickly changed, reversed, etc., making a change—as you really have a different kind of cultivators in this one.

Price, with wheel and lever, only $3.90.

Price Salzer's Combined Harrow and Cultivator, $3.90.

Potato Digger

A great labor saver; uses quickly, is never out of repair, and pleases every body. No trouble to dig 500 bushels per day. It is cheap and effective. Get one for the boys and make the digging of potatoes the "fun of the farm work."

You will like it. The price is very low. Price, only $6.50.

Wing Shovel Plow.

A grand tool, splendid; just the thing for the farmer. Just the thing a farmer wants for hilling Potatoes, etc. Cannot get along without it. When you once use it, you will say, "How did I get along without it." We know it will save you much money, as it will make you much money and will largely increase your crops.

WING SHOVEL PLOW, $2.10.

Price, only $2.10.

Heavy Malta Plow.

There is a great demand for this double shovel plow, and it gives universal satisfaction. The price is so low that it is within reach of everybody.

Price, each, $2.00.

Farmer's Perfect Three-Horse Hitch, for $3.50.

The only three-horse hitch in the world that three horses (working two horses on one side of the other) without a particle of side draft and consequent loss of power. Can be attached to any farm or road wagon, reaper, disc-harrow, or any pole vehicle, taking up no more room than an ordinary two-horse double-tree. Can be changed to a two-horse hitch by simply changing three bolts. Each, $3.50. perfectly equalizes the work of a vehicle pole against one on the other.
Heavy 3-Horse Hitch, price, $4.25. 4-Horse Hitch, price, $5.00.

Tally Ho Tread Power.

There is an increasing demand for Tread Powers. We have the very best make. For one horse, speed 130, weight 1,500 lbs., price $67.50. Two horse power, speed 265, weight 2,000 lbs., price $85. Three-horse power, speed 265, weight 2,500 lbs., price $97.50. Mountings, including pole, weight, 250 lbs., price $17.50. Descriptive circular on application.

The Genuine Famous Boss Harrow.

The greatest harrow in the world. That's what our customers say. It is certainly the cheapest and best harrow that we have ever seen. It is well and strongly made. The bars are 2x4, and the corners 2x4, of the very best seasoned oak. The teeth are one-half inch square steel, with dagger points. Each tooth cuts its own way.

The two-horse harrow consists of center section and two end sections. The four-horse consists of all the sections shown above. It is the most popular, cheapest harrow that we know of, and we heartily recommend same. It is used on our farms to our complete satisfaction. 2-horse harrow, 18 teeth, cuts 12 feet wide, weight, 120 pounds.

Dog Power.

Made single and double, perfect lever device for changing pitch of apron according to weight of animal. Made of steel riveted together. Single, 230 lbs., $15. Double, 360 lbs., $25. We also handle the Wood Frame Spring Tooth, Wood Frame Scotch and Wood Frame Angle Bar Harrows, which we are selling at equally low prices as compared with the famous Boss Harrows. Descriptive circulars on application.

The Advance Chilled Plows.

No. 26—Pony Plow. Shares on Nos. 26 and 29 are interchangeable. Price, only $3.40.
No. 29—Light one-horse Plow. Right hand only. Similar to No. 30, excepting moldboard and share are smaller; cuts 7 inches. Will do good work, and turns a furrow 4½ by 8 inches. Price, only $3.70.

No. 30—One-horse Plow. Right hand only. Well constructed; thoroughly chilled; cuts 7½ inches; turns a furrow 5 by 9 inches. Price, only $4.3.

No. 31 is a very light two-horse or a large one-horse Plow, suitable for gardening or corn and cotton cultivation, and has all the improvements in construction that are used on the other plows. Special pains are taken in the construction of these Plows to make them as perfect in shape and turning qualities as the larger Plows. Price, only $4.73; complete, $5.73.

No. 32 is a medium two-horse Plow. It is especially strong for its size and weight. It turns a furrow 6 by 11 inches. Price, only $5.45; complete with wheel and jointer, $6.45.

No. 33 is a medium two-horse Plow, doing excellent work in all kinds of land, especially clay and heavy land. It has been thoroughly and successfully tried in the Atlantic and Middle States the past ten years. It will turn a furrow 7 by 14 inches. Price, only $5.42; complete, $6.75.

No. 34 is a two or light three-horse Plow; just a size and weight well adapted to general work, and cannot but give satisfaction. It turns a furrow 8 by 14 inches. Price, only $5.50; complete, $7.60.

No. 35, our largest three-horse Plow, is especially adapted to sod plowing and to heavy work. Will cut a furrow 10 to 20 inches. Price, only $6.55; complete, $7.85.

Our No. 20 Steel Plow is a very fine working tool, either in sod or stubble, marsh or rough stumpy soil. It is intended for a light three-horse Plow. Price, only $8.00.

This cut represents one Nos. 23, 34 and 35 Plows.

Hill Side Swivel Plow.

The No. 143 turns furrow's 8 to 10 inches; weighs 22 lbs.; $4.15. No. 152 turns 10 to 12 in.; weight, 95 lbs.; $5.15. No. 163 turns 12 to 14 in.; weight, 125 lbs.; $6.15. Wheels 75c., and jointer, $2.50 extra.

Our No. 20 Steel Plow. Price, complete, $9.00.

Advance Iron Mower.

The frame is cast in one piece, with the bearing for the shafting cast on it and made heavy enough to secure the requisite strength and stiffness to fully guard against breakage.

The gears are the fewest in number possible, and are completely covered, so that at all times they are protected from dust and dirt, and will never wear out if properly oiled. The pitman is attached to the knife by a ball and socket, so that all wear can be taken up. The cutter bar is "all right" and provision for taking up all wear of the knives is made. Steel guard plates are used, which can be ground without being removed from the guards. The pitman lines up with the knives. The cutter bar rolls on wheels. The foot lever works easily. No side draft. It's a great beauty. Cheap as dirt; durable as granite. Price, only $29.50.

Only $28.50

The Advance Balance-Dump Drop-Tooth Rake

Is made of the highest grade of steel, carefully tempered. It has wrought-iron wheel spindles and the axle is stiffened by a truss rod which prevents any sagging. Being a perfect lock lever which can be operated with great ease, a boy's weight will nearly dump it, while the teeth cannot raise except when required to dump. Combination pole and thills.
Price: 20-tooth, with wood wheels, $11.25;
steel wheels, $12.25.
Price: 24-tooth, with wood wheels, $13.00;
steel wheels, $14.00.

Hand Power Hay Press....

Price only $24.00.

Walking Gang Plow.

This Plow complete of "shape 10" bottoms" steel plows with extra strong cast standards. The depth of the Plow is regulated by the operator to suit his work. The purpose of this Plow is to destroy all obnoxious weeds in the land. There is no implement on the market that can compete with the Gang Plow in preparing the ground for spring seeding and planting in even depth and in pulverizing the soil so perfectly. It is constructed on practical principles and built for service. The Plow is shipped in the Knock-Down, so as to get the lowest possible freight rate. Weight 300 lbs. Descriptive circular on application. Price, $28.00.

Walking Gang Plow   Prices only $28.00.

The Wonderful La Crosse Rolling Coulter, $2.50.

This wonderful invention is warranted not to get loose or wear out in the hub as long as the blade lasts (from 5 to 25 years). It is absolutely impossible for this machine to get out of order, and it can be used to any Plow made. We warrant each coulter.
Each, $2.50; 3 for $7.00.

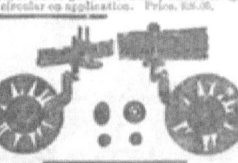

Cummings' Cutter, No. 2.

Immensely popular. Weighs 300 lbs.; speed, 400 revolutions per minute; capacity, 2,500 lbs. per hour. A wonderful invention. Price, for hand, $16.00; as power machine, $17.10; crusher attachment, $9.00; shredder attachment, $14.50 extra.

Cummings' Cutter and Shredder. No. 2.

The Kokosing Cutter.

This is an excellent cutter for ensilage or for cutting cornstalks or straw or any thing loose with bran to feed cattle. It cuts one half inch to an inch, and is a great saver of feed. It has an 11-inch knife, automatic feed, and can be changed in a moment to various lengths. Price, only $10.50.

The Kokosing Cutter. Price, $10.50.

Horse Tail Fastener.

This neat little device is made of aluminum. Is highly polished, very light and durable. Will not rust or tarnish, and is a perfect success. It does not go around the dock, and is the only practical device ever offered the public.

Requires less than one minute to put it on, is adjustable to any size tail, and cannot come down until taken down. This article is entirely new and a great seller. Price 25c.; 5 for 50c., postpaid.

Cow Clip.

The illustration explains itself. No more switching of tails when the cow is being milked. Price, 20c; postage 2c.

Bi-Treadle or Double-Acting Grindstone.

Here is the grindstone of your dreams, the thing you have been wanting on the farm, and it is as cheap as dirt. Double-acting. The complete stone and frame, $4.00.

Root Cutter.

A great many hundred of them are sold annually. They do their work well and save their cost in a week's feeding. They are splendid in every respect. A boy can cut 60 bushels in an hour. Price, each, $6.00; weight, 100 lbs.

GRIST AND BONE MILLS.

Salzer's Warranted Family Grist Mill.

No one appreciates the value of this little mill more than the pioneers of the West and South, and the farmers community generally who live at some distance from a common grist mill. If you own one of these mills, you can have at all times fresh graham flour and corn meal, fresh hominy, split peas, cracked wheat, too table or batter salt; in fact, everything that is ground at a custom mill, excepting fine bolted family flour. It will pay for itself in the tolls you pay the miller. It will pay because you require but a small quantity of meal at a time and want it fresh. Grinds 20 pounds fine meal per hour. The grinding surfaces are very hard, made especially for the purpose designed, and are ground perfectly true, and will last for years. The shaft is made of steel, and every mill is warranted to work as represented. We use it here in the city for fresh meal. Weight, 30 lbs.

Price, $3.50. Burrs, per set, 65c.

Ames Mill.

No. 2½—For grinding coffee, corn, etc. Price, each, $2.50.

Duplex Grist Mill and Corn Sheller.

Where the Corn Sheller and Family Grist Mill are both required, we heartily recommend this little machine. It works like a charm. Price, not mounted on stand, weight, 50 lbs., $4.85; price, mounted, weight 205 lbs., $7.50. One set of extra burrs, 60c.

The Triplex Mill.

This mill shells corn, grinds grain, crushes dry beans, oyster shells, etc. It is splendid in every respect, and being hardened of them are sold annually. Price, mounted on stand like the Duplex, weight 215 lbs., $7.50; not mounted, weight 50 lbs., $5.45. Extra set of burrs, 60c.

Diamond Pony Mill, $44.75.

DIAMOND PONY MILL.

This is the finest small horse power mill for grinding graham flour, corn meal, hominy, cracked wheat and the like in the market. Thousands of them have been sold within a few years, and everywhere they give great satisfaction. It is adapted to be used with our two-horse power. The capacity of this mill with two-horse power is 10 bushels per hour; with a 4-horse power, 20 to 30 bushels per hour. John A. Salzer Seed Co. guarantee this mill to be strong, durable and one of the very best mills made. You will surely like it. Price, each, with 1 sets of block burrs, $44.75.

The Diamond Pony Mill and the 2-Horse Power, to one address, $65.25.

The Kalamazoo Feed Boiler.

We have sold a great many hundred of these and they have given satisfaction wherever used. The price is very low and the workmanship the very best.

No. 1. Height, 34 inches; 9 fires; 15 in. in diameter. Price, only $19.00.

No. 2. Height, 34 inches; 15 fires; 19 in. in diameter. Price, only $25.00.

No. 3. Only $27.00.

The Profit Farm Boiler.

This is not the cheapest farm boiler, but it is certainly the best, as it can be handled with great readiness and ease, as shown, to your use, the water, etc. It heats quickly and is either for coal or wood. A 25-gallon boiler for either coal or wood costs $14.00. A 40-gallon boiler, $19.00.

Write for Granite Feed Boiler.

Dry Bone Mill.

The greatest mill is forty states to grind dry bones. It is unequaled for grinding oyster shells, bones, etc., for poultry. Excellent in every respect for dry bones, and then it's cheap as dirt! Each, $3.00.

NO. 1 MOUNTED. WEIGHT, 50 LBS.

Mann's Clover Cutter for Poultry.

Made entirely of iron and steel, designed upon strictly correct mechanical principles. The knife is made of the finest steel. It cuts any kind of hay or clover either dry or green. Every revolution of the balance wheel produces 12 cuts, which is four times as much as the ordinary clover cutter. Weight, mounted, 80 lbs., unmounted, 60 lbs. Price, mounted, $5.50, unmounted, $4.75.

DUPLEX MOUNTED. Price, $5.10.

Diamond No. 8 Mill.

A wonderful grinder. Weight, 375 pounds. It is perfect in every respect. With a four-horse power speeded at 400 revolutions per minute, the capacity is from 15 to 25 bushels per hour; at 1,000 revolutions per minute, 25 bushels per hour. This has our guarantee, and we are positive will give satisfaction. The price is dirt cheap.

Price, each, with three sets of block burrs, $25.00. Price of burrs alone, per set, $1.25.

Diamond No. 7, one size smaller than No. 8. Price, $23.50.
Diamond No. 9, grinds 25 bushels per hour. Price, $19.00.
Diamond Double King, grinds 40 to 60 bushels per hour. Price, $43.25.

The Osage Jr. Corn and Cob Mill.

A grand mill; weight, 125 lbs.; does its work to perfection. Farmers go wild over it. Capacity 6 to 12 bushels per hour. Price, only $25.00. One set of extra burrs, $2.50.

Diamond Two Hole No. A. Corn Sheller.

the greatest Sheller on earth, that is what dozens of farmers write. Sure to please. Capacity 8 to 600 bushels per day. Works well with our Two Horse Power. Price, $7.00.

Diamond One Hole No. 20 Corn Sheller, price with table, $3.00. Fan, extra, 50c.

Mann's Green Bone Cutters.

Bone Mills No. 1 Balance Wheel and No. 1 and No. 4 Mounted are to cut up green bones by hand power. There is ten times the nutritive and egg-producing qualities in green bones as there is in dry, and for this reason there is ten times as much money made by poultrymen in feeding green bones instead of dry. This mill cuts fresh bone and meat, and these fed to chickens double the number of eggs produced. These mills are perfectly reliable, are cheap and will give tremendous satisfaction.

Price, No. 1, as noted as shown in the illustration, capacity 15 lbs. per hour, weight 50 lbs., is $9.00.

No. 1 Balance Wheel.

This splendid Green Bone Mill is so low-priced, so effective and good that it is within the reach of all.

Weight, 35 lbs., capacity, 15 to 25 lbs., per hour. For hooks of 22 to 25 hens.

Price, $6.50.
No. 1, Crank, $4.90.

Mann's New No. 4 Bone Cutter.

The strong point of this machine is its automatic feeding device. It has an automatic governor that checks the feed as soon as the governor becomes too great. When the governor is released, the feed starts up, keeps on feeding until the pressure becomes too great, when it is again automatically checked. It would cut from 30 to 45 lbs. per hour. Weight, without stand, 100 lbs. Price, balance wheel, unmounted, $12, balance wheel on stand, $17.

NO. 4. PRICE, $12.00.

Bevel Geared Jack.

Weight, 150 lbs.; claimed by those who have used same to be the very best and most in the country. The price is ridiculously low. For 2 to 4 horse power, price, $7.00.

Straight Geared Jack.

Extremely popular. Price, 7.00.

Our Great Two-Horse Power.

OUR GREAT HORSE POWER.

"THE MAYFLOWER."

Weight 700 lbs. This is the greatest horse-power in forty-two states, and all the implements thereon besides. It is perfect in every respect across, very light to run up, ever gait has won wonderful satisfaction. "It would stay. It is being shipped in huge quantities, not only in America, but also to foreign countries. Every farmer purchasing one of them will be delighted with same.

Price of two horse power, 700 lbs., $21.50.
Price of four horse power, 1000 lbs., $28.50.
Price of eight horse power, 1500 lbs., $45.00.

Farmer's Handy Feed Cooker, $8.00.

All-Steel Handy Wagon, $23.95.

The demand for this wagon is simply enormous. Our price is so ridiculously low as to bring it within the reach of everybody. It is strong, well made, of the very best steel, and will carry 4,000 lbs. like a charm. It is easy running, never out of order, and always gives satisfaction.

Price, front wheels 30, rear wheels 34 inches, 4 in. tire, $23.95.
Price, front wheels 24, rear wheels 30 inches, 4 in. tire $23.75
Low Down Part Wood Wagon, 24 and 30 in. wheels, 4 in. tire 18.75

Open Delivery Wagon.

We have three sizes of Open Delivery Wagons, strongly, durably, well built. Prices range according to weight and strength. No. 1, $39.50; No. 2, $58.00; No. 3, $60.00. Full descriptive circular upon receipt of 2c stamp.

OPEN DELIVERY WAGON.

Metal Truck Wheels.

These wheels are very often desired to put onto old wagons or trucks you may have at home. These are good wheels, light, of great strength and durable. We will send illustration for measurement of wheels upon application.

Price, per 4 wheels (front wheels 30 inches, rear wheels 34 inches) $13.00
Price per 4 wheels (front wheels 24 inches, rear wheels 30 inches) ... 11.00
Staggered spokes, extra .... .20

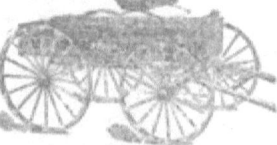

The Piqua One-Horse Wagon.

The one-horse wagon of our fancy and dreams, just the thing for everybody. It is well built, well painted; axles of hollow steel; wheels, select Barren patent, 1½ inch spokes, tire round edged steel Trexbell spokes, Acme box, 2 feet long, 3 feet 2 inches wide, with shaft and spring seat. A wagon that will give satisfaction everywhere. Our price is ridiculously low.

No. A, capacity 1,500 lbs., weight 525 lbs., $26.00
No. B, capacity 2,000 lbs., weight 600 lbs., 22.00

The Salzer One-Horse Solid Steel Axle Wagon.

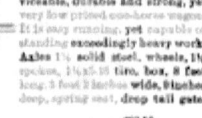

The Salzer No. 00 is a light serviceable, durable and strong, yet very low priced one-horse wagon. It is easy running, yet capable of standing exceedingly heavy work. Axles 1¼ solid steel, wheels, 1¼ spokes, 1¼x1-15 tire, box, 8 feet long, 3 feet 2 inches wide, 9 inches deep, spring seat, drop tail gate.

Price for this wagon complete $32.50
Running gear only 18.00
Descriptive circulars of our farm wagons, 2c.

Salzer Farm Wagon, $38.90.

This is the cheapest and best wagon in the world, wide, well built. Hundreds of these wagons are now in use all over the United States and Canada, and each year adds hundreds of pleased customers. It is the cheapest and best wagon made!

3¼x6 inch skein wagon, complete, 3¼x5 inch tire, 3 feet 8 inch and 4 feet 6 inch wheels, $35.90.

3¼x8 inch skein. A grand wagon. Price only .. $42.40
3¼x10 inch skein. A splendid wagon. Price only .. 48.90

front heel shaft.

Salzer's La Crosse Bolster Springs.

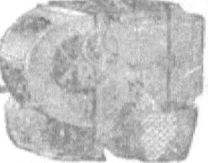

Truly one of the simplest, yet greatest, inventions of the age. It is just the thing to haul milk to the dairy, strawberries, fruits and vegetables to market, or, in fact, anything. It is worth its weight in gold for comfort. It is economy to buy them one see larger than capacity required.

When ordering give width between stakes of wagon.

No. 0, capacity 1,500 lbs .... Per set,	$3.00
No. 1, " 2,500 "	3.85
No. 2, " 3,000 " capacity	4.75
No. 3, " 4,000 "	5.00
No. 4, " 5,000 "	5.50

We have 1 and 1 are the sizes most used.
Have also other makes of Bolster springs.

Farmer's Favorite Mill.

Of this Mill we have two sizes, one with sieve 24 inches wide and one with sieve 30 in. wide. The No. 1 has a cleaning capacity of from 50 to 90 bu. per hour, and the No. 2 of 150 to 125 bu. per hour. This is a magnificent mill for cleaning and grading and separating all kinds of grain and seeds. It is a mill that we know the farmers will be delighted with. It will become at once a great favorite. Each mill is furnished with 2 wheat harp, 1 wheat screen and grader, 1 barley sieve, 1 oat sieve, 1 rye sieve, 1 flax sieve, and clover and timothy sieve.

This Mill retails, the No. 1 at $25.00, and the No. 2 at $40.00. We put these in large quantities, in order that our farmers may have the luxury of a good mill, a mill that will save its cost in the cleaning of grain the first season, we offer them at the following astonishingly low prices:

PRICE:

No. 1 at $14.00; No. 2 at only $17.50.

9 CORDS IN 10 HOURS

SAWED EASY.
BY ONE MAN.

BY OUR NEW, with the FOLDING SAWING MACHINE. It saws down trees. Folds like a pocketknife. Saves any kind of timber on any kind of ground. One man can saw MORE timber with it than 2 men in any other way, and do it EASIER, on each cut.

Price: No. 1, with 5½ foot saw, $10.20.

Excelsior Mill, $11.00.

One of the most popular, and at the same time cheapest mills in use. The feed is large and the sieves are 24 in. For general purposes we believe this mill has no superior. These same contains a wheel feeder with zinc sieve on top, a wheat sieve, an oat sieve, a barley sieve, and the whole loaded of oats, corn, with clover and timothy sieves, costs only $21.00.

THE CLIPPER. PRICE ONLY $19.50.

The Clipper Cleaner.

This is the only perfect Clover, Timothy, Grain and Seed Cleaner that we know of. We are using a great many of them in our warehouse, and would not part with them for $100.00 each, if we could not get others like them. We recommend it to everybody who wants a perfect, easy running cleaner. Send 2c for circular. Price, only $19.50.

THE EXCELSIOR. PRICE, $11.00.

Diamond Saw Frames.

Tilting Table. This machine ships weighs 300 lbs. Can be operated by any power. Constructed with extension table perfectly balanced. 1⅝ in. steel shaft, babbitted boxes, 8 in. pulley. 6 in. face, arbor fitted for saw with 1⅝ in. hole. Can be shipped knocked down knuckle. Price without saw, $15.00.

Sliding Table. This machine is made stronger and heavy with iron slides or bed. Can be shipped knocked. Price without saw, $16.50.

DIAMOND SLIDING TABLE SAW. PRICE, $15.00.

Pole Saw Frame, for cord wood or poles. Can be shipped knocked down, no more freight. Price without saw $15.75; price of Pole Saw with Jack combined shipped in bundle to save freight, without arbor and box, $23.00. Descriptive circular on application.

Gearhart's Improved Darning Machine.

"A stitch in time saves nine." This darner is adjustable. The darn is done when you remove the machine.

Price, 50c; postage, 5c.

Gearhart's Improved Knitting Machine.

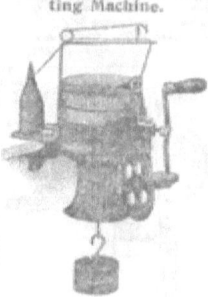

This machine was invented by a party who spent his lifetime in knitting works, and is popular in the meantime that 20,000 have been sold inside of 4 years. It will knit a stocking, heel and toe, in 10 minutes, as also all kinds of household necessities. Printed instructions in German or English, with each machine. Descriptive catalogue, 2c.

Price of machine with one cylinder, $7.50; price of extra cylinder, $1.25; price of Ribbing attachment, $2.00; Heel and Hold down attachment, $4.50; Needles per dozen, 25c.

Western Washer.

This machine is especially manufactured for us, and we do not know of a machine that has had such a run and has given such entire satisfaction as the Western Washer. It is the only machine that is being used in the Salzer family. This machine will be sent you by freight. It is a splendid machine to give your wife so much proweek, as it it is a wonderful labor saver and will make washing day one of delight. Now, we would like to see this machine on every farm and in every home of our customers, and for this reason we have made the price remarkably low.

Price this spring only $3.39; with Daisy Wringer, $3.75.

Daisy Wringer.

Roller, 10x1½ inches..............$1.65

Ball-Bearing Wringer.

Roller, 10x1½ inches..............$2.25

Circulars of other Wringers and Washing Machines, on application.

Everlasting Wick.

Requires no trimming, as it will never burn out. Nothing but the oil burns, as the wick is "mineral wool" which cannot burn and gives no black smoke or soot to discolor the chimney. Gives a white, clean, brilliant light. Retail price, 10c each. We will send three sample wicks for 10c. No. 1 wicks, 30c a doz.; No. 2, 25c a doz., postpaid.

The Ingram Safety Lamp Burner.

The only reliable extinguisher made; simple and durable.

The light is extinguished by turning down the wick, which causes the wick holder to close up, extinguishing the light; the wick cannot drop into the oil, as turning it down, it comes to a stop. They are made in two sizes, the No. 1 taking a five-eighths of an inch wick; the No. 2, one inch. An "everlasting" sample wick free with the first order for sample burner in either size. Price, No. 1, 15c; No. 2, 20c; postage 5c.

The Farmer's Forge.

Here is just the thing, Mr. Farmer, that you have been looking for, a popular, durable, cheap, always ready, warranted, safe, perfect farmers' forge. The hearth is 3 feet square by 12 inches deep and is fireproof. The blower is 11½ by 6 inches. Everything about the forge is A No. 1 and will surely please you. The weight is 260 pounds. Price each, only $5.75.

Seamless Steel Basket.

Can be used for heating water and many other purposes for which it cannot be surpassed. It will outlive a dozen wicker baskets, or the iron basket which is made of a number of pieces and apt to get broken out with hard usage. Made from one piece of cold rolled sheet steel. Weight 5 pounds.

Price....................................$2.00
Galvanized steel basket, weight 5 pounds........3.00
The Goshen Utility Steel Basket, ½ bushel, galvanized, $0.60; Japanned, $0.70
1½ ....$2.00; " 0.90
Galvanized Steel Wash Tub, ...$0.50, $0.75, $0.90, 0.90
Steel Wash Tub and Washboard, combined.....$0.90, $1.00, 1.15

Iron Forge
$5.00.

Fig. 1. Our forge is built especially to our kit. It is 15 inches high by top of bowl, bowl 14 inches in diameter. Weight 45 lbs. We guarantee it the lightest running, strongest blast, and the best forge made for the purpose. Will heat 1½ inch iron in 3 minutes. Price each, $5.00.

Vise.

Our Vise is solid and strong, hardened face, and finely polished. Weight, 50 lbs. Face, 4¼x2¾ in. Jaws 5 in. wide, and open 4 in. Price, $4.50.

Price of complete Iron Worker's Outfit $14.25.

Farmers' Egg Carrier.

Convenient and light, being adjustable, fitting inside the case and armored with a neat, automatic lock, enables one to lock it at any point.
Price each, holding 12 dozen eggs, 30c.

Our Desk and Book Case.

This desk is solid oak, highly polished, and stands 5 feet 6 inches wide, depth 12 in. It has a drop lid and a brass rod for curtains over the book shelves. It is a first-class, strong and nicely finished piece of furniture. It will please you and will surpass your expectations. It is securely crated for shipping and will reach you in first-class shape. Weight, 100 lbs.; price, $5.50; with French pattern plate, $6.14, $6.50.

Out o' Sight "Mouse and Rat Traps."

The secret of mouse and rat catching is the simplicity of traps, holding to scare, and the chief practical beauty of the Out o' Sight is its innocent appearance, nothing about its placed surface which hide the mouse or rat of its approaching danger, catches them coming or going; it will catch those will fed mice or rats that will not go into a baited trap, as well as the hungry ones. Simply place the trap where they come out from behind boxes, back of shelves or any other runways. The material runways for mice is no wood. The trap being made of wood, it is preferred to any other material. It never fails.

Price, No. 1, for mice, 9½c each. 6 for 40c ; 12 for 75c.
Postage on all, 5c ; or 12, 10c.
Price, No. 2, for rats, 15c each ; 4 for 50c ; 12 for $1.25.
Postage on each, 5c.

Dandy Mole Trap.

Better in every way than strychnine to get rid of the gophers. They will not kill everything in the neighborhood not intended, nor evaporate like poison. A few of these traps and gophers cannot exist on the same farm. Especially designed for Dakota Grey Pocket Gopher, but will catch gophers and squirrels equally as well in other states. For general trapping purposes the "DANDY" is unexcelled.
Price, 50c; postage 15c.
Daffodil Mole Trap..............75c; postage, 15c.

Sauer Kraut Cutter.

Made from white selected hard maple, thoroughly seasoned, three knives of high grade finish, sharp, perfect for immediate use, steel edge and iron backing.
painted blue within a half inch of the cutting edge to prevent rusting; set firmly on a rocker. The adjustment is easy, true and tried. A most excellent cutter for family use in making kraut; also for cutting in quantities vegetables of various kinds. No. 3 size, knife, weight, 7 lbs., 90c. No. 5 one, 9x36, weight 11 lbs., $1.40

Victor Meat Tenderer

The Champion Meat Fret.

The Champion Meat Fret makes round steak tender and improves other kinds of steak; it cuts the sinews of round steak without mutilating or flattening the steak or destroying its juices and thereby renders it tender and palatable.
Price, 15c; postage, 5c.

No person willfully buys tough meat. Hard to tell what it is until after it is cooked. The Victor remedies all this; use it on all meat, there is but one result—Tender Meat. Price, 25c; postage, 15c.

Enterprise Meat Chopper.

The demand for meat and food choppers having increased to such a large extent within the past year, we have decided to add to our line so as to give our patrons the choice of different makes.

The Enterprise No. 2, charge ¾ lb. per min. $1.75
 "   "   4, " 1¼ "   "   2.15
 "   "   5, " 2 "   "   2.60
 "   " 10, " 3 "   "   3.00
 "   " 22, " 3 "   "   5.00
Extra plates for No. 5, 30c ; for No. 10....0.50
Triumph Meat Chopper, No. 605, 2 lbs. per minute....................1.65
Universal Meat Chopper or Food Cutter, No. 1....................1.45
 "   "   "   1....................1.50
Surprise "   "   1....................1.25

Descriptive Circular on application.

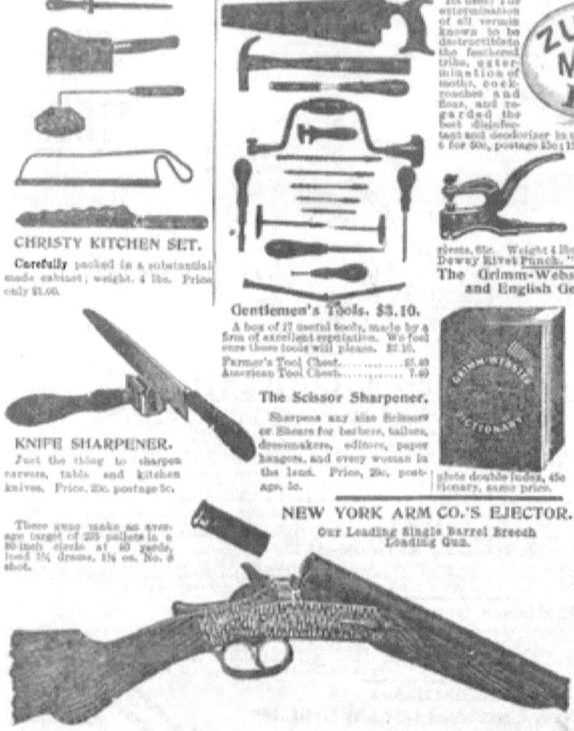

CHRISTY KITCHEN SET.

Carefully packed in a substantial made cabinet; weight 4 lbs. Price only $1.00.

KNIFE SHARPENER.

Just the thing to sharpen carvers, table and kitchen knives. Price, 20c, postage 5c.

These guns make an average target of 225 pellets in a 30-inch circle at 40 yards, load 1¼ drams, 1¼ oz. No. 8 shot.

Gentlemen's Tools. $3.10.

A box of 17 useful tools, made by a firm of excellent reputation. We feel sure these tools will please. $3.10.

Farmer's Tool Chest.............$5.40
American Tool Chest.............7.60

The Scissor Sharpener.

Sharpens any size Scissors or Shears for barbers, tailors, dressmakers, editors, paper hangers, and every woman in the land. Price, 20c, postage, 5c.

NEW YORK ARM CO.'S EJECTOR.

Our Leading Single Barrel Breech Loading Gun.

Pamphlet on other Guns and Revolvers on application.

ZUCKER'S MEDICOL EGG

Its use: The extermination of all vermin known to be destructible to the feathered tribe, extermination of moths, cockroaches and fleas, and regarded the best disinfectant and deodorizer in use. Price, 20c, postage 5c; 6 for 50c, postage 15c; 13 for 90c, postage 30c.

RIVET PUNCH.

This little machine will save more time and money for the farmers and liverymen in mending harnesses than anything on the market. Price, Rivet Punch with box of 50 assorted rivets, 65c. Weight 4 lbs. Dewey Rivet Punch, "loaded," 50c; postage, 15c.

The Grimm-Webster German-English and English German Dictionary.

30,000 words defined in both languages, two complete books in one, compiled by many authorities from the works of the greatest philologists in German and English—Grimm Bros. and Noah Webster—a literary production of the highest standard, an educational necessity, a great and indispensable book of inestimable value for all classes and conditions. Price, limp cloth, 20c. Still stiff cloth with corners, postage 5c. English dictionary, same price. Photo double index, 45c.

Made in 12 gauge, 30 or 32 in. barrel, weight about 7 lbs. Choke bored.

The latest and best single barrel breech loader. They have beautifully case hardened frames, center hammers and AUTOMATIC EJECTORS which throw out the shells automatically on opening the gun for rapid loading. The barrel can be detached from the stock in a few seconds by unscrewing the thumb screw at the side of the frame. These guns have fine experimental lines and balance perfectly. While we advise every one to buy as easily a gun as he can afford, the man or boy carrying one of these beautiful single ejectors can make just as good a target and kill just as much game as his competitor who shoots a $500 gun. They are made in 12 gauge, 30 or 32 inch barrels, and weigh about 7 pounds.

No. 1. Has top lever, blue rolled steel barrel, pistol grip stock, case hardened frame, rebounding hammer, fancy butt plate, choke bored, 12 gauge, 30 or 32 inch barrel, $3.75.

No. 5. Has top lever, fine twist barrel, pistol grip stock, nickel plated frame, rebounding hammer, fancy butt plate, choke bored, 12 gauge, 30 or 32 inch barrel. Price, each, $6.25.

Lightning Lice Killing Machine will give you more and better poultry, lots of eggs, with less food labor and expense. We do not care how you shelter your fowls nor what you feed them, your fowls will never lay as many eggs, never look as bright and healthy as they would if cleaned with this machine. The No. 1 is for cleaning pigeons, cage birds, little chicks and mother hens. Price, $2.50. The No. 3 standard size, used for pet turkeys, etc., and for all sizes of chicks and fowls, price, $3.00. The No. 3 turkey size, price, $4.00.

Lightning Lice Killing Powder, guaranteed to kill any and all kinds of lice on poultry, horses, cattle, dogs and other animals; put up in air-tight cans. One-half lb., 25c; one lb., 50c; package of one-half lb. 10c, on case 20c.

Lightning Lice Murder for coop lice and insects, 15 lbs., $1.50; 50 lbs., $2.75; 100 lbs., $5.00. Descriptive circular on application.

1. The Wonderful Matthews Combined Drill, Cultivator, Plow, Rake and Double Wheel Hoe.

This is the most perfect combined Drill made. In all the errors of old Drills, such as the Planet Jr., and others, are overcome and new additions made to same, so that it makes it to-day the most perfect tool imaginable. In addition to this, the manufacturers, recognizing that the times are close and money scarce, have, unlike other manufacturers, put the price of the tool down to bed rock, so that it is within the reach of everybody. The advantage that the Matthews Drill has over the Planet Jr. are many and so on our own farms and trial grounds the Planet Jr. were entirely discarded, and Matthews used. The simple test of the hopper and index on the Matthews being of such easy access and within reach of your eye and hand at all times, makes it worth double the cogwheel index and hopper of the Planet Jr. Combined Drill. The Matthews is the very best Drill made known.

HOEING BOTH SIDES OF THE ROW   ONLY $7.50   THE MATTHEWS

AS A RAKE

AS A PLOW   AS A DRILL

THIS MACHINE, SIX IN ONE—ALL COMPLETE ONLY $7.50

One Great Advantage of the Matthews Combined Drill is This:

That if you do not wish to use same as a Double-Wheel Drill or Seeder, one of the wheels can be quickly taken off, and it becomes in every respect the same as the Matthews New Universal Garden Drill, illustrated under No. 3. Another is that, when you are through seeding, you simply take away the seed hopper, which is quickly done, and use it as a Double-Wheel Hoe, and it answers exactly the same purposes as the Matthews Double-Wheel Hoe, illustrated Fig. 4.

Six Machines in One, and All for Only $7.50.

That is what you have by purchasing the Matthews Combined Drill. You actually have a combined Double-Wheel Drill, but you have a Single-Wheel Drill, you have a Double-Wheel Cultivator, you have a Hoe, you have a Plow and a Rake. We illustrate in the above cut four of the machines, but it gives you six perfect machines, as here described. The price of this grand tool, 6 in 1 (has John A. Salzer Seed Co.'s guarantee) is only $7.50.

2. Matthews Gem Garden Drill.

There are thousands of people who want a small Drill, who have but a few seeds to sow. This is the Drill to buy. It is low priced, is never out of order, and it works like a charm. It makes the opening, drops the seed and covers it, and does it to perfection—sowing all varieties of seeds, such as Turnip, Carrot, Sage, Spinach, Onion, Parsnip, Beet, Peas, etc., and marks the next row as perfectly as other Drills do. The hopper holds a quart, and can be made to hold more. Price of this splendid little Drill, $4.00.

The No. 2—only $4.00

3. Matthews New Universal Garden Drill.

This is a model. It is splendid in every respect, perfectly simple in construction, neat in design, effective, and is never out of order. It is a larger Drill than the Gem, does its work splendidly, perfectly and without jarring or getting out of order. The flow of seed can be instantly stopped by means of the attachment shown on the handle. The Index is right under your eye, while the hopper containing the seed is easily watched. Price, $5.50.

No. 3.
MATTHEWS
New
Universal Drill.

A magnificent Drill way ahead of Planet Jr.

Price, only $5.50.

4. Matthews Double-Wheel Hoe, Cultivator and Rake.

This is positively the grandest hand Cultivator on earth. It embraces all the good points of older efforts in the same line, and in addition affords very many new features which cannot fail of appreciation. One of these features is the adjusting arch, by an ingenious device, enables the pitch to be adjusted at any single desired. It is certainly without a superior, doing its work as a Cultivator, as a Weeder, as a Plow, as a Harrow, as a Hoe or Scraper, to utmost perfection and complete satisfaction. Any child can run this and do good work.

It is A No. 1 to work both sides of the row at one passing, as the adjustment can be set to suit the width of crop to the cultivator, keeping row midway between wheels. No need of watching the teeth. This is a point no other tool has. The Hoe blades can be set to turn inside or out. A splendid tool for onion cultivation.

There are four Cultivator teeth. Two can be used at desired width to mark out two rows at a time. That's an advantage. The plows can be set closely together for furrowing, turning the ground outward. For cover they can be set to turn inward. The rakes are excellent for fine cultivation, and do better work than ordinary rakes, as they handle the seed angling or straight. The depth is easily regulated. The real plows are provided to prevent the wheel from breaking or injuring large-spread foliage. Price, $4.75.

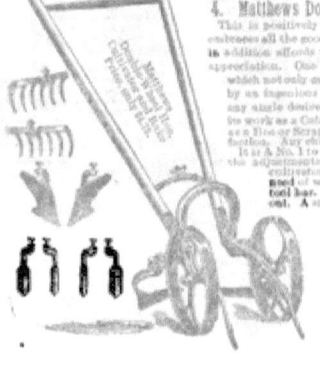

No. 5.
The MATTHEWS SINGLE-WHEEL HOE, CULTIVATOR and RAKE has the following attachments: 1 pair Hoes, 5 Cultivator Teeth, 1 pair Plows, 1 pair Rakes and 1 Vine or Leaf Guard. It is a splendid tool. Price, only $4.00.

Price, only $4.00

The Matthews Single-Wheel cannot be beat as a Cultivator. Price, only $4.00.

Matthews Single-Wheel Hoe.
This is the Single-Wheel Hoe, with Hoe Blades only; no other attachments. Price, $2.00.

Matthews Double-Wheel Hoe.
With Hoe Blades only, $2.75.

Matthews Garden Plow.
Plow simply, splendid. Price, $1.25.

FREE.

The Acme Seed Drill.

Price, $3.00.

When you have but a few packages of seed to sow for a small garden, use the beet, carrot, celery, lettuce, radish and turnip, this drill will sow it perfectly and will do it ten times as quickly as it can be done by hand. It is very simple; a child can work it, and we predict for it a great future. Price, $3.00 each.

SPECIAL PREMIUM

Anybody sending us an order for $3.00 worth of flower and vegetable seeds selected in 3c, 5c, 10c, 15c, and 25c packages (also the flower and garden collections), we will send, free, 1 Acme Garden Seed Drill as a premium. No discount is offered either in seeds or cash on the $3.00 order this Acme Drill as a premium, and only seeds in 3c, 5c, 10c, 15c and packages, and the seed collections, can be selected to entitle you to this.

GERMAN SPINNING WHEEL.

This is a splendid machine for spinning Flax and wool. It is perfect in every respect, made of hard wood, solid and well built; it is cheap and will give immense satisfaction. Just the wheel our good mothers used. Price, $3.25.

THE LITTLE KING.

CYLINDER CHURN.

No. 1. 2½ Gallons	$1.50
No. 2. 4 Gallons	1.50
No. 3. 6 Gallons	1.95
No. 4. 10 Gallons	2.45

RECTANGULAR CHURN.

No. 0. 7 Gallons	$1.40
No. 1. 10 Gallons	2.20
No. 2. 20 Gallons	2.75
No. 2½. 30 Gallons	5.67

The "Little King" Butter Maker..

No. 1. Churn, 2 Gallons	$3.50	No. 2. 3 Gallons	$4.00
No. 3. Churn, 4 Gallons	4.50	No. 4. 5 Gallons	6.00

For full description of above churns send 2c stamp.

Salzer's Home Repair Outfit No. 1, for only $1.35.

BOYS' TOOL CHEST.

Made of chestnut wood, nicely trimmed and varnished, with tray and partitions, containing 20 assorted tools.

Hand Saw.
Smoothing Plane.
Lead Pencil.
Steel Screw.

Gimlet Knife.
Bell Hammer.
Carpenter's Awl.
Mitre Box.
Mallet.
Cold Chisel.
Trying Square.
Fancy Sand Paper.
Twelve Inch Rule.
Iron Square.
Firmer Chisel, handled.
Triangle.
Nails, Screws and Tags.

Screw driver.
Hatchet.
Drawing Square.
Nail Punch.
Nail Grimlet.

Price, $1.15.

Have also a smaller chest with 20 assorted tools. Price, $1.00.

Complete Outfit of Tools for Boot, Shoe, Rubber, Harness, and Tinware Repairing, only $1.35.

CONTENTS.

1 Iron Last for Men's Work.
1 Iron Last for Boys' Work.
1 Iron Last for Women's Work.
1 Iron Last for Children's Work.
1 Iron Stand for Lasts.
1 Shoe Hammer. 1 Bar Solder.
1 Shoe Knife. 1 Bar Rosin.
1 Peg Awl Handle.
1 Peg Awl.
1 Wrench for Peg Awl Handle.
1 Sewing Awl Handle.
1 Sewing Awl.
1 Stabbing Awl Handle.
1 Stabbing Awl.
1 Bottle Leather Cement.
1 Bottle Rubber Cement.
1 Bunch Bristles.
1 Ball Shoe Thread.

1 Ball Shoe Wax.
1 Package Clinch Nails, 1 inch.
1 Package Clinch Nails, ½ inch.
1 Package Clinch Nails, 1 inch.
1 Package Heel Nails.
1 Pairs Heel Plates, assorted sizes.
1 Harness Needle.
1 Harness and Saw Clamp.
1 Box Knitted Rivets, assorted size.
1 Rivet Set for same.
1 Harness and Bell Punch.
1 Soldering Iron. Ready for use.
1 Handle for same.
1 Bottle Soldering Fluid.
1 Copy Directions for Halfsoling, etc.
1 Copy Directions for Soldering.

Weight of No. 1, 30 lbs.

When once you have this great Home Repair Outfit, you will wonder all day long how in "all the world" you got along without it. It's a positive necessity.

ALL OF ABOVE, ONLY $1.35.

Solder and Repair Kit.

Here is something that you have long been looking for. It is cheap and well worth double the price we ask for it. Just the thing you want on the farm and in the house. Price, $1.00.

Household Harness Mender.

A splendid thing for the repair of harness, etc. The outfit contains:

1 Wooden Lever Sewing Clamp.
1 Sewing Awl Haft with Diamond Awl Blade.
1 Saddlers' Round Punch.

1 Rivet Set.
1 Iron. By Shoe Thread No. 10.
1 Ball Wax.
1 Paper of 25 Harness Needles.
1 Package Copper Rivets and Burrs.
1 assorted No. 10.

Price, only $1.00.

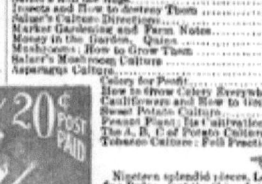

CREAM TESTER.

CREAM TESTER.

The poor cow must go. Here is the greatest invention of the age, and instrument that will test milk correctly and will save its cost a thousand times. By use of this tester you see what food produces the best results, etc.

Price, 35c, sample, postpaid 50c.

No. 2 Outfit.

1 Iron Last for Men's Work.
1 Iron Last for Boys' Work.
1 Iron Last for Women's Work.
1 Iron Last for Children's Work.
1 Iron Stand for Lasts.
1 Shoe Hammer. 1 Peg Awl.
1 Wrench for Peg Awl Handle.
1 Sewing Awl Handle.
1 Sewing Awl.
1 Stabbing Awl Handle.
1 Stabbing Awl 1 Shoe Knife.
1 Bottle Leather Cement.
1 Bottle Rubber Cement.
1 Bunch Bristles. 1 Peg Awl Handle.
1 Ball Shoe Thread. 1 Ball Shoe Wax.
1 Package Clinch Nails, 1 inch.
1 Package Clinch Nails, ½ inch.
1 Package Clinch Nails, 1 inch.
1 Package Heel Nails.
1 Pairs Heel Plates, assorted.
6 Harness Needles. 1 Copy Directions.
Not large size, but actual necessities.

Price, per set, $1.00.

The B Weeder.

The only perfect weeder for extracting dandelions and such weeds as we find in gardens, lawns etc.

Price, postpaid, 55c.
Price, by express, 50c.

BOOKS.

We furnish the following books postpaid at:

Salzer's Pamphlet on Grass Culture	$0.10
Salzer's Bill the Kiss	.50
Insects and How to Destroy Them	.30
Salzer's Culture Directions	.10
Market Gardening and Farm Notes	1.50
Money in the Garden, Quinn	1.50
Mushrooms; How to Grow Them	.30
Salzer's Mushroom Culture	.20
Asparagus Culture	.50
Celery for Profit	$0.30
How to Grow Celery Everywhere	.40
Cauliflowers and How to Raise Them	.20
Sweet Potato Culture	.30
Peanut Plant; Its Cultivation	.30
The A, B, C of Potato Culture	.25
Tobacco Culture; Full Practical Details	.25

New Onion Culture	$0.70
Broom Corn and Brooms	.50
Fuller's Small Fruit Culturist	1.00
Fuller's Grape Culturist	1.50
A, B, C of Bee Culture, a splendid work	1.25
An Egg Farm, Stoddard	1.00
Profits in Poultry	.25
Silos, Ensilage and Silage	.50
Strawberry Culturist	.25
Canning and Preserving	.40
American Pigeon	Each, .40
Feathered Pets	.75
Ferns on the Farm	1.50
The Fruit Garden, Barry	2.00
Grasses, Fodder Crops, Prof. Shaw	1.10
Gregg's Vegetable Gardening	1.25
Spanish Instructor	.40

A Great Offer for 20c.

Nineteen splendid pieces, Lead Pencils of different styles, and Penholders and Pens, and a fine Ruler—just the thing for a city or farm house—all postpaid for only 20c.

ERRORS.

We **make** them—so does every one—and we will cheerfully correct them if you write to us. Try to write to us good naturedly, but if you cannot then write to us anyhow. Our best efforts will be put forth in filling all orders carefully, and with the additional room and facilities we hope to get along the coming season without an error of **any** kind. Let us have your early orders, and we promise to please you.

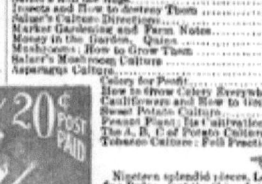

LAST WORDS.

When you sow, you **want** to reap, not sparingly, but bountifully. That's eternally right! It is our honest and earnest endeavor to furnish you with only good, live, vigorous seeds, so that your crop may be generous—yes, bountiful. We believe if any seeds can produce good yields and fine specimens ours can, and we earnestly solicit your orders, and promise same careful and prompt attention.

Truly yours, JOHN A. SALZER SEED CO., LA CROSSE, WIS.

www.ingramcontent.com/pod-product-compliance
Lightning Source LLC
Chambersburg PA
CBHW020753020726
47495CB00008B/2410